STOCK MARKET Mistress

STOCK MARKET *Mistress*

RANDI LYNN BACKALL

Joie de Vivre

Dedicated to my mom and dad,

Ellen and Jerry Backall.

How I wish you were both here to see this.

Love is a fire. But whether it is
going to warm your hearth or burn
down your house, you can never tell.
—*Joan Crawford*

Above all, be the heroine of your life,
not the victim.
—*Nora Ephron*

MISTRESS:

noun: A WOMAN IN A POSITION OF AUTHORITY, CONTROL, OR POWER.

STOCK MARKET
Mistress

Table of Contents

ONE

THE ANNOUNCEMENT

I arrived at the café in time to bump into my boyfriend's wife.

In my defense, it was inevitable that it would happen sooner or later. I just assumed it would be much later, like never. Or after they were officially divorced. Living in separate countries. Perhaps then I would've been prepared. If I weren't in shock, I could've pretended I hadn't seen her, slithered my guilty ass back to my car, and waited for her to leave.

But on this particular morning, with the late November sun ambiguous and excitement bursting out of my pores, I was early. I backed my dirty Toyota Highlander in and out of the same parking spot, hitting the curb three out of the four times it took to get it right, turned off my seventies station, smack in the middle of "Freebird," strolled into the White House Café, and narrowly missed a face-on collision with his designer-clad wife.

There she was. Deenie Gardner, future ex-wife extraordinaire, with honey-colored hair cascading down her back, wearing a fabulous Dolce & Gabbana cocoa-brown blazer and a taupe Hermès Kelly bag. As usual, she appeared polished and flawless, causing me to tremble and wish I were invisible.

"Oh my Gosh! Leah! Hi! It's so good to see you," she gushed.

I swallowed hard and had one second to find my voice, which was hiding deep down in my underwear. "Wow. Deenie. Um. Hi. Thanks again for the referrals." I compensated for the flush creeping up my neck with a dazzling smile. Brain to leg: *STOP SHAKING. SHE HAS NO IDEA.*

"I'm so happy to help! You're the best party planner I've ever had the pleasure of working with. Take care now." Deenie blew me a kiss and left in a cloud of Chanel No. 5, taking my burst of confidence along with her and leaving me breathless and embarrassed. How long would she continue thinking I was wonderful? How long until *I* became the enemy?

My boyfriend got me into this, although there really should be a better word than *boyfriend*, especially at this age. *Lover. Paramour. Boy Toy. Sex God. Man who involved me in his insider trading case.*

So now a family of butterflies had staged a coup in the pit of my stomach—all this before nine o'clock on a Friday. The rich smells of warm cinnamon and roasted coffee beans infused the air as I walked to our regular table and waited for Peyton and Cara.

Meeting at the café was a weekly tradition, fifteen years in the making—seven hundred and eighty weeks meeting my two best friends for breakfast. Fifteen years of free-flowing conversations, from husbands to preschool to sex-toy parties. There were now fewer husbands. Preschool was a faded memory. And the sex? Well, it depended on whom you asked.

Fifteen years ago, I was still in my thirties; my bouncy, dark hair was free from sprinkles of gray, my green eyes didn't yet need readers to peruse the menu, and I could button my skinny jeans—give or take one of the delectable muffins the café was known for. Breakfast was friendship and therapy in a to-go cup. Sacred. Reliable. No pyramid schemes. No insider trading scandals. No secrets. No Howard. Until I traded my predictable life for the volatility of the stock market and a treasure trove full of midlife fantasies.

Cara arrived first, maneuvering her white Mercedes sedan into the first available spot. She pulled down the rearview mirror, tightened her ponytail, swept on a coat of lipstick, hopped out of the car, and breezed into the café.

Peyton, a bohemian badass whom I loved like a sister, arrived next, barreling into the parking lot like a fresh bat out of hell, finding a spot where she believed no one would see her take a hit from her vape pen. She jumped out of the Tahoe and sashayed her way into the café.

A crop of preschool moms, Yogette Coquettes, we called them, walking content for influencers—girls who already traded in their Lulu for Parke and Sporty & Rich, spilled out of their SUVs, the kind with an extra row of car seats in the back, and piled into the next table. Life had escaped in a cold, hard instant. My kids were grown—Lily's wardrobe overflowed with Syracuse sweatshirts, and Asher couldn't speak a sentence without the word basketball. I sighed wistfully, remembering my grandmom's cautious advice about how the days were long and the years were short. The kind of advice I'd laughed at, convinced I knew better, that time wouldn't fly quickly for me. Until it did.

I switched my focus to the other side of the café, where a whiff of charged motivation signaled the Pyramid Girl invasion had also begun its day. Please don't ask me when our favorite breakfast hang had become a place to eat and shop, but around there, you were either a Pyramid Girl or supporting one. I ignored their perkiness and contagious optimism until Heidi, aka Chief Perky, waved. Heidi never gave me the time of day when she was married, but now she needed customers. She'd recently left her second trust fund husband and claimed she joined the ranks of female entrepreneurship to *make a little extra cash*. I waved back, thinking it must've been a hell of a divorce settlement, which is why it made absolutely no sense that she was at the café bright and early to fold sweaters like she worked at The Gap. Plus, I was certain Heidi still had a few good marriages left in her. Maybe we all did.

Once upon a time, I fantasized about getting married again, too. Now, anxiety ambushed those dreams, plaguing them with SEC Interrogations. Jail sentences. Breaking news announcements with my picture on a bad hair day splayed across the television screen. My sordid story in bold print, exposed on the pages of *The Wall Street Journal*.

And no shit, I should've known better. Shouldn't have let him kiss me…

But you know what they say: The only way out is all in. And that's why I was at the café, unfortunately early, to announce Leah Samuels's Second Act. LEAH 2.0. Wish me luck.

"Academy award performance," Peyton said as she joined Cara at our table. Her cocked eyebrow scolded me. "I saw you with Deenie while I was circling the parking lot. Bravo." She clapped once, enough to state her lack of approval.

I didn't mention being on the verge of a panic attack. I had big news, and there was no way I was going to let Deenie or anyone else ruin it. We paused as Franni delivered our customary coffee order in black-and-white checked ceramic mugs.

"I sold my business," I announced, not being able to hold back for another minute, finally releasing the words into the universe. Life of the Party was my dream job. All those years of blood, sweat, glitter, and no social life to build the premier party planning business in the tri-state area, and just like that, I was hanging up my glue gun.

"Why on earth would you sell?" Cara asked. She sipped her iced coffee like it was a fine wine. "Your business is booming. Nobody works as hard as you do. And I've seen your balance sheets." She whispered the last part in her confectionery Nashville twang, accusatory yet sweet, like she had seen my underwear. Black lace thong and demi that day. Just in case.

"Oh no." Peyton's eyes shot daggers at me across the hammered wood table. Our lifelong friendship permitted her to think she knew what was best for me. I had become secretive, and Peyton didn't like it. I wasn't just keeping a secret. I *was* the secret. My whole life had become a dirty little secret.

"Time to move on." I tried to sound nonchalant.

Peyton replied furiously, not taking her eyes off me. "You don't just wake up one day and quit your own business, one you built from the ground up. Next, you'll tell me you're cashing out to become one of Garnet Springs's illustrious Yogette Coquettes."

"SSSHH," I laughed. "They'll hear you. I couldn't do a downward dog if my life depended on it. Curvy is my mantra." Surely, all this sex must've counted as exercise. It would change when I hit menopause, but until then, please pass the cinnamon buns.

Peyton, Cara, and I had real jobs, unlike the Yogette Coquettes, our unanimously coined nickname for the moms who didn't work. Not that we were critical. The moms we knew could do hot yoga and decorate their dining room, but couldn't balance their checkbook.

Yogette Coquettes lived for their workout classes, flaunting their bodies accordingly. They left their kids with nannies so they could get highlights and blow-outs for husbands who didn't notice. Some of them never learned how to smile, but they traveled in packs like a modern-day version of the Pink Ladies.

Peyton took a sip of her mochaccino, tossed a section of her wild auburn curls, and leaned in, the table pressing into her overflowing boobs, attempting to grill me with the proximity of her raised eyebrows. "This is a cry for help if I've ever heard one." A celebrity therapist, Peyton had taken on a professional aura in recent years, especially after her gig on *Good Morning America*. It was quite the transformation from the wild child I grew up with. At just five-feet-four, she commanded the room with her brazenness; a slew of silver bangles jangled when she used her hands to make a point, which was all the time. Peyton could fix anyone's relationships except one of her own.

Cara was as tall as Jerry Hall, willowy and confident, her blonde hair severely pulled back in an aubergine velvet ribbon. The pearls and twin set whispered finishing school, and next to her, I looked like a child. I was the petite one, the good girl, the one who played by the rules, even when it meant I felt like I'd never catch up. No more. It was time for a change.

Cara and I came from different places. I had Yiddish-speaking grandparents who always out-yelled each other. She had an upbringing filled with cotillion classes and debutante balls. Cara was older than Peyton and me and balanced a hefty dose of naivety with the aforementioned Southern charm that allowed her to call random strangers *sugar* without pronouncing the *r*. Peyton said

Cara lacked chutzpah, but her positivity, even in light of her cat-astrophic circumstances, was refreshing, rivaling my deep-rooted Jewish cynicism and Peyton's *don't fuck with me* attitude.

I studied my friends, who'd remained authentic in this play-ground of Botox and pampered bodies. Half of the women our age looked like they just got off the conveyor belt at Mattel headquar-ters. Molly at the next table had so much filler in her face I feared that if she got too close to a burning candle, her face would go up in flames.

Franni came to our table. After I ordered a spinach and mush-room omelet, I turned my head from the inquisitive stares and fumbled inside my pocketbook for something to distract me.

"Sweetie, sprinkle a bit of that *magic powder* on my yogurt," Cara whispered to Franni.

The sweat slid down my back from under my bra. "I got an offer I couldn't refuse," I answered defensively, applying a fresh coat of MAC Trophy Wife lip gloss. It was true. Sometimes, the universe presented itself to you in mysterious ways. *Bashert*, ac-cording to my grandmom. And there had been more than a few of those meant-to-be destiny moments lately. I knew a sign when I saw one.

"You're out of your mind. Why didn't you tell me? What of-fer? What the hell's going on?" Peyton stared icily. I didn't know why I let her get to me.

"It's college money for Asher and Lily." I was in the hot seat.

"Your divorce agreement included college."

"Louis may have used the college money on a facelift."

A few years ago, we told each other more than our spouses. At this very table, I'd announced, over a decadent slice of raspberry coffee cake, that I was divorcing Louis, the cheating snake of an orthodontist. We were sampling the cinnamon streusel French toast when Peyton told us she was finally pregnant, the last of our trio to become a mom. And a plate of decadent pecan sticky buns was being passed around when Cara got the call about the tragic accident that took her beloved Johnny.

"Don't you lie to me, Leah Samuels. This has something to do with Howard," Peyton said, her voice low and seething. She stirred her mochaccino methodically, staring at me like she was trying to piece together a puzzle missing half the pieces. Peyton had a chip on her shoulder the size of a grapefruit. In retrospect, I suppose none of this made any sense. In my cocoon of suburbia, I was Queen Butterfly, an independent woman who'd walked away from corporate culture and surprisingly became the envy of the working girl's circuit. It should've been enough. For all those years, it was enough. Until Adonis fluttered my fragile wings, indirectly causing the part of my brain that separates reason from insanity to go on a sabbatical.

There are no warning signs of the subtle shifts that can sneak up on you. Time can shatter the equilibrium of reliability. You're no longer scared of the unknown. You suddenly want things you didn't know you wanted. But that's the funny thing about reliability—it too becomes unreliable. And it changes everything.

We lived in suburbia, an eclectic mix of mid-level happy marriages and Mean Girls, oodles of them, intent on providing the formerly self-conscious (me) with plenty to feel bad about. On one hand, it was the ideal place to raise a family. Garnet Springs had three synagogues, a Starbucks, a Whole Foods, a four-star Italian restaurant, ten nail salons, a half a dozen yoga studios, a baseball field, and a really good T.J. Maxx. On the other hand, Garnet Springs could be the poster child for prosperous people behaving badly, moral compasses that had lost direction. It was enough to make me question if I belonged, and I often wondered why I stayed, but I knew the answer. My kids. My friends. My business. Sometimes not in that order.

A mediocre sense of envy and materialism, damn, let's call it what it was, good old-fashioned greed, powered through our luxury suburb. To outsiders, it was pristine excellence, yet what lurked inside was an internal competition to keep up with the Goldbergs.

Let's get something straight. I wasn't envious, but I was tired of feeling like a contestant on a giant hamster Wheel of Fortune. One spin away from bankruptcy or a new car. The paltry support checks from Louis, King of the Deadbeats, covered the basics. But after balancing the credit cards and teenage emergencies, I still wondered where all my money went. Sometimes I thought that if I didn't land another client, it would be me and the stripper pole. And I was just the right amount of *klutz* to fall off said pole, tassels and all. It was exhausting. Now was my chance.

"She's going to the dark side," Peyton whispered to Cara, motioning to the beauty queens hawking their wares in the next room. Beauty Queens, otherwise known as Pyramid Girls in my book. They both knew I had little patience for the Pyramid Girls, who I believed were mean girls masquerading as entrepreneurs—annoying ladies with fake smiles perched at their tables with logo-infused banners, their glowing facades outshining the fluorescent lights. A string of boutiques, like those holiday pop-up shops, or an upscale indoor flea market, had sprouted up inside our favorite breakfast spot. Rick, the owner of the café and supposedly, the entire building, had combined two storefronts, turning the café into a one-stop shopping and eating paradise. You could buy almost anything from them, including a scoop of wellness powder—

splashed in your drink or on your food — guaranteed to boost your metabolism or sex life. Peyton and Cara didn't like the term Pyramid Girls, but I was positive their business model was nothing more than a high-end multi-level marketing charade.

"You'll never have to worry about me going to the dark side. I'd love to blow the top off their suspicious organization." I straightened my posture and pushed a piece of hair behind my ear. Franni arrived with our breakfast. Her timing was impeccable, giving me another break to stop talking. I took a long sip of my hazelnut coffee, feeling my nerves calm.

"Explain this." Cara licked her fingers delicately. "Why give up something you're so good at? I mean," another lick of the powder, "you're so talented."

"Please don't do this." Peyton might have been begging.

My burning cheeks were like truth serum. "Can't you be happy for me? This is what I dreamed of."

"Dreamed of when?" asked Peyton. "You never mentioned you were building the business to sell it."

It had been more than twelve years since I designed the giant tennis racket cake for Roxanne Ackerman's fiftieth birthday gala. *Before* Roxanne's husband allegedly caught her in an Only-Fans-worthy performance of oral sex with Simone, the tennis instructor. In their newly remodeled kitchen, no less.

I stared at Peyton, calculating how much to reveal. Rarely did I make a move without deferring to her. It had been that way since the fourth grade. I owed her. Owed them both.

I did a quick 360 degree survey. This place was gossip central for the mothers of Garnet Springs, our fashionable town outside of Philadelphia. When the café opened, we were young and innocent. I had two babies and my whole life in front of me. Innocent.

Maybe not the best choice of words these days. It was time for me to spill the beans.

"I may not get another offer like this," *especially if I'm in jail,* I thought. "This is an amazing opportunity. Daniel from DJ by Design is buying me out. Do you know how long it would take me to make this kind of money?" I knew I was talking too fast.

"The DJ with the tight pants? Ugh. He's slimy."

"Yes, that, Daniel. Stop being so judgmental."

"I am judge-y. He gives me the creeps."

"Why are you attacking me? I need a change. My clients are more demanding than ever. Twelve-year-old *pishers,* novices at best, find ideas on TikTok and Instagram, expecting me to rec-reate them at a fraction of the price." My all-consuming creative spark had waned, replaced with the thought of a promising new life. A second chance. Financial security. I tucked some more hair behind my ear. "Anyway, I passed my Series 7 license. I've been studying for months. Howard got me a job working for him at Arbor Financial." *In for four. Hold for four. Out for six.*

"A stockbroker? Wait. You need experience, training, and gosh, you need to be sponsored, and —" Cara stopped short. "Oh, honey, I thought you were done hanging around him. I mean, I understand the history — the whole meant-to-be story is lovely — but this is serious. Are you sure you're not taking it too far? How's that going to go over with Deenie? I wouldn't mess with that woman." Cara looked like a polar bear had walked into the café and sat next to us. She noticed my leg shaking. "Have you thought this through?" She took hold of my hand, hoping to steady me. "I don't know," she said cautiously. Cara was my accountant. I shouldn't have left her in the dark. But then again, I shouldn't have done a lot of things. It was starting to feel like a sauna in the café. I removed my heavily discounted Rag and Bone army green cardigan and put it on the back of my chair.

"I made my decision. Now, I get to spend more time with the kids. I haven't been to one of Lily's dance competitions in months. My dad crunched the numbers and reviewed the contract, so it's bye-bye, Party; hello, Wall Street."

Peyton wasn't saying much, which meant her mind was calculating the future, and her silence unnerved me. Finally, Peyton spoke. "I think you're making a mistake. A big, fucking, colossal mistake."

"Well, it's a risk I'm willing to take. I took finance in college."

"You hated finance in college."

"It's the next logical move."

"You call this LOGICAL?" Cara put two fingers on her lips, but Peyton got louder. "You're crazy. Go ahead. Sell your business. But I can think of a hundred, no, make that a thousand things for you to do other than working as a stockbroker and with someone, do you hear me? ANYONE other than Howard Gardner. I can't believe your father would support this. Does he know about Howard? The whole connection to him was sweet. Serendipitous even. I get it. But this is not a beyond-the-grave *shidduch*, an arranged marriage, or a ploy for him to be your soulmate. Have you lost your mind? Do you know what they do to women on the trading floor? If you thought the piranhas from preschool were bad… don't even get me started on the sharks in finance."

I picked at my breakfast, which had gone cold. Peyton stopped to close her eyes and shake her head. "Fuck. I wish I still smoked," she said pointedly.

I looked at her like she should know she wasn't fooling anyone. "You do still smoke."

Peyton waved her hands in the air like I was speaking a foreign language. I'd never made a significant decision without her opinion. But Howard had advised me to keep the details quiet. Over forty years of friendship, and I picked the hot guy.

"Good luck, honey. I guess." Cara licked the last of the yogurt off a *magic powder*-covered strawberry.

"I'm so excited." I smiled proudly. "And Howard is a good guy. Decent. Kindhearted."

"Married."

"Not for long."

"You know, most women leave the investment industry at your age, not jump in with their eyes shut and hope for a rewarding career. Do you know how old you are? You'll be eaten alive. You're out of your fucking mind."

"My age is irrelevant. And don't talk to me like I'm one of your sad-ass clients." Our eyes met accidentally. I prayed she couldn't see the betrayal in them.

"I'd rather you become a Pyramid Girl."

"You can either support me or not support me." It looked like Peyton wanted to kill me.

"Hope you know what you're doing," Peyton said in a tone eerily reminiscent of my dead mom. She went back to eating her breakfast, refusing to look at me.

"Change is good. Isn't that what you always say?" I didn't expect them to be happy for me. *I* was happy for myself. It was finally my turn.

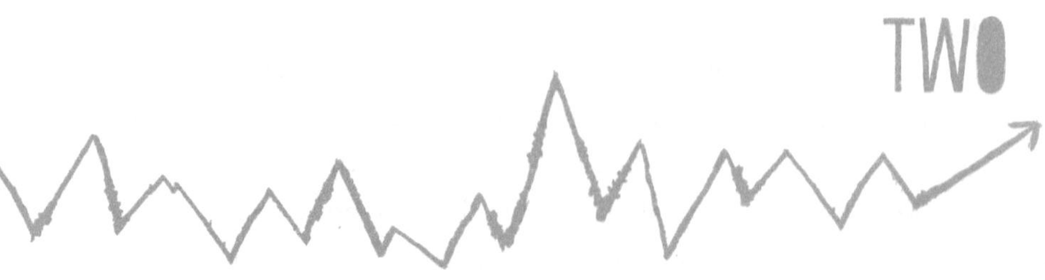

THE MEET-CUTE/ EIGHT MONTHS EARLIER

Deenie Gardner comfortably walked into my house, planting her maxi quilted Chanel on the corner of the table. Her posh black turtleneck dress matched the bag and elongated her neck, giving her a glimmer of superiority. I hoped there wouldn't be any glitter stuck to that bag, which I recognized from the reality show Lily was watching. A status symbol that bag aficionados would classify as an investment piece, but I'd classify as two years of car payments. Her husband, who hadn't spoken since they arrived, appeared awestruck by the intricate miniatures scattered around the room, as if he were in Disney World for the first time. Deenie gave a lingering sweep of my crowded dining room to ensure she hadn't missed a décor option since our last meeting, and readjusted her oversized Jackie-O sunglasses on top of her perfectly golden-highlighted head. "Leah, this is Howard," she said proudly.

Howard was the president of Arbor Financial, and the Gardner name was prominently displayed on everything from private school auditoriums to local sports arenas. If you lived in the tri-state area, you knew about the Gardner Stroke Center, an architect's dream featuring state-of-the-art medical technology and cutting-edge physicians. If only the stroke center were around earlier, perhaps… never mind. Howard was known for his philanthropy. I'd seen pictures of him courtside at sporting events, but also wearing a hard hat and holding a shovel at various groundbreakings. I knew he was handsome, but in person, be still my *When did I get to be middle-aged?* heart, I'd swear the Marlboro Man was standing in my dining room wearing a Brioni suit. The ultimate mix of rugged, sexy, and successful—the kind of guy who made you nervous just by looking at him. I struggled to pay attention.

"Hi, Howard. I'm so happy you could finally join us." He seemed unsure why his wife had dragged him to my house in the middle of the afternoon.

"The pleasure's all mine." Howard winked, making direct eye contact and holding it for a bit too long. "Have we met before?"

"I don't believe so." This man was not the forgettable type. "Let's get started, shall we?" I detected small gasps of awe as I presented the prototypes, which would adorn the ballroom at the Ritz-Carlton in Center City. Howard's mood lightened. Tiny pearls spelled out their daughter Addison's name inside a pink starfish perched on a cake model that seemed so lifelike that he prepared to stick his finger in the Styrofoam layers and taste the strawberry filling.

"No. No. No. You don't want to do that," I said, just in time. "It's a 3D prototype. If it were real, I'd be eating it for dinner."

"Mesmerizing," he mumbled, with another wink. I blinked, keeping my eyes on Deenie.

"If you switch your attention to the screen, we can continue."

I sat in front of my computer and pointed to the oversized monitor. The screen came to life with lavender confetti exploding from champagne bottles, revealing the words *Addison's Bat Mitzvah* dancing across the top. The next shot showed a layout of the thirty-five tables, and I clicked to zoom in on the centerpieces. Then everything went black. I clicked again. Still black.

"I'm so sorry. There have been glitches with this new design program." *Come on, not now,* I prayed to no one in particular. I tapped a red manicured nail a few times onto the keyboard, and nothing happened. I began to sweat.

Howard leaned over my shoulder and said, "Here, let me give it a whirl." The heat from his body added to the moisture I felt on the back of my neck, and I held my breath, trying not to inhale his sultry scent. This was a bit intimate for a first meeting, and I wondered if maybe my fuchsia V-neck sweater exposed too much cleavage. It suddenly felt as suggestive as a bikini top. Deenie's phone rang, and she excused herself to answer the call. Howard and I were now cheek-to-cheek, his stubble grazing my jawline. I noticed the monogrammed initials on his rounded cuff and the gold Day-Date President Rolex on his wrist.

Howard pressed the keys expertly as I shrank into the chair. I recognized that feeling. Less air. More breath. An uneven sensation in my chest. Lust was conspiring to bring me into its orbit, a powerful force linking the space between us. Funny how that feeling could sneak up on you after so long.

"That should do it," he stated as he slowly moved away. Purple orchids in square crystal vases filled the screen.

I exhaled deeply. "Oh my god, you're a lifesaver."

"We use the same program for our presentations. Next time, just press Control D7 three times, and it should do the trick."

"Thank you." We locked eyes just as Deenie ended her call. I regained my composure and continued the presentation. My body was present, but my brain was swooning. I looked up and saw Howard staring. I filled my lungs calmly and stood, pulling myself together to finish on a confident note.

"So, with the swag bags, the total comes to sixty-two thousand dollars. I can modify a few things to bring the cost down if necessary." I tried not to hyperventilate. This was the most extravagant party I'd ever booked, and Howard and Deenie and their blank check budget for their youngest daughter's Bat Mitzvah had allowed my imagination to run wild.

"It's fine." Oh, how I wished Deenie would smile. Although her face was probably frozen in a combination of resting bitch face and a weekly dose of Restylane. I confess she'd been easy to deal with, practically squealing with each of my creative bursts. But in the intervals, her silence frightened me. To say we were worlds apart was an understatement. Deenie Gardner had a sophisticated look celebrities share, like someone styled her hair with four oversized brushes while she slept and ordered her clothes to hightail themselves from the runway into her closet. Sometimes, I picked up my clothes from the floor and wore them for a second day. I wondered what she looked like before she was this shade of blonde and became sculpted by SoulCycle. I'd bet my child support check that she never dyed her hair in the bathroom sink. Or bought her clothes at T.J. Maxx. Deenie had said *"It's fine"* to sixty-two thousand dollars of invitations, decorations, centerpieces, and favors, as if she were saying "It's fine" to the gas attendant filling her car.

"Do you want the full amount now?" Howard asked, equally unfazed. He moved his attention to a display of pastel flying monkeys, lifting one in the air.

The Marlboro Man had morphed into Tom Hanks in *Big*. Luckily, I didn't have a giant floor piano for him to play with his feet. "That's our new *Wicked*-themed party package. It's quite popular."

"I wish I could be popular," Howard chanted, surprising me and finally provoking Deenie to laugh.

"Howard took Addison and her girlfriends to see *Wicked* three times. Even though they're twelve!" Deenie exclaimed.

I was jealous. Louis never took the kids to the movies. His capacity for spending time with his own flesh and blood was limited to an occasional dinner and a trip to the mall.

"I could stay here all day," he chuckled.

"I thought you had a merger to tend to." Deenie had an edge to her accusation.

"Merger. Right. Well… this was definitely more fun. Between you and me," he lowered his voice and tilted his head towards Deenie like she couldn't hear us, "it wasn't worth the argument." Deenie forced a smile, allowing him to go on.

"So here I am in the middle of a huge M&A announcement." He opened his arms to qualify how huge. "And Deenie's having me look at centerpieces." Deenie made a face like a wife who'd just heard her husband tell the same joke for the hundredth time.

"This is the last Bat Mitzvah we'll make, and I want it to be memorable. Plus, you promised Addison you'd come. Just half an hour of your precious time." Deenie looked at me appreciatively.

"It's my precious time that's paying for this over-the-top shindig."

"If you looked up from your phone for ten minutes…"

Howard laughed again uneasily and glanced at me, "I wish I remembered exactly when she began talking to me the way she talked to the help."

The fact that he'd used *help* as a noun declared their tax bracket. Women didn't often drag their husbands to these meetings, and when they did, the men feigned interest to keep the peace. It was easy to figure out who hated their spouse by a few choice words and unspoken gestures.

"Thirty percent upon signing. Another thirty percent four weeks prior, and the balance the week before the party," I said, trying to soften their banter. I wish I could've taken the whole amount from them right then. The American Express bill was due in one week, and it was going to be a close call that month. They probably had the full amount in their change drawer.

"I'll drop it off to you on my way home from work tonight," Howard said with a subtle turn of his lips. *Damn that smile. Breathe.*

"Whatever's convenient," I answered as professionally as I could muster.

Howard continued walking around the room and suddenly was not in any hurry to leave. He studied a collage of cake flavors, with mouthwatering icing options. In the early years, I baked everything myself. Now, I designed the cakes, but a commercial kitchen did most of the baking. Howard moved his attention to the publicity gracing the walls. Word had spread quickly, turning my silly hobby into a thriving business. I took pride in my accomplishments, but it came with a price.

He read aloud as if I didn't know every single word by heart. "Leah is at the top of her game, guiding people through the corridors of party heaven, down to every last confetti-strewn detail. The travel agent of the party circuit." Howard continued, "Planning a party with Leah was seamless, like taking a world trip without the jetlag." His eyes were intentional. Penetrating. "How do I sign up for that trip?"

"I think you already did," I joked. *I should turn the thermostat down a few notches.*

"Thanks for everything. It looks fabulous!" Deenie interrupted. She adjusted the sunglasses onto her nose, a stroke of dismissal that I wasn't sure was directed at Howard or me.

"One second, I'll give you the contract." I tapped a key and heard the printer start.

"Handle it, Howard. I'll be in the car," Deenie said before letting herself out.

I wondered how someone so charismatic and—I did say handsome, right?—could be married to someone so formidable. Howard's face was chiseled and strong and close to perfection.

The contract shot out of the printer, and Howard moved to claim the pages. He walked with the swagger of an old-time movie star and was certainly out of my league. This was a man who obviously had a personal trainer. My knees were on the verge of buckling as I contemplated the size of his arms. The wide structure of his shoulders.

The truth was, I'd never been part of the so-called popular crowd, yet there I was planning parties for the type of people who never would've invited me. Howard wore a bronze-like glow of someone who had recently visited the Caribbean, and I felt I could melt in his eyes with those specks of gold. A smattering of salt and pepper lined his temples. Straight teeth. My turn to stare.

I reminded myself of Rule Number One. No flirting. One insecure Bat Mitzvah mom's wrath would never be worth ruining my reputation. No matter what exquisite shade of green his eyes were. Malachite.

"Just a signature on the last page will suffice. I'll email Deenie a copy." I handed him a pen.

Howard signed the contract and then put out his hand to

shake mine. "My merger announcement forgives you." Before extending my hand, I rubbed my dewy palms on my floral skirt. Howard's hand was large and strong. It felt like a heated muffler. He held on a few seconds longer than necessary. God, he was sexier than he should've been. "Are you sure we haven't met before? You remind me of someone. I can't quite grasp it." Was that a lame pick-up line or what?

"I'm positive."

"Where did you grow up?" His eyes narrowed.

"About fifteen minutes away from here."

"Hmm. Okay, maybe just a familiar pretty face." Howard picked up one of the Life of the Party promotional chocolate bars displayed on the table, asking permission with a tilt of his head.

I nodded and said, "Of course, help yourself." He walked out of my house, turned around, opened up his jacket to show me he'd actually swiped a few of the bars, shrugged his shoulders, and smiled one last time as he got into a silver Maserati, where Deenie was impatiently waiting, presumably barking orders into her phone. Shaking my head as I silently added the sixty-two thousand to my memorized checking account balance, I moved to the side of my window so they wouldn't see me watching. Usually, I ignored showy displays of wealth. Peyton would've made a noise like she was puking, but that time, I smiled at the vanity plate as the Gardners pulled out of the tree-lined cul-de-sac. **NVR-ENUF.**

An hour later, Howard Gardner was a distant memory, wiped away by my new client, Cecelia (call me CeCe) Silverbloom. I'd had to stop myself from laughing at her stripper name.

"This is my daughter Gigi," CeCe said. Okay, so they were going to be a mom-and-daughter stripper act.

"Mom, stop calling me Gigi. Hi, Leah. It's nice to meet you. I'm Georgia. And I don't want a girly Bat Mitzvah." I liked Georgia instantly, but didn't know if she'd win this battle. I often played therapist in addition to party planner.

Cece, wearing a pink rhinestone-encrusted jogging suit that was a good two sizes too small, pulled out a purple bedazzled phone and tapped the screen with a set of gold-frosted talons, the same shade of gold as the stars on her sneakers. A mood board appeared, one that I was positive Georgia had never seen before. "Let's alternate the tables in shades of pinks and purples. When I had my Bat Mitzvah, everything was pink and purple."

"Mom, stop. We talked about this in the car."

"Okay, add in a bit of orange—but not a lot, because ya know orange can be, like, so garish and we want classy. Then we can have one of these tablescapes," she tapped again, "to incorporate all the colors together like this one. Whadda ya think?"

"Interesting." The mood board looked like every Bat Mitzvah from the nineties. Georgia examined a few strands of hair, which were tinted dark blue, and quietly put her nose into the novel she was holding.

"Gigi, darling," Cece said, "would you please pay attention?"

"It's Georgia! And I said no pink!"

"You have to have pink. My Bat Mitzvah was pink. My Sweet Sixteen was pink. My bridal shower was pink. And they'll be pink place cards and pink ribbons on the back of the seats. And your dress will be pink, and we'll trim the cake with a little pink…"

"Mom! STOP! I'm not you!"

"Gigi, darling, we can't turn Beth Chaim into one of your weirdo fantasy novels. Everyone will talk about it, and then I won't be able to show my face at a sisterhood function ever again."

It was time for me to intervene while maintaining the delicate balance between puberty and *Looney Tunes*. It wouldn't be the first time a twelve-year-old walked out of my house sulking because of a bejeweled helicopter mom. But I also knew who was signing the checks.

"Listen, Cecelia," I said cautiously.

"CeCe," she corrected.

"CeCe, sorry, let's nix the pink. Honestly, pink is soooo overdone. You wouldn't want overdone, would you? I mean, you've seen one pink glitter ball; you've seen them all, right? There are interesting palates we could choose that'll be more appealing to Georgia's tastes. And I promise you, it'll be spectacular." I focused on Georgia, trying to drum up some inspiration.

CeCe looked like Beebe (no relation) Gallini, being told by Mike Brady that no, her building couldn't be in the shape of lipstick or a powder puff.

I walked to the other side of my table and pulled out a basket of fabric swatches, selecting colors to match Georgia's personality. Terracotta. Marine blue. Army green. Charcoal. Georgia's eyes lit up as CeCe's dropped.

"Here's what I'm thinking…" I stopped and stole a peek at the cover of Georgia's book. "I'll incorporate the covers of Georgia's favorite books into centerpieces. Each table will tell its own story. I'll place foliage on green tablecloths and spray-paint the branches. We can use the same foliage on the invitations. Then I'll take a variety of different-height candles and cluster them around gold chargers and gold cutlery. It'll be quite magical."

Georgia smiled for the first time.

"But at my Sweet Sixteen, we had pink mints with my initials on them."

"We'll have chocolates in metallic-colored wrappers on the table. The place cards will be gold-dipped leaves, and they'll hang from bamboo trees. It'll appear as if your guests have entered an enchanted forest." Through Georgia's thick glasses, I could see excitement forming. "Best of all, I've never done this design before. It'll be a Georgia special."

CeCe's ears perked up. "No one had this before?"

"No one."

Georgia's face came alive. Mission accomplished.

"Will my gown match the room? It's hot pink with a tulle skirt." CeCe said, her eyes widened with excitement.

"That will definitely stand out."

"Can I still wear my tiara? Cause I was gonna get my hair done in an updo with a tiara and maybe, ya know, some loose tendrils hanging down. And my nails and toes must match everything. Ooh, maybe I'll get gold chandelier earrings!" I realized CeCe had completely lost sight of whose Bat Mitzvah it was.

"I'm sure it'll be truly exhilarating." I was running out of adjectives for CeCe. She was one degree away from crazy. The moms were getting more difficult, as the celebrations began to rival The Met Gala. Everybody had to outdo each other. Yes, it made my business successful. I was grateful. But the money people spent to commemorate a religious rite of passage for a thirteen-year-old was mind-boggling. Gone were the days of a small luncheon after the service. Or an intimate backyard party complete with someone's Bubbie making a pot roast and a giant plate of rugelach. Somehow, it had evolved into themed parties with sushi chefs and food trucks. Personalized mocktails and ice sculptures. Live entertainment that cost more than a year of college. My creativity was on overdrive.

"I'll put a proposal together and make some prototypes. Think about favors, and we can incorporate them into the color scheme. It's a pleasure to meet you. This'll be a lot of fun. I promise." I winked at Georgia, who mouthed "thank you" to me.

I handed CeCe a bag with a Life of the Party mug and a chocolate bar as she continued discussing what color shoes would match the place cards.

"OOOHHH, can I have one for my husband?" CeCe asked.

"Of course," I answered. I handed her another bag and led them both to the door. Then I watched CeCe chomp down both chocolate bars before she pulled out of my driveway.

It wasn't a secret that I wouldn't have been able to stay in my four-bedroom house without putting up with all kinds of clients. Louis and I had bought the house pre-construction, pre-babies, and pre-cheating. "An investment that'll pay off one day," he'd promised. Yet, he ended up in a rental with his bimbo du jour, and I worked around the clock to make the mortgage payments.

The last meeting of the day was with Nina and her son, Cooper. A single mom like me, Nina showed up to our first appointment with a bag of envelopes stuffed with twenty-dollar bills. She worked at Starbucks for the benefits (and the tips), substituted at the junior high, drove the camp bus, and, last I'd heard, was driving for Uber on weekend nights. But don't tell anyone that part. Cooper, a lanky blue-eyed boy who looked like he hadn't hit puberty yet, was polite, agreeable, and protective of his mom. The gossip mill stated that two years ago, Nina's husband, Todd, had attended his high school reunion and hooked up with an old girlfriend, who *accidentally* got pregnant. Within three months of her giving birth, he'd moved to Colorado to work on a horse farm, leaving Nina with no money and Coop with a new brother he had never met. Nina wasn't even forty but had a multitude of bags under her eyes and a sadness etched around her lips. I understood. It could've been me.

"Leah, I can't begin to thank you for staying within our budget. We're…" Nina's eyes welled up, and Cooper finished the sentence for her, "appreciative that you're helping make my Bar Mitzvah special. I told my mom to skip the party, but I know how much she wants to do this for me. Next week, I start babysitting after school, so I'm happy to contribute."

Nina beamed at her son. "You keep that money, Coop. I'm sure this bill is due before you'd save enough." The pride in her eyes was touching.

Cooper wanted a race car theme. I could do it with my eyes closed, which was good because there was no budget. This party was teetering on pro bono, but I'd make it up with the Gardner party. Nina had confided in me that she'd have to put the house up for sale after the school year. Cooper would be devastated. A little bit of kindness was just what she needed. I threw in some T-shirts and marked her file **PAID**.

By the time the doorbell rang six hours later, I'd forgotten Howard's impromptu promise to return. CeCe had left me with a headache. I'd taken off my makeup, changed from my skirt and heels to sweats, spent a few hours sketching designs, and was deep into a game of Scrabble with the kids. It was my turn, so Lily answered the door.

"Mom, there's a man here with an envelope for you."

Thinking it was Mr. Pomerantz, the new next-door neighbor with a piece of misdirected mail, I barely looked up before I realized Howard Gardner was standing in my living room. I quickly pulled out the scrunchie and fluffed my hair.

"Hi there," I tried to sound blasé, but I wasn't sure if those two words came out of my mouth in the correct order.

"Your daughter's beautiful. You look like twins."

"Thanks." Changing the subject quickly, I said, "Hold on a minute. Serious game going on here." There were only a few plays left on the board. I needed to concentrate—something hard to do with the stud muffin standing next to me.

"Scrabble?" Howard asked, amused. He leaned in behind me, watching me move the tiles around on the rack.

"Hey, no cheating!" said Asher.

"Wouldn't dream of it," Howard laughed, as he removed his Burberry coat and draped it across the sofa. "I'm a bit of a Scrabble maven myself."

"JOVIAL! Thirty-two points!" I boasted. I arranged the letters on the board.

"Good one," Howard said, obviously impressed.

"I guess that's the game," Lily said. She'd used up the last of her tiles to spell LEARN.

"You win, mom," Asher said, tallying up an inconsequential four-point NOD on the board and revealing a rack full of useless vowels. "Good game, but I've got homework to finish."

"Me too," said Lily. She dumped all the tiles into the pouch and ran for the steps.

"Wow, game night on a weekday. I used to play with my father."

"We try to play once a week. With our busy schedules, it guarantees some time together, and it definitely helps them with their vocabulary skills. Sorry to keep you waiting. You could've mailed the check." *He's married*, I reminded myself, as I felt a fever coming on. Or maybe a hot flash.

"First," he leaned in a little closer to me, "your kids are priority. Second, you need to call me Howie. Third, if I mailed it, I wouldn't get to see you again," he said softly as he pressed the check into my hand.

I couldn't remember the last time I'd felt such a powerful attraction. Maybe never. Not with Louis, that was for sure. However, the passionate part of my marriage had become one big, ugly blur. I thought about how you convert a decade of marriage and two kids to a ledger sheet of who pays for the allergy shots and the math tutor and whose year it is for the Jewish holidays. After being left broke and completely disillusioned, the last thing I wanted was a romantic relationship with anyone. Nonetheless, there I was, standing in my living room, holding the largest deposit I'd ever received, struggling to speak in complete sentences, and wondering what Howard looked like naked.

"My wife thinks you're a miracle worker. And she's not easy to please."

I wasn't about to respond to the insult about his wife. "A little glitter can make anyone happy, and glitter pays the bills." I laughed nervously at my joke.

"So, no husband?" His eyes poured into mine until I had no choice but to look away. Howard was teasing. I was fairly certain Deenie had given him the inside scoop.

"Happily divorced."

"Deenie said you were a single mom and a workaholic. From one workaholic to another, I commend you. You don't know how many of my kids' activities I missed." Howard shook his head. "On second thought, you probably do. It's also why I try to carve out time to do special activities with Addison. I worked crazy hours when my older girls were growing up. My dad wasn't around much when I was a kid. I had a slew of nannies." Of course, this man had grown up with a silver spoon in his mouth. A mouth that I could imagine… Oh no. I needed to compose myself. Howard's vulnerability was like a giant magnet. An authenticity pulling me in. It was wrong. Six foot two inches of wrong.

"I do what I have to." You'd think we were having a smile competition.

"Well, if you ever need help investing your hard-earned money, or you just want to talk Scrabble strategies," Howard winked, "give me a call. My cell number's on the back." He handed me a matte black business card and grabbed his coat.

"Thanks, Howard. I'll keep that in mind." My voice cracked as it was now hijacked by my fourteen-year-old self, trying to find the courage to ask a boy to dance.

"It's Howie," he repeated as he leaned down to kiss me good-bye on the cheek.

I was so startled that I moved my face toward him, and the kiss landed closer to my lips than intended. Okay. *On* my lips. Unless it *was* intended. *STOP IT. MARRIED. BUSINESS. DANGER, WILL ROBINSON!* Oh, but his lips were soft and… *STOP.* Not many clients kissed me the first time we met. Unless they were drunk and God knew, it was never the attractive ones, not that it should've mattered. I shuddered, remembering one disastrous client's scruffy, potbellied husband, who, still wearing his yarmulke, had cornered me in the coat closet, boldly asking for a blow job as I packed up my supplies. I'd heard they were divorced three months later.

I got a whiff of Howard's cologne again and almost lost my

balance. It was unlike any scent I'd smelled before. Probably some bespoke product he'd had custom-made in Paris. I wasn't a fan of cologne generally, but this was musky, smoky, and smelled like sex should smell.

"Howie," I whispered as a gold-flecked eye caught mine. "Got it."

"Jovial. Thirty-two points. I have to remember that one," he replied as he headed out the door. I couldn't help but giggle.

THREE

SECRETS

"No, it's fiiiine," I repeated, imitating Deenie to Cara and Peyton, "… can you imagine?"

"Well, your work's worth it," Cara replied. "Stop undervaluing yourself."

"Sixty-two thousand dollars? I had built in enough for them to remove a few things."

"That's my girl," said Peyton. "Coffee's on Leah today!"

It was the morning after the kiss, and we were at the café. I was in leggings and a messy ponytail, knowing my day would consist of sitting on the floor decorating seashells. I looked up from my carrot cake muffin, opened my mouth to say something about the kiss, and decided against it.

"What? Cat got your tongue?" Peyton didn't miss a beat.

"It's the Gardners. They're dripping with money. Deenie's a tough read," I continued. "I mean, she's nice, but how do the snooty girls get the irresistible guys? Howard's great. I don't know, for being such a big deal financial guy, he doesn't take himself too seriously. He showed up during Scrabble last night. And, holy shit, do you guys have any idea what he looks like? I've seen his advertisements, but they don't do him justice."

"Oh no, not the sacred Scrabble night. You don't let anyone interrupt that." Peyton could burst any bubble.

Cara was happy to fill us in. "Deenie, or Adena Fishman, when I knew her, was quiet and sweet when we were in college. I don't think she's a bitch. I think she's reserved. Southern grace."

"I forgot you knew her!" I suddenly remembered seeing a humbling picture of Deenie in Cara's Vanderbilt yearbook.

"Adena was inseparable from one of my sorority sisters, Jen Wiley, this adorable girl from Chattanooga. Adena had a boyfriend, Chad. Darling boy. Our parents are friends. He was simply dashing, like a summer dream." Cara's eyes brightened. "We had several classes together, but then I left for my master's, he went to law school, planning on joining his daddy's firm, and Adena became Deenie." I loved the way Cara told a story with a drawl.

"And? Out with it." Peyton was impatient with details.

"Deenie was in New York interviewing for an internship. Chad and Jen were involved in a car accident. Deenie assumed Chad was cheating on her. Chad tried to explain that he'd never slept with Jen, but Deenie wouldn't listen." Cara paused, challenging her memory to recall the events. "It was a nasty break-up. Deenie wouldn't speak to Chad and even went so far as to date several guys in his fraternity as payback. Deenie cut ties with Jen, too. Jen couldn't handle the embarrassment and transferred the following semester. After graduation, Deenie took off for New York City, and I didn't see her again until I moved here with Johnny. We're on the board of several charities together. I've done a ton of work for the Gardner Stroke Center. Deep pockets."

Cara paused as she momentarily drifted back to Nashville. "Gee, it's been years since I've seen Chad. I don't think he ever got over Deenie."

"Well, it looks like she did okay for herself," I added, thinking about her giant emerald-shaped diamond ring, eight carats at least, not to mention the big-ass Chanel she'd slung over her shoulder like a gym bag. I suppose Envy did have a seat at our table that day.

Cara continued to indulge us. "My momma used to say Deenie looked like she was harboring a whole lot of secrets in her crinoline. Though it looks like the years have been kind to her. I wouldn't cross that woman. I heard she keeps a tight rein on her husband."

"I don't know how tight."

"Why?" Cara and Peyton both said at the same time.

"No reason." I considered telling them about the kiss, but stopped myself. It was my secret, and just this once, I wasn't telling my friends anything they'd use to keep tabs on my personal life. Or lack of one. I took a sip of my coffee, looked around the café, and waved perhaps a bit too enthusiastically at Roxanne and Simone, who walked in, still wearing tennis clothes and smiles as big as Texas. I contemplated conversing with Barbie, this month's newest Pyramid Girl, who flaunted a collection of *to-die-for* CBD oils. I'd do almost anything to avoid an interrogation from Peyton, but then I'd be in for a month's worth of grocery money to fund the CBD deliveries.

"Stay away." Peyton was using her *I'm in charge of you* voice.

I took another sip of coffee, holding the oversized mug against my mouth long enough that Peyton wouldn't see me smirk.

"Do you hear me, Leah? Stay. Away."

"Don't worry. I've resigned my position as the president of the Bad Judgement Boyfriend Club. That's why I'm a workaholic."

"Howard Gardner's dangerous with a capital D." Peyton's voice got louder. I hated it when Peyton used her authoritative tone toward me. You'd think I'd be used to it by now.

"Do you know something? Is he a client? Oh—is Deenie?" I felt my heart leap and then drop, knowing better than to ask. Peyton would never divulge client information, but my curiosity persisted. I tried to shake it, but couldn't. A little male attention was refreshing. And that smell. I swore I'd smelled it on the check when I deposited it at the bank that morning. I would've left it on my night table if I didn't need the money so badly.

Peyton gave me the evil side-eye and pointed her finger. "I know enough to warn you to stay away. Trust me. Guys like him will chew you up and spit you out. And you'll be left heartbroken and humiliated. That type is attractive, successful, and just the right amount of available. As if adultery is a privilege for them. I've seen it a million times, and it ain't pretty."

"You just don't want me to have any fun."

"I want you to have plenty of fun… with a nice, eligible, Jewish single man. You know what? He doesn't even have to be Jewish. Plus, my schedule's so booked these days that I'll have no room to take you on as a pro bono patient."

"Don't worry. I need this job too badly to screw things up. I do have a reputation to uphold. I simply mentioned how charming he was. Not to mention unexpectedly funny."

"He's a snake charmer."

I pretended not to hear. Peyton took a giant bite of her bagel and lox, mastering the Jewish eat-with-your-mouth-full diet.

"I've heard stuff. Something about financial wizardry. Bernie Madoff–level shit. There's a long list of people who allegedly," she made air quotes, "lost a fortune because of him. That business is a lot of smoke and mirrors. You know I can't reveal my sources. I've had some pretty influential clients, and it can't get out that I've repeated anything I heard in confidence. But I do get paid to listen, and you're messing with fire. Do your job, take their money, and *arrivederci.*"

"She's right; don't even think of giving Howard another thought. I've heard rumors about his business, too. I know he's worshipped for his stroke centers, but be careful," Cara whispered.

I didn't want to believe this fascinating man could be involved with anything illegal. He looked like the definition of success. And he made me laugh.

"Don't mess with Deenie either. I think Howard's full of himself, and he looks nothing like Louis."

"Exactly. My tastes are refined now." Hearing Louis's name in the same sentence as Howard's repulsed me. I didn't remember being attracted to Louis, but it was the nineties. Everyone wanted to look like Brad Pitt. My mother said Louis Perloff was so in love with himself that there wasn't room for him to love anyone else.

Peyton agreed with her. And so, as much as every ruthless bone in her body cringed with disgust, Peyton begrudgingly walked down the aisle as my maid of honor. When she gave her speech, I prayed that she wouldn't make any wisecracks and set up a wager on how long our marriage would last. But Peyton behaved, smiled virtuously for every picture, and then stood by me for eleven mostly miserable years.

Peyton and I met Cara when Louis opened his first dental office in a strip center owned by Johnny's company. A few years later, some faulty wires and a malfunctioning crane caused a horrendous accident that took Johnny's life. Louis called 911 and assisted the first responders before calling Cara with the news. Somehow, Cara handled it with a level of calm and composure no one could understand. She grieved and then picked herself up and moved on with her life. "What else am I supposed to do?" she asked us when we tried to sit vigil with her. "Bad things happen. Life goes on. I have to take care of my son." She was the kind of no-nonsense friend we needed.

Peyton was with me when I found the incriminating emails Louis left in plain sight on his computer. It was Peyton who hid behind a tree and took pictures of Louis with the Invisalign rep. Peyton took it upon herself to change the locks, sparking the threats Louis left on my voicemail day after day. *You'll be moving in with your father, Lea-AAHH." "See you in the welfare line, Lea-AAHH." "Do us all a favor and die young like your mother."*

"Told ya. The bigger the bicep, the bigger the asshole," Peyton reprimanded, loudly, as we walked out of the county courthouse, divorce papers in hand. "Hold your tears. Don't you dare give that prick the satisfaction of seeing you cry. And get rid of his last name. You don't belong to anyone but yourself." I switched back to my maiden name the following week.

My dad negotiated my divorce settlement in a way only a legendary prosecutor could. But it was Peyton and Cara who kept me sane, especially when I almost reconsidered. Louis begged to come back during what must've been either a weak moment of self-reflection or a tip from his lawyer about what the divorce was going to cost him. Peyton and Cara took turns coaxing me out of bed when I got too comfortable. Not showering for days. Watching marathons of *Sex and the City*. Eating the entire Sara Lee strawberry cheesecake with a fork straight out of the box. I accused Peyton of being happy that my marriage blew up. She accused me of settling. *The unthought known*, she called it. In the end, damn her, she was right about everything. It was easier to commiserate with Carrie Bradshaw than to actually get in the shower. But little by little, I did. And that's when I started grief baking. And had a serendipitous meeting with Roxanne Ackerman's husband.

"Okay, can we talk about something else?" I needed to divert the conversation and get my mind off Howard. After his daughter's Bat Mitzvah, I'd probably never see him again.

Cara motioned to Franni for a second glass of lemon water. "What's the first thing you're buying with the sixty-two thousand dollars?"

We all laughed, but Cara realized how thin my profit margins were, no matter how busy I was. I looked at my watch. I had a peaceful few hours of decorating shells before setting up for the Levinthal engagement party. It was a beach theme, and I had one hundred and seventy-five pounds of sand in my trunk.

It got noisier in the café as a dozen women passed around a mirror at Raina's Turn Back the Clock table. We heard the "oohs" and "aahs" of women realizing that the wrinkles around their eyes were gone! Three hundred and seventy-five dollars multiplied by twelve customers later, the noise dissipated. The Pyramid Girls were multiplying right in front of our eyes.

I hated these multi-level marketing scams. My mom was a sucker for all this nonsense. Back then, it was Tupperware. Mary Kay. My mom was the quintessential Avon Lady in her day, spending her time hosting parties and lining up teeny, tiny white lipstick tubes and white ceramic lambs filled with perfume to deliver to her clients. The only way to get her attention would be to place an order for a set of mixing bowls. Peyton knew I had my own set of conspiracy theories concerning their arrival, including a suburban mafia contingency. If only these walls could talk.

Now it was SHAKETOWN. CBD NATION. EYEMAZ-ING. GOGO ATHLETE. Every month, a new company invaded our space with their *Don't take no for an answer* brainwashing techniques. Women who ignored me at social functions were dying to sell me their secret to happiness, followed by a subscription plan that would put my credit card over the limit. Some sold clothing I wouldn't be caught dead wearing; others pushed life-changing Korean skincare products. Their carefully concocted Kool-Aid was handed out in electric-colored Stanley knock-off tumblers, which, by the way, were also for sale. One smile, and I'd be signed up for a starter pack of facial creams. Last week, a doe-eyed merchant asked me what kind of neck cream I used. I wanted to scream, "It's a new company called There's Nothing Wrong With My Neck, Bitch." Instead, I was polite and excused myself. The funny thing was that these girls didn't appear to need money. I looked at Heidi, smiling and folding away. Nobody did that except Marie Kondo. However, Cara seemed to be falling for it, too. Each time a new vendor set up shop, Cara was the first in line to introduce herself like she was the brand ambassador Grand Poohbah. Ever since Rick increased the café's space, I swore it was like an episode of Pyramid Girls Gone Wild.

Blair, the proprietor of SHAKETOWN, organized packets of the newest flavors. It was the latest health craze for flat abs, and after she'd shed a whopping fifty-five pounds on the program, Blair had become the ideal spokesperson. I wondered if she realized she was in an establishment known for small-batch muffins and zucchini bread. Just the sight of these tables made my blood boil.

Cara opened up the Houzz app on her phone. "I need some opinions."

"I have some of those." Peyton tossed her head back. An over-sized pair of gold hoops shimmered, catching the light from the fluorescents.

When my phone rang, Cara had just pulled up pictures of upholstered beds for the third renovation of her bedroom since Johnny died. Currently, it looked like a cozy nook in a bed and breakfast straight out of a Pat Conroy novel. I wasn't sure why she was at it again. But the bank was calling, and I couldn't ignore it.

"Leah Samuels speaking. Uh-huh. Are you positive?" I felt the color drain from my face, which Peyton and Cara closely monitored.

Peyton mouthed, "What?"

"I'm sure it's a mistake." Peyton edged closer to hear the voice on the other end.

"Of course. I'll look into it right away and be in touch. I appreciate the call."

Peyton's radar went up. "Let me guess. Louis signed another support check with a pencil?"

I set my phone on the table. "Nope. The Gardners' check didn't clear. Sorry, I have to go." I stood quickly, reached into my wallet for a ten, and left my empty mug and muffin wrapper on the table.

I felt my insides twist, not sure if I was excited or nervous to call Howard. Or maybe I should call Deenie. I needed to stop being dramatic. It was a simple misunderstanding. "I'll talk to you later."

"Snake charmer!" Peyton called after me, animated enough for the whole café to hear.

I got in my car, and Peyton texted: DO NOT CALL HIM!

Louis often wrote support checks from an account with insufficient funds. I never knew if his account was overdrawn or if he wrote the checks from a closed account on purpose just to hear me beg, but why was Mr. Megabucks writing bad checks?

I raced into the house, intent on not letting my mind go wild playing *what if.* The last thing I needed was to do business with someone who bounced the deposit check. Not cool. I'd call Deenie. She was the client. Not the guy with the seductive eyes… the well-defined lips. Fuck it. My inner flirt took over, and I dialed his number and hung up, feeling like I was fourteen for the second time in twenty-four hours. *Breathe, idiot. It's a bounced check, not a pregnancy test.* I redialed his number.

"This is Howard." His deep, husky voice caught me by surprise.

"Howard, hi! It's Leah from Life of the Party. I'm sorry to bother you."

"Are you calling to talk about Scrabble?"

I pictured Howard in a large corner office, lounging in an overpriced executive chair with his feet up on the desk, his Italian leather loafers the same color as the mahogany.

"I'm calling about the check."

"Did Deenie add more favors? Twinkle lights? How much do you need?"

"No… She didn't add anything. It's just that, well, the bank called, and your check didn't clear." I was nervous but didn't want to stop hearing his voice. Ever. Every inch of my body was ablaze from hearing his voice.

"Not the impression I was hoping for." Howard laughed. "I'm sorry. My assistant must've taken a check from the wrong account. I'll take care of it immediately."

What I didn't picture was Howard's compliance manager, Nathan Sterling, sitting in front of him with a bigger problem than a bounced check.

I'm sure that Howard's smile faded before the line went dead. He switched screens and typed his account number into the computer.

Account Frozen… Access Denied flickered in neon green lights.

"Fuck," he said, looking directly at Nathan. "It's starting."

FOUR

THE FIRST KISS IS THE DEEPEST

oward's call came on the heels of another panic-fueled call from CeCe concerning Georgia's Bat Mitzvah dress matching the tablecloths. It would be a long few months talking Mrs. America off her insanity ledge. I nearly dropped the phone into my coffee mug when a deep voice said, "Good morning, sunshine."

The butterflies that visited my stomach yesterday escaped into my diaphragm.

"Howard… Good morning." My voice had an undeniable lilt to it.

"I'm at an appointment nearby. I can drop off that replacement check. Be there in fifteen minutes." I took a few breaths, rationalizing that the smart thing to do was to tell him no.

"Don't go to any trouble. Just drop it in the mail."

"I've got coffee. Twelve minutes."

"Great." *Not great*, I thought, running up the stairs two at a time to brush my teeth again. And douse my ears with a hint of perfume because, well, just because. I couldn't remember the last time I had a case of jitters like this. I threw on a pair of ripped jeans and tried on four shirts before settling on a black fitted T-shirt as the doorbell rang.

Howard stood at my door with a bag of toasted almond croissants and two iced coffees. Navy blue suit pants. Impeccably crisp white shirt. Ferragamo loafers. Like he leaped off the pages of *Esquire* and onto my body. I mean doorstep.

"After seeing those cake samples, I got the feeling you had a sweet tooth. You're going to invite me in, right?"

"Of course. But I'm working on a design proposal. Fair warning that I'll kick you out once I finish my coffee."

"I'll take my chances," he said with a flirtatious smile.

I led him to my kitchen and placed two plates on the table. I arranged the croissants and grabbed two forks and two knives. Then I put the fan on. *Hot flash*, I thought. The iced coffee was the perfect remedy. "Sit, please."

"I'm terribly sorry about the check. So many expenses for the Bat Mitzvah; it was just an account mix-up. I gave my assistant hell for it."

"It happens. Don't worry about it." I had worried enough for both of us. I took a bite of the croissant, which had ricotta cheese stuffed inside.

"So, tell me, when did you become a superstar—what did that article call you? The travel agent for the party circuit?" I blushed, realizing he remembered the exact wording.

"Well, first, I was a public relations executive. It was a decent job in a field I loved. Then Lily, she's my oldest, was born, followed by Asher eighteen months later. I was juggling work and daycare, and Louis, my husband at the time, who's an orthodontist, was busy opening a chain of practices. At least that's what I thought he was doing. Then, on top of everything, my mom got sick. The work was consuming. I missed my babies, and I was trying to spend time with my mom. At that point, I was too overwhelmed to enjoy anything."

Howard watched me closely. "That must've been so hard for you."

"You could say that."

"I swear, you remind me of someone. I can't put my finger on it. It's driving me crazy."

I shrugged my shoulders and pressed my lips. "I have no idea."

"What was wrong with your mom?"

"Cancer. We had a difficult relationship, and I was taking time off to accompany her to chemo appointments, trying to mend years of resentment. She never had time for me when I was growing up, and now she needed me. My brother and sister live in New York, so I dropped everything to help. She was doing well, but she kept complaining about pain in her legs. It's not very common, but the chemo caused blood clots, and then . . ." My voice began to crack. Howard put his hand on top of mine.

"She had a stroke."

"How'd you know?"

"It's the mission statement of the Gardner Stroke Center to know all about the risk factors, to do our best to prevent strokes from happening, and when a stroke does occur, to give the patients the quality of life they deserve." The silence hung in the air.

"I wish your center were around when my mom needed it."

"How is she now?"

I shook my head. "My dad couldn't take care of her by himself, so we moved her to a facility for stroke patients. Louis said we couldn't afford for me to stop working. I offered to help manage one of his orthodontist offices—and was quickly rebuffed. It would've saved money and given me the flexibility to spend time with the kids and with my mom and still have a career. But it would've blown his cover. Me working all the time gave him more time for his extra-curricular activities if you know what I mean." Howard's chin tilted toward me suspiciously.

"So you're juggling two babies, a job, and a sick mom, and he had a girlfriend?"

"Not just one. Office managers. Patients' moms. Hygienists. The guy couldn't keep it in his pants. It was pretty easy to catch him. Which we did—red-handed."

"We?"

"My friend Peyton and I. She always hated him, so she was happy to set up a sting operation of her own. She's a pro with an iPhone camera. You don't want to mess with her."

"I'll take that under advisement." Howard was absorbing everything I said.

I took a few sips of the iced coffee, which was a scrumptious mix of vanilla, caramel, and hints of butterscotch. "This coffee's incredible. Your turn. How'd you become *the* Howard Gardner? Is there anything in this town not named for you?"

"My story's not nearly as remarkable as yours, just a bunch of lucky breaks and one not so lucky. My dad was an inventor. He had patents and trust funds but hated doctors. By the time he was diagnosed properly, no one could do anything for him. He had several small strokes followed by one massive one. I watched him suffer while listening to my mom's self-loathing regarding the upending of her life of luxury. Eventually, we also put him in a place that specialized in stroke patients. I was fortunate enough to be able to visit him all the time before he died."

"I'm glad you had the time with him."

"Now I do my part to make sure no stroke victims lose their dignity and suffer the way my dad did. We've come a long way, but there's still a long way to go. It's why I try to balance the seriousness of my job with some good-old-fashioned fun. I teach Addison to be lighthearted — told her she has plenty of time to be serious. Deenie used to laugh at my jokes; she was the lighthearted one. That's the Deenie I fell in love with… not…" He paused to think. "Rigid. That's what she is now. We met in New York. She was doing an internship, I was a rookie stock trader, and I swear she was the sweetest thing I'd ever met. We got married within the year. The Plaza. Society pages. A true power couple. I got an offer to run a start-up office, so we moved. Started a family. But then something shifted. No one warns you that the spark dims when you're not paying attention."

I nodded, knowing firsthand how love can turn to indifference.

"So did you confront your husband?"

"Not right away. My mom took a turn for the worse. Louis was unsupportive, making it difficult to visit her. Then she died, unexpectedly. I quit my job six months later and just went through the motions. I could only do one crisis at a time."

"Did you try marriage counseling?"

"Ha," I laughed. "I'm pretty sure he slept with the therapist, too. Or at least tried to."

"I'm so sorry."

"So that's when I filed for divorce."

"You are a badass."

"Not really. But, enough about him. I was alone a lot. Baking relaxes me. Something about the layering and the design process—it's one skill I learned from my mom. It was grief baking at its finest. And I was making elaborate favors and personalized gifts for friends just for fun. I didn't think my hobby was an actual business."

"So what happened?"

"Louis threatened to sell the house out from under me." I shook my head. "He claimed the practice was losing money. I couldn't prove he was hiding money, and giving up my job didn't look good, but I couldn't go back full-time and afford the daycare on one salary. I was desperate. I applied for part-time jobs at the mall. Then, an old friend begged me to plan her parents' wedding anniversary party. I turned her entire house into Studio 54, complete with cut-outs of Andy Warhol and Liza Minnelli. Cher. Mick and Bianca Jagger. Strobe lights. Seventies music. It was insane."

"How'd you think of that?"

"I'm a sucker for nostalgia. Old movies. I love all that old Hollywood glitz and glamour, and once I get an idea, it takes off."

"*Casablanca. An Affair to Remember. Some Like It Hot.*" He ran his hand through his hair. "The classics. I used to watch them with my dad, along with playing Scrabble. He was a true Renaissance man. I'd be lucky to be half the man he was."

"I played Scrabble with my mom, too. It's a family tradition." I recognized a moment of unity and then continued. "Anyway, this was before Instagram was so popular. But coincidentally, one of the guests was the owner of a country club. He was throwing his wife a fiftieth birthday party and insisted I take the job. It was a tennis theme. No one guessed Roxanne, his wife, was already involved with Simone, the club's tennis pro, and I rattled off fifteen different ideas during our first conversation. He gave me an unlimited budget. The party was a smashing success. And by the time the night was over, I had a dozen people ready to hire me. Before I knew it, I had an LLC, a tax ID number, and voila, my dining room was transformed into glitter headquarters."

"What an amazing story. You're one impressive lady."

"One exhausted lady." Howard hadn't taken his eyes off me. I could feel the heat from his gaze. "Your dedication is admirable, Howard."

"I could say the same thing." My skin was tingling. I felt like we'd never run out of things to say.

"I'm just trying to put food on the table for my kids. Survival of the fittest, you know."

"Speaking of food." Howard reached over and brushed a few almonds off my lip. His touch sent a jolt through my face. This was better than most dates I had been on. He was worldly and secure. I was finally speaking to a man who was interested in what I had to say. Louis and I couldn't finish a conversation without saying *Fuck you* to each other. But enough, *Mr. Kill me with his smile* needed to leave.

"Sorry to cut this short, but I have a presentation that needs a few finishing touches." I stood, waited for him to do the same, walked into the living room, rubbed the silver glitter off an uphol-stered chair, and leaned against it.

"Glitter?" he asked, moving closer.

"Yes, lots of glitter," I giggled. The second cup of coffee had me wired.

Howard cupped my chin in his hands. I swallowed, not meet-ing his eyes, and then, not knowing how else to respond, looked right at him.

He leaned down and kissed me tentatively, waiting for me to kiss him back, which I did. His mouth was warm and inviting. He expertly prodded the inside of my mouth. Unhurried and deliberate. Exceptionally handsome businessmen didn't just appear in my house for a make-out fest. The butterflies were in an uproar. My ligaments melted, then began to shake as I felt my world spin out of control. I couldn't let this happen. I pulled away first.

Howard dropped his voice to a whisper, "I've been dying to do that. I can't get you out of my mind." Suddenly, the confidence he exuded so well was replaced with apprehension. The unexpected vulnerability made me want him even more. This was dangerous. I divorced a cheater. How could I even consider this, whatever *this* was? Every receptor in my brain told me to stop. But I couldn't help myself. It had been so long since I'd had a proper kiss. I had all but given up on passion. I reached up on my tiptoes and kissed him again, deeply, knowing I may never get this feeling again. He pulled himself into me, and I closed my eyes, letting my body relax. Feeling his weight on me, I suddenly wanted him to do things to me I hadn't done before.

We knew we were entering reckless territory. I considered the five-star testimonial he could give me: *The centerpieces came with a quickie on the kitchen floor!* I knew this had to stop, or I didn't know what would happen next.

Flustered, I pulled away again. I couldn't let my emotions undo all I had worked so hard for. Good girls don't kiss clients. "I can't," I said breathlessly. "Not yet. I mean, no. Just no."

Howard lifted my chin again with his hand and brushed a few more croissant crumbs away. "I'm sorry. I don't know what came over me. You are so beautiful." No one had called me beautiful in a long time. My whole body shuddered. Something told me that not many people had rejected this man before. Howard lowered his hand and grabbed my hand to shake it. "A pleasure doing business with you." He walked himself to the door.

"Thanks for the check. And breakfast." I didn't want him to leave.

"My pleasure. You can deposit it today. I'm truly sorry for the inconvenience. Talk to you soon, sunshine." I pressed my burning cheek onto the ice-cold door as I closed it after him.

I took a shower to get myself back into work mode. The Silverbloom proposal wasn't going to write itself, but I couldn't concentrate. I put on the TV to watch what was happening in the stock market. If I ever talked to Howard again, I wanted to sound like I knew a thing or two.

Eight hours slipped by. I did half as much work as usual and remained in a romance-fueled stupor, making me late to Asher's basketball game. I slid into the front seat of my car, peeking up at myself in the rearview mirror at red lights. The mirror revealed an unexplainable smile. A guilty face! The whole world would know he kissed me. Either an elephant was doing push-ups on my chest, or a full-blown panic attack was starting, and I contemplated pulling over.

Instead, I changed my radio station for the tenth time. AH… Barry Manilow (yes, really). I turned the volume louder, listening to him sing about taking a chance again and how you get what you get when you go for it. Now I was shaking my head to the beat and tapping the steering wheel, my foot pressing the gas pedal in tempo, pretending my legs were not made of rubber when *crunch!* I plowed into the car in front of me.

"Fuck! Fuck! Fuck!" I muttered, gripping the steering wheel. I turned down the volume to see better. I knew this day was too good to be true. I couldn't have guessed it was about to get worse. The shiny black Mercedes pulled onto a residential street, and I had no choice but to follow suit with my 100,000-mile, hopelessly dirty Toyota.

The sun was setting. There were no streetlamps or other cars nearby. It didn't look like too much damage to the other vehicle, but I knew I had to pull myself together and get out of my car to ensure the other driver was okay. This crazy schoolgirl crush was to blame. *Damn you, Howard Gardner!* I unbuckled my seatbelt, grabbed my purse, and opened the car door. The other driver beat me to it. Calm and confident, the tall blonde had already surveyed her back bumper and was walking toward me. Blondie's deliberate walk was familiar but was so out of context that it took me an extra moment to realize it was none other than Deenie Gardner.

Fuck, no. *Serves you right.*

"Oh my God, Leah! Are you ok?" Her concern startled me.

"I'm fine, I'm so sorry… Are *you* ok?" I was fired. I knew it. Game over.

"Fine…" Deenie removed her tortoiseshell sunglasses and examined the bumper again.

"I'm so embarrassed. I'll get my insurance card." This was not happening.

"No. Don't worry about it. I don't know this part of town very well. I… I'm late to an appointment, so I must've stopped my car short. I'm just so glad you're not hurt, sweetie." Was it my imagination, or was Deenie the one who seemed flustered now?

My voice was missing.

Deenie looked me squarely in the face. "It doesn't look like there's any damage. I'm in a bit of a rush. Let's just keep this between the two of us, shall we?" Her cornflower-blue eyes looked at me hopefully.

I couldn't believe my ears. "Are you sure?"

"I'm sure." She looked at her white Cartier watch. I'd noticed it at my house, but outside in the withering daylight, it looked like a giant sundial slapped on her arm. "I must get going. I'm so glad you're okay." She replaced the large glasses on her nose and got back into her car.

There was that *fine* comment again. Was everything in Deenie's world always fine?

I examined the damage and got back in my car. My car was loaded with dings and scraped tire rims. It was an occupational hazard of always being overwhelmed. Okay, I was a horrible driver. But this was a sign, and I might not be so lucky next time. *Stay away from Howard Gardner.* Peyton was gloating. Her and Cara's warnings were still fresh in my head. And I could hear my mom's voice: "*The best intentions yield the biggest mistakes.*" It wasn't the time to be taking advice from a dead woman. God knew I never took it when she was alive.

I'd never talk to Howard again. Starting immediately, all communication would be with Deenie. I had ten minutes to get to the basketball game and forget about any ridiculous fantasies I had conjured up. I knew better. I'd remove all thoughts of Howard from my head. Forever. After all, nothing happened. It was just a stupid kiss.

As if on cue to test my resolve, my phone rang. It was Howard. I let the call go to voicemail and pulled back into traffic. What in the world had I been thinking anyway?

DEPARTMENT OF JUSTICE

BACKGROUND NOTES

EDWARD GROSSMAN, CEO OF VG INDUSTRIES

Details were vague concerning how Edward made his fortune. He arrived in Garnet Springs forty years ago, fresh off a short-lived stint in Vegas with a now bankrupt casino. He refused to discuss his questionable background, stating, "ancient history belongs in the past." He eventually married Sunny, a local high school teacher with a disposition as bright as her name, quickly producing four sons who shared his great size but not his business acumen. Sunny volunteered at the local nursing home and often brought administrative work home. Edward claimed he never paid attention to his wife's work, and she didn't question him about his.

Headquartered in Las Vegas, with factories worldwide, Vitamin Global, also known as VG Industries, an international vitamin and health products behemoth, was, by all accounts, an exemplary business, and currently the number-two supplier to GNC. Edward owned a total of twenty-two companies, all headquartered in Las Vegas. Some were spun-off divisions of Vitamin Global. Others boasted banking alliances. All were public companies listed on the OTC market.

Every Thursday, weather permitting, he played golf with Howard Gardner, whom he considered his fifth son.

Eddie, as Mr. Gardner affectionately called him, stated his business relationship with Howard was a trusted one, then laughing, added, "like a marriage, but without aggravation. It's a mutual attraction, a romance of Machiavelli's proportions." Edward's contacts propelled Howard's status at Arbor Financial, and his generosity provided the seed money for the Gardner Stroke Center.

Howard managed Eddie's portfolio as well as executed Eddie's speculative stock trades. Some of the hunches panned out, and some did not. Eddie had the kind of money that it didn't matter. Eddie claimed he was careful and would never risk trading on anything but legitimate information. But he had the arrogance of a greedy man.

Mr. Gardner remembered a typical golf outing, with Eddie not playing well. It was never his style to be presumptuous, but he hoped it wasn't a health scare. He often joked with Eddie about his unhealthy eating, but Eddie dismissed his concerns.

"Part of my charm. Nobody wants a dirty joke told by a skinny guy eating a salad."

Eddie remained vague about that day. "Nursing homes. Well, I suppose it's possible my sources mentioned there were a few on the chopping block. But I'm always strategizing, so nothing specific rings a bell."

Howard claimed he questioned the sources, but revealed Eddie was uncooperative; it was common knowledge that Edward Grossman never revealed his sources.

Howard didn't recall precisely if Banyan Pharmaceuticals was discussed. Or if Eddie ever mentioned them in the same conversation as the nursing homes. He claimed that Banyan Pharmaceuticals was just one company in a long list of healthcare companies he routinely invested in. His research and development team provided him with the data, but Howard claimed it was purely a series of lucky guesses.

Eddie invested big. Howard invested bigger, with what he proudly called OPM. Other people's money.

FIVE

SERENDIPITY

So much for not speaking to Howard again. When he called the day after the fender bender, I assumed Deenie had confessed, they were hiring another party planner, and I'd be in negative territory for the month. I was so stunned at Deenie's laissez-faire attitude and eagerness to keep it a secret that I couldn't remember how much damage there was to her car. But Howard never mentioned it.

He called again the next day. And again, three days later. Each time, the conversations got longer. Howard was a relentless tease but also intuitive and funny. And I couldn't be rude to a client.

I was on the floor unpacking a box of embroidered sweatshirts, listening to Howard mull over a few long-lost relatives he'd added to the Bat Mitzvah list, when I received a text from Louis.

Dickhead: You need to tell Asher I have to go out of town and won't be able to take him to the Sixers game on Wednesday. Asher had been looking forward to this game for months.

Me: You tell him.

Dickhead: I'm at dinner. I don't have time to explain. Just say I have a scheduling conflict.

I punched the carpet three times. "DAMN IT! I have to hang up."

"What happened? Are you okay?"

"It's nothing." I got up and kicked the box, barefoot, possibly breaking a toe. "Ouch."

"Doesn't sound like nothing. Can I help?"

I took a deep breath. I didn't really want to give Howard a peek into my hatred for Louis, but my anger had its own agenda. "It's Louis. He cancels at the last minute. It's always some made-up conflict, and he doesn't have the guts to tell the kids. So he makes me the bad guy. He promised to take Asher to the basketball game with three other dads. And now he's going to be mysteriously out of town. If you ask me, he never bought the tickets. Asher's going to be crushed."

"I'm sorry you have to deal with this. Can't you buy the tickets?"

"Nope. Not in my budget. I need to go talk to my son and hopefully calm him down. You know, be the responsible parent. I'll talk to you soon."

At ten o'clock the next morning, a messenger delivered an envelope with two courtside tickets to the basketball game. It had to be Howard. No way was I accepting them.

I called Howard on his cell and said, "I'm assuming these tickets are from you?"

"What tickets?"

"Howard, I can't accept these tickets."

"Please take them. The firm has plenty—it's not a big deal."

"How would I even explain where they came from?"

"Just say it's from a very appreciative client."

"I don't know what to say. Thank you. It's very generous."

"Rule number one—never disappoint your kid if you can help it."

I'm not certain where Howard and his kindness came from or what I'd owe him, but the look on Asher's face when I gave him the tickets was worth it. I just hoped he wouldn't get used to it.

The next call was from Deenie, who explained she couldn't pick up the invitations and that Howard would come in her place. If I didn't know better, I'd think he planned it that way.

Howard arrived halfway through Scrabble night with the kids. The grin on his face was intoxicating. "Scrabble again? Are you prepping for a tournament?"

"Mom taught us to play when we were little. She said that it will keep our minds sharp and we may need that one day more than we know," Lily answered.

"That it does, and critical thinking. She's right. You have a very smart mother," Howard replied. He studied the board, trying to get a feel for our skill level.

"Watch my tiles while I grab the invitations?" I asked.

"Trust me not to take your turn?" Howard laughed.

"I trust you." Asher was winning tonight. I was so proud of the way my kids took the game seriously. I'd caught Asher studying the Scrabble dictionary, looking for new ways to beat us. Lily's vocabulary amazed me, which made sense since she was planning on majoring in journalism. I disappeared into the dining room to get the invitation boxes and carried them back to the living room, placing them on the cocktail table.

"Here, let me help you." Howard approached the table but

stopped short in front of my wall unit, admiring a collection of family pictures. "What a lovely family. You all have the same..." Howard's voice froze. He lifted a silver-framed eight-by-ten picture of my mom and dad taken at my wedding. "Candace. Oh my God. Of course."

"Did you just say my mother's name?" The kids stopped rearranging their tiles and looked at Howard.

"Did you know my grandmom?" Lily asked, shocked.

Howard lifted the frame, bringing it to his face, examining it closer, and said, "I can't believe this. I... When did you say your mom died?"

"June will be fifteen years." Howard got a faraway look in his eyes. "You're scaring me. What?" My body was transported to that horrible time. How could he have known my mother? He didn't have a stroke center back then.

"What hospital?"

"Medical Center of New Jersey. It wasn't convenient, but they had the best protocol at the time."

"My father was a patient there, too. He died six months before your mother."

"I'm confused, Howard. I thought you were from New York. How would you know that?" Both kids had their eyes glued to him. Howard removed his coat and sat down on my sofa, still holding the ornate frame.

"It was the best facility. I wanted my dad closer to me. Board games, especially Scrabble, are therapy for stroke patients. It helps them with dexterity, slows cognitive decline, and improves short-term memory and word recall. My father was failing, but Scrabble kept him alive. I visited every day. I brought my older girls every weekend. We played Scrabble like it was an Olympic game. It brought him so much joy."

I winced, remembering that my kids never got to spend any time with my mom. The stroke wing was no place for babies. "I played with my mom, too. My mom lost her ability to speak, and the only way we communicated was through the words she made with the tiles."

Howard continued, lost in his memory. "My dad got worse. He had an old, original Scrabble game. Believe it or not, he was friends with the inventor. I brought the game with me every time we visited. Didn't want to leave it there. It was quite valuable, even had an inscription to my dad on it. Anything that would have kept his memory vibrant was important."

The room was silent. Like we were having a séance and the spirits could break through at any moment, interrupting the tension.

"Anyway, my dad died. I was broken. I couldn't stop going back to the hospital. He was gone, but the essence of him was still alive in the hallways. I'd roam the corridors day after day, trying to make sense of it all. And then I stumbled across your mother's room."

My hands flew to my mouth. This couldn't be happening.

"A young woman was inside playing Scrabble with her. I remember her long, brown hair. I could tell she was carrying the entire weight of her mom's illness on her shoulders."

"It was me. My sister doesn't play." My voice was barely audible. Howard was replaying a part of my life I had buried.

"The nurses wouldn't give me much information. HIPAA laws and all. But they told me Candace was better on the days she played."

"My father came when he could. He wasn't retired yet. My

brother, sister, and I juggled visiting, but there were days… I felt so guilty… she was alone… I couldn't get there."

"One day, I stopped in with my sixty-plus-year-old Scrabble game. Candace had a smile that beckoned me. I let her feel the texture of the tiles. The original tiles are different, you know? Smoother. Glossy. Did you know they were made of solid wood? The racks made from floor molding? The inventor made them in his kitchen." Howard looked at me. I shook my head. I didn't know any of this. "My dad worked on the patent for the double and triple point squares with the zigzag lines. They were designed so you wouldn't have to lift the tile to see the reward."

"This is fascinating."

"Your mom was alone with her thoughts. She perked up when I arrived. So I sat, and we started to play. She was quite good. And then I came back the next day. And the next. I couldn't do any more for my dad, but I could help someone else. It was during these games with your mom that the idea for the stroke center began percolating."

My hand was still on my mouth in disbelief. The kids were staring. "It was you? The nurse said someone was coming in to sit with her when we couldn't be there. She said he wanted to remain anonymous." How had our paths never crossed before?

"I didn't want to intrude on your grief."

"I can't…" It felt like a giant rock was stuck in my throat. I sat next to Howard, touching my mom's face in the picture.

"So I kept coming. For six months. I told myself I'd come forever if it could brighten her day. And then…" Howard searched my face for confirmation. "I arrived on a Tuesday. It was raining heavily, torrential storms. I had been there on Saturday… we had an out-of-town wedding… I got back late on Monday… I knew she didn't have much time left… and I… I couldn't let her be alone."

I felt the tears start to drip down my face. "I was there on Friday. The nurse called that night. They knew it would be soon." I looked at the kids. They knew this part of the story by heart. The hatred. The guilt. "I planned on visiting on Saturday. Asher had a fever. I needed Louis to stay with the kids, but he had an *emergency* and was gone all day. I called him, sobbing, begging him to come home, and he didn't pick up. I was a mess. Louis didn't return home until after visiting hours. I called the hospital, and the nurse said she was sleeping peacefully. My mom died Sunday morning. Luckily, my dad was with her. The funeral was on Tuesday. In that horrendous storm." The tears fell freely. I felt like I was losing her all over again. My past and present converged.

"When I got there on Tuesday, the nurses told me. I was gutted. The torture of losing my dad and the pain of losing Candace were intertwined. Obviously, I had missed the funeral, and going to Shiva seemed like overstepping. I said Kaddish for her for a month."

This stunning man said Kaddish, the Jewish prayer for the dead, for my mother. I needed to let that sink in. "I never went back to the hospital. I couldn't bear it. I wasn't there when I should have been. I could never forgive Louis. Not ever. I knew damn well where he was that day." The hatred was seeping out of my pores, taking possession of my voice box.

"Your father sent quite a sizable donation when I opened the first stroke center. Apparently, he was able to finagle my name from the nurses."

I smiled softly. "My dad would definitely be able to do that. He never told me that part."

"This is the coolest story ever!" exclaimed Lily. "I'm going to write about this one day."

"My daughter's a talented writer."

"I'm sure your mom would be so proud. Of all of you. Especially that you've continued the Scrabble tradition." Howard stood. "By the way, whoever spelled *hierarchy* missed the second *r*."

"Oh man! Well, no one challenged me, so I'm good!" Asher explained.

"Brain not working on full capacity tonight," I said, still in shock. I stood too, dwarfed by Howard's imposing height.

He handed me back the picture frame. "Candace. I still can't believe it. You're so lucky to have had her for a mother."

"I didn't realize it at the time."

"None of us do. Finish your game. I'll be on my way now."

I was numb, but I silently walked Howard to the door. What are the odds? The universe was flashing a sign. I just didn't know what it was saying.

SIX

NO WILLPOWER

I couldn't wait to call my father. The story spilled out of my mouth with a passion he had forgotten I had. "Can you believe this? Our mystery Scrabble angel. In my house. While we're playing Scrabble! His daughter's Bat Mitzvah—it's the most extravagant party I've ever worked on."

"I'm sure you'll do a phenomenal job."

"He told me you sent him a donation."

"I did. He said he was going to do something special to honor Mom, and I told him he did enough while she was alive."

"And you never reached out to him again?"

"Sometimes you need to put trauma in a place and only visit it when you feel it's important. I figured we all needed closure, and you were so distraught with the divorce that there was no reason to keep bringing up the end of her life. I was worried about you enough, *ziskeit.*"

I loved it when my father called me the Yiddish name for sweetheart. It made me feel safe.

"It was a bad time."

"And look at you now. If you happen to speak to him again, please send my regards."

"I promise I will, Daddy."

The next morning, I met the girls for a quick breakfast. They both knew about my mom's mystery Scrabble player and were shocked that it was Howard.

"Oh my gosh, it's like a romance novel!" said Cara.

"Exactly!" I said.

"Not exactly," piped Peyton. "It's a touching story, but I don't need to remind you he's a married man, with a family and a very powerful reputation. It definitely shows a lot about his character, but remember to exercise some caution."

"Must you ruin everything?"

"That's my job, Pollyanna."

The calls with Howard continued. He convinced me I should transfer my money to his firm. I was positive he'd do better than my dad's stodgy financial advisor, where my divorce money had been resting comfortably for years. Howard didn't waste any time. The transfer forms appeared in my inbox by the next morning, but I decided to wait until after the Bat Mitzvah, as a conflict of interest could be messy.

"How about I come over and play a quick game. I'd love to see your smiling face."

"You're flattering me, but it's not a good idea. Maybe another time."

Howard often called late at night. Although I stood my ground and consistently said no to a visit, it was easy to fall into a comfortable conversation. I poured myself a glass of wine and curled up in my bed, the phone nestled between my ear and the pillow.

"Tell me why you won't see me. Is there someone else sharing that bed of yours?"

"You're married," I said firmly, realizing that didn't matter to him.

"Not for long."

"There's a line if I ever heard one."

"I'm serious. Deenie's only interested in looking like the ideal wife. The most generous donor. We haven't behaved like married people in a long time. I don't know the last time we had a conversation that didn't revolve around the Bat Mitzvah or an appearance at a charity gala. The minute the flashbulb goes off, we barely look at each other. It's a marriage of convenience. We're roommates, not lovers. We live parallel lives. And the minute this Bat Mitzvah's over, we are over."

I knew what he meant by parallel lives. I'd played that charade, too. I didn't answer.

"It's the truth."

"Ah, the age-old 'just staying until the Bar Mitzvah is over.' How many women have you said this to?" I'd heard that one before. Look great for the pictures, and then within three months—POOF—one spouse files for divorce.

They weren't fooling anyone. Not the friends who watched the relationship unravel slowly. Not the photographer capturing the picture-perfect moments and a few not-meant-to-be-seen moments. And certainly not the kids. I'd yet to meet a teenager blindsided by their parents' divorce.

"Eighteen."

"Eighteen what?"

"You asked how many women I've said this to."

"For real?"

"No, silly. I haven't told anyone. But we aren't doing anyone any favors by pretending we have a stable marriage. Deenie is dealing with some, um, personal issues. How do I put it? She's fragile. Every few weeks, she goes to a special spa in Nashville to get back on track. She's not the woman people think she is. A touch of…" Howard's voice became a whisper. "Mental illness. Depression. She has her moments. We all walk on eggshells. I've probably stayed longer than I should have. I don't want to hurt her, but we've been talking about this divorce for a long time."

"I'm sorry. I didn't realize any of this."

"Everyone wants the world to think they have it all. The Bat Mitzvah? I know it's over the top. But that's what people expect. Deenie and Addison are happy. It's the least I could do."

"I don't know what to say. You seem like the perfect couple."

"Perfect? Fourteen points! Without any double or triple points."

"Maybe I should start writing these down."

"Seriously. Don't get caught up in illusions, Leah. I don't want to have regrets. There's too much life left to live and no one to share it with."

His introspection struck a chord. I realized he had so much and so little at the same time.

"What would you do?"

"What wouldn't I do? Learn to fly a plane. Ride a motorcycle naked. Take a leave of absence and climb Mount Everest. I work hard. I want to enjoy life."

"Naked naked?"

"That's the part that interested you?"

"No, definitely not." *Yes, definitely.*

"Our family vacations are a joke. My Black American Express card deserves its own seat in first class. I go to the gym. Play golf. Deenie gets a massage. It's been like this for way too long. A polite hello in the kitchen. We don't sleep in the same room anymore. It wouldn't be that way if I were with someone down to earth. Someone I could talk to. Like you."

I tried to be empathetic to someone complaining about their luxury vacations. But his vulnerability captivated me once again, and I closed my eyes for a brief moment and wished I were lying next to him. "But… you…"

"How come I'm the only one pouring my heart out? What do you want in a relationship?"

"Who said I want one?"

"Tell me you don't." I thought about it for a moment. Howard made me feel safe. I didn't feel embarrassed about revealing my private thoughts. Something told me I could trust him.

"Not to pretend."

"I don't follow you. Why would you have to pretend?"

"Because sometimes I think nothing is real." I heard Howard inhale and exhale loudly.

"That ex really did a number on you."

"Worse than you think. And Peyton doesn't let me forget it."

"Why does Peyton need to remind you of your mistakes?"

"She's my best friend, she's just looking out for me, but she'd have my head on a platter if she knew I was talking to you. She's warned me about guys like you."

"I'm not like other guys," Howard said firmly, "Trust me, Leah. I'm not."

The calls got serious. It started with Eddie, Howard's stand-in father and mentor. The man with the Midas touch.

"How'd you meet Eddie? He just arrived one day with a suitcase full of cash?" I was on the floor of my dining room, sketching Georgia's welcome sign and deciding between fonts.

"I don't remember, but suddenly, Eddie was everywhere. The golf course. Charity functions. The VIP lounge at the airport. If I didn't know better, I would've thought the old man was stalking me. He reminded me of my father. Same hairline. Same wired spectacles perched halfway down his nose. The same Borscht Belt era jokes. Trivial things, but enough to spark a friendship. In the back of my mind, sometimes I feel like it's my father I'm talking to. Or that my father sent Eddie to me. I know it sounds bizarre."

"No, I get it. There are times I'll have a creativity block. And I'll sit for hours, sometimes days, waiting for inspiration to hit. And then I'll have a dream with my mom in it, and suddenly the ideas will pour out of me. Or I'll be decorating a cake and think I see my mom watching, guiding my hand, telling me where to put the flourishes. Sometimes I feel like we get along better now that she's dead. It's eerie."

"That's what happens when we miss someone. We find ways to bring them back where they're needed."

"Yeah."

"Yeah."

"So you think Eddie's your dad coming back to haunt you?"

"Not haunt. I think mentors fill a void we didn't know we needed."

"I never thought about it like that." Or that just maybe my mom sent me Howard.

"I was intrigued by Eddie's connections, so I pitched him my idea for a stroke center. Before long, Eddie was writing checks and introducing me to architects, hospital CEOs, renowned doctors, and stroke experts. I never could've raised the money myself. I had a good position at the firm, but I wouldn't be where I am now if it weren't for him."

"And where's that?"

"In a golden tower handcuffed to a woman I don't love."

I began to feel sorry for him. I couldn't help myself. I'd never had a man show his vulnerabilities to me before. "Why you? Didn't you ask Eddie where all the money came from?"

"I didn't need to. He sat on the board of several public companies. People love to throw money into philanthropy projects. A little altruism goes a long way. You don't go around asking millionaires where their money came from. Eddie didn't like his name on too many projects. And I wanted to be the guy to leave a legacy. You know what I mean."

I didn't, but I said I did. "Of course."

"The checks got bigger. Eddie stayed anonymous. He said he'd made mistakes when he was younger and was lucky to start over, so he brought me in as an investor in some of his deals. Eddie's business insight is second to none. I don't know how he does it. There's a pharmaceutical company and a nursing home. He thinks they're on the verge of merging—" He paused. "I'm sorry. I must be boring you."

"Not at all. I love that you're so passionate about what you do."

"Remind me how you're still single."

"I work all the time. If I don't work, my kids don't eat. You're passionate about your work. It's different."

"I'm passionate about a lot of things." That was my cue to end the call. His voice was deliberately suggestive. We'd begun stumbling toward something I wouldn't be able to resist.

"Alright, Casanova. Time to hang up."

The weeks flew by, and now I was talking to Howard at least once a day. There were days I convinced myself he was buttering me up so Addison's party would be beyond expectations. On other days, the conversation flowed like we were a couple who had been together for decades. The connection to my mom was a link to my past that I felt needed to be brought back to life, as if I now had my mother's seal of approval to continue talking to Howard. Soon, the intensity of the calls increased to a full-fledged phone affair. A platonic one, but the calls became an addiction.

Howard mentioned confidential research reports and stock recommendations. At first, I felt uneasy listening to him reveal financial information. It was just a lot of jumbled company names. But the more we spoke, the more I wanted to learn.

Before long, I had a firsthand account of who Howard's big clients were, as well as their finances, all secretive information he shouldn't have been sharing with me. Instead of seeing this as a red flag, I took it to show how much he trusted me.

"Did you ever consider going into the business?" Howard asked one Sunday morning, while driving to the golf course, to meet the mysterious Eddie.

"Finance?"

"You'd be terrific. You're a quick learner and personable. I could use someone like you."

"I entertained the thought more than once, actually, but Louis told me I didn't have the guts to work in a man's world, and that was the end of the discussion. I like what I do, for now. I need to pay for college."

"Don't listen to anything that moron said. I'm telling you, you'd make a lot more money."

"Probably." I tried to keep my constant battle with the budget to myself, but he had to have figured out I was living on the edge. And not in a good way.

"Work for me. The clients would love you."

"I should go make dinner for my kids."

I checked my phone constantly for missed calls. Funny emojis. Scrabble trivia. Tracking the NASDAQ. Peyton accused me of being distant. This was my brain on Howard.

Two weeks before the Bat Mitzvah, I met with Deenie and Addison to review the final touches. Addison was warm and courteous, not usual for many thirteen-year-old girls. Deenie mentioned the connection to my mom and how she remembered it being such an integral part of Howard's stroke center idea.

She also appeared to be a doting mom and a faithful wife. I wondered if she knew Howard was planning on leaving her. Perhaps her charm was a well-rehearsed act or merely a façade to help save face during adversity.

Seven days before the Bat Mitzvah. I was working sixteen hours a day on the details, but one night, after a few glasses of wine, Howard crossed the line.

"Okay, pretty lady, why don't you tell me what turns you on?" All the business talk was well-played stimulation. "I'm sorry. I didn't mean to make you feel uncomfortable."

"I think you know exactly what you're doing." Infatuation crawled through me, landing between my legs. I didn't know if it was the wine, the suppressed vixen in me, or if I had subconsciously waited for this all along. I felt his breath through the phone. Waiting. Knowing he unlocked something in me. It was after midnight, and the kids were asleep, but I got up and quietly closed my bedroom door, fell into the comfort of my bed, and whispered in a voice I didn't know I still had, "Tell me what you want."

Howard's voice dropped. "Close your eyes, Leah. Clear your mind and don't think about anything except the sound of my voice. Are they closed?"

"Mm hmm."

"Good. Now picture me slowly unbuttoning your shirt. I want to watch your body shiver as I step behind you to take off your bra. It's lacy, isn't it? I want to slide my hands around your back and touch your breasts as I kiss the back of your neck. Do you feel what you're doing to me? I want to rip your skirt off. And then I want you to beg me to touch you. Can you beg me, Leah? How bad do you want me to touch you? I want to turn your body to face me and rub my hands up your thighs. How wet are you now?"

I couldn't speak. I was losing myself in his voice. In the thought of him. I should've stopped.

"Don't touch yourself. Just picture what my fingers would feel like teasing you. Slowly dipping my fingers inside you. I want to make your knees go weak. And then I'm going to grab your face and kiss you as you've never been kissed before, and I want you to feel my body pressed against yours. How bad do you want me? Can you tell me, Leah?"

"Howie, I can't."

"Shh. Of course you can. Stay with me. Now touch yourself. Let me hear you breathe. Don't stop touching yourself until I tell you to."

"Oh God." I opened my eyes. My heart was racing. Desire flooded my body. "I need to go to sleep."

"Sweet dreams."

I tossed and turned all night, unable to think of anything but Howie making love to me on a beach. On a plane. Rich people's places. And then any place at all.

Embarrassed, I kept the next call brief. Two days later, he reverted to all types of sexual innuendos and then picked up where he had left off. This time, I did nothing to stop him.

"Close your eyes again. Think of me kissing you. Picture yourself putting your hands on my waist and then kneeling in front of me. I hear how deep you're breathing, yes, baby, keep going. Now, picture taking my pants off. That's it. I want you to feel every inch of me. I want to picture your face while I'm inside you."

I couldn't breathe. The conversation escalated to full-fledged porn. Howie heard me unleashed and uninhibited, bringing things to another level. It was just harmless phone sex, I told myself. He'd probably have sex with his wife when we hung up.

For the next seventy-two hours, I worked around the clock. Addison's Bat Mitzvah was finally here, and for all I knew, I'd never hear from Howie and Deenie again.

SEVEN

CELEBRATE GOOD TIMES

eenie's gown was the most beautiful dress I'd ever seen. Layers of spun champagne lace formed a strapless sheath that accentuated her almost nonexistent hips, overlaid with hints of shimmering paillettes strategically positioned. Her hair, a waterfall of curls, metallic gold ribbon braided throughout, added to her chic elegance with a finesse that made me self-conscious. I was positive Deenie, wife, socialite, and enchanted hostess, did not eat Tate's cookies in bed. I found it hard to believe the implications Howard made about her mental state. Or that he was not sleeping with her. *Lies*, I told myself. *All lies*.

The party looked like a red-carpet paparazzi event. Professional photographers feverishly flashed, making sure everybody, from a second cousin to an old business acquaintance, would ultimately be recorded at this year's social event. The room was a masterpiece of lights and sparkles. It was the defining moment in my career.

Daniel Ross was the entertainment, so the night was sure to be a blast. His packages were overpriced but legendary. Daniel was booked a solid two years in advance and was a hot commodity in the party world, and the only person I knew who was busier than I was. He was difficult to reach, and I teased him that he must have a booty call near every wedding and Bar Mitzvah in the Delaware Valley, and he just winked and answered, "Lucky Lady or Lady Luck, they're both my pleasure and my pain."

But wow, Daniel could get a party going. He had an awkwardness to him, like the nerd in every John Hughes Brat Pack movie, but once the microphone was in his hand, his energy lit up the room as he swiveled his hips to a discerning tempo. Daniel had a magnetic personality, making every person from the wallflower at table six to your eighty-three-year-old great-uncle Saul think they were on *Dancing with the Stars*. The dance floor was on fire. He had unique hats and funny glasses, and the most original inflatable props, keeping every guest engaged. He was a powerhouse in tight pants and high-top bedazzled sneakers and was "worth every penny," according to his website's testimonials.

I couldn't help feeling envious when I saw Howard walk into the ballroom like he owned the place, wearing a custom-fitted tux and a bow tie made from the same fabric as Deenie's gown. Adrenaline rushed through my veins. Howard charmed everyone in his path with a smile and a self-assured presence cultivated over years of experience, and I was no exception. I couldn't fall for it tonight. The muscles in my chest tightened. Our shared history was not part of this equation. Howard stepped onto the dance floor and did a few steps from the Macarena. He grabbed Daniel's microphone, crooning his best Sinatra rendition of "The Way You Look Tonight" to test the sound, and then helped Daniel rearrange the speakers. He was like a kid at a carnival. I watched Howard put on a large pair of goofy glasses and pose with a sombrero for the photo booth, bringing the attendant into the picture with him. I laughed but knew I couldn't let him distract me. Every centerpiece needed to be secured so that nothing would catch on fire or fall into the lap of even the worst of mothers-in-law. I'd hired eight assistants for this party. Place cards positioned alphabetically. Check. Two hundred votive candles lit. Check. Swag bags arranged before the guests arrived. Check. I spotted a tiny crack on the sign-in board and made a swift exit to retrieve a glue gun from my glove compartment. Howard was surveying the bar. I didn't realize he followed me. As I leaned up from the passenger seat, he grabbed my waist from behind. Please, not now. Oh my God. This was crazy.

"Hello, beautiful."

"Okay, I know you're not talking to me." I spun around. My hair was pinned up. My work uniform consisted of black jeans, a black bodysuit, sneakers, and the understated diamond-stud earrings I inherited from my mother. Strands of purple ribbons hung loosely around my neck. Velcro wrapped around my wrists like bangle bracelets. There were scissors in one pocket, a roll of tape in the other, and most likely, a smattering of glitter on my face.

"Mazel Tov! You look great!" I may have needed a defibrillator instead of a glue gun.

"The ballroom's fabulous. I don't know how you do it."

"All an illusion." After the initial contract, Deenie had added life-size snow globes and a photo wall made of starfish and flowers, bringing the total to over seventy-five thousand dollars. Excessive yet tasteful. And the best affair I'd ever put together. No pun intended on the word *affair*.

"I can't thank you enough." He moved his face closer. I could smell the smoky flavor of top-shelf whiskey and remembered what those lips felt like.

"Do you want to join me for a spin around the dance floor?"

"Now?"

He took hold of my hand and twirled me around. "Not tonight. But one night. Maybe every night."

I breathed heavily, not trusting myself anymore to decipher whether he was kidding or flirting. Whether I was infatuated with him or just a fool, this was no joke.

As we stood in the parking garage of the Ritz-Carlton, I reprimanded myself for every intimate detail I revealed over the past few weeks. It was a grown-up game of truth or dare.

I felt my face redden, thinking about how his deep voice urged me on to the point of no turning back. I couldn't decide if I regretted it or not. He noticed my blush, steadied my arm with his hand, and then swept back a glitter-covered loose strand of hair from my eye. A few specks had surreptitiously fallen onto my eyelashes. It was May, but I was trembling. He lifted my chin and said, "I know this isn't the time or the place, but what are we going to do about the fact that I can't stop thinking about you?"

I ignored my instinct to analyze his words. Ignored the gnawing envy eating away at my insides. Instead, I smiled and said, "It's going to be one hell of a party."

JUST A LITTLE OLD-FASHIONED ENVY

It wasn't like me to be jealous of clients. I was happy. Happy enough.

I needed a diversion to keep myself from imagining Howard and Deenie together all night. It was precisely the type of event that pulled you closer. I'd watched it firsthand, a stark reminder of all they'd built together—what *they* shared. It was as if two hundred grand's worth of baby lamb chops and filet mignon, plus over three hundred people doing the Cha Cha Slide, was the secret potion that made you realize the latent discourse and daily squabbles of family life meant nothing. That it was all worth it. The smile on your kid's face. The bunkmates who solidified their camp popularity. The cousins from overseas. The childhood friend you'd never be friends with now, but history had a way of finding itself on guest lists. The symbolic lifting of the chairs into the air. Candle lighting ceremony to memorialize dead relatives. A celebration steeped in tradition. Hands shaken, kisses blown, glasses clinked. It's why I did what I did. But tonight's party was a world I'd never be a part of.

I pulled up to Peyton's house and let myself in. When we were kids, Peyton often walked into my house without ringing the bell. My mother would scream, running to protect her precious samples.

"I don't care if it's Robert Redford, you ring the damn bell. What if we were doing something in private?" Those crazy companies. The meetings. The recruiting. The parties. Like she was a CIA agent instead of an Avon Lady.

"Like what? Are you clipping coupons for the mob?"

"Tell your friend if she wants to come in; she rings the bell."

"Peyton, Mom. She's my best friend! She's practically my sister."

"You have a sister." I hated to admit that Rachel and I never connected the way Peyton and I did. Rachel designed sets on Broadway. We talked a few times a month, but it wasn't even close to my bond with Peyton. I hadn't even told Rachel about Howie's connection to our mom yet.

Peyton's husband, Leonardo, a world-class chef and cookbook author, was outside grilling steaks. Jadyn and Cassie, two miniature Peytons with the same bouncy cherry curls, ran to hug me. I took off my shoes and melted into my surroundings. I pulled the clip out of my hair and felt the weight of the past few months lift. These were my people. Peyton's billowy skirt skimmed the floor as she made her way toward me. She handed me a glass of wine; her grip was forceful. "Spill."

"Like the freaking Met Gala, but with kosher food. Privilege wins. You'll see the pictures on my website. And Instagram. And everywhere."

"And?"

"And what?" I sipped my wine, a fruity, light-bodied pinot grigio Leonardo had chosen.

"Are you and Jason Momoa going to finish this Harlequin nonsense and ride off into the sunset together?"

"I don't know what you're talking about."

"You know exactly what I'm talking about. You've been walking on air for months. I haven't seen you like this since you met Louis, and we know how that turned out."

I bit the inside of my lip. If I told Peyton the truth or at least some version of it, she'd stop thinking I was hiding something. "You think something's going on with Howie?"

"You call him Howie?"

"He told me to."

"What else did he tell you? Wait, no. Let me guess." Peyton put her hands up, resting her fingers on her temples. "He's miserable in his marriage."

"They've already met with the attorneys. They're technically separated, just waiting until after the …" I put my wine down so I could pull my hair back up.

Not listening and still with her fingers on her temples, Peyton kept going, "You're refreshing. You're smart. And now the connection to your mom, that's the icing on the cake. He can't stop thinking about you. His wife doesn't understand him. He'd like to get to know you better. They don't have sex anymore." My jaw dropped. "Should I go on? He's getting a divorce. Just has to work out a few things. Jesus, do you know what I do for a living? Do you know how many smart, successful, independent women I've had to pick up off the floor, literally?"

"Nothing happened."

"Yet."

"Nothing happened. A few flirty phone calls. Totally harmless. I promise."

"That's what they all say."

IT MAY AS WELL BE SPRING

$\mathcal{S}$pring buzzed by like summer was daring it to disappear.

I did my best not to miss our weekly breakfast. It was sidewalk sale season; the café opened outdoor seating, and the Pyramid Girls were multiplying once more. I watched a new batch of vivaciousness schlep Rubbermaid boxes of merchandise from their cars to curated table displays. Rick watched proudly, tallying profits in his head. Ivy, a close friend until three months ago when the Pyramid Girls abducted her, had informed us that, in addition to rent, Rick got a percentage of the sales.

Cara wrapped up a purchase at the FOREVER LIP table, nodding in agreement with Lyssa, a new consultant. Lyssa had previously worked as a receptionist at the local hair salon and sported a new hairstyle every other week. This week, it was a trendy bob. She was a former Yogette Coquette, not a very nice one either. We were in the self-checkout line at Whole Foods last month, and I knew she pretended to be on the phone so she didn't have to say hello. A few days later, when she saw me at the café, Lyssa was so friendly you'd think I offered her some bone marrow.

A Mean Girl. Shameful. Malicious. Unkind. The type of woman who stopped inviting me to dinner parties when they got wind of my divorce. Didn't they know that being cheated on isn't contagious?

Cara got back to our table, breathless and excited. "This lipstick. You have to try it."

"I'm begging you—don't involve me with this crap. And newsflash: Lyssa's a bitch. She's nice in public and nasty in private."

Cara continued while examining the milky pink tube. "You put this lipstick on in the morning, and you don't have to reapply it all day—eight whole hours. You can drink coffee, eat, and even kiss; it won't rub off! You don't need any other lipsticks."

"You sound like you're on QVC." For someone with a master's degree in finance, I expected more. But she was effusive, so I was gentle. "Cara, you know that lipstick is made with shellac? As in polyurethane. Furniture varnish. I use it to seal centerpieces to keep the beads from falling off. Why do you think you need to buy their industrial-strength lipstick remover? You'll wind up ripping the skin on your lips off, and you're right—you'll never need any other lipstick because your lips will be gone."

Peyton perked up. "Leave her alone. It's just lipstick."

We both cut Cara a lot of slack. Filling the void of her dead husband with retail therapy was one thing; her fascination with these products was a lesson in futility. And now the parties. She was obsessed.

Cara didn't seem to mind my negativity. "I'm having a private party for Lyssa, and you can see for yourself when they launch their new products."

"I love you, but please don't invite me. These businesses should be investigated."

"Lyssa's trying to get back on her feet since her husband got laid off a few months ago."

"Fired," I added. "For cause." I stole a piece of bacon from Peyton's plate and ate it.

Lyssa's husband, a beloved coach, was under investigation for stealing from the Garnet Springs Soccer Fund. He claimed it was an honest mistake, but the timing seemed coincidental with the purchase of their new in-ground pool.

"She's down on her luck, and this lipstick's fabulous. I see no reason not to help."

"You know you can buy shellac at Home Depot and brush it on your lips for the same effect? Much cheaper too."

"I'm hosting a tea next Wednesday at my house, and I expect you to attend. Lyssa's bringing a few new consultants. It'll be heaps of fun."

"Is Jim Jones deejaying?"

Peyton kicked me under the table.

"And whatever you do, Leah, please don't call them Pyramid Girls. It's downright disrespectful."

"But that's what they are — cult leaders with a license to steal. It's multi-level marketing. You should know better. I'm telling you, they're pyramid schemes. My mom was their biggest supporter when I was growing up. She lost so much money, you have no idea. And then she'd bounce back and join another one. I lived in this world. It almost ruined us. It's a scam."

"Tea starts at six."

"No promises. I'm overloaded with work."

Cara looked like I slapped her. Peyton kicked me again.

"Okay, I'll try."

"Everyone's just trying to make a living," Cara said defensively.

I wasn't lying about the overload. Luckily, my business was booming. Unluckily, my finances were still on shaky ground. I couldn't afford the lipstick starter set even if I wanted it.

The letter from Louis's lawyer arrived two weeks after Addison's Bat Mitzvah. It was a double-edged sword. Louis stalked my Instagram, attempting to assess my income, and then filed to reduce the child support again. It was a vicious cycle. At this rate, I'd never catch up.

As expected, the Bat Mitzvah had been the event of the season. Deenie had sent me five referrals so far. Addison was photographed wearing a deep purple mermaid gown, lying across the head table amid a flurry of sequins, and a meringue concoction made of crushed seashells and whipped glue, spelling out her name in shades of lavender. Life of the Party was splashed across more Instagram feeds and influencer posts than I could count. I couldn't pay for advertising like this. Howie texted me a selfie next to the five-tiered tie-dyed cake edged with dollops of turquoise whipped cream. He was drunk, but it made me wonder why he was texting me while partying with family and friends. I felt guilty. Homewrecker. Hussy. Life was a conflict of emotions. I had a busy few weeks ahead and needed to focus on two graduation brunches, the Silverbloom fiasco, and Cooper's party, which I'd make no money on.

Howie's calls continued. I couldn't resist the rousing sound of his voice. No doubt, the kids had picked up on my upbeat mood. Cara and Peyton asked what kind of happy pills I was taking and said I was perkier than a Pyramid Girl. My father said I sounded blissful. It was a tough lie. But by this point, I was lying to everyone.

The following Wednesday, as I got ready for Cara's insufferable tea, I overheard Asher on the phone with Louis. They usually ate at the kids' favorite restaurant, Coco Bella, a family-owned Italian restaurant known for its bruschetta and mozzarella-stuffed meatballs, which used to be my favorite restaurant when Louis and I were still on speaking terms. Now, it was too risky to show my face there. I didn't need any confrontations, and who knew who Louis would be with?

"Did Dad cancel again?"

Asher looked cagey. My baby had grown to be an athletic and muscular man who towered over Lily and me. Gone were the pudgy cheeks and freckles, but what remained were sensitive, pale blue eyes carrying a hurt I couldn't erase. Lily nodded her head, encouraging Asher to answer. Her graceful body slouched a bit, admitting defeat. She was selective about divulging what went on at their dad's house. She thought they were protecting me, but failed to realize it was they who needed protecting.

Asher ignored her, fidgeted with the waistband of his basketball shorts, and said, "No, he's coming." The kids' car was in the shop, and I needed my car tonight, so Louis had to pick them up.

"He's bringing someone," Lily confessed.

"Huh? Bringing someone where?" I was clueless, which, based on my preoccupations over the past few months, was par for the course.

Lily licked her lips, contemplating how much to say. "Dad's dating someone."

"Your dad's always dating someone."

"He wants us to meet her. Her name's Jackie."

I felt a pit form in my stomach. The kids were collateral damage after Louis's last divorce. The man just kept moving on, and I spent Saturday nights watching twenty-five-year-old rom-coms, every limb in my body aching after setting up and breaking down parties. Whereas Louis had no problem finding a perpetual parade of available women, all averaging fifteen years younger than him, I was caught up in an endless loop of *Sweet Home Alabama*, *The Wedding Planner*, and *How to Lose a Guy in 10 Days*.

"I'm sure it won't last. Your father's not so great with commitment."

"This is so annoying. I don't want to go." Lily plopped down on the sofa, throwing her head back in exasperation and scooching her mini skirt up way too high.

"Are you wearing underwear?" Please let her be wearing underwear.

"Ew, Mom. It's my dance leotard. I'm staying home."

"It's just dinner. You'll survive." If Lily stayed home, Louis would blame me for meddling. Plus, *When Harry Met Sally* was on later. I might need to watch it again. Just for reinforcement.

Louis pulled his shiny new BMW convertible into the driveway, and I strained to see what the latest eye candy looked like. An endless pile of dark curls, deep cleavage, and a playful smile. How he racked them up was beyond my comprehension. I called out to the kids to be kind and returned to my closet to get dressed. I had a tea to get to.

Cara had a knack for decorating. The fragrance of peonies danced with hints of roses. A subtle whiff of lavender drifted into my nose. Splashes of pink intermingled with serene white daisies. Her house looked like an English garden, but it didn't stop me from feeling like I had walked into the seventh-grade cafeteria. I'd chosen a ruffled sundress with pink carnations on it, so I considered leaning against the wall and pretending to be wallpaper. Waiters held silver platters stacked with scones and fresh berries. I headed to a cucumber sandwich display, where Peyton was immersed in conversation with three women complimenting her on landing a new podcast. She narrowed her eyes and switched her attention to me.

"Nice of you to show up."

"I wouldn't miss it." I would have killed to miss it.

"What happened?"

"Nothing." I thought I used enough concealer, but Peyton saw right through me.

"What kind of nothing? Looks like you were crying."

A new set of tears formed in my throat, and Peyton excused herself and guided me to the bathroom, where a gaggle of ladies were trying on lipsticks in the cool powder-room light. We looked over our shoulders to see Cara hugging an unfamiliar woman. Realizing the coast was clear, we went upstairs to Cara's bedroom. Upholstery samples were strewn across the floor.

"Louis is dating some new chick with lots of hair and lots of boob."

"Unoriginal. Why do you care?"

"I don't, but he brought her to dinner with the kids tonight. Why does..." I tried to keep my voice from faltering.

"Leah, the problem isn't Louis. It's you. Move on. Join a dating app. Go to a singles dinner. Go on freaking Tinder for all I care. Go to Israel with a group of women. You spend all your time with so-called happy families planning their top-tier affairs." Peyton lifted her fingers, using air quotes to make the point clearer. "You're watching everyone's life from the sidelines and wondering why you're still alone. Just like Jennifer Lopez in that silly movie."

"It's a really good movie."

"Here's my advice. And I charge big money for this, but for you…this one's free." Peyton winked. "Reframe your thinking. Think about what you want and how you're going to get it. You're a smart girl, but your comfort zone is other people's happiness. It's about time to find your own."

"I don't know how." Peyton put her arm around me. The tears started up again, and I grabbed a tissue from Cara's bedside table. "I'm so busy, and the kids are going off to college, and I'll be all alone, and I finally feel seen by someone, and I know he's still married…"

"Do you realize that you're letting something nice Howard did for your mom over fifteen years ago cloud your judgment? There are plenty of people who'll see you for what you are. Don't do this the wrong way. You're a superstar. Not a victim."

"Louis is always trying to undermine me."

"I don't want to hear another word about Louis. Fuck him. This is about you. Go to The Meet Market—a new bar that recently opened. I heard it's a great place for middle-aged women."

"Who're you calling middle-aged?"

"You. Embrace it. We all have to because there's no alternative. Unless you're dead."

"Why do you have to be mean?"

"I'm not mean. I'm honest. You just don't want to hear it. And no one's going to tell you like I will. Two divorced moms opened The Meet Market after they couldn't find an age-appropriate place to go when their exes had the kids. Give it a chance." I pursed my lips, debating whether to divulge that I already had.

"I went once and was too embarrassed to tell you. Half the women were wearing tight skirts and crop tops they stole from their daughters and prancing around letting the world know their vaginas were still open for business. I was home in an hour in my pajamas, watching *The Way We Were*. No, thank you. I'm done."

"Oy, Leah. Maybe it was just a bad night. Try again. You can't let one bad husband, one bad date, one bad anything deter you from living your life."

"You don't understand."

"I do understand. I do this for a living." Peyton turned my body toward the giant gilded mirror on the wall. "Your smile lights up the room. You're sexy. You own your own business. That's huge. You have two amazing kids that you raised completely by yourself. That's admirable. You're comparing yourself to other people. Don't you realize how appealing you are?"

"Not really."

"You have this notion of waiting for someone else to make your life complete. Stop chasing some notion of a spiritual soulmate. Your happiness is out there waiting for you, and it's bigger and better than you can imagine. Just stop looking in the wrong places."

"Like my mom always said, to find my own joy?"

"Yeah, well, maybe Mary Kay was on to something. I promise it will work if you know where to look. And one day, you'll find your Prince Charming and look back on this conversation, and I'll remind you I told you so." Peyton surveyed the mess on the floor and added, "Let's get out of here, or we'll be stuck choosing between paint samples." I hugged Peyton and followed her downstairs.

We wandered through a tight group of women chatting. They all held glossy gray bags with violets embossed in the corner. Their faces looked fresh and rejuvenated. As if these little shopping events could transform their lives. I thought back to my mom's makeup parties. Peyton and my mom were right. I was going to find my own joy.

TEN

BETTER MAN

By the following week, I had a profile on two dating apps and had mastered a new set of dating lingo. I now knew what *rizz* and *kittenfishing* meant and could use the term *breadcrumbing* in a sentence. (It had nothing to do with veal Milanese.) After painfully scrolling through pictures of men without shirts or leaning against their cars, I finally swiped, had a somewhat interesting conversation with a man named Max, and scheduled a date for Wednesday night.

Howard continued to send me cute texts, but when he called, I told him I was too busy to talk. I was sure he'd get the hint, eventually.

Coincidentally, Max lived a few miles away and worked at the high school, and I agreed to let him pick me up. Thirty minutes before Max was scheduled to arrive, I heard a car door close. I hadn't decided on what I was wearing yet, and half my clothes were on the floor. I peeked out my bedroom window and was shocked to see Howard's Maserati Quattroporte in my driveway. I'd designed enough car-themed parties to recognize the Trident logo and knew his car was luxury at its finest.

I threw on a forest-green off-the-shoulder dress that complemented my eyes and raced to the front door, prepared to tell Howard he had a lot of nerve showing up unannounced at my house. He greeted me with a bouquet of silvery pink tulips, a dashing smile, and a scent that could knock me off my feet. I didn't have the heart to scold him.

"I never did properly thank you for all your hard work." He looked inside my house to see if anyone was home. He knew the kids saw Louis on Wednesdays.

"Howard, these are gorgeous." I took the bouquet out of his hand. "I was just doing my job. Deenie sent me a bunch of referrals. That's the best thanks I can get."

"Can I come in?" he pleaded.

"I'm getting ready to go out." I looked past him to make sure Max wasn't about to show up, too.

"Big date?" Howard laughed.

"Actually…" I turned my body, placing the flowers on the entryway table, not wanting him to come in. Not trusting myself if he did.

"You're going on a date?" He looked like he had the wind knocked out of him. "Now?"

"Yeah. In about twenty minutes." I started to feel lightheaded. Maybe I could still cancel.

"But… why… I mean… who… where…?" For the first time, Howard was unnerved. "Let me guess. He's something safe. What is he, an accountant? English teacher?"

"History teacher." I couldn't meet his eyes.

"Sounds like some riveting conversation." The sparkle in his eyes came back. "Could I take him on? Who'd win in a duel? I may have a sword in my trunk. You know, from my swashbuckling days. Hold on…"

I finally laughed. "Howie. You need to go."

"History teacher? Really?"

"I'm going with an open mind. It's time for me to get back out there. I have to stop…"

"Stop what? Thinking about me?"

I felt my lungs contract and closed my eyes, wishing away the craziness I felt whenever he was near me. I shook my head. "I can't do this. You're married. This is wrong, and we both know it."

"How wrong? Tell me." His face got closer to mine. My heart somersaulted.

"He's going to be here in fifteen minutes. I have to get ready. Please."

"Will you let him touch you like this?" He adjusted the sleeve on my dress and smoothed some hair away from my face, lightly grazing my cheek. His hand was on fire. Like the insides of my body. "…Let him kiss you like this…?" He brought his lips closer. He was one second from kissing me. I wanted it so bad.

"No." I swallowed. "Stop. I'm done romanticizing." I felt the ropes tugging at my heart.

"If you say so." Six feet two inches of defeat slouched on my doorframe. "Promise to text me if you need saving from a medieval castle discussion. I'll be home ironing my puffy shirt."

"I'll remember that."

"Puffy. That's sixteen points."

"Good one."

"I could probably kick his ass."

"Goodbye, Howard," I said, shaking my head.

"And Leah…"

"Yes?" I whispered.

"I'm getting divorced. We can stay friends. For now. But don't write me off. I'll prove it to you." He turned and got back in his car, backing it out slowly as I watched him leave.

Max arrived looking part academic, in corduroys and a button-down, and part cowboy, in a distressed pair of boots. Something was endearing about him. He was nice enough. Attractive enough. Interesting enough. Just not *Howard* enough. I tried to pay attention, but the thought of Howard's lips almost touching mine again made it difficult to focus. Max dropped me off, and as a gentleman, kissed the side of my cheek and said he'd love to see me again. "Sounds good," I replied.

As I was dozing off to sleep, Howard sent a picture of Captain Jack Sparrow, sword in hand, with the caption…*Ready when you are.*

I went on another date with Max. I was enthusiastic but bored. Howard continued sending texts. Scrabble words I didn't know. Pictures of Zorro. Captain Hook. Movie quotes. Cute reminders that he was thinking of me during the day. Nothing provocative. He was courting me the old-fashioned way.

Date number three with Max, and I couldn't take it any longer. He mentioned a Revolutionary War reenactment, and that was a dealbreaker. I cautiously resumed the phone calls with Howard, warning him there'd be absolutely no sex talk. He agreed, but it was obvious he was seducing me with his restraint.

I wrapped up the last two parties of the school year. Cooper's father, Todd, showed up with his fifteen-month-old son in a baby sling, along with his pregnant, again (oops), fiancée. Nina kept her composure with the help of her girlfriends, who rallied around her and formed a human wall whenever Todd attempted to approach her. I watched as Todd dumped a pile of soft pretzels meant for favors into the diaper bag and somehow convinced the caterer to let him take the leftover cheese wheel from the cocktail hour. I'm not sure how he got the cheese wheel through TSA, but Cooper got the last word, omitting his dad from the candle lighting ceremony.

Secret texts with Georgia Silverbloom gave me the inside scoop into the world of magical realism, allowing me to replicate a mythical kingdom into life-size cutouts, which I wrapped around the perimeter of the dance floor. Georgia was thrilled. All in all, the night was a success until a drunk CeCe flew off the chair during the Hora, the traditional dance where people are lifted into the air, landing in a splat of fuchsia tulle and sparkles and informing the entire sisterhood that she had gone commando.

Ah, the life of a party planner.

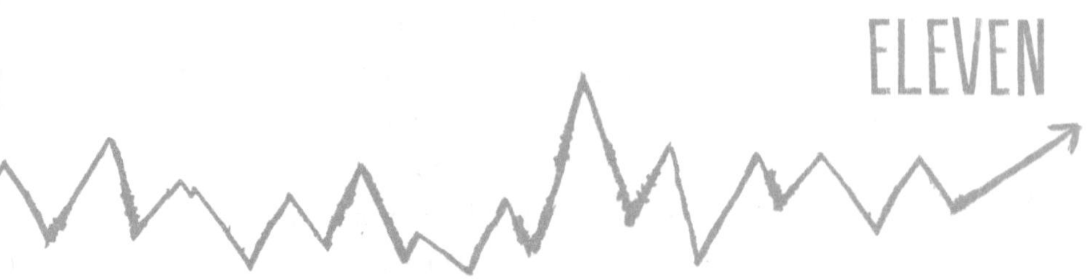

ELEVEN

AN AFFAIR TO REMEMBER

I t was early on a Sunday morning when my father called. "Leah, I completely forgot to tell you something about your friend Howard. He left an old Scrabble game in Mom's hospital room. Apparently, it was the board they played on. I'm not sure if it was left there by mistake, but the nurses packed it in her box of belongings. It must be in those boxes I gave you when I moved to Florida."

"The Scrabble game is in my house?" I never opened any of those boxes.

"Yes. It was very old. I'm not sure of the condition."

"It's an original set. Howard's dad worked with the man who invented the game."

"Well, talk about a buried treasure."

"Maybe it's time to dig it up."

I jumped out of bed and headed for the basement. I remembered the boxes were shoved in a storage closet after Louis moved out. I'd never been able to bring myself to go through them, although I assumed it was just leftover junk from my mom's businesses.

I grabbed a step stool and took a few boxes off the shelf, one at a time. The first box held my mom's yearbooks, diplomas, and old family photos. Maybe Lily would be interested in organizing them one day. The second box held three baby blankets: mine and two more belonging to my siblings, Rachel and Mitchell. I smelled the blankets, inhaling remnants of baby powder, Shalimar, my mom's perfume, and the saturating aroma of sorrow. I squeezed my hand under the pile of fleece, and sure enough, I felt a box.

I felt like I was unwrapping a fragile piece of history. It was a burgundy box, with the Scrabble name in a circle, very different than the large, deluxe plastic version I now played on. The corners of the lid were slightly warped, but the blankets must have prevented any moisture from getting in and doing real damage. I opened the box slowly and carefully lifted the game board out and unfolded it. In the left-hand corner, directly under the tile distribution, was an inscription: *To Gene: My eternal thanks. Your buddy, Al.*

I ran my fingers across the smooth board, knowing the very last people to touch it were my mom and Howie. Together. It was exciting and heart-wrenching at the same time. I could picture her long fingers placing the tiles just so. Her eyes shimmering with delight and speaking the words her voice wouldn't allow.

The discipline of keeping my distance from Howie, avoiding all elements of temptation, went out the window. I sent him a text.

Me: Can you come over?

Howie: Are you okay?

Me: Yes. I have a surprise for you.

Howie: I'm on the golf course. Be there in an hour.

One hour later, Lily, Asher, and I sat around the table listening to Howie's oral history of this particular set. Howie's face looked like he had opened a sealed time capsule. He repeatedly shook his head in disbelief. "See the zigzags? They're actually triangles called pips. The double squares have two triangles on each side, and the triple squares have three. It's a patented design that my father worked on."

My kids were captivated by Howie's knowledge.

"No one knew what happened to this set. I asked every nurse, every doctor, every orderly. I even checked the cafeteria. It was like it disappeared into thin air. Eventually, I gave up and just hoped that it made its rounds through the hospital to all the patients who needed it."

"I still can't believe it's been in my house all this time."

"Each of the Gardner Stroke Centers has a game room. One location has a room called Candace's Corner. For your mom. We sent a letter to your dad when it was being dedicated, but the post office sent it back."

"Oh my God! For my mom? You never tried to reach him? Or us?"

"I tried. There was no forwarding address. I think they tried to track you down, too. If I recall, you had a different name?"

"My dad sold the house and moved to Florida. I changed my last name after my divorce."

"Here's the thing I've learned about charity. Some people like to shout their generosity from the rooftops. Others are private with their grief or wish to remain anonymous. The Gardner Stroke Center respects that. Our main focus is enriching the lives of our patients."

"Can we see the game room one day?" Asher asked.

"Absolutely. I'll give you all the royal tour."

"This is literally the coolest thing ever!" exclaimed Lily.

Howie caught my eye. I'm not sure whose eyes held more layers of emotion. "I think this calls for a celebration game!"

I couldn't turn him down now. Asher and Lily were enthralled with the new development and were equally eager to show off their skills. I felt sorry for my kids, who never enjoyed a family game like this with both of their parents. The void was not lost on me; I was doing the best I could. We finished the game — Lily won — and Howie prepared to leave.

"Pack up the tiles and get a shopping bag for Howard, Lily."

"Oh no. This is for you. It's only right that Candace's family becomes the rightful owner."

"Thank you. We promise to take good care of it." I smiled graciously as my heart flipped over a hundred times.

Two weeks later, Lily and Asher left for camp in a flurry of excitement. Lily was chosen to be the head content creator of the camp newsletter, and she hoped the experience would provide some inspiration for her college essays. Asher, worried he'd miss crucial basketball practices and jeopardize his place on next year's team, contemplated staying home, but as soon as we arrived at the pick-up location, he joined his buddies in a huddle and ran onto the bus, barely saying goodbye to me.

I pulled up to my house to find Howie waiting in the driveway, holding an assortment of bags from Coco Bella, the bakery, the wine store, and the local bookstore.

"What are you doing here?" I had to be firm. He didn't belong here. Oh, but how ecstatic I was to see him. My left brain was telling him to drop the bags and march back into his car. But my right brain was undressing him.

"I knew you'd be lonely after dropping the kids off. Hopefully, this'll take the edge off. I went through this with all three girls. You want them to be happy and independent, but it shatters you not to have them around."

"This is so thoughtful."

"I'll help you unpack, and then I'll leave. Promise." *Don't come in. Don't come in.*

"Okay. Come in." Howie followed me. I was shaking. I was afraid he could hear my heart thumping. We arranged the food in the fridge; there was enough for lunch and dinner for a week. He put the wine on the counter. I took a bite of a chocolate chip cookie as he emptied the last bag, revealing three books I'd mentioned I hoped to read this summer. "Why are you spoiling me like this?" I looked up at him slowly. The tension between us was palpable.

"You deserve to be spoiled. And cherished. And adored. And…" he put his hands on my face. "Jesus, Leah. This is…"

"I know… I…" I didn't stop him this time. I was burning with desire. I reached up on my tiptoes to meet his mouth. Months of phone foreplay washed over me. His tongue was fierce, guiding its way from my lips to my neck. He whispered how long he had waited for this. Waited for me. His muscular body pressed into me with a yearning I'd never felt before. My hardwood floors felt like quicksand. There was no turning back, for he was an animal, and I was his prey. Hunted. Willing. Aware that Mr. and Mrs. Pomerantz could see in my sliding glass doors, I found my balance and knowingly took his hand and led him upstairs. When we got to the top of the stairs, Howie lifted me into his arms and carried me into my room. There was no time to think. No time for a shred of remorse. Howie lifted my sundress over my head in one swift move, removing his clothes with one hand and caressing me with the other. His breath was hot and minty, and his tongue did not stop. He held my arms firmly over my head. Inspected the curve of my thighs methodically with his fingers, allowing the invisible hairs on the small of my back to rise to attention. After sharing our lives through a telephone line, spreading my legs felt natural. Howie entered me without hesitation. I shuddered, closing my eyes. Every intimate detail we'd shared exploded in my extremities like a match to a forgotten box of firecrackers. It's possible the Earth tilted off its axis or stopped spinning altogether. This is what ecstasy was. I opened my eyes, taking in every inch of this man who made me feel like my whole life was preparing me for this. Then everything stopped. Quiet. My hectic life switched to mute. I could breathe. The world shifted, and at that moment, my life shifted along with it.

Howie fell into an easy sleep. I alternated between searching his naked body and surveying my surroundings to remind myself it was real. Soon, I was asleep too.

The buzzing woke us, puncturing the serenity of our self-made love nest. His phone vibrated violently with a barrage of announcements. Howie removed my hand from his chest and looked at his phone; a wrinkle in his forehead gave him away, and I should have expected the next part would come.

"Sorry. I have to leave."

"What? Now? No." I didn't want to sound needy, but he had just done things to me that would have me blushing for days.

"Family issue." His words declared an assault. Humiliation. Second best.

Peyton warned me about clients with hot adulterous affairs

and what it does to them psychologically. "It doesn't matter how strong you think you are," I remembered Peyton reprimanding, "men fuck with their dicks, and women fuck with their hearts."

Howie kissed me slowly, thinking he was kissing away my doubts, then jumped out of bed to put on his pants. "I thought Deenie was in Nashville," I whispered, twirling my hair.

"She is." He buckled his belt while looking at his phone. "Tune-up."

"Then why the quick exit?"

"Hey, look at me. No sad faces. This is just the beginning." Howie was preoccupied with his screen. A lump formed in my throat. It was a bit late to be playing hard to get.

"Whatever," I said softly.

He buttoned his Zegna shirt, which happened to be the identical color as his eyes, wiping away any telltale signs of what just happened. He paused, seeing the disappointment on my face. I pulled the sheets up to my chest.

"Oh, screw 'em," he said, tossing his phone onto my nightstand. Howie got back into bed and wrapped his arms around me, allowing me to bury my head in his chest. "You're more important." He pulled the sheets off me and gave me another orgasm, this time with his tongue.

"Okay, lover, you can go now," I teased.

Why is it that a man has sex, smooths over his hair, adjusts his waistband, and looks like he's ready for the boardroom, and I look like I had a gangbang in a carwash? My body had turned into Jell-O. So, I stayed in bed and watched Howie walk out the door. Silently cursing Deenie as though it were her fault that I just had porn-quality sex with her husband when I should be cursing myself.

What did you think? I asked myself. *What the hell did you think?*

SUMMER LOVIN'

Oh God. What had I done? Was I a cliché? Was it a temporary lapse in judgment? Was I an easy middle-aged conquest? Were the dredged-up emotions about my mom making me extra emotional, or was it my hormones? Would Howie even call? I wasn't going to wait and find out. I tapped out a text: We both know this was a mistake. Unfortunately, it can't happen again. Something kept my finger from pressing send.

I'd gotten this out of my system. No one needed to know. Tomorrow, I'd tell Howie I couldn't see him again. I'd tell Max I changed my mind. I'd learn to play pickleball.

Tomorrow, I'd work on my fall schedule. Hire a full-time assistant. Except lately, work was feeling tedious. I was beginning to resent my job and considered taking Howie's advice and looking for a finance job. Then I shut down the ridiculous thought, desperately trying not to think about him, struggling not to have his smell seduce me again. Just when I was sure I could put this behind me, I received a text:

Howie: I can't stop thinking about you, and I can't wait to see you again.

I had the emotions of a teenager. The rationale of a love-starved middle-aged divorcee with a medicine cabinet full of estrogen pills. A conscience misguided by old-fashioned lust. When Howie asked to see me two days later, I figured, well, maybe one more time.

And so went my tug-of-war summer.

Deenie and Addison were in Nashville for the summer. Howie claimed the divorce was in progress, and I embarked on an un-inhibition tour, the kind I should've taken after my divorce. It was the kind of love affair you see in the movies. Nancy Meyers had nothing on me. We spent hours in bed, playing Scrabble, watching old movies, feeding each other delicacies he'd surprise me with, exchanging family histories, sharing dreams I believed had been tucked away forever. Howie was not your stereotypical Wolf of Wall Street, and I let myself fall deep into his universe, presuming this was what a real relationship felt like. An expensive bottle of perfume was left on my vanity. A massage gift certificate was taped to my bathroom mirror when I was stressed. Truffles were arranged on my bed in the shape of a heart. Bags of gourmet coffee appeared in my refrigerator. New pillows for our love nest. More books. No one ever paid this much attention to me. And the sex kept getting better. *Just don't fall in love*, I reminded myself.

Seven weeks. I justified my actions with a looming and finite expiration date.

Ten parties were scheduled for September, four more than usual, and for the first time, I considered turning away business.

My predictable world was replaced with spontaneity. And I was loving every minute of it.

When I wasn't working or having orgasms, I lounged at Peyton's pool, pretending everything was normal. My porn queen summer gave me a reason to exercise. I treated myself to a new black and white strapless bathing suit and felt more self-assured than usual when I walked into Peyton's backyard after spending the past two nights in a multitude of uncharted positions with Howie.

Peyton, in a wide-brimmed black straw chapeau with an extra-wide red bow that made her look like she was out for a romp in St. Tropez, eyed me up and down like she was judging *America's Next Top Model.*

Cara, in a demure navy one-shouldered maillot with a matching sarong, said, "You look prettier than a peach today."

Leonardo, in a loosely buttoned pineapple shirt, proudly showing off his grizzly chest, placed a tray of prosciutto-wrapped melon in front of me. "Wow, new smell?"

"Huh?" I said, distracted by Leonardo's charcuterie plate. His nose made him a culinary expert. Now that famous nose was going to expose me.

"Darling, you smell fabulous."

"Must be the suntan lotion."

"Sunscreen isn't laced with high notes of patchouli."

"Oh," I said, uncharacteristically flip, "a client gave me a bottle of perfume as a thank you." I reached for a piece of melon and popped it in my mouth.

"Really?" Peyton chimed in, knowing if Leonardo picked up on it, it wasn't the run-of-the-mill perfume you'd find at Bloomingdale's. "Which client?"

"It's been in the box for months. I decided to try it last night. I'm surprised you can still smell it on me." A cloud of deceit quietly blocked the afternoon sun.

"Where were you last night?" Peyton was busy consulting for her new weekly podcast, coincidentally called *Women Who Stray*. There was a lingering veil of secrecy to our time together. A constant dew of misplaced equilibrium. As much as I tried to ignore it, something had shifted in our friendship, and it was all my fault.

"It's from the Gardners," I blurted out. Peyton removed her sunglasses and crossed her arms. Cara put down her cabernet and *Southern Living* magazine.

"From Howie," I added, testing the waters and immediately regretting it.

"Oh my God, you slept with him."

"It's not like that."

"YOU FUCKING SLEPT WITH HIM? I FUCKING WARNED YOU!"

"Oh my, Leah, he's married! How could you?" Cara looked like she was about to cry.

"I didn't say I slept with him. And he's getting divorced."

"So, you didn't sleep with him? Are you kind of a virgin? Did you fuck him or not?"

"It's complicated."

"Algebra's complicated."

"Why is it any of your business?" I knew I was on treacherous ground. This was mine and mine alone. I had to lie. "I didn't sleep with him. I swear. We kissed a few times. And then it started to get out of hand. Don't worry. I'm not going to do anything foolish."

"Sounds like you already did."

"He's my friend. Why do you care?"

"We're your friends. We aren't good enough for you any-more?"

"He's just different from anyone I've ever known. Half of our discussions are about business. It's quite the aphrodisiac." No one answered. It was a trap. "And he sees me. He listens to me. You just don't get it." Still no response. I had to get out of this.

"Anyway, it's harmless, and now it's done. Promise." They were letting me hang myself. "Although I may let him invest my divorce money." I trusted Howie's expertise and signed the trans-fer papers weeks ago. He assured me my money would be safe with him.

"I'm begging you, BEGGING YOU, don't give him your money," Peyton threw off her hat, got up, and stomped to the edge of the pool.

Leonardo gave me the *she's your friend* shrug.

Cara delivered the fawn-in-the-headlight look, discreetly leaned over, and said, "I'm happy to recommend some reputable financial advisors."

"DO NOT invest in companies that are part of this so-called harmless pillow talk! You don't know what you're getting your-self into," Peyton yelled before jumping into the water, ending our discussion.

It was too late. I knew exactly what I was getting into. Howie's investment knowledge empowered me. My friends didn't know him the way I did. Gentle. Rough when it counted. Kind. Carefree. Firm when needed. The Scrabble connection untethered me, but the financial talk had unleashed something new in me. I watched the market fluctuations all day long. I wanted to be part of it. The volatility. The excitement. All of it. I couldn't get enough of it. Or of Howie. It was my turn to have the life I thought I deserved. I didn't know which was worse, the lies I was telling my friends or the lies I was telling myself.

THIRTEEN

FALLING

As the summer progressed, Howard continued divulging confidential details about SHINE, an invitation-only group of traders who accounted for over fifty percent of his assets under management.

Howard spoke of media mogul Frank Masterson and his artist wife, Rita. Howard said there were more zeros in their portfolio than I'd ever seen. Whenever Howard had a bad day, it was tied to a disagreement with Frank. I asked why he didn't just tell him to find a new broker, and Howard said it didn't work that way. Frank knew too much.

Bud Westin was Howard's favorite client. Howard said Bud's daddy made his fortune in oil, a Texas wildcat, explaining the nature of risky oil drilling. With Howard's help, Bud multiplied that fortune several times over. I was fascinated by each person's story. These were the kind of men you read about in the business section of *The Wall Street Journal,* which, incidentally, I had begun reading to impress Howard.

Avi Segal Moskovitz, a tech and crypto maven who'd be the next Zuckerberg, gambled like the stock market was a casino. Howard said Avi was a genius and that the world would be talking about him one day.

Don, a supermarket scion who was conservative and trepidatious. Howard called Don a neurotic investor. He said he finally got Don right where he wanted him. Whatever that meant.

I knew the ticker symbols for every stock Howard traded. Howard explained the difference between value stocks and growth stocks. He introduced me to clients over the phone, referring to me as a new high-ranking associate in the mergers and acquisitions department. The calls were made from my bed, and it took every ounce of willpower not to giggle while Howard carried on an entire conversation while he was in a compromising position. I also noticed how he took their calls at all hours of the day, including nights and weekends.

"They're VIPs. I need to be available."

"They sound like a bunch of degenerate gamblers."

"I like to call them risk takers."

"How do they trust you so freely?"

"I know how to schmooze them. And their wives. It's all fun, games, and expensive real estate until someone files for divorce and their statements get subpoenaed." I wondered how he was going to handle his so-called divorce.

"Are there any women in SHINE?"

Howard laughed. "God, no. They don't have the appetite for this type of trading. Too emotional."

"But I thought the wives had their own money. Who invests that?"

"The women are happy letting the men control the money. They're not interested."

"How do you know?"

"It's just not the way it works. I've got several women clients, but I got them by default. Widows. Divorcees. A few inheritances. They don't want to be bothered. I send them a Christmas gift each year, and if they need money, we cut them a check."

"It sounds like you're missing out on a whole lot of business."

"Do the husbands usually come to discuss party planning?"

"That's different."

"Not really."

"You did."

"That was a one-time thing to make my daughter happy. Now my job is making you happy." He reached over and kissed my nose.

"Okay, but I think you're missing the bigger picture."

"You didn't ask how your money was invested."

"I don't have a lot of money. A few mutual funds but…"

"The women don't care about this. At least not the ones I deal with. I'll show you where the real money is." Howard opened a portfolio on his computer. He explained how the portfolios fluctuated and how he could manipulate the numbers by showing comparisons of hypothetical trades and entering a series of filters to show favorable results.

I pointed to a group of yellow shadings on the screen. "What's this mean?"

"Creative financing."

"So you're a loan shark?"

"You watch too many movies."

Toward the end of July, Howard began discussing Banyan

Pharmaceuticals. He and Eddie "were in deep" and it sounded like they'd made a killing. Slowly, I began to understand how much was at stake.

"It's massive. Our research predicts that Banyan Pharmaceuticals will acquire several independent nursing homes. But Banyan is in talks with several big pharma companies who want to merge. They haven't disclosed the nursing home expenditure, so it values their company at a lower multiple."

"Isn't that fraud?"

"No, it's business."

"How do you know this?"

"We have our sources. Don't worry your pretty little head about it. It's for the big spenders, like my SHINE group."

The SHINE guys were betting on margin, investing with money they didn't have, but Howie confided in me that he was loaning them short-term funds to make larger trades and charging less interest than traditional margin accounts with less oversight. Each transaction was classified as part of the monthly fees in an algorithm that nobody cared to dissect. He called them Howie Loans, and he was incredibly proud of himself. "This way," he explained, "they never run out of money."

"I could use a Howie loan."

"Stick with me, kid, and you won't need one."

"Do the clients have to ask for the Howie loan? Isn't that a conflict?"

"No. It's assumed that when they hit a certain level, the Howie Loan goes into play. We have a banking arm. They trust me. And nobody complains when they see the profits."

"Is this legal?"

"Of course."

"It seems complex."

"That's the point. It's so complex that no one knows what questions to ask."

"And that's legal?"

"Absolutely."

Then the clincher came. On a sweltering Sunday morning in August, I got out of the shower to find a new white silky robe draped over the hook in my bathroom. I put it on and walked into my bedroom to see Howie waiting in bed, with rich, buttery croissants, crepes with orange zest, a bowl of strawberries, half of a leftover quiche, and a pitcher of mimosas arranged on a tray I got for my wedding shower and never used. "I can't wait to do this with you every day."

"Serve me a traditional French breakfast in bed?"

"Well, you said you've never been to Paris. So I brought a little Paris to you. I'll never stop wanting to surprise you. I want to be with you all the time."

"All the time? How would that work? You're still married. And I'm a busy single mom."

"I'm not getting any younger, you know." It was the first time he acknowledged the age difference between us.

"I didn't think this would turn into anything serious."

"It was always serious for me. I'm falling for you, Leah. I want a life together."

It was as if every birthday candle I ever blew out, and every star I wished upon, wrapped themselves in a gift box and were sitting on Howie's chest, waiting for me to open it.

"I want that too, but... have you thought this through?"

Howard lifted my chin and looked directly into my eyes, "I

planned on leaving Deenie years ago. We were comfortable, but not in love. I began looking for a house nearby. Then, one sentimental night and a bottle of wine, and two months later, Deenie discovered she was pregnant with Addison. So I stayed. Hoped things would get better. Joined more boards. Poured all my energy into the Gardner Stroke Center. I realize I'm wasting my time. I'm sixty-four. I'll never abandon my kids, but I'm spending my life with a woman I don't love anymore."

"Why me? Your wife looks like a supermodel."

"Why not you? You're spectacular, Leah. You make me feel like anything is possible. We make one hell of a team."

A vision of my kids flashed in front of me. Lily, in a Little Mermaid costume. Asher dressed as Elmo. Lily, dancing her heart out to the Backstreet Boys. Asher's face when he got his first basketball. For a second, I forgot how old they were. How old *I* was. The thought of my kids leaving terrified me. But now… I didn't owe anyone an explanation. It was my turn to live on my terms. I lowered my eyes.

"Did I say something wrong?"

"No. I'm just afraid it won't last." *I'm afraid you're going to break my heart.*

"You're not getting rid of me so quickly. I have a plan. Be patient. I promise."

I took a bite of my crepe, tasting a delicate hint of Grand Marnier. I batted my eyelashes and looked up at Howie lovingly. "I guess we'll always have Paris."

"Yes, Leah. We'll always have Paris."

SEC Interview #1

Howard Gardner

SEC: How long have you been employed at Arbor Financial?

Mr. Gardner: Thirty-nine years.

SEC: Your capacity? Current marital status?

Mr. Gardner: President. Married.

SEC: Happily?

Mr. Gardner: Is that a trick question? Of course.

SEC: When did you meet Edward Grossman?

Mr. Gardner: We met twelve years ago through mutual business associates. I'm on the board of a dozen Fortune 500 companies. It was inevitable.

SEC: Why inevitable?

Mr. Gardner: We're serious about providing the highest financial outcome for our clients and, in his case, his shareholders.

SEC: What do you know about Banyan Pharmaceuticals?

Mr. Gardner: Just what the yearly shareholder and earnings call reports say. Our private equity team knew about Banyan before it became public. Seems like a good, stable company. Substantial earnings ratios. Impressive shareholder value. Growth potential.

SEC: Any other information?

Mr. Gardner: A few speculative articles. My research guys analyzed them. The Banyan CEO has appeared on the usual investment-related TV programs. Nothing out of the ordinary. Solid financials. That's all we care about.

SEC: Are you familiar with the nursing home industry?

Mr. Gardner: It's not a sector I follow.

SEC: What's your relationship with Leah Samuels?

Mr. Gardner: Who?

SEC: Leah Samuels. Her name's listed as a client for whom you purchased Banyan Pharmaceutical stock.

Mr. Gardner: Oh, right. Nice girl. I don't know her well; we met once or twice. She was the party planner for a family event, and then, out of the blue, transferred a small amount of money to the firm. Too small for me to be bothered with. My wife must've bragged about me. That's usually how I get random new clients. I'm not sure I'd even remember what Lisa looked like.

SEC: Leah.

Mr. Gardner: Right, what Leah looked like.

SEC: And you never discussed Banyan with her?

Mr. Gardner: Why would I discuss business with a party planner? Another broker probably made the trade as part of an overall portfolio allocation.

SEC: Mr. Gardner, did you have insider information on Banyan Pharmaceuticals before any of the trades you made? Did Edward Grossman or another individual provide you with information that would cause you to amass such a significant stake in the company?

Mr. Gardner: Absolutely not. Why would I be stupid enough to risk my career on that?

SEC: Thank you for your time.

Mr. Gardner: My pleasure.

fourteen

AN AUTUMN CHILL

etween four Bar Mitzvah celebrations, two Sweet Sixteens, and Lily's college applications, my life took a 360-degree turn from the romantic days of summer. I was busier than ever, and seeing Howard four times a week was reduced to once a week, and last week, only a lustful fifteen minute, in an empty parking lot. I had become as uninhibited as someone half my age. But my home life was suffering.

The air conditioner condenser began leaking. I asked Howard to take a look, and he laughed, saying he wouldn't know a condenser from a can opener.

Asher returned from camp with a video game addiction. His tousled hair, still speckled with glimmers of summer sun, covered his eyes as he begrudgingly looked up when I walked into his room. He didn't need me. I'd become a vessel for stocking the fridge. He grew six inches over the summer, another reminder he'd be leaving before long. My baby. With facial hair. He would've needed a lobotomy not to know what I was doing. My brother Mitchell offered for Asher to come to New York and attend one of his basketball clinics. It was a good idea to get Asher away from the video games and spend some time with a reliable male role model for a change.

Lily and I pretended that I didn't know that she knew what was going on. She returned from camp with a fresh mouth, and I felt her slipping away. Lily was my best friend. It had been the three of us against the world when Louis left. I tried my hardest to give them as much of my time as possible. But Life of the Party had been growing, and I couldn't afford to turn away business, so spending lazy Saturdays with my kids got preempted by someone else's kid's party. In the early days, I dragged them along. Lily loved to help, but now she'd rather lust after boys than assemble balloons and pour chocolates into giant martini glasses. I couldn't blame her.

The second week of school, Lily asked to borrow money to become an ambassador for ShakeTown. Her friend's mom, a high-ranking executive, aka cult leader, began recruiting the senior girls to promote the shakes on TikTok. My daughter wanted to be a Pyramid Girl. Karma smacked me on the side of the head with a handheld blender.

"You don't pay to work. You get paid to work."

Lily looked at me the way you pray your seventeen-year-old will never look at you. The former pig-tailed mini-me may as well have said she hated me. "Mom, you're such a hypocrite."

I pretended not to apply the innuendo to my personal life. "Get a job where you don't scam people."

"You're the one stressed about money. I'll ask Dad."

I'll ask Dad—three magic words with the power to launch a migraine and a colitis attack.

I told Howard. "She'll lose all her money."

"A little entrepreneurial spirit is good. If she loses it, she'll learn the hard way."

"I hate these companies. They ruined my childhood."

"Everyone's entitled to make a living. Don't fight with Lily. It's not worth it." I didn't want to admit how far apart our moral compasses were on this subject.

Lily gave me the silent treatment. I refused to give in, although it was hard to be ethical when I was the one half-naked, bent over my married lover's desk late at night, a stream of light from nearby computer screens outlining our silhouettes.

Howard was increasingly busy. When I couldn't sneak out, we spent hours on the phone while I worked, long after midnight, discussing confidential reports. I loved the highs of the industry, of our relationship. The problem was that the lows teased how this all could end. The thought of not having Howard in my life was terrifying, but I wondered if my summer fling had run its course, and I should end it before it was too late. I wasn't cut out for this. I felt like everyone was taking advantage of me, and my life was spiraling out of control. I considered confessing to Peyton. But then irresistible Howie would surface again, goofy and carefree and tender, chasing my doubts away, and promising me a future. Howard had a hold on me that lacked definition. Because none of this second-guessing was enough to derail my thinking that we were meant to be together. I was falling in love. Fuck, who was I kidding? I was in love.

All I wanted was to turn off my phone and curl up alone with a pint of Ben & Jerry's, a big bag of Nestlé Crunch, and watch a good old-fashioned rom-com.

That's when the shit hit the fan.

THE FAN

$\mathcal{S}$eeing Louis's name on my phone made me nauseous, although it didn't actually say Louis; this week, his name was programmed to A**hole.

> A**hole: We need to talk.
>
> Me: Talk to my lawyer.
>
> A**hole: No. In person.
>
> Me: Not interested.
>
> A**hole: Leah, please. It's important. I'll stop in when
>   I pick up the kids for dinner.
>
> Me: I'll meet you outside. The prick wasn't
>   setting foot in my house.

When Louis pulled up fifteen minutes later, the kids weren't ready. I walked outside and stood firmly on my driveway, arms crossed, eyes ready to roll. Louis had a fake tan that looked like someone smashed a sweet potato into his face. He leaned in for a casual kiss, from which I pulled my body away as far as it could go without falling into the asphalt. He was drenched in cologne. "Get away from me. What do you want?"

Louis looked at me sheepishly, his eyes sad and pleading. "I need to defer the support payments, and you need to pay for Lily's college applications. I'm in a financial jam."

"Absolutely not. Take it up with the courts."

"Then we'll both have to pay attorneys, and it'll take you longer to get paid. Please, Leah. It's important. Give me three months, and I'll pay you back. I promise."

"Your promises mean nothing. You've canceled the past few weeks. You're not reliable. I don't trust you."

"I had a medical procedure."

"You mean another facelift? Or was it lipo this time? Get off my property, Louis."

"If you aren't flexible, you'll leave me no choice but to file for a permanent reduction. You don't need this house. You could sell it. The kids are leaving for college."

I hated sharing the same air as this reptile. "I can't afford to do this."

"I'm sure you can. Seems like business is booming. I'm handling something deeply personal."

Louis looked defeated. All my fantasies about his demise came to the surface, and for a split second, I felt sorry for him. Maybe he was sick. He got me in a moment of weakness. If there was something seriously wrong and I refused to help, he'd turn it around and tell the kids I was selfish. Paint me as the bad guy. God, I despised him.

"Fine—three months no support. Not one minute longer."

"Thank you." He smiled a genuine smile. The kind that made me forget what a *putz* he was. The kids ran outside and scampered into his car. This was why he insisted on picking them up instead of Lily driving. Lily shot me a quiz-worthy look, meaning *Why in the world are you talking to him*? He was the effervescent Disney Dad once more. Everyone's favorite orthodontist. Fake as they come.

"Work on your college essays, Lily! Stop procrastinating."

"I'm waiting for inspiration to hit!" she responded.

My phone rang a minute later. Howard. "Be there in five minutes."

"I thought you had a meeting tonight."

"Change of plans. I picked up sushi from Blue Tuna." My favorite sushi. Something was wrong. I had the strange sensation that things were about to get messy.

We ate in silence. I noticed a light was out over my kitchen table. I was pretty sure Howard had never changed a light bulb, so I didn't mention it. I devoured the spring roll and picked at my Rainbow Roll as he inhaled his shrimp dumplings. The air was tight, the mood somber. It was over. I knew it. Deenie found out. At least he had the balls to break it off in person. Of course, he had to make sure I wasn't going to do anything rash. Hell hath no fury. I could relate. A woman scorned, baby. Right there. I should've done it first. I should've called Deenie and come clean. Why didn't I write down everything he said about her? I should've… could've… a thousand things…

Howard put down his fork, unbuttoned his collar, and shook his head. He peeled himself off the chair, opened and closed the refrigerator three times. Took an investigative stroll to the front door, looked outside, and scuttled back to the kitchen. Opened the fridge again, assuming a magician had appeared and refilled the food. He paced, looking for an emergency exit.

I'd never seen him like this.

"Are you going to tell me what's wrong?" This was the first time I raised my voice. His pacing made me anxious, and I wanted him to leave. *You might as well get the ball rolling. Just rip the Band-Aid off already, mister. I've got two pints of Ben & Jerry's in the freezer. I can handle this. I'm a big girl. This isn't my first rodeo.*

"It's the SEC." I didn't see that coming. "There's an inquiry."

I should've said I was sorry. I should've said I couldn't be involved. Except that was the point. I was. "What can I do?"

"There's nothing to do. I'll fix it. Don't worry."

Even I knew you didn't just fix an SEC inquiry. "Too late. I'm worried. You've got to stop pacing. You're making me dizzy."

Howard let out a guttural scream. He sounded scared and desperate. And completely unsexy. He wasn't going to listen to reason. I'd gotten a feel for his foul moods before, but I handled it by hanging up the phone. This felt different. This was personal.

"I'm telling you it's a mistake. I've dealt with this before. The firm files some papers, and it goes away. I have a clean record. Almost forty years in this business. Forty years." He banged his fist on my kitchen table.

Howard didn't mention that his record was perfect because he'd never been formally charged. He *had* been questioned before. And the frozen accounts? More than once, I'd eventually find out.

"Then why are you so upset?"

"I don't have time for this. And the clients have to be questioned, and—"

"Which clients?"

"You wouldn't understand." He banged his fist again in rhythm. "Forty years! Do you know what that means? You weren't alive when I got into this business! Forty God damned years!"

I *was* alive when he started, except I was playing with Barbie dolls. Well, not quite. I stared at him in disbelief. I didn't have any answers. Nor did I know why he was attacking me.

"You've been discussing Eddie and the SHINE investments for months."

"I shouldn't have told you." Howard walked to my kitchen window and looked outside.

"Who are you looking for? Is someone following you?"

Howard twisted his body as if he was giving himself an adjustment, then pulled his shoulders back until his elbows met. He looked around my kitchen. Horrified. Like he'd just realized my house wasn't as fancy as his. He ran his hands through his hair and took a seat. "I bought this stock for twenty clients and in my girls' accounts."

"What stock?"

"It doesn't matter." Ouch. "I dabbled in it before. I bought it in my personal account too. It was questionable the first time. A few accounts were frozen. No big deal."

"No big deal?"

"Don't look at me like that! It's a compliance protocol. The dust settled. The freeze came off. So I bought more. I allocated the shares, but most of them went to SHINE, my trading team."

"I know about SHINE. I've spoken to them. From my BED! Oh my God! Is my house bugged?"

"I don't think so."

"Don't think so? WHAT?" I may have been shrieking.

"Stop talking, Leah. Just listen. I also bought it for a few special *wink-wink* clients. The stock dropped. Big." Howard paused. "So, I bought more. That's what I do. I buy on the dips. Shit. WE ALL DO! I moved some Howie money in and bought more for everyone. And more for myself. Two days later, the stock became a five-bagger—through the fucking roof. Home-fucking-run! It was a lucky shot, but we all made a fortune."

"Eddie, too?"

"Of course! And now the SEC's asking questions. They look for patterns. Fuck me. Oh, God. Why now? WHY?" Howard put his head down on the counter.

Attempting to digest all this information, I instinctively asked, "Did you buy it for me?" I heard an inaudible jumble of consonants. "Did you?"

"Yes," he answered sheepishly. "Just a little." He picked his head up and looked at me thoughtfully. "I thought you could use the money. It seemed like a good play. I didn't realize how good."

"A good play? You promised me my money would be safe. Am I going to be questioned?" I held my breath as I said it.

Howard didn't answer. He was pacing again. He stopped and banged his head on the counter. And again. It's a good thing my kids weren't home.

"Stop banging your head! You're going to give yourself a concussion!" He banged it three more times, refusing to look at me. I was watching him come undone. I wondered how I would explain to the paramedics that my millionaire married lover bashed his head into oblivion on my fake quartz countertop. "Stop it, Howard! Just stop it. Pick your head up!" He stopped banging. "Don't play games with me. Am I going to be questioned?"

"I'm not sure."

"Look at me!" I felt a burst of outrage. "Tell me the fucking truth, Howard."

"Shit, Leah, I don't know. Please don't look at me like that. Yes, probably."

"Yes, or yes, probably?"

"Okay, not probably. Yes. You'll be questioned. Maybe. Yes. I mean, no, I didn't know this would happen. I thought I was helping you. I didn't mean to involve you in… in this investigation… in any of this. I'll protect you."

I felt like I did when my mother's doctor said the word *inoperable*. Like I was kicked in the throat, and my words were held hostage by my lips.

"What stock?"

"Banyan Pharmaceuticals."

"The nursing homes? With Eddie? The big merger you've been talking about the entire summer. Do you think I wasn't listening? Why'd you buy it?"

Howard hesitated. "Is this an inquisition?"

"Call it what you want."

"Same reason why I purchase any stock. I think it'll make money. That's what I do all day. Make people money."

I tried to remember the details about Banyan, but they were fuzzy. So many details. But this stock always excited him. I felt excited, too, but I was excited for *other* people. It never occurred to me that he'd use my money.

I felt like our relationship had just boarded the Tilt-A-Whirl at the amusement park. Everything was upside down and sideways, and I was about to puke.

"If you bought it for me, I'm involved, I'll ask anything I want." I tried to remain calm, but then Howard screamed again.

"I can't do this, Leah. I just can't. FUUUCK!" Cool, confident Howard suddenly turned into frightened, nervous Howard. I wasn't sure if I liked him at that moment. For better or worse didn't apply to concubines.

"HOWARD!" I finally raised my voice to match his. "You're not making sense. You can't do what?"

"I could fucking lose my fucking license. Or a suspension. And Eddie—oh my God, Eddie, he's not going to be happy."

"So, you had inside information?"

"NO!"

"Okay, so, what's the problem? Don't you take risks all the time? Do you mean to tell me that the SEC breathes down your neck whenever you pick a good stock? I know how it works. I follow the market!" I was shouting now. I started following the market to impress him and have something to add to our conversations. My TV was set to CNBC instead of HGTV; my inspiration was now less Martha Stewart and more Jim Cramer. Watching the highs and lows of the stocks gave me a bigger shot of adrenaline than decorating a cake.

"What about Eddie?"

"What about Eddie?" His back went up in protest.

"Stop yelling at me!"

"I'm not yelling! Damn it, Leah!" He ran his hands through his messed-up hair and looked out the window again.

"Someone better not be watching my house. What did you involve me in? What does Eddie say? You tell him everything."

"This has nothing to do with Eddie." I had a feeling it had everything to do with Eddie. "The big guys in the New York office are involved. They want me to hire an independent lawyer. I didn't do anything wrong, and they're going to make it look like I did. People are jealous, don't you see? I'm extremely successful. They love to think I've got something up my sleeve when I make this kind of money. They forget how much money went into the Gardner Stroke Center. All the money I give to charity."

The air was like frozen nougat. Thick. Opaque. I couldn't think straight, let alone see straight. Both of us stopped talking, trying to make sense of it all. Make sense of each other.

"You may need a lawyer, too. Not yet."

"You've got to be kidding me."

"I'll pay for it."

"That's not the point. Are you sure you didn't have insider information?"

He looked at me wildly, his eyes bulging like a deranged Jack Nicholson in *One Flew Over the Cuckoo's Nest.* "No! You believe me, don't you? Oh, God. Leah!"

"Of course, I believe you. Why wouldn't I?"

"I'm sorry to involve you. I work my ass off trying to please my clients, and there's always someone, some asshole, trying to bring me down." He started to breathe normally again.

"I don't see why you're so upset," I said, trying to process it all calmly. "It seems like you do pretty well to me." There was an anxiety minion party in my stomach, and by all accounts, they were trashing the place.

"I won't tarnish the Gardner name. The timing's not good. We're opening more stroke centers. The thing is, clients love me when I'm making them money hand over foot. But the minute their account's down, it's all my fault. So now," he paused, "when I have a good play, it's too good to be true. I can't win."

"Do you have to give the money back? Do your clients have to give it back?" It just occurred to me that I was included in that group. I tasted the spring roll I ate half an hour ago.

"Only if it's proven that I traded illegally. Which I didn't. I swear. I wouldn't lie to you."

"How much money are we talking about?"

"I don't know. A few million or so."

"WHAT? How much of my money did you invest?"

"This isn't about just you," he snapped.

"How. Much. Of. My. Money. Did. You. Invest?"

"Not a lot."

"Not a lot doesn't mean the same to me as it does to you." I put my hands on my hips.

"Maybe twenty thousand. I don't know exactly. Don't you look at your statements?"

"TWENTY THOUSAND DOLLARS? That's a big percentage of my money." The divide between us got bigger. He didn't know *exactly*, and I knew, to the penny, how much money was in my bank account. His charmed life of golf and fancy cars dwarfed the fact that I reused my aluminum foil. Only bought things on sale. I had to live within my means. Forget the fact that I hadn't looked at my brokerage statements once since I transferred my money.

I knew better, but that account had never fluctuated much. After my divorce, my father bought a few mutual funds, and I barely noticed the monthly gains and losses. It was for college and retirement, if I could ever afford to retire. I assumed Howard put me in better funds, never occurring to me that he'd invest it along with his high-roller clients. "And now it's worth a hundred thousand?"

"Around that. Maybe more." He looked pleased with himself.

I felt a rush. The kind I felt after landing a big client. Which took months of hard work. Money didn't just appear in my account like I'd won the lottery. I hadn't told anyone I actually transferred my money to Howard's firm. Convinced myself it was best to keep it private. I wasn't sure why it unnerved me so much that he didn't waste any time making major decisions with MY money.

"I'm guessing you invested more personally?"

"You could say that." He didn't want me to know how much. "Look, I'd never do anything to hurt you financially."

"I know you wouldn't." Or did I? "But what if I can't get my money back? I trusted you. Oh my God." Then I screamed, "WHAT IF THERE'S A FAMILY EMERGENCY?" Suddenly, all my financial insecurities drummed into my head since childhood came crashing into my kitchen like the Kool-Aid Man.

"If you need money, I'll give it to you. I still have plenty." With his thumb and forefinger, he motioned that there was still a little left, then opened them up to mean more than a little. I forged half of a smile and looked up to meet his eyes, which miraculously had turned from his usual comforting shade of malachite to inauthentic circles of dirty water. This was what guilt looked like.

"I don't want your money. I want my tiny safe amount of money!" I wanted my life back from an hour ago. I wanted my life back from six months ago.

Howard shot me a look of pity. Like I should want better.

"What about the Howie Loans?"

"Did I say this has anything to do with the Howie Loans?"

Oh shit, he was guilty. What did Peyton call him? A snake charmer. How could I have fallen for this guy? *I love him. He's guilty. I love him. He's innocent. I love him. It's all a mistake. Just be supportive.* Fuck. FUCK. I had to hold it together. I had to be calm.

Howard sat down at the table and put his hands in mine. He rubbed his thumbs up and down slowly around mine. His breathing slowed. "If only—"

"If only what?"

"If I had someone like you working for me, this never would've happened. You're so calm. Smart. Your attention to detail rivals that of the amateurs in my office. What would I do without you?" Everything about him softened.

"Be home having this conversation with Deenie?" I couldn't help myself. I needed to know where I fit in.

"She has no idea. They're freezing accounts, and I bought Banyan in our joint account."

I winced at the words *joint account*. "Freezing? My money?"

"Sometimes they'll freeze the money until they prove it was made legally. It's standard protocol. Happens all the time. And then they take the freeze off. No biggie."

"No biggie?"

"They unfreeze it once the investigation's clear. My lawyer takes care of it. There are limits as to how much they're allowed to freeze." I reminded myself I didn't even know about the extra money, so surely, I wouldn't miss it. But still.

Then I remembered the bounced check from when we met and wondered if this was just business as usual for him. "Deenie hasn't noticed your lovely mood?"

"No. I've been at the office late every night reviewing my records. That's why I've been..." He hesitated. "Distant. I didn't want to involve you. There could be subpoenas. And I told you, Deenie and I barely see each other. It's as if I'm not there."

It always came back to that, and now probably wasn't the time, but it was never, ever the time. So, I blurted it out anyway. "How much longer is *that* going to take?"

"I'm taking care of it. This throws a wrench in my plans. I can't do anything suspicious. Separating now will make me look guilty."

"Because no other stockbroker in the world is divorced?" This was our sore point. My marriage failed, I got divorced. His marriage failed, he made excuses.

"You're going to start with me about that now?"

At the end of the summer, Howard announced he'd hired a new divorce lawyer, the biggest name in Philadelphia. The kind you see on TV, escorting high-profile clients while shielding their faces with a stack of legal briefs and a Gucci briefcase.

Things hadn't progressed. There was always one more family birthday party. One more charity event. One more vacation. (Like the one he hadn't told me about yet.) Howard brainwashed me that it was complicated, and he had to listen to his attorney so that not only could Deenie not find out about us, but she had to ask for the divorce, not him. In retrospect, that should've been a huge red flag of *his* lack of integrity. Retrospect. Why do we only use that word *after* the shit hits the fan?

"Trust me. I've got it all under control. Just be patient. I have a plan."

"You always have a plan. You should fill me in if it involves me. Unless it doesn't?" I wasn't sure I wanted to hear the answer.

"Of course, it involves you." At least he wasn't breaking up with me. I needed to give him the benefit of the doubt.

"You're sure Deenie doesn't know about us?"

"No chance. I mean, she wouldn't care, honestly, but, no, she doesn't suspect anything."

I looked at him with pity. Did I want this? Howard was a mess. His face was ashen, and his considerable five o'clock shadow mirrored a face that hadn't been shaved in a few days. How could I be so foolish? I could end this now and go on an actual date in public. Or have sex without worrying about getting caught. A clean break from all this romantic *mishegas*. The craziness. Plead innocence by stupidity. Hire a lawyer. Let my dad, Sid Samuels, do his stuff.

I had planned a future with a man who'd never seen me doubled over in pain with cramps. Or with unwashed hair. Unshaven legs. Maybe none of it was real. Perhaps I wouldn't miss him. The sex, yes. Him? Pick door number two, Leah. Door number two.

Howard leaned over to hug me. I tensed up, but then my shoulders dropped, and I gave in; my body snuggled into him. He wrapped his arms around me and kissed the top of my head.

Door number two was closed. He smelled like power. Rugged and musky, a sweetness I couldn't even describe. The man was a chameleon. I closed my eyes. RUN, LEAH! RUN! A million thoughts swirled around my head, one of them being the sound of a heavy metal jail cell slamming shut.

I straddled two worlds now. And even though my head was exploding, even though my conscious knew better than to trust him, even though the word *guilty* was stamped on his forehead in indelible ink, even though every receptor in my brain screamed to get the hell out while I had a few shreds of decency left, even though I heard the words *snake charmer* being repeated over and over, I let myself be swept ever so gracefully deeper into his web of lies. Somewhere in my inner consciousness, a voice laughed:

Welcome to the insider trading jungle, Leah Samuels.

Reason found its way back to my brain, and I broke away from Howard's strong embrace. "You need to go. I have to think this through clearly. Just give me some time."

"I understand." Howard's eyes were hollow with fear as he picked up his coat and walked out the door.

SIXTEEN

THE FAN Continued

It was my turn to come undone. I raced into my office, a small alcove off my dining room. My desk was a mess. I found the pile of white envelopes featuring an abstract arborvitae with the words Arbor Financial expertly positioned at the roots, signifying that your financial position will grow if you invest with Arbor. One would hope. My hands trembled as I ripped open the most recent statement, looked at last month's balance compared to the previous balance, and stopped myself from falling off my chair.

Please don't let it be so… Howard had invested fifty thousand dollars of my money, in three increments, not twenty thousand, as he'd said, making me a profit of two hundred thousand dollars. *TWO HUNDRED THOUSAND DOLLARS*. If he lied about the amount, what else did he lie about?

My mother's voice hummed, "*If it seems too good to be true, it usually is.*"

How dare he! I picked up the phone and slammed it down. By

now, Howard was home discussing it with Deenie, and if I called him, he'd be busted. I had to think this through. Rationally. I could only imagine how much he invested in total—no wonder the SEC was involved. Seeing it in black and white was infuriating. Did he think I wouldn't notice? Maybe he could afford to play around and lose money on a speculative stock, but this would've wiped me out. Anger seethed out of me. Gambling. It was a tale I knew well.

Believe it or not, I was no stranger to the shady side of this industry. PopPop Harry and his brother Abe were stockbrokers. My mom referred to Uncle Abe as a *gonif*. A cheat. A gambler. She said stock trading was a fool's game. Harry bailed Abe out of trouble over and over. Abe always had a deal too good to miss.

Although my mom was doing her own version of gambling. She plowed through my dad's money, constantly reinvesting all the profits from the businesses, hoping for a windfall, saying *"It could all be gone in a moment"* as she snapped her fingers. It was the mantra of my youth. My mom was right. Not just money. Your health. Like hers. One bad scan and, *snap*, her health was gone in a moment.

My father didn't know I transferred my account. Maybe I'd confess. He knew all the top lawyers in Philadelphia. At least he used to. His colleagues were retired and living in Florida now.

But then, for a split second, I thought about what I could do with all that money. *It's not yours—give it back,* the Monopoly man sitting on my shoulder purred. Maybe I wouldn't have to. A sliver of excitement crept back in; oh, the things I could finally do. I could pay off the second mortgage, the one my dad had cosigned. Life would be so much easier.

At the same time, my brain was intricately peeling back the

layers to expose Howard. Could it be an honest mistake? Did I go with what I felt in my gut or what I felt in my heart? Was there a difference? The SEC made mistakes, didn't they? All that money to the Gardner Stroke Center. What better legacy was there than saving lives? But did he make it legally? How do you ask someone straight out if he's a crook? I shook my head until it hurt. I'd need more than a pint of ice cream. As much as I didn't want to believe it, the universe flashed a warning light: Howard was bad news, and I was in love with him. There had to be a way out.

Night has a way of igniting irrational thinking, unleashing the worst-case scenario into a minefield of disaster; mysteriously, morning has the power to erase it. The idea was simmering when I woke up at four in the morning. It didn't seem relevant whether it came to me in a dream or was there all along. *My* perfect plan. Mascara remnants were all over my pillow, but my headache was replaced with an urgent sense of how I'd help Howard fix everything, save his business, and win his heart. Did I have the guts to go through with it? My last words to Howard were that I needed time. I attempted to put all of the pieces together rationally, but fell into a deep, peaceful sleep until the garage door opening brought me back to reality.

SEVENTEEN

ENOUGH

Footsteps running up the stairs signaled Lily and Asher's return. I needed to pretend my whole world wasn't flipped on its head since last night. But Lily and Asher had news of their own and didn't notice my blotchy face or that I'd slept in my clothes.

"Mom! You'll never guess what happened last night! Dad and Jackie got engaged!"

"Who?"

"Dad and Jackie! You wouldn't believe the ring! Princess cut. It's huge. And gorgeous."

"Who the hell is Jackie?"

"Dad's girlfriend. Well, fiancée now."

I fought back vomit for the second time in twelve hours. "I thought her name was Pam."

"No, Pam was like two girlfriends ago. Pam was after Dana before Jillian."

Dana was the Invisalign rep Louis swore he wasn't sleeping

with. Dana, whom he married less than thirty days after our divorce was final. It lasted three years, and she supposedly took him to the cleaners. No prenup. It couldn't have happened to a nicer guy.

"They bought a house and said the wedding's going to be in Cabo!"

While my tongue was busy tying itself into a thousand knots, my brain was doing handstands. This was the financial situation? How did two men play me on the same night?

"Let's go, Asher. We're gonna be late for school. See you later, Mom!" Lily's green eyes sparkled, and she blew me a kiss before the door slammed. Quiet returned. Along with a rage that wouldn't subside. This was why women killed their husbands. I should've poisoned Louis years ago. Plead insanity and been out by now. But this was no time to be making jokes about jail.

Still processing the news, I picked up my phone, scrolled down to A**hole, and pressed call. "Are you fucking kidding me? Is this the sensitive personal matter you needed money for? You've got some nerve thinking I'm giving you even one day off from paying support."

"Thanks for the congratulations. By the way, we're registered at Crate & Barrel!"

I could picture the smug look on his face as my blood boiled. "I'm serious, Louis. No deferring payments. It's out of the question. Next time, talk to my lawyer, not me. Never mind. There won't be a next time."

"You said three months without support."

"I thought someone was sick. I take it back. You lied to me."

"Did I say someone was sick? You and your fantasy world."

"Fuck you. I can't afford to do this."

"You agreed. And by the way, I was taping you, so I have

proof that you agreed to it."

I hurled the phone across the room, smashing a picture frame on the windowsill. Twelve hours. Two men. Both swindled me out of my money. It was shaping up to be a banner day.

There was no question about what I had to do. I changed my mind about needing time and called Howard on his private line, knowing he'd probably been in the office for hours.

"Good morning, beautiful." No sign of last night's hysterics.

"We need to talk."

"Listen, I'm sorry about last night, and I understand you need some time. The New York office has reconsidered and already has its lawyers working on it." Howard's voice was calm and soothing.

"I didn't sleep much. I may have a better idea. I'll stop by the office. See you at eleven?"

"You remember where to go in the daylight?"

"Yep. I look for the giant dollar signs on the road."

Operation Save Howard entailed a black body-hugging dress, a pair of high-heeled black suede pumps, and a stylish tote bag. Sexy. Confident. I could do this.

It wasn't the New York Stock Exchange, but the Arbor Financial complex buzzed with electricity. Everything spelled prestige from the lush gardens intricately cut to spell the word ARBOR, to the gold chandeliers hovering over the spiral staircase and lining a hallway of elevators, lending just the right amount of opulence before entering a more informal office space.

I strolled past a dozen of Howard's protégés, and one hot guy lingering with a coffee cup in his hand, who looked like he didn't belong. Leather jacket. Brooding demeanor. A mysterious wolf who lost his pack on his way out of the office, but he turned, and

I could feel his gaze on the curves of my dress. The rest were Stepford brokers. Finance bros, to be precise. Black pants, crisp dress shirt, Patagonia vest. Indistinguishable yet trendy haircuts and barely visible facial hair. The most incriminating feature was their cocky attitudes. Closer inspection may have yielded their slip-on loafers, a Whoop band, a Troubadour backpack within reach. I heard a male voice say "slay" and received a few questionable glances as I made my way to Howard's office, one noticeably from BethAnn, who, by the disapproving look on her face, was not happy to see me.

BethAnn was shorter than me with shimmering silver hair, severely cut shoulder-length, with skin the color of luxurious face cream. Her eyebrows were severely penciled, as was the deep red line around her lips. She wore an indigo tailored two-piece ensemble with creme flats. Her demeanor was authoritative, abrasive, and protective. I knew BethAnn had worked for Howard for a long time. I knew little else about this woman except for her irreplaceability, and I instantly disliked her. In my imagination, she was an invisible force, not one that required a description. But now, I realized she looked like she was best friends with Miranda Priestly.

Luckily, Howard was waiting outside his office in an Armani navy windowpane suit tailored to perfection, prepared to quell her questions with his gigantic smile, quite a sharp contrast to the man crying in my kitchen fifteen hours ago. Howard stuck to traditional attire when he had meetings, but seeing most of the office in casual garb and monogrammed fleece had me thinking his look was more of a power play.

"BethAnn, meet Leah, party planner extraordinaire." The mention of my job relaxed her, realizing I couldn't be much of a threat unless I had stashed a few poisonous cupcakes in my tote bag.

"Don't take up too much of his time."

"Hi," I put out my hand, "it's nice—"

"BethAnn, hold my calls." Howard took hold of my elbow and guided me past BethAnn's desk and into his office. One wall was glass, allowing light to wash over the remaining walls, which were covered with awards highlighting Howard's four-decade ascent to top producer.

"Sorry, BethAnn's job has become increasingly stressful with compliance breathing down our necks. Everyone's a prospective ticking bomb. She's afraid that if I lose my license, she'll be out of a job."

"She knows?"

"Of course. She's my right-hand woman. Confidante. She knows everything."

"Everything?"

"Everything."

I digested the information that she knew I was having sex with her boss. Sometimes in this office. After hours. I gasped, opening my mouth to respond before Howard laughed and said, "No, not that, silly."

"She knows everything that goes on in here." Howard swept his arm around the perimeter of the office. That's why she gets paid the big bucks. I trust BethAnn with my life." He motioned for me to sit in a Herman Miller charcoal gray ergonomic chair, a mini replica of the larger executive version across the desk.

"She seems scary."

"Nah, just a bit apprehensive. She and my compliance manager, Nathan, are thick as thieves. They know what's going on before I do. Nothing happens in here without her seal of approval."

"Hire me."

"Excuse me?"

I leaned into the large desk, uncomfortable with the space between us. "You've said I should come work for you." Howard put up one finger and looked in a few corners to see if the office was bugged.

"Go ahead," he said, satisfied no one was listening.

"Why don't I get my license? I'll be your assistant. It can be part-time, so I don't have to give up my business. I'll sub some of the work out. You know I'm bored and frustrated. Maybe it's time for a change. This could help both of us. You can trust me. And you won't have to worry about me ever stealing your clients."

"Stealing my clients. You're funny."

"So if you get a suspension, I'll continue making your trades until it's restored. Do your schmoozing. Your clients wouldn't even have to know."

Howard shook his head. "No. It doesn't work that way."

"Why not? You've told me a million times you wished I worked for you. I quote, 'You're wasting your brain on such a small-scale operation.' Didn't you mean it?" When Howard initially commented, I was hurt, couldn't believe he'd minimize all I built. Now, I realized he was right. I could use my strategic planning skills to make a hell of a lot more money for myself.

"Of course, but this is serious. The last thing I need is another assistant. And the SEC—"

"But then you wouldn't have to worry about... especially if—" I saw him silently nod, acknowledging you know what, so I continued. "We'd be a team. I'll take the financial tests. I'm a quick learner. I feel like I already know your big clients. It's your expertise, but my execution—the perfect plan to save your credibility.

Plus, it's for our future." I flashed a sexy tilt of my head.

"I can't ask you to do this for me. I appreciate it." He paused. "This will blow over. Sometimes, they don't have a solid case to pursue. Or, I may get off with fines. A small settlement. Most of these cases never go to trial. Or they wind up not prosecuting. I did nothing wrong. And it could take a long time before the investigation is complete."

"I know, but I saw how desperate you were last night." Desperate was an understatement. "If we were a team, I'd cover for you. Just if you know… you couldn't trade… even if it's temporary, and then when things get better, I'll step back. You can teach me the business." I considered kissing him and telling him some other things he could teach me, but with one glance out of the imposing glass, I knew we were under the watchful eye of Sergeant BethAnn. "Think about it. Please." It was as casual as asking for a puppy but as monumental as offering a kidney. I was about to give up everything I'd worked hard for to save his ass. In my murky world, if that wasn't love, I didn't know what was.

There was a flicker of relief on his face, a realization that I *could* be the answer.

"You're a genius." Howard reached for a bulging black file and handed it to me. "Everything you need's inside. Testing dates. HR Forms. Log-ins with passwords."

"So you were planning this?"

"Not planning. Hoping. One day. We were updating that file for new hires, but it has everything you need."

There was a knock on the door, and we both saw BethAnn pointing at her Apple watch. "Noon lunch meeting." Howard stood first, signaling the end of our discussion.

I exited his office feeling triumphant. I flipped my freshly washed and blow-dried hair back and strode past BethAnn towards the lobby. I took a peek around the lobby for Hot Fonzie and his leather jacket, just to give him something to look at, but he was nowhere in sight. Screw Louis and Jackie or Pam or whoever the whore of the month was. I felt more secure than I had in months, knowing I was on the path of something exhilarating. I hadn't thought about how I'd tell my clients or family; my only thoughts were about how my plan would help Howard. I was starting over again. Only this time it wasn't so scary because Howard was in my corner. I didn't realize it then, but with this innocuous request, my fate was sealed and rested in Howard's hands. God help me.

DEPARTMENT OF JUSTICE

BACKGROUND NOTES

BETHANN O'CONNOR, OFFICE MANAGER

BethAnn O'Connor grew up in the Albany foster care system while she waited for her parents to reclaim her. She made up elaborate stories of her parents living the glamorous life, promising herself she was one Christmas away from being picked up.

By the time BethAnn was sixteen, she knew they weren't coming back. All the years of holding onto hope had built a wall around BethAnn, and she vowed never to trust anyone again. One morning, she skipped school, hopped on a bus to New York City, and never looked back.

BethAnn had been sleeping in a soup kitchen near Central Park in exchange for helping out at mealtimes and was scouring a discarded newspaper left on a park bench for a job when she witnessed a standoff between a spoiled toddler and his nanny. His eyes tugged at her.

She sang a verse from the only song she remembered her mother had sung to her.

"I want you to be my nanny!" the boy proclaimed, no doubt angering his actual nanny. The boy was Howard, and his innocent words changed her life.

"We don't talk to homeless people," the nanny replied. She grabbed Howard's hand and headed away from BethAnn, but not before Howard rattled off his address.

BethAnn showed up at the Gardners' residence the next day, looking like Mary Poppins in a borrowed dress and a hat securing her unruly ebony hair. When Eugene Gardner opened the door to their Park Avenue townhouse, Howard wrapped his arms around BethAnn. "Daddy, meet my new nanny."

After six nannies in as many months, Eugene had nothing to lose. There were no references to check about a singing, malnourished girl whom his son took a liking to. Howard and BethAnn became inseparable. BethAnn was determined to look out for Howard in a way she felt her parents had fallen short with her. She sat in with his tutors and accompanied him to music lessons. Eugene made sure BethAnn had fresh clothes and whatever else she needed. Before long, BethAnn became the older sister Howard never had.

BethAnn stayed on the payroll after Howard left for college, doing housekeeping and personal assistant work. Eventually, Mrs. Gardner convinced Eugene to move out of the city. They had no use for the former nanny who was now in her thirties. She promised to give BethAnn a glowing recommendation, but Howard did one better. He used his trust money and sent BethAnn to college. The day after graduation, Howard hired her as his manager. BethAnn would do anything for Howard. Take a bullet. Anything.

TOO GOOD TO BE TRUE

I was in the checkout line at the market when Daniel Ross called for the third time. I asked if he was having a slowdown in his social life. He laughed, saying that he was so impressed with the press from the Gardner party that we should strategize marketing our services together.

I agreed to meet him the following Wednesday at my house while the kids were with Louis. Daniel arrived in a beaten-up Kia covered in bumper stickers, carrying two antipasti, a giant order of spaghetti and clams, and a garden-variety bottle of wine. I waved to Mrs. Pomerantz, who had taken up spying on me.

"Yoo-hoo, Leah. Everything ok?" Mrs. Pomerantz was sporting a peacock blue floral housecoat and a perm that looked like she had washed it before the required waiting period. I had too much on my mind for chit-chat.

"All good." I gave her a thumbs-up in gratitude. After all, it wasn't a bad thing that someone was looking out for me.

Daniel on a Wednesday night was a far cry from Daniel on the dance floor. He nervously looked at his phone a few times and apologized for it "blowing up with clients."

Daniel claimed every centerpiece idea was "the best he'd ever seen." We sat on the floor, and after toasting to our mutual success, he flashed a pearly white grin and said, "I really admire what you've done with your business. Would you consider selling it to me?" He clasped his hands together in a prayer position and placed them under his chin.

"What?" I coughed, choking on a piece of garlic bread.

"I know this may come as a shock to you." Shocking, yes. Out of the question? Not the way this week was shaping up.

I took a large gulp of wine. "I don't understand. You have a business. Why do you want mine? I've heard about DJ by Design's deluxe package."

"You're the talk of the party circuit. I'm jealous. I've been in this business a long time, and I don't get half the press you do. Maybe it's time to cash out. Unless you're not ready."

"No offense, Daniel, but could you afford to buy me out? And how much are we talking?" I did some mental calculations about college and my mortgage.

"A group of investors approached me. They're interested in building a one-stop party showcase business. From what I understand, they're acquiring several independent party-planning operations. Building a venue. Imagine the business this would bring in, and you could be involved as little or as much as you want."

I pondered the idea. Being a small, personalized business is what got me where I am. But if I started working with Howard, this would be perfect timing.

"So if I don't sell, I'd be competing with them?"

"Sounds like it. You could probably name your price."

That got my attention. "I wouldn't even know how to value my business." But I knew who could. I tried to comprehend what he was offering.

"Listen, Leah. Sometimes, you should pay attention to when to hold something and when to fold 'em." Daniel often talked in song lyrics. I noticed that about him before as a way of compensating for his awkwardness. "I want to be a DJ powerhouse. I'm talking to a few other people." He glanced at his phone again. "But you're my first choice."

"I'm flattered, Daniel. And I appreciate you thinking of me. This is just so unexpected."

Daniel morphed into his best Kenny Rogers impersonation. "You should know when to walk away."

It was hard getting my thoughts together enough to get a sentence out. "Absolutely. I know what you mean."

"They need a profit and loss statement and the profit on your average package."

"With or without the Gardner party?"

Daniel looked perplexed.

"The Ritz-Carlton—with all those sushi stations?" He paused for a minute and then laughed. "Right. I made a killing on that one."

"It paid my mortgage for four months," I joked.

"You really shouldn't count your money," he tapped out "while you're sitting at the table" on his knee.

"I get it, Daniel."

"I'm sure it would be worth your while. You wouldn't have to give up your weekends anymore. Think about all the things you could do with your time."

"Yes." If he only knew. "Where're you off to next?"

"I'm heading to Atlantic City to meet with prospective clients, so a little business, and who knows, maybe a little pleasure." He shook his hands like he was rolling the dice at a craps table. "I'll chat with you after the weekend. Sin City awaits." He was weird, but I did find myself humming "The Gambler" in my head.

"You know Sin City is Vegas?"

"Same thing."

I shook my head. "No promises, but I'll think about it. Have a good trip. And thanks for dinner." I walked outside with Daniel and noticed Mrs. Pomerantz watching from behind her curtains. The woman was Gladys Kravitz reincarnated. Daniel was texting before he got into his car. *A weeknight booty call*, I thought as I went back inside. Like I should talk.

I pulled out my binder, curled up on the sofa, and got to work. The next thing I knew, it was three in the morning, and I had a calculator stuck to my face. I felt like I was on the verge of a new life. Howard was away for a few days. I couldn't wait to tell him my news. It seemed like things were finally coming together for me.

Three days later, Howard called. It was the old Howard. No sign of *bash-my-head-on-the-kitchen-counter Howard*. I knew not to pry about his meetings. A lot of lawyers and compliance people. And loan sharks for all I knew.

"I have amazing news! An investor wants to buy my business!"

"That's wonderful! Do you need an accountant to help you figure things out?"

"My best friend's an accountant."

"Right. I knew that. If you're ready to sell, we could create a more permanent situation. I just don't want you to give up a business you love. For me."

"I don't love it anymore." *Don't you see? I love you.* We hadn't gotten to the point of professing our love for each other. I was afraid to say it and have him not say it back.

"You're going to be fabulous in my business. I just know it."

"I have to hope it's a real offer. I'm not sure how Daniel can afford it."

"Who?"

"Daniel Ross. The owner of DJ by Design from Addison's Bat Mitzvah?"

"Hmm. Cost a pretty penny, if I remember correctly. He's got a hell of a racket going."

"I suppose. Anyway, he wants to buy me out, a party powerhouse or something like that. The timing couldn't be better, don't you think?"

"This is terrific. Life-changing. I'm so proud of you."

The finance networks were my new obsession, and I kept the TV on mute throughout the day while I worked on party proposals. I finally asked Cara how to value my business, mentioning an interview I watched with a party store CEO. She recited mathematical equations by memory as easily as if I were repeating my mother's chicken soup recipe. EBITDA. Capital assets. Net assets. Discretionary earnings. Forward earnings. I wrote them all down and stared at them, confused. I began googling and got frustrated. I knew my dad would put it all in perspective for me. I'd put this off long enough.

"Hi, Daddy. It's not Poker Sunday, is it?"

"*Ziskeit!* It's about time you called your old man."

"Sorry. I'm busier than normal. Do you have a minute?" Just the sound of my father's voice let me know I was in good hands.

I began with Mitchell inviting Asher to participate in his basketball clinics, then dove into Lily's latest college choices, including UCLA. My dad heard the trepidation in my voice. I imagined him interlocking his broad, Florida-age-spotted fingers behind his amply covered silver head. He still had all his thick hair, looking dashing and younger than his eighty-three years.

"Gotta let them fly, Leah. Remember that your mother didn't want you to go to Washington. And that was only three hours away. Lily will be fine. But why the West Coast? I thought the dream was Syracuse?"

"I think it has something to do with a boy." Toby, her camp boyfriend, went to UCLA.

"Ah, of course. It's always about a boy, isn't it? If I remember correctly, you went down that same path." If he only knew.

Sid Samuels was an eternal optimist, and most importantly, he let all three of us kids make our own decisions. He saw the beauty in failing, using it as a learning tool instead of admonishing us with his own opinions. Rachel was three years younger than me. Bursting with talent, she took off for the lights of Broadway after high school, her family being the cast and crew of her latest production. My dad was exceptionally proud of her, especially when she invited him to the Tony Awards a few years ago.

Mitchell, the baby, married his college sweetheart. His wedding was the last time we were all together as a family before my mom's stroke; her frail body, draped in long-sleeved navy chiffon, matched the exposed veins she'd tried so hard to hide. She looked ravishing that day, even as she struggled to stand and complete the mother-son dance to Elvis's "Can't Help Falling in Love." There wasn't a dry eye in the room. I still can't listen to that song all the way through. Now, Mitchell teaches at a private school in New York and runs a basketball clinic for promising athletes. I don't see him nearly as much as I'd like to.

When I got divorced, my dad never said *he told me so,* which my mother would've done loudly, even from a sound system six feet under. Life had handed Sid Samuels a basket overflowing with misfortunes, yet he remained upbeat, finding his latest live-in girlfriend, or whatever you call it when you're over eighty, on a Jewish dating app. You had to admire his open-mindedness and spunk.

It was now or never. The abridged version trickled out. "Remember I told you about Howard, the secret Scrabble player? He convinced me it was time to handle my finances a bit more aggressively."

"Not a bad idea. He was quite successful, if I remember correctly."

"There's more. An investor wants to buy my business. Do you think I'm nuts?"

"Brazil or Pistachios?"

"Daddy!"

"Whoa. Great job, sweetheart."

"You don't think it's a mistake?"

"If you have one good idea, you'll have another. You're young."

"I'm studying for my Series 7 license."

"That's quite a divergence from party planning."

"I need to see how much I can get for the business. Then I have to pass the exam. But there's a job offer waiting for me. With Howard."

"Well, I think the world could use a female Warren Buffett.

Now that he's retired, he should move to Boca."

"Okay, Daddy. I'll let him know when I see him. Can you help me value my business?"

"Keep it simple. Don't get caught up in crazy algorithms. Take an average of your last two to three years' gross sales and multiply it by four. Be firm. You're worth it. And don't jump at the first offer."

I called my dad ten times over the weekend to review the numbers. I could hear him tapping away on his adding machine and ripping off the paper tape. I reminded him that my child support for Lily would end next year, and he upped my asking price accordingly. I was shocked when he suggested five hundred thousand dollars.

"It never hurts to ask. That's the power of negotiating. Ask for the stars; settle for the moon." If anyone was an expert in negotiating, it was my father.

Daniel called a few days later for an update.

"I believe five hundred thousand dollars is a fair price. I can provide additional backup if you need it."

"They already know you're worth it," he said evenly. "I'll be in touch."

By the end of the week, Daniel called with an offer of the full five hundred thousand dollars. This was too good to be true. I'd be out of my mind not to accept.

NINETEEN

CH-CH-CHANGES

oward walked through the door with two dozen magenta tulips, a bottle of champagne, a pound of dark chocolate coconut clusters, and an overly zealous kiss. "Look at you selling your business for a cool half a mil."

I blushed. It was nice to finally have a man who recognized my accomplishments. We settled into a ritual of sex and dinner, with studying replacing our Scrabble games. I had finally started beating him, too. There was plenty to learn, and Howard quizzed me by text during the day to see how fast I would respond. The new terminology poured out of me. I was determined not to let him stump me.

Unable to hide the changes in my behavior any longer, I took both kids for a chicken parmigiana dinner from Coco Bella. Louis was away at a dental convention, so the coast was clear. I high-lighted the perks of having a structured nine-to-five office job, carefully mentioning that career choices often change.

"That's it!" Lily exclaimed.

"What?" I asked, assuming I would once again need to defend my choices to her. I'm not sure whose raging hormones were worse these days—hers or mine. Everything was an argument.

"I'm going to write my college essay about selling a business and starting over at your age. How a creative brain can flourish in a corporate environment, and the ability to change. How the children of parents who make changes are more adept at handling change themselves. I have so many ideas already. Gee, Mom, thanks for the inspiration! This is going to be awesome. Maybe they'll publish it in the high school newspaper, too."

"Wow. But what happened to inspiration from camp?"

"Mom, writing about Color War and who is hooking up during Shabbat song session is not what will get me into college."

"True. I'm thrilled you see this as a positive." Whatever Lily wrote would be spectacular. Her writing never ceased to amaze me. I just hoped she didn't find out this was a covert operation to help save my boyfriend's ass from jail.

Surprisingly, Lily and Asher became part of my study routine. They were equally excited, offering up flashcard drills during dinner and study sessions replaced our weekly Scrabble games, too; a little financial literacy would do them well.

The kids were giddy about Louis's destination wedding, but I was so busy with my new career plans that it didn't bother me when they talked about the planned beach ceremony and the ever-growing guest list. I begged them not to tell their father what I was up to. Louis had loose lips and an urge to screw me over any chance he got. He'd find a way to discredit me. I reminded myself that if I made enough money, I could tell him to take his child support and shove it.

The kids spent the Jewish holidays with Louis, and I spent them at Peyton's with Cara and Leonardo, who was trying out recipes for his new cookbook. Howard promised that by next year, we'd be hosting the holidays together. The mood was festive, and I felt like Peyton and I were in a good place.

We were halfway through dessert, an apple, caramel, and hazelnut torte, when Peyton began discussing her upcoming podcast. "So this woman, Darcy, vice president of a publishing company, was juggling four affairs, along with four kids. I was exhausted just interviewing her. I thought to myself, Jesus, lady, can't you just buy yourself a vibrator?"

Cara twisted her lips like she had swallowed a gulp of sour milk.

"I mean, how does a busy career woman and mother find the time?" Her gaze was stuck on me.

"This is my busy season."

"Uh-huh. And where's the illustrious Mr. Gardner spending the holidays, Dubai?"

"Probably with Deenie's family. I haven't spoken to him lately." I shot Cara a look of compatibility. And avoided Peyton's accusatory tone. I spoke too soon. We had made it all the way to dessert without an interrogation.

"Couldn't you just do the handyman?"

I knew Peyton was on her fourth glass of wine, so I didn't bother answering.

Instead, I turned to Leonardo. "Can you please pass me another slice? With extra whipped cream."

The next day, Howard was relaxing in my bed. He'd taken an early morning flight back from Nashville to spend the day with me. Lily and Asher slept over at Louis's, opting to spend quality time with the new fiancée. The thought of it put my blood pressure on a roller coaster.

"I forgot to tell you. I'll be in Turks and Caicos for Thanksgiving. It was scheduled over a year ago. I tried to get out of it, but I can't disappoint the girls."

"So you won't be around for Thanksgiving? I was hoping maybe you'd stop by to meet everybody."

"I'm really sorry. Deenie and I agreed not to disappoint the girls. It's our last family vacation. Ever. I promise."

The next four weeks raced by. My dad reviewed the contract, and once he made his red pen notations, it was in DJ by Design's lawyer's hands.

The Securities Industry Essentials test and Series 7 exam were scheduled. I spent every spare minute studying and passed them both on the first try.

It was finally me in the audience at Lily's dance competition, cheering her on as she won her last high school trophy. This time, I didn't have to race home to meet with new clients. Back-to-back parties were scheduled right up until New Year's Eve. A press release was scheduled announcing the sale of Life of the Party, along with a personal letter to my clients explaining the transition. Howard called three times a day, saying his trip was a mistake, and he couldn't wait to get home to see me. Everything was falling into place. It was time to let the girls in on my secret.

TWENTY

THE ANNOUNCEMENT... Part Two

An hour after my big reveal at the café, I heard a car door slam, and a furious Peyton barged in through my front door.

"Here we go again, Leah. Do you realize what kind of mistake you're making? Didn't you learn the first time? Do you remember what your marriage was like? What you put us all through? Maybe you forgot the crying and the pleading to make something work that never had a chance. Maybe you could block it all out. The self-respect you gave up for that scumbag. All the wasted years when you could have had a guy who treated you like you deserved. Maybe you were young and stupid then, maybe you forgot, but I don't. I remember every horrible minute of it, and I cannot, not for the life of me, figure out how you can let yourself get caught up with Howard. It's a big, fat train wreck waiting to happen."

"You don't understand. I'm different. Howard's different. And it's a great opportunity. I need to do this. Can't you understand

I'm tired of struggling every single day? I'm tired of working so hard and still not having enough to pay the bills."

Peyton famously treated a news anchor with a habit of sleeping with her co-anchors. This catapulted her into writing a book titled *Spare Me* and the ability to charge a cool four hundred and seventy-five dollars for a forty-five-minute session. Peyton didn't reuse her aluminum foil.

"You have a habit of confusing orgasms for love and infatuation for security."

"I'm tired of not having a life. I finally feel alive, for the first time, and you can't even be happy for me. I've been waiting for a change forever."

"Forever's an abstract destination."

"Why do you always think you know better than me? You're not *my* therapist, and we're not in junior high anymore." I crossed my arms in resolve.

"No, we're not." Peyton stopped yelling and took a step back. And then it hit her.

"Oh my God. You're in *love* with him."

"It's not that simple."

"I'm sorry. I can't watch you do this to yourself with another guy. I just can't. We all know how this ends."

"Stop worrying about my relationships for once and worry about one of your own. Before it's too late." It was a low blow, but I had no choice. And with that, Peyton walked out of my house in a rage usually reserved for other people. She didn't come to breakfast for the next two weeks and didn't answer my calls or texts. Cara made excuses, but I knew what Peyton was doing, and it wouldn't work. My mind was made up.

Peyton had never been close to her mom. Annabel Meyers was not the force of nature her daughter was, but she was a legend in her own mind. A few small leads on Broadway convinced her she was star material. Finally, a role on *Peyton Place,* and Annabel was bound for stardom.

Annabel got pregnant the same week her husband was offered a residency in Philadelphia. In what she called an unfair twist of fate, Annabel left the Great White Way for a white picket fence and a daughter named for everything she gave up.

Peyton and I grew up in identical two-story colonials featuring manicured lawns, basketball hoops in the driveways, and enough mylar wallpaper à la 1970s glam to inexplicably tell you if you had food in your teeth. I never felt we had an extravagant upbringing; it was the type of house expected of a lawyer with three kids (my dad) and a pediatrician with two (Peyton's dad) in a planned neighborhood akin to where we live now.

Peyton loved drama as much as the fictional town she was named for. She also claimed her mother resented her for needing to put the whims of a wisecracking and opinionated daughter in front of her potential Oscar-worthy career. By the time we were in junior high, Annabel was back in New York, auditioning for soap operas and commercials. And missing every milestone in her daughter's life. She'd settled for community theater in more recent years, but still believed her Gloria Swanson moment was right around the corner.

I'm sure Peyton and I bonded because neither one of us had

mothers who had time for us. It was no coincidence that Peyton chose the profession she did.

At the café, the Pyramid Girls were multiplying again. Holiday pop-up fever was upon us. I pretended to enjoy the camaraderie of female entrepreneurship, for Cara's sake. Inside, I was seething at the rapid expansion of the women's empowerment club. It all seemed sketchy.

The day my business sale was finalized, Peyton left for vacation. It was the longest period we'd spent not talking to each other since we were ten years old. The lawyer, a limp, spot of a bespeckled guy with a handlebar mustache, walked me through a pile of documents. Like my divorce, years of effort, a couple of signatures on the dotted lines, and it was all a memory. This time, there was no congratulatory girls' dinner toasting the next chapter. I didn't feel good about it, but it was my turn to take charge of my destiny. With or without Peyton's support. She'd come around. Hopefully.

Life of the Party was officially a subsidiary of DJ by Design, and my bank account was, for the first time, at a level where I didn't panic every time I went to the supermarket. The money was deposited in my new account at Arbor, and Howard assured me it would be invested conservatively and with my consent.

On the first night of Chanukah, I received a text from Peyton: A Chanukah miracle. I'm spending the holidays with my mom. She says hello. I'm going to try to give her a chance. I guess I'm giving you one, too. Go get 'em, Leah, and good luck. (You'll need it).

It was the best I could hope for. Chapter two was finally beginning.

TWENTY-ONE

JUST AN OLD BOYS' CLUB

I officially started my career at Arbor Financial feeling like Mary Tyler Moore and a million dollars, which was not much more than what I spent on my new outfit. I admit I was nervous. After all, the last time I started a new corporate job, my working girl role model was Murphy Brown, and the Spice Girls were at the top of the charts.

I chose a silk Diane von Furstenberg charcoal wrap dress that screamed Wall Street chic with Peyton-mandated Prada pumps and a classic Chanel bag. My hair was long and straight, my bangs swept to the side, and I let Cara pick out a new lipstick color for me. Sans formaldehyde.

"Live a little," Peyton and Cara said in unison as they coaxed me into buying the extravagant items.

"This'll be more than my first three paychecks combined," I protested.

"Chances are you'll have the bag and the shoes longer than the job," Peyton quipped.

BethAnn met me at the elevator door and walked me to an open workspace of razor-sharp dressed brokers. Eleven of the twelve people in my section were male, and many were half my age. Last night, Howard reminded me for the hundredth time that we couldn't look suspicious. I was a trainee. He had a plan, and I was instructed to sit tight and not attract any attention to myself. I reminded him he didn't have any problem with the attention he had spent on me in my bed just a few hours earlier.

I couldn't help but flash Howard my best come-hither smile. He barely looked up from the cluster of finance bros surrounding his desk.

Within one minute, I received a text from Howard. Giddy and already blushing, I opened it inside my pocketbook so no one would see.

DO NOT DO THAT AGAIN. I was quickly becoming aware that there were two Howards. The fun-loving one who couldn't wait to tear my clothes off. And the one who pretended he didn't know me. Fine, let him do his best to Danny Zuko me.

Sorry. I tapped back—heart emoji. Delete heart emoji. I put the phone back in my bag.

Sergeant BethAnn appeared just as I positioned a framed picture of my dad, kids, and me, taken last winter in Florida. Accustomed to hearing Howard call her BA, I silently christened her Sergeant BA, Sergeant BadAss. I was terrified she'd make me regret this decision, especially after reviewing the employment contract I was required to sign, which explained that I was on probation for the first sixty days. Doesn't sleeping with the boss count for anything these days?

"Don't get too comfortable," she said, not blinking and turning her back to me.

My dad called at 10 am. "How's the first day going?" he asked eagerly.

"I'm the low man on the totem pole," I whispered, watching my surroundings cautiously.

"Ah, *ziskeit*," years of wisdom poured out of him in the space of silence, "the bottom symbol of the totem pole is the most important. The most prestigious of people are the ones at eye level."

"I hope so. It's a little intimidating."

"Has Carl Icahn invited you to dinner yet? Do I need to put in a good word?"

"Daddy! You know him?"

"No, but we go to the same cardiologist. And your mom's cousin knew Michael Milken back in the day."

"I don't think that will help me."

"Probably not. But, you've got this." He blew me a kiss that I could feel across the twelve hundred miles that separated us.

The hum of the terminals fueled my enthusiasm. My body sizzled with excitement for what lay ahead. The office was noisy. Tickers crowded the screens. TV monitors flanked the giant Arbor Financial logo on the wall.

I smiled broadly at the guy next to me. Howard said Arbor's hiring standards were high; Ivy material, with impressive resumes, summer internships, and the ability to kiss some major ass. This guy looked like he still lived in his college frat house. His biggest decision of the day was half zip or quarter zip. I pictured him pounding his palms on the desk, counting Dow points as he was egging on his bros to do more shots. It also occurred to me that Lily could be less than a year away from dating a guy just like him. She loved this look. Early aughts Abercrombie. Probably on the rowing team. Sandy-colored hair falling loosely into hazel eyes.

"Hey. Reese Hollander. Glad to meet you. Welcome to the Newbies," he said warmly.

"Newbies?" I asked.

"New hires. Anyone who's been here less than four years. I hear that's how long it takes before they take you seriously. Or know your name. I've been here almost three years and still get nervous whenever I walk through those double doors. You're shadowing me. So cozy in!"

The camaraderie routine wasn't convincing. This was six feet five inches of pure arrogance.

"Nice to meet you, too," I said. Reese gave me a nod of familiarity, probably thinking I looked like someone in his mother's book club.

Just before eleven, Howard made his obligatory rounds. I watched him make small talk, knowing this would be the extent of his coming near my work station. "Leah, I'm so happy you've joined the team."

"What, no corner office?" I joked.

"In due time," Howard said with a wink as he walked away. I watched, hoping no one noticed me checking him out, feeling thrilled that I knew exactly what color boxer shorts were under all that pinstripe.

I wasn't the only one watching him. Reese's gaze followed Howard. Reese whispered, "I still can't believe I'm working with *the* Howard Gardner. The man's a legend."

"Yes, he is legend material." I smiled back, hoping my face

didn't give anything away. I was ready to work and sink my teeth into this job, and the lack of anything meaningful to do was unsettling. I was used to being productive. I had to remind myself that I'd only been there for two and a half hours. From what I could see, everybody stayed in their pod, staring at their terminals. Howard hadn't told me I was shadowing a child.

Finally, Nathan approached my workstation. "Leah. Zoe. Brent. Compliance meeting in the conference room in ten minutes. You can tag along, too, Reese." The word *compliance* was starting to make the hair on my arms stand at attention.

Zoe was seated on the other side of me, and it was obvious she spent more time studying FINRA rules than *Vogue's* latest trends. Zoe was a free spirit and looked cut from the same tie-dye cloth as Asher's junior high music teacher. She was his first crush, and he was heartbroken when she moved to New Mexico with her husband. Zoe's radical dark hair rivaled the length of her maxi skirt, definitely more Stevie Nicks than *Forbes*, and I liked her instantly. She smelled like incense. I hoped we'd be friends. She didn't acknowledge me.

Brent jumped to attention. He was not much taller than me with prematurely thinning hair. He zipped his midnight blue Arbor fleece vest almost to his chin. "Yes, sir. On my way. Can I help you with anything?" He had *kiss-ass* written all over him.

Whatever was left of the stereotypical suit mentality went out the window with COVID. Business casual, with an emphasis on the casual, was now an acceptable option. I knew I had to be careful. I was probably overdressed, but also one inch of cleavage away from Sergeant BadAss sending me home to change my clothes.

My coffee had gone cold, so I quickly stopped to get a fresh cup. "Excuse me," I said to a man leisurely stirring his coffee, blocking the creamer station. Hot Fonzie turned, flashing me a mischievous grin. He sported a heather gray scarf and a camera around his neck. A pair of gloves dangled from worn leather pockets. "I'm sorry. I…"

"No problem," Hot Fonzie said as he stepped to the side. I reached for the vanilla creamer and knocked over my coffee. "Ow," I cried as I felt the hot liquid on my hands. Nathan poked his head in, reminding me that the meeting was about to start. "Coming," I replied, flustered.

"Here. Let me get that." Hot Fonzie appeared by my side with a wad of paper towels and a fresh cup of coffee. I was still squeezing my hand, hoping I didn't have third-degree burns.

"First day jitters," I said nervously.

"Want some ice for that hand?"

"No, I think my cool embarrassment will heal it."

"Good luck on your first day." He stared at me a little too long, his eyes piercing, making me feel like he knew exactly why I was there. Although it didn't look like he worked there. He didn't have on anything fleece or trendy. It must have been my paranoia kicking in.

"Nice jacket."

"Thanks. It's vintage. Like me."

I laughed. "Me too. I'm going to be late. Thanks again." Did I mention this delicious man was hot? I was going to have to talk to my gynecologist about this. My dopamine transmitter needed an adjustment. I'd like to think my prowess had improved over the past thirty-plus years, but it seemed like the jury may still be out. I headed for the conference room, determined to forget Hot Fonzie.

Nathan Sterling had the demeanor of a man who couldn't take

a joke. He plopped a *Sears* catalog in front of each of us, settled himself in front of the conference table, and began with the obvious. Compliance. Ethics. Employee Loyalty. Insider Trading. Regulatory Commissions. SEC. Most of this was still fresh in my mind from studying. It seemed like common sense.

The *Sears* catalog was a prop—all 600 pages of glossy stock. Everything was available for us to read on the firm's website, but he was proving a point as to how long he had been in this industry.

Nathan looked squarely at us and planned his level of *scaring the shit out of us*. He walked over to a dry-erase board and wrote KISS on the whiteboard. Thinking I knew what it stood for, I raised my hand. I quickly realized that raising my hand was out of fashion.

"Keep. It. Secret. Shithead." Nathan was dead serious. "No discussing information with friends or family members who work or have sources at any public company." Nathan had worked for the SEC for over twenty years. He took his job seriously. "If any of you Gordon Gekko wannabes are considering using Arbor Financial as a clearinghouse for something questionable, you can leave the conference room right now and keep walking. Arbor has been in the business for forty-two scandal-free years. We plan to keep it that way for the next hundred and forty-two, so if your cousin's husband's friend works for Facebook and they're about to announce a new feature, I don't want to know about it. You don't want to know about it. You're not doing your clients a favor if you tell them about it. Keep. It. Secret. Shithead. We'll hear about it when the *Journal* breaks the story."

Reese said, "So what about Beau, my roommate from Harvard. He's in tight with the Winklevoss twins." I was sure he was joking, but Nathan ignored him. I realized my Ivy assessment was accurate.

"Your brother-in-law works for Price Waterhouse? Great! But you don't want to know about the audit for the REIT that owns the local shopping center. You don't want to know Old Navy is closing half its stores. Tell the Shithead to Keep It Secret. Tell him not to talk to you. Not even in a conversation at your mother-in-law's house for Sunday brunch. Ask about his tennis game. Compliment your mother-in-law's new drapes. Sit at the children's table if necessary. Do. Not. Engage."

We got the picture, but Nathan kept going. "Your best friend's mother was part of a clinical trial for a new cholesterol drug from a Big Pharma company everyone has heard of. Wish her well and change the subject. Please don't talk to neighbors at their kids' birthday parties who have a tip and offer to split the profits with you. This information will cloud your judgment. Even when you think it won't. Trust me. The information will be there waiting, lurking, in the back of all your cum laude cortexes. It's forbidden fruit, and you're dying of thirst, but I beg of you, walk away. Anything that seems too good to be true always is. There are cameras everywhere. People panic and fess up, and the next thing you know, they leave friends and family holding a bag of money in a parking lot outside a Starbucks with surveillance waiting across the street. I've seen it. The SEC has ways to track this shit down. So does the FBI. And the Department of Justice. They work together. Insider trading is a crime. Everyone gets hurt."

I was intrigued by Nathan's colorful scenarios. It sounded like a pep talk for a sting operation. It was daring. I could taste the danger and could've listened to his stories all day, and wondered if these were hypothetical stories or bona fide cases. I wanted to ask, but knew better than to make light of anything. Plus, I was already involved with Howard's case and assumed Nathan knew the details. If these were scare tactics, they were working.

"Any questions?" Nathan looked at the four of us, waiting and hoping no one would ask a stupid question.

Nathan was too good-looking for such a serious job. His ruffled, salt-and-pepper hair made him look like he just finished a workout, ripped off his headband, and shook his head. An older version of Andre Agassi. Scratch that. Andre Agassi was that old now. And bald. Nathan's eyes were kind, a pale cerulean, tranquil like the ocean. He wore olive slacks, loafers, and an olive and black crew neck sweater with a collar peeking out. He didn't wear a tie but looked polished and wore his years of experience on his clean-shaven face, each line representing an accomplishment. I was a little scared of him, which I guess was the persona he was going for.

Howard had said that Nathan had the most stressful job at the company. They often bickered, with Howard usually relenting to whatever Nathan proposed. I knew that Howard had generously persuaded Nathan to leave the trenches of the SEC. Arbor made him an offer to switch sides, which he couldn't refuse.

"Nathan keeps the whole place in line, so I don't have to."

It seemed like a no-brainer to me. I mean, how hard was it to follow the rules? It consoled me to think Howard made too much money to risk it. Plus, it all funded the Gardner Stroke Center. The SEC inquiry had to be a mistake.

"Compliance is simple," Nathan said. "If you have to think about it, don't do it." He adjourned with a lingering thought, "I hope I don't get to know any of you too well."

The following weeks progressed slowly. Howard continued to ignore me at work.

When I asked him for details about the case, he replied that things were going in the right direction and, once again, to be patient. Howard's mood in the office was volatile. I liked him better as a sex toy.

I hated that I was bored at work, waiting for directions. I hated that I wondered if I had made a mistake, even though I told everyone I loved my job. I hated that sometimes I loved this man and sometimes I didn't. I had no choice but to believe he knew exactly what he was doing. I also had the uneasy feeling that Howard wasn't the only one calling the shots. I hated that I had given up my power.

It's strange to give something away that you didn't realize you had. A defining character trait that most women spend their whole lives waiting for, and mine was there for the taking. Somewhere between my divorce, my business, and years of struggling, it had quietly emerged, and therein lies the problem. It was a quiet power. An oxymoron at best. It should never have been quiet. It needed to be fierce. And loud. And I had to get it back.

The snow dropped eight inches of heavy, wet slush, and I was unable to get out of my driveway. I texted Howard, who told me the stock market doesn't have snow days and that he'd send his "guy" over to shovel. I trudged into an empty office at noon.

"Where is everybody?"

"They don't have a guy," he laughed. "Don't worry. Nathan will be here. He's never missed a day of work."

"I was watching CNBC this morning. Why aren't you buying Apple and Microsoft?"

"That's the point," Howard explained. "We have plenty of Apple and Microsoft, and all the tech stocks. The Wealth Portfolio Division buys the stocks you hear about on TV. I spent most of my career buying them. My SHINE group is taking positions in smaller stocks that fly under the radar. The positions are too small to garner attention."

"I thought that's what happened before. They caused attention."

"They weren't supposed to." He paused before indulging me with more. "We're wondering if there's a mole. I think someone was on my computer. IT is working on it, and then you're on my team."

"Do I finally get to trade?"

"Slow down. We're making a few additions to the advisory panel for SHINE. Their interests are high-risk, and we often rotate people for their input. You'll buy the sexy stocks—the Apples, the Facebooks, and the big-name tech stocks, the ones everyone and their cousin are buying these days, as part of the allocation, along with what I instruct you to buy. Reese will be working with you. And Barry weaseled his way in for a change. You haven't met Barry yet. He'll be back tomorrow. He's attending another Rock and Roll Fantasy Camp Week."

"Fantasy Camp?"

"Barry was one of the founding members of the firm. But he still thinks he'll make it on the road." Howard rolled his eyes.

"What does that mean?"

"Barry participates in Rock and Roll Fantasy Camp a few times a year. It's for charity. Rich people pay a lot of money to spend a few days with their idols. It used to be a big networking thing for him. Now, it's just a way for him to play guitar, smoke pot, and seem cooler than he is. The board's trying to get him to retire, and he won't go. He's past his prime."

"Why do they want him out?"

"He's too conservative. He's not willing to try new things. No crypto. No alternative investments. He just walks around the office pretending to be important. It's a wonder he knows how to use computers. He's happy living in 1976."

"It was a good year."

"If you're going to make it in this industry, you must take risks. If you don't, someone else will. That's why I have a stroke center, and Barry doesn't." Howard's ego was showing. "Anyway, you're going to officially be working with the SHINE team. You'll execute the trades from your computer."

"Are we still buying Banyan Pharmaceuticals?"

Howard shook his head, annoyed. "No. We sold the positions, secured the profits, and moved on. We're hoping the SEC's attention on Banyan will go away."

"Did you sell mine, too?"

"Yes. We're done talking about Banyan."

"I thought we discussed not trading in my account without talking to me first."

"That was before we were partners." He winked and smiled. "Everyone got out. Trust me. I know what we're doing."

I thought about it for a minute and replied, "But if those gains were obtained illegally and used to buy other stocks, doesn't that muddy the new purchase?" I didn't study around the clock for nothing.

"Leah, you're overthinking this."

"Yes, but—"

"Stop assuming anything was illegal. This is how the business works, sweetheart. I told you they'd probably drop the case. Nathan agrees. It takes time. We're traders. We buy and sell. The SEC has no proof, and no proof equals no case. The SHINE group is aggressive. We'd call more attention if we suddenly held something too long."

"Okay, Boss." I vaguely remembered hearing a story about a mistress/concubine/*what am I these days*? not being forced to testify against her lover. Or was it that she was forced *to* testify? He was trying to shut me up. *Well*, I rationalized. *I'm not technically a mistress. We're partners.* At least, that's what he kept telling me. I didn't know how the SEC would see it.

The next day, Barry and I met over a tray of bagels, and a monumental decision concerning the lox or the chive spread.

"So, you're the mysterious Leah. Welcome. Whatever you need, just ask. I'm the one with the biggest office and the best stories!"

Being well past retirement age, Barry resisted the urge to cut his hair, allowing his long gray locks to make a statement. He shaved when he felt like it and had given up on the suit and tie before anyone else did. He wasn't obsessed with looking younger to woo new clients. I assumed he was a high-functioning pothead, judging by his laid-back manner and the lingering smell of weed from his office.

Barry's door was always open, and depending on which corridor I took to the elevator, I could hear him strumming the faint sounds of Crosby, Stills, Nash & Young on his guitar.

Barry's smile was inviting, and his office was filled with signed guitars and framed memorabilia from all the top rock bands. Grand Funk Railroad. The Allman Brothers. Grateful Dead. He wasn't your typical Wall Street type; he was the real deal, authentic, most certainly, an original. It was obvious Howard didn't like Barry. But I did. In this buttoned-up finance world of men, it was clear not much had changed in a hundred years. At least women were allowed in the industry now. A mere handful of us. I thought I could learn a few things from Barry.

"Tell me about Barry," I asked Howard the following Wednesday night.

"Barry's a has-been."

"What does that mean?"

"Once upon a time, Barry played backup as a session musician for Loggins and Messina. Torn between his finance degree and his love of music, he cozied up to the managers and set up 401K accounts for the artists. I think he knew Geffen or Azoff. One of those guys. Anyway, these musicians were in their twenties, making boatloads of money, and far more interested in drugs and getting laid. Being out on the road, the last thing they had time to do was get a financial advisor."

"That's amazing."

"I guess. If you're into that kind of thing." I was. "Back in the day, Barry went on tour with the legends and set them up for when the road became too hard. The money's been growing for years. Now that artists are selling their catalogs, Barry doesn't have to do a thing. The money just rolls in. We laughed at his obsession, but in hindsight, it was genius."

"Does he still play?"

"Don't you hear him in there?"

"I mean professionally."

"He plays gigs with his band on weekends. Vintage Whiskey or something like that. Mostly a bunch of old guys, along with his son, a hotshot journalist or something. It's not my scene. The son's a loser. He tried to include me in an exposé a few years ago, but I wasn't interested."

"Can we go see Barry's band play?"

Howard shook his head in disregard. "Don't involve yourself with people who aren't looking out for you like I am."

A few days later, I reported to the conference room, where I joined Reese, Brent, the kiss-ass, an older man with a generous amount of silver hair named Stu who bore an uncanny resemblance to my Uncle Abe, and Barry, who walked in humming "You Can't Always Get What You Want."

While we sat around a shiny oval table covered with an assortment of fruit and gourmet pastries, Nathan and Howard took turns explaining that we'd be concentrating on stocks in the wellness category. I discovered that Reese was an expert in data analytics, and Stu used to be a forensic accountant. They were in charge of the analysis. Brent and I were in charge of patterns. Once Howard greenlighted the positions, I'd execute the trades. It seemed simple enough. It looked like Barry was in the meeting because he had nothing else to do. He spent a lot of time examining his cheese Danish. Howard and Nathan dismissed us with a list of prospectuses to review. Brent tried to fist-bump Howard, but Howard ignored him. Just as I got up to leave, Howard told me to meet him in his office in ten minutes.

The power lunch, also known as the two-martini lunch, was dead. To make up for it, there was a never-ending supply of food available. Reese's college roommate, the aforementioned Beau, worked in the merger and acquisition department of Skylar Holdings, our sister company in New York. Beau worked in our office once a week and invited me to tag along when they went out, but I was too afraid of Sergeant BadAss to sneak away.

I poked my head into Howard's office to see Sergeant BadAss and a heavyset man with shoulder-length coiled hair and ebony skin conversing behind Howard's desk.

Howard introduced us. "Leah, meet Kai, my IT wizard. If you have questions regarding computer accessibility or any technical problems, he's your guy."

Kai nodded. "Good to meet you."

"And—" Howard winked at BA, who looked defeated and shrugged her shoulders. "I'm giving you access to SHINE as well as some earnings reports. You'll be able to access the trades I want you to make from my computer. Kai will set you up with the passwords and fingerprint access. Don't discuss this with anyone." Kai typed in a series of codes, and Howard's computer responded.

"I want you to study the SHINE group. Get a feel of what they trade, how often, and how much, as a percentage. Start taking their calls."

"Great. I can't wait to meet them all." Sergeant BadAss looked at me as if I had six eyes.

"Prepare to allocate the trades over the next week. We rotate in and out. In the meantime, look at their holdings, and if there's something you think will complement what they have, buy it. If you think they're too heavy on a position, sell it. I'm giving you the stocks to buy; it's your job to allocate them. Stick with the pool of stocks I give you, don't get cute or go rogue on me. And don't be afraid to press the button. You can always sell. We're only worried about the net."

"Do we have the authority to do that?" I asked. BA shot Howard another look of annoyance. Like, *why in the world did we hire this dimwit?*

"These accounts are specifically earmarked for this type of trading."

"What about tax efficiency?" I could feel BethAnn roll her eyes.

"We're traders, not accountants."

"What if there's not enough money in the accounts?"

"There's always enough money. We talked about this, remember?"

Right. Howie Loans. Clearly, it wasn't common knowledge with everyone else.

"And they don't care which stocks we buy?"

"Not if they're making money. Green is green. Capeesh?"

"Okay, Boss." I smiled, knowing BA was watching me. "I guess I have some work to do," I added as I turned to walk out of his office.

"That's what you're here for," BethAnn said.

DEPARTMENT OF JUSTICE

BACKGROUND NOTES
NATHAN STERLING, COMPLIANCE MANAGER

Nathan Sterling was well-versed in the world of corruption. Nathan graduated from Cardozo Law School and jumped between firms until he settled at a little-known company based in Texas named Enron. Nathan watched how fraudulent moves were orchestrated. He watched people make risky transactions with no fear of consequences whatsoever. Nathan questioned the unethical behavior, and his questions went unanswered. He reviewed accounting practices and fought to avoid legal loopholes. Nobody wanted someone who played by the rules. He found it increasingly hard to do the job he was hired for.

Nathan's father, Jerry Sterling, worked for Drexel Burnham Lambert, home to the notorious Michael Milken. In the late 1980s, buried amid the scandalous headlines, Jerry went to jail for someone else's mistakes.

Intent on proving his father's conviction was a set-up, Nathan left Enron (just in time) and joined a law firm specializing in securities fraud. Unfortunately, Jerry died of an apparent heart attack in jail, and Nathan never had the chance to see him vindicated. By 1990, Drexel was forced into bankruptcy. Nathan watched furiously from the sidelines as the Boeskys and Milkens of the world were paid hundreds of millions of dollars for breaking the law.

Nathan knew there was only one place left to go: the Securities and Exchange Commission.

The dot-com bubble of the early 2000s terrified Nathan. He knew the players in the financial industry were taking advantage of the system, and it was just a matter of time before they were caught. He wouldn't draw the same short stick as his father. He had a vengeance that catapulted him to create a high-profile task force.

Eventually, he was assigned to SAC Capital. It seemed like a home run of indictments. Ten years later, a handful of their top traders were charged and sentenced. The best Nathan's division could do was get a guilty plea from the firm, punish them with a fine, and close it to outside investors. No matter how hard the SEC tried, they couldn't build a case against the billionaire owner.

Nathan took it personally. His dad was dead, and billionaires were dancing on his grave. When Nathan was offered a compliance job managing a small office outside of Philadelphia, he thought it would be just the swan song he needed to end his career on a positive note. He never dreamed he'd be caught up with a man like Howard Gardner.

Nathan knew all the ins and outs of the industry to keep a man like Howard in line. He also knew just how to allow him to get away with it.

TWENTY-TWO

TURNING THE WORLD ON WITH A SMILE

alfway through the probation period, it still bothered me that I was the odd woman out. I was beginning to believe that's why it was easy for Howard to hire me. If I was invisible, I didn't exist. Nothing but another middle-aged woman, who disappeared into the background, overshadowed by the alpha male synonymous with the industry. Peyton was right about that. I had to make my mark. Prove myself. Use my power. But, no matter how hard I tried, the bros had no interest in talking to me beyond a few pleasantries in the snack room. Zoe barely spoke at all. Arbor really was the epitome of an old boys' club. No girls allowed. No matter what their head count was.

This was the hazard of being the old woman on the trading floor. Conversations stopped when I walked by the young traders. There was the daily football toss through the Newbie Pit, and although I ducked the first time, not realizing what was whizzing by my face (thank you, Marcia Brady), it was never thrown my

way. I learned that the proverbial football was a notch of entitle-
ment for a profitable trade. The same finance bros threw hundred-
dollar bills in the air for sport. Not that I planned on making lifelong friends or wanted to go out for happy hour—I had kids at
home who needed dinner—but it would've been nice to be asked.
Reese and Barry were my only friends.

On the plus side, nobody was making a pass at me. I wouldn't
have to endure anyone patting my ass or propositioning me for a
blowjob at the coffee station. So, as good as I thought I looked,
I was, after all, a woman of a certain age. The age of most of my
coworkers' mothers. Vivian, an ancient woman at the end of the
corridor, rarely came out of her office. Nathan, whom I decided
was hot in his own scary, enigmatic way, was polite but guarded.
Barry, who, if I weren't here because of Howard, would be the
man I'd call my mentor. The senior executives, the ones who still
wore the power suits and shared hearty laughs, rich with an air of
industry longevity, kept their distance.

Being a SHINE trader was different from being an ordinary
stockbroker. We were an elite group trading in a small sector. VG
Industries was our top position.

"Where's our information coming from?" I asked Howard one
evening when he saw me working later than usual.

"Research and development," he answered casually.

"I know that," I answered breezily, "but from where?" I'd
been spending all my spare time researching. And counting how
many female clients there were.

"It's internal. We have an interest in this category; it's emerging, and the clients trust us."

"What kind of interest? I'm just trying to be thorough."

"R&D is thorough. You've read every earnings statement.

You have access to my computer. You've memorized the launch calendar. I swear you're one credit short of a doctorate in VG Industries and all their spin-offs. Just allocate the trades. Keep doing what you're doing. You're killing it."

"Okay. But I still want to know who R&D is." Our success rate was phenomenal. Sometimes, I wondered if it was beginner's luck or if I had a predisposed knack for this.

"If you want to be part of the SHINE team, let go of the interrogatories. We have enough information to know these are good investments. That's the point. We invest in companies before they're hot. That's how you make money in this industry. Being first. You do realize how many people in this office want to be part of the trading team?"

"Well, not really, since no one talks to me. It's like I have the plague or something."

"They're jealous. You started as an assistant, and within a month, you're doing the kind of work someone with years of experience does. Do you know how many people would kill to be my protégée? You don't need anyone to talk to you. Remember why you're here."

"Yes, Boss," I teased, "But I still wish people were friendly."

"It's not a popularity contest, Leah. It's a job."

The pace picked up. Being part of the SHINE team became a daily sprint with high stakes. I quickly got the gist of trading, and the team began welcoming my suggestions. They didn't know my information came from Howard. Reese began complimenting me in front of the other traders. Little by little, the other team members were nicer to me. It was a slow thaw, but I gladly accepted it. Reese was brilliant; he had incredible insight and timing. He was more thoughtful than I originally gave him credit for. He delighted in bringing me homemade cookies from his mom. We were an unlikely match, but Reese and I worked well together. He was patient but quick, and we fell into a mutually respectful volley of picking the right stocks at the right times. I'd given him access to my computer when my screen wasn't responding. Reese could fix anything without me having to bother Kai in IT or Howard.

Reese was from Ohio and had lost his father when he was six. By the age of eleven, he worked in the local supermarket. Every penny he made went to help his mother. Reese's mom raised him and his disabled older sister, ZuZu, alone. I knew that ZuZu was the name Reese made up for Suzanne because he couldn't pronounce her name. He beamed with pride whenever he mentioned her. Reese was driven, a superstar in every way, but I could tell there was a lot of sadness behind all his confidence. He told me that he spent all his college internship money to pay for a new wheelchair for ZuZu. He went to Harvard Business School on a full scholarship, where he met Beau. On his desk was a twenty-year-old faded picture of Reese, ZuZu, and their father. He got his chiseled features from his dad, but I knew he got his motivation from ZuZu. Reese had confided in me that he paid for the special facility ZuZu now lived in.

As the weeks progressed, I began to understand Howard's mercurial moods. There could be a downturn in the market any day; it was inevitable, but we were bulls, and bulls charged. A dip would force us to buy more. I could feel myself riding the same roller coaster and promised myself I could handle the fluctuations without taking it out on anyone, especially my kids.

After Lily wrote her college essay, she pitched an in-depth version for the school paper. I'd come home exhausted, but she'd curl up in my bed. I'd run my fingers through her hair, just like when she was a little girl, while she'd grind through a list of questions about my job. My long-term goals. It's impressive how she took my simple answers and turned them into a swoon-worthy piece about women's adaptability in a man's world. Her angle was sharp and insightful. The school paper ran her story on the front page. It was great to see her so excited about me for a change. Howard was wary about my saying too much. I told him it was harmless and he had nothing to worry about.

Asher came home the day the story ran with a strange look on his face. "Mom, my history teacher saw Lily's byline and asked if you were the party planner from Garnet Springs. When I said yes, he broke into the biggest smile I've ever seen and said to say hello. The whole class began singing *'Asher's mom and Mr. Rubenstein sitting in a tree.'* How do you know him?"

"I don't."

"Mr. Rubenstein. He's got wavy gray hair, a mustache, and beard, and he wears cowboy boots."

"Max?"

"Um… yes, Max Rubenstein. My history teacher. Oh no… Please don't tell me you're seeing him. All he talks about is his dating escapades. I'll die of embarrassment."

"We met last year and had a bite to eat once or twice. You're safe. No spark."

"Gross."

The winter freeze lifted, and my probation period ended. Sergeant BadAss had less of a hold on me, or maybe she lost interest. There was an uncomfortable moment in the ladies' room when I thought I saw her smile, but she followed it up with an abrupt, *not sure what you are still doing here* turn of her lips. Howard's stress level receded, and he was loving and flirty again. He said new developments were happening every day. I felt a new stroke of confidence, believing I was needed there and not just to cover for Howard. Arbor was the structured environment I didn't know I craved. I should've known not to get too comfortable.

COLD AS ICE

The ice bitch came out of nowhere. It was after six, and I was leaving the office for the night. We stopped and stared at each other. She looked like a hundred women I knew—striking, with a body sculpted by Pilates. She was obviously in a hurry, but stood tall in a tailored black blazer over a knit pencil skirt, finished off with a silk leopard print scarf. It was unlikely I would've missed a female coworker who looked about my equal. But with a much better sense of style.

A few days later, I jumped onto the elevator, preoccupied with the upcoming premarket earnings call, when the ice bitch, now wearing a fabulous black and gold leopard print blazer I recognized from the latest Neiman's catalog, and a baroque pearl choker, walked onto the same elevator cautiously, looking around, making sure the coast was clear.

She was younger than me, but not by much. She had flowy chestnut hair that looked like she put hot rollers in every evening and possessed dark, uncomfortable eyes focused intently on the brightly lit elevator buttons. Her body language sent a stark refusal to my affable demeanor. I offered an upbeat "Good morning."

She turned, shocked, and muttered in what sounded like a whisper, "Morning." She didn't get off at my floor, barely moving to allow my exit. Barry, who was also on the elevator, watched the whole thing transpire and got off with me, humming his trademark Stones song.

"Did I just get an ice shower?" I asked when the elevator door closed.

"It's just Staci."

"Does she work here? Is she new?"

"Staci used to work on our floor. She was transferred upstairs. She's not exactly approachable. At least, not anymore."

"You can say that again. I was just trying to be nice."

"Don't take it personally."

"Why was she transferred upstairs?"

"Oh, office politics. You know what I mean."

"No. I don't." I stared at Barry, waiting for an answer.

"Sometimes it's easier to pay the piper, so to speak, instead of dealing with the issues. I've been at Arbor a long, long time. Sometimes I think too long; I know some people here think the same, but one thing I know is that they come and they go. When Staci started, she was great, but you can never tell. It's not like it says troublemaker on her resume. Don't fill that pretty little head of yours with worry."

"I'm not sure I follow you, Barry."

"Staci needs the job. She's a single mom. No one's going to fire her. She's upstairs in accounting now." I felt a twinge of camaraderie and waited for more information.

"Maybe I'll bring her a coffee."

"Listen, Leah, you're new. You're smart. I've heard that management likes your team. But don't be naïve. And don't trust anyone. This is a rat race. Everyone wants to kiss up, be promoted, get bonuses, and move into the executive offices. There's a right way and a wrong way. Let's just say, Staci did it the wrong way. I'll leave it at that."

"Well, do you think—"

"I wouldn't spend any time worrying about Staci." Barry winked. I followed him to his office, hoping he'd offer additional information in private. As I approached his office, I realized we weren't alone.

"D-man!" Barry cried. "You're back!" Barry gave a hearty handshake, which turned into a giant hug with a man wearing a leather jacket, a camera, and a messenger bag slung across his chest.

"Leah, this is my son, Dylan."

Dylan. Of course. Otherwise known as Hot Fonzie.

Dylan was a replica of Barry, just younger. Long hair. Laissez-faire attitude. Suddenly, it all came together. The seductive charm, like Matt Dillon, for those of us of a certain age. A throwback to the kind of heartthrob I would've lusted over in college. For a split second, I forgot where I was or that I was planning a future with Howard. I reminded myself I wasn't technically single, and smiled widely. "It's so nice to meet you."

"Ditto. Dad, is this the Leah you keep talking about?" Dylan, like his dad, needed a shave. "The gorgeous girl whom I rescued from a tsunami at the coffee station?"

I felt my face go pink. Barry was talking about me?

"The one and only." Barry winked and turned to me, "You

really should come see us play. When the D-man isn't away on assignment, he sits in with his old man's band. Let me tell you, he missed his calling."

Dylan laughed and replied, "I suppose being an award-winning photographer will never be good enough. Most Jewish fathers want their sons to be doctors and lawyers. I get the dad who wants his kid in the music business. He wants to live vicariously through me."

"Do you work here part-time?" Barry's office felt twenty degrees warmer than the rest of the office.

"Nah, I just come to visit my dad when I'm around. Plus, you never know when a big story will break. I like to be in the middle of the action." He had an enticing way of holding his body like nothing at all would rattle him.

"Well, I doubt anything exciting ever happens here. But I need to get back to work. Barry, we'll continue our conversation another time, okay?"

"What conversation?" He winked, and I knew that was my cue to leave.

"Come see us play. You won't regret it," Dylan called after me.

Later that week, Howard was tinkering on my keyboard after most of the office had left.

"Do you know Staci, who works upstairs?" He didn't look up, so I added, "The pretty one with the long, dark hair?" It was odd that I'd never heard him mention Staci. He spoke freely about his thoughts on everyone in the office. I watched his fingers freeze. "She was rude to me on the elevator."

"Please don't interject yourself with office drama. You're above that."

"So you know who I'm talking about."

"Of course I know. I run this office. I hired ninety-five percent of the people who work here, or at least had a say in hiring them. How do you think you got this job with no experience? You don't even have a resume that would pass human resources for an administrative position."

"Don't talk to me like that," I said.

"I'm sorry. I didn't mean it. But, you know why you're here."

"But—" I felt deflated.

"This was your idea. I went to bat for you. You're here to work with me, not build a career for yourself, or worse, get your teeth cut on us and then hightail out of here for a bigger position elsewhere. I've told you that you're part of a bigger plan. You're doing better than I expected. None of this is a joke. I mean… please, honey, just don't mess it up. Things are perfect." A glimpse of Howard's vulnerability was showing again.

He was right. I had no experience. No relevant degree. Sure as hell, not a recent one. Howard wasn't only my lover; he was my gift horse. "Maybe I'll introduce myself."

"She's trouble. Stay away from her. The last thing you need is to get caught up in office politics." He took my hand, surveyed the office to confirm no one could hear, and added, "We'll be together publicly, soon. Everything will work out. We have a big trip coming up. I can't wait for you to meet everyone."

With those magic words, I forgot all about Leopard-Loving Staci. At least for now.

TWENTY-FOUR

SPRING IS SPRUNG

The café was bustling. The Pyramid Girls' tables increased again, making it noisier than usual. And, what was this? A Pyramid Man? A new svelte vendor (probably someone's husband) spoke to a dozen men about the benefits of his overpriced elephant pills with an automatic renewal plan, which would magically make the stack of Belgian waffles waiting on their plates have zero calories. Dad bods be damned.

I arrived at our table and slipped into the empty chair, just as Franni delivered three piping-hot cups of coffee. My hair was thrown up in a scrunchie, and I was thrilled to finally be make-up-free, in yoga pants and an oversized sweatshirt from Syracuse, fresh from Lily and Louis's visit last month. I was wrong in thinking this job would free up more time, leading me to surrender and send Louis to visit Syracuse, the trip Lily and I had planned for months. Lily had been accepted, and I wasn't home when she got the notice. Another score for Louis and an extra helping of guilt for me. Then again, Louis hadn't been around for bedtime in fifteen years.

The GlammerMe table had a neon seventy-five percent off sign, and women were stuffing eyeshadows into bags while shoving cash into Amanda's or Alana's (I couldn't remember, and honestly, they all looked the same to me) hands. Her chipper face was a mortified shade of WTF, and what was normally a magazine-worthy, color-coded display of chic makeup was a heaping mess of bargain-basement finds.

Rick came out of the kitchen wearing a black-and-white checked apron that matched the awning logo and the dishes, looking quite pleased with himself. He stopped at our table, greeted us with his usual, "Of all the gin joints in the world… you walked into mine" with a hearty laugh, and set a plate of oozing caramel biscuits for us to try. He often joked about how he named the café White House because it translated to Casablanca. Rick was a portly, jovial guy who took great pride in his food. I had to hand it to him; since he took over, the café had become a gold mine. I struggled to see how the vendors made any money, yet there they were, cheery and optimistic as ever (except for Amanda/Alana) and willing to give up their time to make a pittance.

In the opposite corner was a large group of men, wearing turquoise polo shirts with the word ROMEO embroidered across their hearts. My father was part of the same group in Florida: RETIRED OLD MEN EATING OUT. It was a weekly unscheduled event, no different than my breakfast ritual. The ROMEOs stopped by the Pyramid tables, hoping to learn something new or score a trinket for their wives.

Although I relinquished my files to DJ by Design, Daniel still called for details on upcoming events. I thought I'd been thorough, but the truth was, he was in way over his head. There were repeated emails from a sender I didn't recognize, increasingly frantic that I should call them as soon as possible. I was torn between being polite and forwarding them to Daniel to handle.

I took a sip of the steaming coffee, closed my eyes, and said, "God, I missed you guys."

"How's the Stock Market Maven?" Peyton asked teasingly.

"Not a maven yet, but I'm great. I love it. Best decision ever."

"I'm so proud of you, Leah. Starting over in your fifties, and look at you now," Cara gushed. "I'm sorry I doubted you."

"Thanks," I said, waiting for Peyton to include herself. She didn't.

"So… what's it like?" Peyton asked.

"A little overwhelming, like learning a whole new language."

Franni came to take our order. I was dying for substantial food. "I'll take the garden omelet with pesto. Fruit. Rye bread with the homemade strawberry preserves. And bacon."

Peyton looked at me over her reading glasses.

"I'm starving. I haven't had time to eat a proper breakfast or lunch, and I'm too tired to cook dinner when I get home."

"Make that two," Peyton said as she closed the menu.

"Three," added Cara with a giggle.

"Making any friends?" Suddenly, Peyton was interested.

"One or two." Peyton could tell she had hit a nerve. I thought for a minute before continuing. "It's not that kind of atmosphere, and let's just say I don't fall into the friend demo."

"What's that mean?" Cara needed everything spelled out.

"It's a little worse than going back to seventh grade."

Cara must have loved seventh grade. She'd probably joined the Junior League by then. She didn't realize that, for most of us, seventh grade was a torture chamber.

"I'm too old to be friends with the finance bros fresh out of college. So that leaves Barry–he's a musician. I love him. He doesn't judge anyone; he walks around the office pretending to be interested in what's going on. He's got to be in his late seventies, but still smokes pot. So, mentor? Definitely. Share a joint? Possibly. Friend? Questionable. Maybe you guys will come with me to see his band play."

"I'd love that," said Cara.

"Road trip!" exclaimed Peyton. The old Peyton had returned.

"Anyway, Howard doesn't like him at all. He says business is changing, and Barry doesn't like change. Whenever I go to Barry's office, I feel like I'm cheating on Howard. But it's the place I feel most comfortable. Last week I met his son, Dylan. That man is smoking hot."

Peyton licked her lips and said, "You need your hormones checked. You're definitely in menopause, lusting after men like this. You're going to be like that woman with four lovers on my podcast."

"I don't think so."

"Go on."

"Reese sits next to me. He's the homecoming king, the All-American star you love to hate but have a crush on at the same time. He's uber-smart, Ivy League, MBA, you get the picture. I can see Lily dating someone like him. God help me. He swears Howard's a legend and hangs on to every word he says. The young brokers either want someone to drink beer with or to fuck. I'm not available for either."

"Why the hell not?" Peyton asked. "You've got to let go. You wanted a second act… why settle for monogamy now? It didn't work last time."

I shot her a look that said to fuck off.

"Then there's Beau, Reese's college roommate. Another super smart guy. The two of them have helped me transition from a newbie who didn't know anything to a respected member of the team. I could get an MBA just by hanging out with them and listening to their conversations. They're mesmerized by Howard." Peyton rolled her eyes at the praise of Howard.

"The older executives are worldly and smart, but I feel intimidated starting a conversation with them. These guys have been in the biz for forty or fifty years, which is why the firm's bringing in so many young hotshots."

"How about the women?" Peyton asked. "Sharks?"

"I think I've counted seven women."

"Seven women in the whole office?"

"Yeah, I know. One female receptionist and two assistants. There's one senior woman broker. Vivian. I think she's like a hundred. Barry said she's gifted. She started the Arbor Hedge Fund. I saw her in the bathroom adjusting her bun. I think the bobby pins have been in her hair since the sixties. If you pulled one out, her head might fall off. She stays in her office all day and doesn't interact with anyone."

"Maybe that's why they hired you."

Peyton caught me off guard. I shook my head. "Definitely not."

"Are you sure? MeToo has every office clamoring to up their female presence."

"I don't think that's the case with me. The other woman is Zoe. I think she's harmless and looks like she stopped by the office on her way to a Dead concert. She just graduated from Penn. Zoe's interested in going to business school next year, but not interested in making friends with someone her mother's age. Last-ly, we've got Sergeant BadAss. Otherwise known as BethAnn. She's Howard's bodyguard. I'm not sure she'll ever warm up to me."

"No one needs a bodyguard unless there's a reason to be pro-tected. He's a freaking stockbroker, why would he need a body-guard?"

"Come on, Peyton. It's an expression. She knows everything he does, everywhere he goes, and controls whom he talks to. It's not normal. Howard says she's just protective."

"Sounds like you're threatened."

"No. But I feel like she hates everyone. OH! I almost for-got! Leopard-Lovin' Staci from upstairs! The ice bitch with good clothes. And oh my God, you should've seen the leopard-print Louboutins she wore last week. I don't know what her problem is, but she hates me!"

"Why would she hate you?" Cara asked. "What'd you do to her?"

"Nothing. I swear." I took a bite of the bacon, finally delivered to our table. "The first time I saw her, I didn't realize she worked in the office. The second time, I said hello, but she ignored me."

"I know the type. Stay away from her," Peyton said with her mouth full.

"I'm obsessed with her leopard-print Valentino boots. I'm talking fabulous. Maybe I need a signature look."

"You wear your heart on your sleeve. That's your signature." I threw a grape at Peyton, missing her face.

"Anyway, Barry said she was transferred due to office politics. He knows all the office secrets. However, when I asked, he was evasive."

"Don't get involved."

"Howard was weird when I asked about her."

"He's sleeping with her."

"NO!"

"She's sleeping with someone."

"Why do you always think everyone's sleeping with some-one?"

"Because they are."

"You're wrong."

"Wake up. You even said it's an old boys' club scenario. And there's nowhere worse than the finance industry."

"Hmm. I wonder who it was."

"Or still is. It's possible they couldn't fire her without risking a sexual harassment lawsuit. I'll bet she got a big fat bonus to keep her mouth shut. Why do you look so surprised? Your knight in shining armor could be tarnished?"

"Shining armor? Howie? Oh God, no. He's not sleeping with her."

"How do you know?"

"He's not like that. Anyway, I have a few ideas about bringing in more women clients. I'm just not sure who will listen to me."

"Listen, Leah, I don't know what you are or aren't doing with Howie or whatever nicknames you lovebirds have for each other. I don't care anymore. But I'll tell you this: If you're going to work there, this damsel-in-distress bullshit isn't going to fly. Enough with the women don't like you crap. Enough with being scared of strong women. You're in the major leagues. You need to play hard. You're the badass. Not some over-the-hill *need to be laid* of-fice manager. Or someone with good shoes. Don't you dare let anyone intimidate you. Be the best damn woman in finance they've ever seen. I know you've got it in you. I watched you take a four-dollar Betty Crocker sheet cake and turn it into a half-million-dollar business. If you want to attract women clients, don't wait for permission. Do it. I guarantee nobody will turn away business."

It was the first time Peyton acknowledged my capabilities. I guess she always was my biggest supporter; she just never said it out loud. "You're right. And I'm working on it. I just need to wait for the right time."

"This omelet is truly delicious. The pesto takes it to the next level," Cara said.

"All I know is, maybe I should've gone to the dark side. Would you look at all the people waiting in line?" The Pyramid Girls were collecting money faster than a slot machine.

When I finished eating, I walked over to Ivy's table. I felt bad about our friendship fading away, so I asked where her daughter, Bailey, was going to school. I should've known better. The vultures saw me coming and turned on the charm. Each woman had something positively life-changing for me to try. I told myself to keep an open mind; like me, they were all just trying to earn a living. One eye cream stick at a time. I politely accepted brochures and business cards from three women and a small bag that I admit smelled like a slice of pineapple heaven before I escaped back to the table, where I carelessly dropped them.

The check came. As I reached into my bag to get my wallet, I casually mentioned that I'd be away for a few days for work.

"That's fast for perks," Peyton replied, her antenna in full bloom.

"Arizona. It's a yearly event for SHINE, the private group I'm handling."

"One hotel room or two?"

"It's a business trip. Two."

"Liar."

"Fine. One." I felt a rush of heat on my face, I just couldn't hide it any longer. Maybe getting it off my chest would bridge the gap in our friendship once and for all.

"You owe me twenty bucks," Peyton said to Cara.

"You're betting on my love life?"

"No, that was last year. Today, we're betting whether you finally told us or not." Peyton looked proud of herself for getting this tidbit of information from me.

"There's been some talk that Deenie and Howard are separating," Cara said wistfully. It hadn't occurred to me that the news would've seeped its way into the neighborhood gossip. And why hadn't they indulged me?

"Where'd you hear that?" I asked defensively.

Cara leaned in, "Y'all know I'm on the board of a charity fashion show. Last week, at the country club, I overheard Deenie talking to some women in the bathroom. It wasn't much, but I heard her say, 'It'll be over soon enough.' You can take that for what it's worth, but honestly, it doesn't sound like she's too upset. The other women didn't seem surprised. Word has it, it will be a nine-figure divorce."

I stopped to count on my fingers. No wonder Howard was taking his time. Nine figures?

I wondered if Howard knew Deenie was discussing their impending divorce. He did say that he was pacing his moves so as not to upset her frail mental health. Maybe Deenie was trying to save face. No one wants to be the jilted wife. I knew that first-hand.

"I told you it was a marriage of convenience. I'm not a home-wrecker." I pleaded. "He was practically divorced before I met him."

"Right. Divorced, still living in that mansion, and going to Turks and Caicos."

"There's more to it." Howard had begun storing personal items at my house. More than thirty boxes, meticulously arranged, had taken up residence in my basement in the past month. This was proof he was moving out. I opened my mouth to tell them about his personal belongings and changed my mind.

Peyton lifted her coffee mug, "To the next Mrs. Gardner." Her tone held a warning that I chose to ignore.

I scooped up the business cards and shoved them into my hoodie pocket. But before I did, I noticed that although they were all different companies, each card had the same distinct logo on the bottom right corner. Violet and Gray. The words were layered on top of each other in rich hues of violet and gray. I was sure this was the same business card from the Lipstick Tea at Cara's last year.

"What's the face for?" Cara asked. I must have looked perplexed.

"I've seen this business card before."

"Of course you have. They leave their cards everywhere; it's their marketing strategy other than saturating everyone's Instagram feeds."

"Whatever makes those perky girls happy."

Car reached for my hand. "Just promise me you'll be careful, okay?"

That's when the anonymous emails started getting serious.

DEPARTMENT OF JUSTICE

BACKGROUND NOTES
BARRY SORKIN, EXECUTIVE VICE PRESIDENT

Barry Sorkin's profile reads like an IMDB. Barry had a mile-long rap sheet dating back to the 1960s. Possession of marijuana. Possession of controlled substances. Possession of paraphernalia. Intent to distribute. Disorderly conduct. Resisting arrest. Sit-ins. Bail-jumping. Disdain for authority. Protest organizer.

Barry was one of the top marijuana dealers and top guitar players in Laurel Canyon during a time when it mattered. He came from an Orthodox Jewish family but traded in his tallis for a guitar pick before he was fifteen. After being busted for marijuana for the third time, he cut two deals: one with the police to give up the name of his supplier and one with his father to go to college. He majored in math, assuming he would resume dealing pot on a larger scale when he graduated.

Barry thrived in college. He had a knack for numbers that surprised everyone. He graduated from UCLA in 1969, cut his hair, and took an upstanding job at the accounting firm where his father worked. Three months later, his best friend convinced him to drive to a small town in upstate New York for a life-changing music festival. Barry couldn't resist. He fired up the Volkswagen and took off for a seven-day jaunt across the country. Barry made contacts at Woodstock that he kept for life. Sitting in with legends at night and hanging with their managers all day gave Barry insight into the unscrupulous world of money for nothing and chicks for free. He decided to go back to college and get his MBA in finance.

By the 1970s, the music world was on fire. The musicians trusted Barry.

One more arrest and Barry decided his pot-dealing days were over. He teamed up with one of his attorneys and formed the most extensive portfolio of musician-based tax-deferred investment vehicles in the financial world. By 2000, one out of every three musicians had three names on their speed dial. Their agent. Their lawyer. And Barry Sorkin.

Barry's friends included high-powered names like David Geffen, Irving Azoff, and Jon Landau. But his client list boasted more recognizable names. Joni Mitchell. Phil Lesh. Stevie Nicks. Bon Jovi. Eddie Vedder.

Barry married singer and songwriter Tamar Stone and moved with their two young sons to Pennsylvania to be closer to his wife's family. He joined Arbor Financial the year it opened. He can still be found playing his guitar at the Stone Pony, Jones Beach, and Irving Plaza.

In the past few years, Barry has been the target of business and personal lawsuits that stem from a world rife with greedy and unscrupulous behavior. The vendettas of those defendants keep us monitoring Barry's moves. In and out of the office.

TWENTY-FIVE

PARADISE

I flew to Arizona alone. Howard arrived earlier in the week to meet with prospective clients. Flying first class and spending three days at the Princess Spa, alone with Howard for more than a few stolen hours, waking up in those incredible arms, was a luxury worth flying alone for.

A black S-class was waiting for me at the airport. The trip to the hotel was barely long enough for me to close my eyes. A white-gloved bellhop opened the door and extended his hand for assistance, as my bags were whisked away, presumably to my room. I watched as a group of divas exited a fleet of Uber Black town cars and knew it had to be the SHINE wives.

Howard appeared in his golf attire, slim-cut pants in a shade of sapphire, a white belt, and a white polo shirt adorned with tiny flamingos wearing polos in the same eye-catching shade of blue, and escorted me to a private honeysuckle garden surrounded by intricately woven bamboo structures. Howard expected me to look professional. I was glad I opted to travel in a flattering color-blocked tank dress with a pale pink cardigan and comfortable wedges, not my usual travel leggings and hoodie. As we entered the garden, we were met with a round of applause. One by one, the SHINE wives took their place next to their husbands. It was the most astonishing display of arm candy I'd ever seen.

Howard cleared his throat. "Ladies and gentlemen, welcome to the annual SHINE retreat. I'm overjoyed to see all my favorite faces here." He turned to admire the scenery and continued. "As you can see by this breathtaking background of Camelback Mountain, we've arrived in paradise. It's my great privilege to introduce you to Leah Samuels, a phenomenal new member of the Arbor team and your new SHINE liaison. I know you'll be as impressed with her as I am." More applause. I wasn't expecting the fanfare, and I felt a blush emerging, but knew it would be appropriate to respond.

"Thank you. I'm looking forward to meeting all of you and hope I can provide you with the level of expertise you've come to expect from Arbor Financial." Howard handed me a glass of champagne. I lifted it and said, "To SHINE!"

They all responded with "To SHINE!" The guests began to mingle. A bamboo screen was wheeled away, revealing a wooden table covered with Aztec-decorated stone bowls and plates that looked like they were made of turquoise. Lunch included guacamole and tortilla chips, a giant display of shrimp cocktail, Caesar salad with grilled pears, a Santa Fe chicken dish, platters of poached salmon, and an abundance of vibrant colored berries arranged next to pastry shells.

The SHINE brokers wore looks of devotion on their faces. Discretion was rule number one. Howard mentioned that a few years ago, he'd banished a member for mouthing off about a particular investment. When asked about the specifics, Howard looked pleased with himself and replied, "It's my elite trading circle. I make the rules, and I get to enforce them. If they don't like them, they can find another broker and be happy with mediocre returns."

The men were complimentary, bordering on flirty, but self-aware enough to hold back in front of Howard. The women, polished and primped, segregated themselves. They all knew each other and were accustomed to attending these retreats where the men disappeared for golf and meetings, and they were happy being left to their own devices, leisurely breakfasts by the pool, and hours of spa indulgences. Today, it was painfully apparent they were interested in me, speculating about my role here. They kept their eyes on me in between whispers. I was equally sizing them up and down, wondering if they knew what their husbands were up to, often trading millions of dollars at a time. Howard had said the women controlled some of the money, but only what they knew about.

Howard put his arm around my waist and turned my attention to the men. He whispered in my ear, "Talk to the money. You can socialize with the women later."

Fat Frank. Big Hat Bud. Diligent Don. Geoff, the giraffe. Odd Avi. M&M. Howard had prepped me for weeks, and I had started a cheat sheet on my phone to keep track of who was who. "Schmooze them," he said. "It'll soften the blow when things are down. Remember their birthdays. Kids' names. Anything to butter them up and convince them to give more money and ask fewer questions."

"Leah, how does Howard manage to get such good-looking associates?" asked Fat Frank, the oldest of the SHINE crew and by far the wealthiest.

If the average trade was fifty thousand dollars, Frank Masterson's was two hundred and fifty thousand. The bulge of his stomach matched the bulge in his eyes, and he looked like the definition of a dirty old man, Harvey Weinstein in the flesh, but I was instructed to play along.

"He's harmless. Stroke his ego. Schmooze the money right out of his pants," Howard whispered. The thought of stroking anything on this vile pile of flesh turned my stomach. Business, I reminded myself. My face hurt from forcing a smile.

"Well, Howard, ol' boy, I know I missed the game today, but why are you playing golf when you could be playing hole-in-one with this darling young thing?"

I hoped my face didn't give away my disgust. Upon hearing her husband's voice, Rita Masterson watched me closely. I could tell she was used to her husband's remarks, but she waited for my response. Rita wore her platinum hair in a pageboy with bangs sweeping over a pair of curious eyes, heavily lined. She, too, was round, but a long, multi-colored caftan hid her curves. Howard had told me she was an artist. The layers of silk looked like they could have been painted by hand, and her jewelry was an extravagance of eclectic style, hammered silver, exquisite stones in jade and coral, but more importantly, I could tell that she was a force to be reckoned with.

"Mr. Masterson," I began.

"Frank, darling," he interrupted, not hiding that he was looking at my cleavage. "Mr. Masterson was my father and a cheap son of a bitch." He howled at his joke.

I swallowed hard. "Frank, you're every bit as charming as on the phone."

Geoff interrupted as if his sole purpose there was to rescue me from Frank, "Geoff Lembeck, Leah." He stretched out a large hand, golden-brown tanned with fingers twice the size of mine. I shook his hand, which was warm and not as intimidating as I had guessed. Geoff looked like he played basketball, with a mop of curly brown hair that added another few inches to his imposing height. Peyton would call him a hot nerd who got better-looking with age. I remember reading that Geoff sold his cell phone company, probably too early, for seventy million dollars. That number had swelled since Howard had brought him into SHINE. Now, he was on the verge of selling an app to Microsoft.

A line formed around me, each man vying for my attention.

"Bud Westin, as close to Texas royalty as you will get." Howard tilted my body slightly to make eye contact with Bud, who was appropriately wearing a Stetson and looking like he could be J.R. Ewing's twin brother.

"A pleasure, sweetheart," Bud said in a confident drawl straight out of Dallas. "I reckon we'll be gittin' to know each other *real* good." Bud winked, and Howard interrupted with a paternal, "Bud, I'm sure you'll be pleased with Leah's business skills. Don't make me regret bringing you here."

Don, my favorite SHINE member, whispered something in Howard's ear, which made his eyes squint. Rita approached us and said, "Leah, join us. We're ready for another round and are dying to hear all about you." I glanced at Howard for approval, who, being deep in conversation with Don, nodded for me to go. Rita placed her arm around my neck and guided me to the women's table. I made a split-second decision to keep myself off the hot seat.

"I've been talking to your husbands for the last few weeks, but I'd really love to get to know all of you better," I said earnestly.

One by one, the women took over, eager to share the spotlight normally reserved for their husbands. Rita said, "I'm an artist and a sculptor."

Misty, Bud's wife, interrupted, "She's being modest. Ask her about her pieces in MoMA!"

Rita volleyed with "I'd rather discuss the Young Artist Scholarships I award each year. My *Forbes* Woman of the Year award was tied to the number of students I've sponsored."

"Congratulations." I wasn't expecting that.

Misty, wearing a fuchsia and kelly green striped mini dress and a pink bow in her bouffant hair, boasted, "I'm the founder and CEO of MISTY and MAY Nail Products!" Another surprise. She looked like a pageant contestant.

"Wow, I had no idea. My daughter and I love that brand."

"Why, thank you, sweetie. I'll be sure to send a package of goodies to your daughter."

"Hi, Leah, I'm Taffy, Geoff's wife." Taffy had a permanent scowl on her face. They seemed quite mismatched. "I have a pharmaceutical device company. Soon to go public."

"I have a string of boutique hotels," Gabrielle, Don's wife, said modestly. "I also do entrepreneurship TED Talks."

"My sister and I own shopping centers," Avi's wife, Shira, said.

"I own a fashion brand and dabble in real estate on the side," remarked Natalia, Morgan Maynard's wife. "And I have a podcast." Morgan (M&M) had been a child actor. It wasn't clear exactly what Morgan did now or how he made his gazillion dollars, but Howard said not to ask questions and just take his money.

I was blown away. I had been impressed with the men, yet the wives were next-level. They were being treated as appendages instead of equals. I wondered if Howard knew how accomplished these women were. Why was he only focusing on the men? I knew this was the opportunity I was waiting for. It was possible Howard would kill me, but the words fell out of my mouth too quickly to worry about it. "Why isn't there a Women's SHINE?"

A hush came over the table.

"We've been asking our husbands the same question for years," quipped Gabrielle.

"Are all of your investments in joint accounts? Or do you have your own accounts?"

The women remained quiet. Misty and Taffy refolded the napkins on their lap. Natalia cleared her throat and looked away. Rita said, "I have a brother who manages my trust and the family money. But don't tell Frank. He doesn't know how much money I make from my art pieces. He calls it my play money. So, he pays the big bills. And I play." Rita winked at me. I was stunned.

"Same," said Shira, a whisper of a girl with olive skin, a dimple, and long limbs. "Avi's too busy to pay attention to all our money. He has accounts at so many different investment houses, I think he forgets who has the money. I mean, obviously, Howard has the most. I let Avi pay for the kids and me. He's young but old-fashioned. In the early days, everything my business made was reinvested, but now we're profitable, so the money has grown, untouched for years. Oh, and I was recognized as a top ten star to watch in 40 Under 40 this year."

"So where's the money?"

Shira's voice got lower, "Some is in the house. In the safe."

"In cash?"

"Shhhh." Shira smiled, her dimple more pronounced.

"Ours too. Hidden, of course," said Natalia.

"Our money is in joint accounts. But I have a *pishke*," Gabrielle announced. "It was wedding advice from my mother."

"Good for you." I smiled. "My grandmother used to say every woman should have her own *pishke*!"

"I want a pushcart!" cried Misty.

"Pish-ka," said Gabrielle. "It's your own secret nest egg away from your husband."

"Oh, I want that too," Misty said, embarrassed. "If Bud will give me one."

This was my chance. Howard said the wives didn't know the half of what the husbands did. This was proof that the men didn't know half of what the women were capable of. They had enough of their own money to have a seat at the table. And if Howard didn't want to give them one, I'd make my own table. I had to figure out how to do it.

I felt Howard come behind me and whisper that it was time for our couple's massage.

"Ladies, I can't wait to see you all at dinner tonight, where we can continue this conversation."

"We're counting on it," said Rita. It was going to be an interesting trip.

TWENTY-SIX

THE WOMEN

"**T**his is ours?" My voice bubbled over with delight as Howie led me into our room. The ground-level suite boasted a breathtaking view of the mountain and was bigger than the square footage of the first floor of my house. The late afternoon sun warmed the room, which was overflowing with vases of hibiscus in shades of orange, pink, and red that looked like they were plucked from a rainbow. Howie lifted me, bringing my body close to his, and swung me around.

"It's going great already. I can feel it."

"I know. I have so many ideas I want to discuss with you."

"Pleasure first..." Howie whispered before kissing me deeply. "I thought we'd have our massages on the terrace before the sun sets."

"Are you sure it doesn't look bad that we're sharing a room? I'm not accustomed to luxury like this."

"You deserve it. I can tell they love you. And everyone here is aware Deenie and I are separating."

It was three days jam-packed with activities. I just hoped the looming SEC threats wouldn't be hanging over Howie's head here, and we could finally enjoy ourselves.

An hour later, we were naked and asleep under the crisp, cool Frette sheets. Every inch of my body had been prodded and pulled. I felt dizzy. The massage, the scorching sun, and the excitement had taken their toll. "I want to discuss an idea for the wives," I remember saying aloud before dozing off.

When I woke up, Howie's arms were crossed in defiance as if he were in a raging argument when he was struck with a sudden stroke of exhaustion. I kissed his neck, wriggling my way into the crook of his chest, and kissed him again. I felt him stir and kept kissing, slowly making my way down toward his stomach. Howie woke up, just long enough to engulf me in his arms, and then drifted back to sleep. I wished I could close my eyes and fall back to sleep with him, but my brain was racing with a new sense of determination. I could tell Howie was agitated. It must have been the conversation with Don. I tried to wiggle out of his grasp, but Howie's arms held me tight, and I was no match for his strength. "Howie," I whispered. "We've got to get ready for dinner." I started to panic. I needed an hour. At least.

Last week, I rifled through my closet, showing off everything I planned to bring on the trip.

"Maybe it's time you start playing the part." Howie smiled. The kind of smile he knew made my knees weak. "You do understand the clientele I deal with. Perception's everything. Dress for the job you want, not the job you have. Buy some appropriate clothes for this trip. Don't you have a friend who can help you?"

Ouch. "It doesn't sound like I can afford what you're asking for," I said. I wasn't accustomed to spending the kind of money he was alluding to. I doubted he owned a pair of dress shoes that weren't Brunello Cucinelli or Tom Ford. Even his underwear was designer.

"You never had a problem with my clothes (or lack of them) before," I said. This was a man who'd have sex with me without taking my clothes off.

"Here. This bill comes to the office. Three nights of cocktails and dinners. Poolside lunches." He reached into his pocket, pulled out an American Express card, and tossed it to me.

"No! I can't."

"Don't be silly. It's a business expense."

He was turning me into his own Eliza Doolittle.

"Do I have a budget?" I was the budget queen. A deadbeat husband could do that to you. He doesn't know who he's dealing with.

"No budget. And no TJ Maxx." He smiled devilishly. Like he could read my mind.

"Don't knock it till you try it," I answered.

"Make an appointment with Sima at Neiman Marcus. I'll let her know you're coming."

"A private shopper?" Oh, what the hell. You only live once. "Thank you," I said.

That was last week, before I racked up seven thousand dollars in three hours at Neiman Marcus. It was official. I was *Pretty Woman.*

And now I was going to be late. I nudged Howie, whispering the time. I was about to push my way out of bed, jump in the shower, and let him sleep a little longer when suddenly, in one swift motion, he lifted himself onto me. I couldn't resist as he covered me like a shadow; whatever anger or frustration he had been wrestling with while he was asleep now shifted into a consuming motion inside me. I responded to him, kissing him softly. I leaned back, closed my eyes, and savored every last minute.

Sima had chosen a dress in a deep eggplant with tiny splashes of pink and black. It skimmed my calves and hugged my body without being too tight to breathe, the neckline scooped just enough to indicate I had cleavage. Howie was adjusting his tie, a bold floral print, when he said, "That dress is missing something."

"I am absolutely not changing my clothes." I put my hands on my hips.

"How about some sparkle? Eighty-nine points. Triple word. Seven letters."

"No time for games, Howie. You're going to be late to your own party."

Howie pulled a long black velvet box from his suitcase, an impish grin on his face.

"What are you doing?"

"Open it."

"Now?"

"No, for Chanukah next year. Of course, now."

Inside was a magnificent diamond bracelet. Seven carats at least. No one had ever bought me jewelry before without me begging for it. Howie beamed as he lifted it out of the box. "Let me help you put it on." He attached the clasp and kissed my hand. "Now, you're ready."

"Howie, I… It's breathtaking… but…"

"But nothing. You needed a little sparkle. That's all. Let's go. SHINE's awaiting."

There was still no breeze, and the ombre sky set the stage when Howard and I entered the courtyard, his hand cradling my back and holding me and my four-inch heels upright. Champagne poured freely. Waiters with overflowing trays of hors d'oeuvres discreetly wove in between the guests. "Partners," he whispered. "Follow my lead. Smother them with your charm."

"Ah, so that's what you brought me on board for."

"Don't mention the Howie Loans in front of the wives."

"Why?"

"Just don't mention it tonight."

Avi Segal Moskowitz looked like he was barely old enough to vote, let alone have enough money to trade ridiculously huge sums each day. He was the only one not dressed to impress, unless you counted a pair of khakis and Air Jordans impressive. He had bushy black hair and looked like he didn't own a hairbrush. In contrast, Shira, in a turquoise gown with a slit up to her *pipick*, her belly button, looked like she stepped off the red carpet.

"Don't be fooled by Avi's appearance or lack of social skills. The guy's a genius, a true visionary, a prodigy," Howard whispered as he handed me a stuffed mushroom. I smiled warmly, remembering that Odd Avi never engaged in small talk. Short and sweet. It made my job easier.

Avi was talking about Bitcoin. Something about the blockchain and how cryptocurrency transactions were recorded. The men were huddled around him, hoping for a shred of intellect to fall into their laps. Avi was highly selective about whom he shared intel on his company. It was humbling to watch a group of millionaires trying to impress him.

Morgan stumbled over to us. He was already plastered as he struggled to form a cohesive sentence. Howard led Morgan to a chair before turning my attention to Larry, Don, Yussi, and Kyle. "Ah, my dream team," Howard stated with a chuckle. Under his breath, he said, "Young, stupid, money. Yussi and Kyle are a couple. This is Larry's first year. He's not even thirty, my youngest SHINE member. His AI program was recently acquired, and he doesn't know what to do with this much money."

Geoff appeared with Taffy. Her straggly hair had already fallen out of the blowout and was stuck to her neck. Her cheeks were hollow, her eyes were lifeless. The chartreuse silk slip dress accentuated her sagging body. Her husband was worth hundreds of millions of dollars, and she didn't own a proper bra or a pair of Spanx. But she was wearing a fabulous pair of sixteen-hundred-dollar Manolo Blahnik sandals and a Bottega bag that I salivated over in last month's *Vogue*. You could tell she was the most miserable one of the bunch.

Don was nursing a Jack on the rocks. He flashed me a self-assured smile. Don's voice oozed with patience. Even when he was upset, his voice remained calm, which seemed to be more and more the case lately. He owned a chain of supermarkets up and down the east coast. I looked forward to Don's calls more than anyone else's. You could tell he was no stranger to manual labor, a muscular guy who looked uncomfortable in dress clothes. The warmth he exuded was so intense that I felt like hugging him instead of shaking his hand.

The yarmulke perched atop Yussi's head was the only distinguishable feature between him and Kyle. They looked more like twins than lovers. Mid-thirties. Slicked back hair. Gucci Horsebit loafers. They stood close and held their drinks like trophies. Yussi was a diamond dealer from New York and was complimentary and friendly. He immediately noticed my bracelet, and I realized that Howard may have not only purchased it from Yussi but had him hand-deliver it here.

Finally, dinner was announced. Howard's hand appeared on my back again, guiding me to our table. As luck would have it, we were seated next to Don and Gabrielle. Howard and Don were deep in conversation throughout the meal. I couldn't determine what they were talking about, but I could see the furrows forming in Howard's forehead like trenches.

The music began, Howard excused himself from the table, and led me onto the dance floor. He sang in my ear, mimicking the band, glossing over the part about being simple and free, and whispering I was everything he ever dreamed of as he tilted my face into his.

The band took a break, and Howard resumed his discussion with Don. I found Rita at the dessert buffet, where a waiter had poured alcohol onto a chafing dish and set it on fire. Rita was wearing another hand-painted caftan, this time in jewel tones, along with a large gold and opal heart necklace. She waved and motioned for me to join her at the table. The wives were waiting.

Rita assumed the role of unofficial speaker for the group. "Leah, we've discussed it, and we're fascinated with your interest in SHINE. What can we do to be included?"

"I've been thinking about this all afternoon. I don't think you should be included." A gasp of disappointment followed. I studied their anxious, painted faces and took a breath, cautiously not saying too much without authorization. "I think we should set up an elite women's trading group. It will be tailored to your individual interests and risk tolerances. Although it may overlap with what we do in SHINE, it won't have the same level of volatility. I need to figure out the specifics, but I think there's a great deal of opportunity for you."

"How soon could we start?" asked Misty. She seemed the

most interested in getting her money away from Bud.

"I'll have to discuss it with Howard and my superiors, but we can work on the basic ideas this week and I'll finalize it once I get back to the office."

Rita added, "I'd like my own autonomy. My own statements. I've been married for fifty years, and I stopped telling my husband everything years ago. I'm not sure how the other women feel about that."

"My business. My money," said Shira proudly. "It's about time someone cares about me, not just what Avi is selling the world. Can my sister be in the group too?"

"I'm in," said Gabrielle, a radiant smile forming on her lips. "Let me know how to send you the money."

"Me too," said Natalia.

Taffy looked suspicious. Her eyes darted back and forth. I wondered if she would say something stupid and ruin the idea for everyone. "I'll have to move a few things around, but I'd like to consider it too."

Misty said, "I'm getting a pushcart!" Everyone laughed, but we all knew her pushcart would be one of the biggest in the group.

I didn't know how Howard would respond when I told him I just created a women's SHINE division, but, as he taught me, green is green. If the SEC dismissed Howard's case, I didn't know what my role at Arbor would entail. Time to put a little job security into our plan.

Howard played an early game of golf while I slept, but left a note in the bathroom reminding me about lunch with Eddie. According to everything I'd heard over the past year, Eddie could part the sea. I was anxious to see how he measured up to all the hype.

Breakfast was served overlooking the golf course, and the wives were deep in conversation by the time I showed up. I ordered a hot tea before realizing Gabrielle was missing.

"Are we waiting for Gabrielle?" I asked.

Rita offered in a hushed voice, "Don and Gabrielle will not be joining the group today."

That had to be related to Don and Howard arguing last night. What could've happened with Don in just a few hours? I strained to remember if he and Gabrielle were on the dance floor after I met with the wives. They must have made an inconspicuous exit. Rita noticed my bewilderment and put her hand on top of mine. I felt the weight of several clunky rings. "Everything will work itself out, dear. It always does."

Rita changed the subject. "So, Leah, we're dying to know more about you."

Howard had warned me to be careful about sharing too much, so I recited the Howard-approved version of my bio. "I worked in the party industry for several years before selling my business. I decided it was time for a career change and went back to working in finance, which I studied in college. (Just a tiny white lie) I have two teenagers, Asher and Lily. I'm thrilled to have found a home at Arbor Financial."

"I think having a woman entrepreneur on our side is just what we've been waiting for," said Natalia. "I'd like to put you on my podcast."

"I'd love that." Howard might not. He wasn't thrilled about Lily's article. He was paranoid someone would figure out why I was hired. I didn't tell him I'd already spoken to someone at the local paper who wanted to do a feature.

I was so busy fielding questions that I barely had time to finish my frittata before a waiter whisked it away. I was on the verge of saying goodbye to freshen up before meeting Eddie when I overheard Natalia say, "I like her. She seems far more suited for Howard than Staci."

Hearing Staci's name procured goosebumps in the 100-degree heat. Maybe I heard incorrectly. They must've said Deenie, not Staci, but that fear was confirmed when Taffy said, "Geoff heard Staci got a promotion and a payoff with a confidentiality agreement. Honestly, I don't want to know. What did she think would happen? He feels so bad about how she was treated. Geoff still emails with Deenie; she's open about the separation but she made it clear she didn't want to be involved in any of Howard's business dealings. Seems like they do a good job getting rid of the women."

The blood must have drained from my face, and my lips parted in disbelief. Could it be the same Staci? *The* Leopard-Lovin' Staci? Barry said she was Trouble. Howard acted as though he barely knew her. Then it hit me; this was precisely what Peyton was talking about. Damn her.

I picked up an ice-cold glass of water, wishing I could pour it over my head without being obvious, and drank it in one gulp. I needed to find out what happened with Don, then Howard would have to come clean to me about Staci.

TWENTY-SEVEN

STILL PARADISE

I had less than ten minutes to get back to our suite, splash cold water on my face, reapply my lipstick, and make it to the poolside bar. Howard's face shone with pride when he saw me approaching.

"Here she is. My star assistant."

Eddie's face lit up, too. "It's been a long time since I've seen Howard so happy. You must be doing something right. Welcome to the family!" Eddie lifted his glass to me.

Eddie was privy to our relationship. Within the first five minutes, he made me feel like I was the only person in the room. "Howard told me how fast you're moving up the ranks at Arbor and that you've become an expert on VG Industries. I hear you're my number one cheerleader."

"Thank you. I'm encouraged by what your company stands for. It seems cutting-edge, incorporating all the most recognizable beauty industry segments into one company. I believe there are some prime takeover targets as well. But all in all, it makes for a profitable company, and I'm pleased to be able to educate our top clients about everything you have to offer."

"I told you she'd be an asset, not a liability."

"You do have a knack for picking winners." Howard winked at me, and I knew he was pleased that Eddie was impressed.

"That leads me to a new venture I'd like to discuss with you."

Howard opened his mouth to say something, but Eddie seemed mesmerized and said, "I can't wait to hear it."

"The wives want to be in SHINE." Eddie and Howard both laughed.

"I'm serious. You have a company geared toward women and aren't targeting them to invest in it. They probably understand the business more than the men who just see numbers on a chart."

"The numbers on a chart are what stock trading is about."

"How much of your business is women?"

"Leah, honey. We've been through this. I'd say ten percent. The majority of women are not interested. I know what I'm talking about. Let them have their jewels and fancy houses and let the men do the heavy lifting with the money."

"I'm telling you, you're missing out. These aren't trophy wives; they're serious businesswomen. They want to be seen. Heard. I want to set up a women's version of SHINE. I guarantee you, if you don't want their money, someone else will."

"Brains and beauty," Eddie said to Howard.

"Okay, you can try. But don't be disappointed. Just because the wives seem enthusiastic while we're footing the bill for their vacation doesn't mean they'll follow through."

"I think they will."

"Give it a shot. But your priority is SHINE."

"Got it, Boss."

The next two days flew by too fast. I spent hours talking with the wives about their financial goals and discovered they all wanted accounts separate from their husbands. Shira went so far as to insist she only wanted statements to go to a PO Box. They all provided me with cell phone numbers and email addresses. I promised that as soon as I had approval to proceed, I'd be in touch.

Howard and I flew home together. He claimed that Gabrielle was scheduled to speak at a TED conference, and she and Don were only scheduled to be in town for one day. It seemed odd they didn't say goodbye, but I didn't press him about it. I needed to know about Staci. It was eating away at me.

"What's the deal with Staci? Why does everyone discuss her with hushed voices?"

"Oy, Staci's a touchy subject."

"Did you have an affair with her?"

"Absolutely not. She was invited to a SHINE retreat a few years ago, drank too much, and flirted with the men too eagerly, so she was asked to leave."

"That's it?"

"It was unfortunate because Staci's a smart woman. I saw her as an embarrassment, and I insisted she resign, but she refused. Management was afraid of a wrongful termination lawsuit. She had violated her employment contract, but they didn't want to risk any bad publicity—this industry has enough of that—so they decided to move her to another division. There's nothing else to know." I had no reason not to believe him. No proof of a payoff.

The trip was just what Howard and I needed to recharge. And what I needed to fall more in love with him. But the wives. They needed me. It was clear from our conversations that the Women's SHINE division was going to be a game-changer for them and for me. One thing was for sure: If I had any doubts about upending my life, selling the business, and starting over, I left them all in Arizona.

YOU DON'T OWN ME

Howard was in Washington to meet with another set of lawyers. It was time to put my plan in motion, and there was no doubt who would be my best option to discuss it with.

Barry's door was ajar. If I wasn't mistaken, I thought I heard the faint sounds of a vinyl LP going around a turntable. I poked my head in, "Hey, Bar, got time for a few questions?"

"All the time in the world."

"Did you know I was in Arizona?"

"Yep. Surprised those retreats aren't in Vegas. Did they eat you alive?"

"Actually, just the opposite. Can you tell me how much of your business is women?"

"Thirty percent. Why?"

"I'm thinking of setting up a women's trading group. Like SHINE, but for women."

"It's about time. I've been saying for years there's a huge, untouched market in women's investing, and no one wants to hear from the stoner with the guitar."

I saw a flash of light and shielded my eyes. "Would you help me figure this out?"

"I'd be thrilled to, but you should really talk to…" another flash of light. Was I getting a migraine, or was it delayed jet lag? I turned my head from the light and realized that Dylan was in the back of Barry's office snapping pictures, the flash creating a starburst of white crystals.

"Dylan, are you taking pictures of me?"

"Sorry. Just adjusting the ambiance. Your face is luminous when you're talking business." I rolled my eyes. "Plus everything's copy, you know?"

"Okay, knock yourself out." I turned back to Barry and continued, "I should talk to who?"

"Vivian."

"Vivian Vivian? I'm not going down that hallway. It looks like she stepped out of a Hitchcock movie. There might be birds in there."

"Leah. Stop letting appearances fool you. Vivian's the queen of women's finance."

"Isn't she like a hundred? Hasn't she been here forever?"

"How do you think she got so wise?" I stopped to think about it. He was right. If I wanted a woman's group, I'd need a woman mentor.

"Okay, but if I disappear in there, it's on you."

"I'll take my chances. Kamish?" He opened a tin of small crescent-shaped cookies with poppy seeds—the kind my grandmother made. I grabbed one and took a bite.

"Yum, tastes like my childhood."

"Mine too," said Dylan as he tilted his camera and took another picture. He flashed a mischievous smile. "Last one… promise."

"Guess I'm going to see Vivian. Wish me luck." I saw the flash go off again as I walked out the door.

I decided to go straight to Vivian's office before I lost my nerve. Her office was situated at the end of the corridor, far away from my workstation. It was the only executive office without glass floor-to-ceiling windows. I noticed the brass nameplate on the door, Vivian Rosen, Senior Vice President. I knocked twice before a velvety voice commanded me to come in.

"Hello, Ms. Rosen, my name is Leah—"

"I know who you are. Can I get you a drink? Vodka? Scotch?" It was 11 am.

"Um, no, I had coffee, thanks."

"Ahhh… coffee won't cut it in this business." I heard the clink of ice cubes as she poured herself a drink from a crystal decanter. Her office was ablaze with color, and I felt like I was in an art gallery. Large paintings graced the walls. Warhol. Picasso. Dalí.

"What can I do for you, dear?" Vivian was wearing a crepe suit with an ivory silk blouse, a bright Peter Max scarf neatly tied around her neck. Sensible, stylish shoes. The tip-off about her age was the suntan pantyhose, the color usually found in a large plastic egg container like my mother used to buy. Vivian's onyx hair was stiff, but pulled back in a loose chignon with bobby pins older than me. She was intimidating, but her eyes were kind, and I could tell she was a force in her day.

"I'm new here, and I was thinking of creating a women's finance department, and I was wondering how much of your business…" My voice was not steady.

"Sixty percent of my business is women. Is that what you're asking?"

"Yes. And um, how would you…?" This wasn't going well.

"Leah, sit down. It's a great idea. I've been pushing for it for years. No one listens to me anymore. But they didn't listen to me when I set up the Arbor Hedge Fund either. Didn't listen when I wanted to change the commission structures. So I did it myself. My fund has beaten some of the largest funds in the industry for over thirty-five years. And the honchos all want to take credit for it. They nearly laughed me out of the conference room when I suggested it."

"I'm sorry. That's cruel." I took her advice and sat.

"You get used to it. They think my best days are behind me. But they're fools. Crypto Shmypto. They want flash. Do you see my masterpieces?" She pointed to the wall.

"Yes, I was just admiring them."

"Most of the men in the office have never seen my paintings. But I've seen their Porsches in the parking lot. I have art for *me*. So I can enjoy beauty. That's my joy. Not to impress other people." She was making more sense than I thought she would. "Leah, you have to realize that women are commodities. Not end products. Use them for good, and the possibilities are endless. Men want to make a splash. Women want security. Men want action. Women want calm. It's a known fact that women's emotions hold up better in a bad market."

"Ms. Rosen… If the women actually send in the money, will you help me?"

"Absolutely, let's show these *putzes* with the snazzy watches what they're missing."

"I really appreciate this."

"You're tougher than you think, Leah. You just don't know it yet. Stick with me. I'll show you how all that glitters is not gold."

Arbor had been an Old Boys' Club for too long. It was time to let the women in. Vivian and Barry helped me create the building blocks for a women's division. Letters were sent to the women explaining the process and how the money wouldn't be invested all at once. Rita sent texts to me several times a week, outlining new ideas. She had become the unofficial liaison with the wives. We were putting together a team, and although I'd be their point person, I knew I didn't have enough experience yet to make all the decisions, and I wouldn't have Howard's computer telling me what to do. Howard was away when the money started rolling in. BethAnn began a new habit of walking around my station, intent on spying on me. Within the first two weeks, over forty million dollars was wired to the firm. I began meeting with Vivian every day. The women's trading division wasn't just an idea anymore. It was a reality.

TWENTY-NINE

A WOMAN SCORNED

The email came from AF@AF.com, the same as the last few, which I had unceremoniously ignored. This was the fifth email from the same address, but this one grabbed my attention. I did a quick search and pulled up the history.

> **We need to talk. Urgent. I don't think you realize what you're caught up in. AF**
>
> **Please help. AF**
>
> **VERY important. Must discuss soon. AF**
>
> **You can't let this happen. Please respond. AF**
>
> **Please call or email me. Important. AF**

I didn't have time for nonsense. Daniel needed to have a better handle on the transition, and as much as I said I would help out, I was too immersed in work and with the kids to comply. A clean break was better. I hit forward on the latest email and signed off for the night.

I had a pile of paperwork to do before work the next day, and the money was coming in faster than I planned. The wives had mothers, sisters, and friends who wanted to join our new team. And, Nathan was breathing down everyone's neck about new compliance rules.

Howard was away again for more meetings in Washington and New York. I missed him, but I was busier than ever. There was a different vibe in the office when he wasn't there. The meetings were top secret, he said, but he assured me that by the time he got back, everything would be straightened out, and we'd be back to business as usual. Our future was being dangled in front of me again.

Another email appeared from the same address: **This will not fix itself. AF.** Oy, Daniel… I forwarded the email to him, but then I couldn't concentrate.

My curiosity piqued, and I logged back on, retrieved the forwarded email, and answered: **Who are you?**

A quick response: **This is of an imperative matter.**

Me: **I don't have time for games. What do you want?**

AF: **It's confidential. It's about your involvement at Arbor.**

I froze. I put the top of my laptop down, refusing to engage with whoever this nutjob was. I wasn't in the mood for office drama. I wasn't answering. I didn't remember giving out my email to anyone at work. I never did have any willpower.

AF: **Leah, please. It's in your best interest. I promise.**

A personal plea. Fuck.

Oh my God. They knew my name. And who the hell was AF? I needed to talk to Howard. But something told me not to. Howard was adamant that everything was on schedule, and before he left, he gave me the name of a real estate agent.

"You'll help me find a rental—the sooner, the better. It'll be a fresh start," he said, "I just have to do it slowly and not upset Deenie."

He went from being evasive about moving out of his house to discussing his plans daily. In the past month, Howard brought another thirty boxes or so of personal belongings to my basement. It was all there, concrete proof he was leaving Deenie and making our relationship official.

"Right," I answered happily. "What's in all these boxes anyway?" I asked when I saw him huffing and puffing his way up and down my basement steps. I didn't need him having a heart attack in my house.

"Just stuff. Old photo albums. Records. Sports memorabilia. College stuff. Awards. Family heirlooms."

"That's an awful lot of heirlooms."

"Over sixty years' worth," he said with a wink. "All the sentimental stuff. Plus, the Scrabble set is already here! I don't want to take a chance on Deenie tossing anything when she realizes I'm moving out. Although it's mutual, her illness often makes her irrational. These are irreplaceable… things from the kids… you know… that old hell hath no fury like a woman scorned mumbo jumbo."

"Oh, I know all about it," I said as I remembered smashing a glass bottle of Windex against my wedding photo. I also smiled victoriously at the memory of Peyton helping me pack Louis's belongings and driving the boxes to the dump three miles away. It was one of the happiest days of her life when I announced he wasn't coming back.

"I refuse to be that mean," I had told her when she suggested that we trash everything. "It's not worth it. Just leave his stuff. I'll give it to him when things calm down."

"He should've thought about that before he threw your marriage out like yesterday's trash," Peyton said triumphantly. "You're not letting the motherfucker in here again."

I had to admit it felt good when Louis called, looking for his missing things, begging me to allow him to come over and search the house himself. It wasn't easy keeping a straight face when he showed up. After four hours of rummaging through the house and basement, he gave up, relenting that maybe the old boxes were thrown out years earlier. However, two days later, I noticed two pieces of jewelry he'd given me were missing from my hiding spot in my pajama drawer. Touché, Dr. Perloff. Touché.

"Fuck him," said Peyton when I told her the jewelry was missing. "Jewelry's replaceable. Revenge is priceless. Why would you need a few lousy trinkets that he picked out anyway?"

I knew all about being vindictive. It amazed me that Howard was thinking that way, too.

I glanced at the screen. Another email. God, this person was relentless.

> **Meet me at the White House Café. 7:30 tomorrow morning. I'll be in the back near the private room. Please come alone. I won't take up much of your time. Please.**

Whoever it was, they knew something about my schedule. AF. Of course! Arbor Financial. It had to be Staci. I should've known. Who else at work would want to warn me about anything? I typed **Okay** and hit send.

It felt like a mere five minutes later when my alarm went off at 6 am. I double-checked my email to make sure the meeting was still on. The only new mail was from Miriam, the newspaper reporter Lily was working with, confirming the date for our interview at my office. I answered her, then showered and got dressed for work, taking extra care to wear something I believed was equally as fabulous as Staci's wardrobe. I settled on a sophisticated navy linen number with buttons up the back. Howard wasn't expected back until the end of the week, and I was spending every spare minute with Vivian, discussing new ideas for the women's division.

The parking lot was empty except for a Ford F150 with an out-of-state license plate. I was sure I saw Staci park an Audi SUV in the office lot. I pulled down the vanity mirror, reapplied my lip gloss, and exited my car.

I peeked through the café window and saw Ivy and a bright-eyed Pyramid Girl setting up their wares, but other than that, the café was empty. Maybe a Pyramid Girl needed a job. Perhaps I could hire someone my age. Get that female quota number up. Either way, I needed to get this over with. I walked in, looked around, and was about to leave when I noticed a small table by the back exit. The back of a woman's head wearing a baseball cap caught my attention. Facing her was a blonde-haired man in a tweed sports jacket. Immediately, he lifted his arm and motioned for me to come over to his table. As I approached, he stood, and a look of relief spread across his face. Wait, where was Staci?

"Leah?"

He looked like an All-American boy next door, more like Robert Redford in *The Natural* than a stalker who was going to stuff me in the trunk of his car. Inquisitiveness burned in his eyes. What the hell was going on?

"Yes?" I answered with trepidation.

"Chadwick Turner." He handed me a business card.

"I'm sorry, I'm not sure what you're selling, but I'm meeting someone here."

He looked at me cautiously. "I'm aware. I won't take up much of your time." He pulled out the chair for me to sit next to the lady in the hat. He didn't look like a murderer.

I glanced at the card before stuffing it in my bag. Chadwick Turner, Esq. If I hadn't been so preoccupied looking for Staci, I would've noticed the SEC emblem.

Maybe Staci was running late. I hesitated before sitting, glanced at the time, and decided I'd give him the benefit of the doubt. "Just for a minute. I need to get to work. Is this a legal matter?" I was hoping for an investigation into Louis. Workers' comp or tax fraud. Anything to teach the son of a bitch a lesson. How I'd love to see him go down. Chadwick motioned again to the chair, and half flabbergasted, half in a coma, I sat.

The baseball cap may have thrown me off, but the oversized Jackie O sunglasses were a dead giveaway. It was a good thing I was sitting because I might have passed out. I quickly stood up, using the table to steady myself. "Deenie… I'm… I'm… sorry… I…" All those extra layers of confidence since I started working with Howard and Deenie could strip them away in a heartbeat. Speaking of, I think my heart stopped beating for a minute. My jaw was locked in place, prohibiting anything coherent from coming out of my mouth.

She quickly laid her hand on top of mine. "Leah, wait. Please don't go."

This was not happening. It was inevitable that we'd run into each other again. Not today. I wasn't prepared. I had imagined a thousand scenarios in my head of how that would play out, and none of them came close to this. I flashed back to the first time I laid eyes on her, standing in my dining room, so sure of herself. A redoubtable opponent. She always held her head high. Back then, I related it to snobbery. I remembered how beautiful she looked the night of the Bat Mitzvah. Ethereal. That was before. Before Howard confided in me about the fragility of her mental state. Before I slept with her husband. Before I started working at Arbor. Before, I earned my confidence wings. Before her husband's possessions made their way into my basement. Before he picked *me*. Damn, it wasn't supposed to be a competition.

"Deenie, I'm so sorry," I muttered. It was the best I could come up with. What was the right thing to say to the woman whose husband you stole? *Sorry* didn't seem enough or even appropriate right now. Was I sorry? I didn't think so. I was too busy helping myself to the lap of luxury courtesy of Howard. Since the *Pretty Woman* expedition, I had been using his credit card right and left. I felt like the air was being siphoned out of my lungs with a silly straw. Howard swore she didn't know about me. Obviously, he was wrong.

"Leah, this isn't what you think."

I had no choice but to sit down again and listen, mainly because I was so dizzy I was about to lose my balance and fall in her lap.

"I kept getting emails from someone at work. The email address is AF. From Arbor. Staci, I think…"

"They're not from Staci. If she's emailing you, that has nothing to do with me. I thought they got rid of her. AF, that's me. Adena Fishman. It said Fishman on all the party proposals. Fishman's my maiden name. Deenie is Howard's nickname for me." I felt stupid.

I forgot that Cara always referred to her as Adena.

I looked out at the parking lot again, but it was clear. There was no Staci in this scenario. Deenie took off her sunglasses. I wasn't accustomed to seeing her bare-faced. Her hair was tucked into a Vanderbilt Commodore baseball hat, but a few tendrils of gray escaped. Deenie's eyes were clear, her lashes simple and uncoated, giving her a look of innocence I'd never noticed before.

"I know you're with Howard. I've known for months. You'd think he would've gotten better at hiding these things from me after all these years." Deenie sighed and shook her head.

I looked at Deenie with surprise. Years? Plural? I straightened my body. I opened my mouth, but once again, no words escaped. *Hold it together*, I thought. *Don't be the victim.* But I was dumbfounded. Frozen in a thousand thoughts that didn't make any sense.

"Oh, my Lord," she said with a southern drawl that I was also not used to hearing. "You think you're the first?"

I swallowed hard. Still unable to speak. It was better that way.

"I don't know what he told you, but it's gotten more complicated since he moved out. I'm sorry you're involved in this mess."

"Moved out?" I felt a sharp pain sear into my chest.

"He moved out in the beginning of April. You didn't know?"

"April?" I repeated. Everything was happening in slow motion.

"Leah, let's get you a cup of tea."

I nodded. April? That was last month. Something didn't add up.

I didn't need to let Deenie watch me fall apart. I needed to call Howard and sort things out. *She's just upset. Her dates are wrong.* Maybe she was spiraling without her medicine. I reached for my keys.

"We have a pied-à-terre in New York. I assumed he was staying there. But then some forwarded mail came back to the house, and I saw he was living in Princeton."

"Pied-à-terre? Princeton?" I spoke like I was learning a new language.

Chadwick cleared his throat. "Ladies, let's not forget the real reason we're here."

I felt the room get darker. Did the lights just flicker? Maybe there was a power outage.

"We're investigating Arbor Financial and its sister company, Skylar Holdings. You are one of several employees whose actions are under scrutiny. Although this isn't normal protocol, as a favor to Deenie, I'm alerting you to our investigation. Any information you provide is separate from the scope of the subpoenas filed with Arbor. We want to allow you the opportunity to help."

"You're mistaken. Howard said that was all taken care of. I didn't work at Arbor then."

"Then?"

"I know about Banyan. It happened before I worked there."

Deenie rolled her eyes. "Howard wouldn't know the word *honest* if he were being given an intravenous drip of truth serum."

"He's in Washington. The inquiry is practically settled." I should've stopped speaking.

"I'm afraid we're talking about two different things."

Deenie made an unladylike snort. Chadwick took a small notebook from his coat pocket and fished a pen out. He seemed old school in a comforting sort of way. "The case I'm talking about hasn't even been filed yet. We've had many leads. Many of them were not substantial. But there have been some developments lately. Troubling information about the earnings reports in a sector where you make most of your trades."

"What kind of information?"

"That's confidential, but you do know what a whistleblower is, don't you?"

And there you had it. The mole that Howard was worried about. I felt the color drain out of my face. "Do I need a lawyer?" Howard told me I wouldn't need one on the Banyan case.

"That's certainly up to you. This is off the record. The whistleblower mentioned your name as someone to protect, someone to give a heads-up to before charges were filed."

"Who is it?"

"I can't tell you that, Ms. Samuels. However, Deenie saw your name in my notes, unofficially, of course, when we were discussing the case, and she also chose to warn you. She thought you could help. It's not the usual way I conduct my business, but, well, anything for Deenie. We're old friends from Nashville." Chadwick stopped talking long enough to wink at Deenie. "You have my card. I'd be very careful who you talk to. Go to work—business as usual. Make sure there are records of who's directing your trades. Phone conversations. Emails. Office correspondence. Make a copy and save it on your phone. Don't trust anyone at the office. They've probably already started deleting files. If anything seems out of the ordinary, email me."

"Uh-huh."

"And it would be best if you do not discuss this with Howard Gardner."

"But, how am I supposed to… Why?" I looked directly at Deenie. "Why are you protecting me?"

"I know how charming he is. He's had lots of practice. And you're a single mom. That seems to be who he goes after. He gets to be the knight in shining armor. I don't want to see you in deeper trouble than you already are. I was so impressed when

I met you, Leah. The way you conducted your business. You made sure every last detail of Addison's Bat Mitzvah was tended to. I'm sure I wasn't easy to deal with. When Howard said you sold your business, I was heartbroken. And then, little by little, I started to put the pieces together." Chadwick shook his head, alerting her not to say anymore.

Wait, Deenie Gardner was impressed with me?

"If you want to be with him, go right ahead. You can have him. He's not all he's cracked up to be. I filed for divorce months ago."

I gasped. I should have been thrilled, except I was in shock.

"Let me guess," Deenie chuckled, "he said he was waiting for the right time? He doesn't want to disrupt his family? He doesn't know how to be truthful, Leah. I've watched him manipulate people for over thirty years. He's a pro."

It was Chadwick's turn to talk, which was a good thing. My mouth muscles had forgotten how to operate. "Ms. Samuels. It seems you were just the amount of vulnerability Mr. Gardner needed to keep this charade going."

"Charade? But it was my idea to get my license. And then once I got the offer to sell my business, it seemed like a good time to make a career change." My strength was coming back. "He was supportive, but you can't tell me he had me working for him planned. It was one hundred percent all my idea."

"How much do you know about the sale of your business?"

"I sold it to Daniel Ross, the DJ. It was a great deal," I answered proudly.

Deenie and Chadwick looked at each other. I could sense they were holding back.

"How much do you know about VG Industries?"

"Does this have anything to do with Eddie? I just saw him

in—" I stopped myself, thinking anything could be a trap. I didn't know if Deenie knew I had been in Arizona with Howard, luxuriously slinking my way into what should've been hers.

Chadwick waited for me to continue, but I shook my head, trying to absorb all this information. I decided to keep my mouth shut. There was no way VG was under investigation. I read all the R&D reports because I found them so interesting. They were on track to be one of the top players in the beauty, wellness, and supplement industry. Their profits surpassed expectation and their finger was on the pulse of the industry. A few smaller underperforming divisions may eventually be spun off, but the press was astounding. Pretty soon, VG was going to be a household name. It was the affordable version of GOOP.

"So, I need a lawyer."

Chadwick leaned forward and said, "The way I see it, there are two ways you can play this. You can go running to Howard. The majority of women in your position do. That would be a poor choice. Unwise. Perhaps you'll be implicated in more ways than you realize."

"Is that a threat?" My guard suddenly went up.

"Not a threat. A warning." He clasped his hands together and stretched them out in front of him. "I suggest you go to work and try to limit your interactions with Mr. Gardner. Don't divulge the specifics of our meeting. And most importantly, try to hold off on trading anything related to VG Industries."

"That's the bulk of my trades. People will notice I'm not doing my job."

"Do something else."

"We're looking into some banking issues as well. We don't

believe Howard's the only one involved. Or, who knows, maybe Howard isn't involved at all. But if he's not, someone high up at Arbor is."

"What do I tell the clients?" SHINE was accustomed to stellar returns from VG. And now I had a personal relationship with all of them. And the wives. They trusted me.

"Tell them there will be a very promising announcement soon. I'm sure compliance will put a hold on the trades."

Howard and Eddie had mentioned a big announcement. It was a takeover of an exercise equipment company. But it was confidential. Maybe the deal was falling apart. I was already strategizing.

"We need your help, Leah. Our people are watching. We believe you can help our case. You are closest to Mr. Gardner. And you're privy to information about Mr. Grossman."

"You can't expect me to…"

"We've been watching them both for some time."

"Nathan would never allow it."

Deenie rolled her eyes. "Nathan."

"I don't believe you. There's no way anything illegal is happening. Not on his watch. And not with BethAnn watching."

"Ugh. That horrible bitch of a woman. Only one who can control him. Always did." I couldn't believe Deenie was talking like this.

"You have to be mistaken."

"I wish I were. But I have to follow all leads. From time to time, it's a disgruntled former worker looking to retaliate. We don't take any of this lightly. It's a slippery slope of what you can and can't do in this industry. If you choose to help us, we can offer some immunity."

"Immunity? I didn't do anything."

"Just be careful who you trust. If our leads amount to any-thing, you'll need to consider what side you want to be on." Chad-wick Turner stood up, signifying to me to do the same.

Deenie put her hand on mine in solidarity and eked out a forced smile. "I'm afraid greed has lifted Howard to a level of ig-norance that will come crashing down on him. He always thought he was unstoppable. I do trust you'll make the right decision, Leah." And with that, her sunglasses went back on.

THIRTY

PANIC ATTACK PENDING

I fled the café, angrily brushing past Ivy and the unfamiliar Pyramid Girl, eagerly wishing me a too-perky *please buy some-thing* good morning. It was like an ant colony multiplying before my eyes.

"Why isn't anyone investigating *these* companies?" I shouted. I was too agitated to care; I couldn't get out of there fast enough. I collapsed in my car just as my phone flashed two texts from Howard. Without looking, I threw the phone into the backseat and turned on the ignition. I put the car in drive instead of reverse and hit the curb at an alarming speed.

"FUCK!" I wailed as the steering wheel jammed into my rib cage. I shifted into park and got out of the car to examine the tires and make sure the front ones weren't flat. I was sure that was captured on the café's surveillance cameras. I carefully drove straight to Peyton's house. How many times had she warned me? How many times did I disregard her warnings? She was the only one who could help figure out these new developments. An emergency session with the esteemed Dr. Peyton was warranted.

I walked through Peyton's front door, intruding on her breakfast with Leonardo. He jumped out of his seat, thrilled to set another place at the table. Peyton took one look at me and said, "Uh oh."

I felt my composure slip away. "He's a fucking liar. A fucking fucking liar. How could I be so stupid?"

Peyton didn't speak. She waited while I processed what was happening. She was unflappable. I was a raging lunatic.

"FUCKING LIAR! He said he was moving out as soon as he found a place. He didn't want to upset Deenie due to her mental state. He lied. He moved out weeks ago. The promises—the whole romantic fantasy in Arizona. The real estate agent. The boxes piled up in my house. And the liar had already moved out! LIAR!" I felt snot drip from my nose. I was starting to hyperventilate. "And Deenie filed for divorce months ago. MONTHS AGO!"

"Is that it?"

"What do you mean?"

"Sounds like you got what you wanted. He moved out. It's not like he decided to stay in the house with his wife. That's what most of them do. Isn't this what you wanted? And she filed for divorce. Again, just what you wanted. What's the problem?" Peyton calmly took a bite of her breakfast.

I stopped my rant to think about this. Leave it to Peyton to be cool. Leave it to Peyton to make me seem like the hysterical one. Hysteria was an understatement.

"Did you ask him about it?"

I shook my head. "No, I ran into Deenie, and she told me he had moved out already. I didn't know what to even say to her other than that I was so sorry."

"You ran into Deenie again? God, that couldn't have been good." Peyton answered like we were discussing a pair of shoes. She continued eating.

"You could say that." I didn't mention the business accusations. I couldn't bring myself to believe any of it could be true. In retrospect, that was precisely the part I should have been thinking about. The fact that I could be the target of an investigation. That he could go to jail. Or I could. Not the fact that he'd already found a place to live. "Why would he lie to me?"

"Why don't you tell me? He's your boyfriend. Ask him."

"How do you always stay calm? I'm losing my mind here."

"I told you. I've seen this before, every scenario you can imagine. Any guy who cheats on his wife is not exactly the honest type. Do you think you're the first person to go through this? Take the blindfold off, Leah."

"Does it ever work out?" I asked as tears began to drip down my cheeks.

"I guess it depends on how bad you want it to. First, why don't you ask why he lied to you? Maybe there's a logical explanation."

"Why are you defending him? You hate him."

"I'm just looking at it rationally. Something you never did. Your heart was in control. And, are you sure you can trust Deenie? How do you know she's not the one lying? It seems like there are a few sides to this story. Hurt people like to hurt other people."

Leonardo placed a freshly baked slice of frittata and two slices of avocado on my plate.

"Eat, love," he said as he discreetly stuffed some tissues into my hand.

I didn't think I could eat a morsel of food, but Leonardo's concoctions were enough to make anyone's troubles disappear.

"I guess you're right." I blew my nose. "Howard texted me a few times, but I didn't answer. And I'm supposed to be at a work meeting in ten minutes."

"Calm down. Where's your phone?"

"I threw it into the backseat of my car. I thought about throwing it out the window. Oh, and I may have cracked my bumper." I looked at Peyton sheepishly.

"Again? Oy. Give me your keys." I swear my mom was standing there, shaking her finger at me.

"Love, let me ask you, it's not my business, but is he worth it?" Leonardo stood in front of me, wearing an apron that said *Bow to the Cook*. I felt my eyes well up again.

"I thought so." It was an admission filled with uncertainty. Maybe it had been too good to be true. I wished I could turn back the clock and leave the menacing email in the trash. Ignorance would have been better than how I'd begun to feel with my new knowledge.

"I never thought of you as a quitter, love."

He was right. I needed to see if there was a valid explanation before I went mad.

Peyton returned with my phone, which now had two more missed calls and four new texts from Howard.

> Howard: Are you ok?
>
> Howard: Where are you?
>
> Howard: Honey?
>
> Howard: Leah, please answer.
>
> Me: Sorry, horrible migraine. Late for meeting. Talk later.
>
> Howard: Thank God. I was so worried. Feel better. XO

Maybe Deenie was just fishing. Stirring up trouble. After all, she was the jilted wife. Her psychiatric issues could be spearheading this, and this might have been her way of seeking vengeance. I took a giant swig of the fresh-squeezed orange juice Leonardo had poured for me. I knew I had to pull it together and get my ass to work. I excused myself to the bathroom. Peyton appeared and handed me a concealer and some translucent powder. I fell into her for a hug.

"Enough, my little Stock Market Mistress. Fix your face, go to work, and act like the badass you're trying so hard to be. Then, confront his lying ass," she said happily. "You know where to find me."

SEC Interview #2

Howard Gardner

SEC: Mr. Gardner, you previously mentioned you weren't familiar with Leah Samuels. Isn't it true that she's currently working in your office?

Mr. Gardner: Yes. Leah works for Arbor Financial.

SEC: Did you get her the job?

Mr. Gardner: No. All applicants go through HR. I don't get involved. Leah's in my division now. She's a hard worker. Smart girl.

SEC: What's the nature of your relationship?

Mr. Gardner: She's part of our trading team.

SEC: Are you sure you don't wish to amend that response?

Mr. Gardner: I'm sure.

SEC: So you're stating your only relationship is professional?

Mr. Gardner: Look, you know how it is. A little office

flirtation. It doesn't mean anything. Everything was consensual.

SEC: How long did this flirtation, as you call it, last?

Mr. Gardner: Just a few weeks. We knew it was a mistake. No harm. No foul.

SEC: So there's no future planned with Ms. Samuels, either romantically or professionally? No plans to bring her in as your partner?

Mr. Gardner: Partner? (Laughter) That's a good one. I have a very powerful position. Women are drawn to me. Especially the single ones. Maybe they think I'm their meal ticket. But it was brief and completely consensual. We agreed it was just an indiscretion. A mistake. I'm a happily married man. She's single and a bit on the prowl if I do say so myself. I don't think I'm any different than anyone else in a position such as mine. We work long hours. A little extra-curricular activity is expected in this industry.

SEC: How many of these extracurricular relationships have you been involved in?

Mr. Gardner: Just this one. And like I said. It was a mistake.

SEC: How familiar is Ms. Samuels with your clients?

Mr. Gardner: She takes their phone calls. I'm a very busy man. She's licensed, so she can accept trades. She picks up the overflow from the other traders. We don't expect more from her at this point.

SEC: Thank you for your time, Mr. Gardner.

Mr. Gardner: My pleasure.

THIRTY-ONE

DISBELIEF

I got into my car and sent Reese a text.

Me: Running late. Cover for me, please?

Reese: It'll cost you, Mamacita.

Thank God for Reese. Sometimes I didn't know if I'd make it through the day without him.

Reese had become my work husband. He was competitive, but the whole culture was competitive. Reese was the type of guy with a calculator for a brain, and not only was he quick to figure out returns, but his statistical analysis of risk was mind-boggling. He was amazed by the timing of my trades. "How could anyone be right this percentage of the time?" he had asked. We all had our strengths, and I was known as the VG expert. I couldn't tell anyone that the information was all on my computer.

As we got to know each other, I discovered Reese was exceptionally kind. He brought me a maple syrup sampler from his fraternity alum ski trip in Vermont. Magnolia cupcakes after a meeting in the New York office. There was no good reason to butter me up, but he confessed that he had a soft spot for single moms.

I made it to the office in record time, dropped my bag at my desk, and quietly slipped into the conference room. Reese had saved me a seat and had a bottle of water and a cookie sitting on top of last week's report. I smiled with relief. Reese leaned over and said, "You didn't miss much. I printed the files you needed from your computer."

"Thank you," I mouthed as I took a bite of the cookie.

The retreat resulted in several large donations for the Gardner Stroke Center and a staggering influx of cash into the SHINE accounts. I knew the Howie Loans were used until the funds settled. Howard explained that people with this level of wealth frequently invested with different strategies. The accounts I handled were just a partial picture. Our goal was to get a bigger piece of the pie, and we accomplished it.

The biggest surprise was that every one of the wives decided to take my advice and open up their own women's trading accounts. I was now going to head up the Women's SHINE Division. There'd be no Howie Loans. Full transparency, I decided.

I was intrigued by the numbers being written on the whiteboard. It had been a record month. All quotas were met. Bonuses would be paid. Not counting the newly transferred money. The room erupted like we'd won the Super Bowl.

"Gonna pay my momma's mortgage with this bonus," Reese whispered as he doodled a picture of a truckload of dollar bills on a conference room napkin. "And ZuZu and her friends need new iPads."

I smiled at the thought of him spending his hard-earned money on his mom and sister. Reese would make a great father one day. What a *mensch*.

The excitement kept me from worrying about my early morning meeting. I looked around the room, trying to figure out who the mole might be. Chadwick said it was an accounting issue. If that were the case, it wouldn't be anyone in my group; it would come from the statistical desk upstairs. Like Leopard-Lovin' Staci.

Once I had (mostly) calmed down from the morning's freakout, I decided I didn't believe everything Chadwick Turner said. I promised myself I'd do some sleuthing later tonight to set my mind at ease, and more importantly, I decided not to mention it to Howard. He had enough on his plate, and as Chadwick said, the SEC had to follow all leads. I was still sure Howard would be exonerated. I'd bring it up in person. It was very possible Deenie was stirring up trouble as divorce leverage. I couldn't blame her. Hit Howard where she knew it would hurt.

I was certain no one in my group would sabotage such a booming organization. As I walked back to my desk, BethAnn gave me her usual look of disapproval, and that's when it occurred to me. The mole could be BethAnn. I sat down at my desk, thinking about what BethAnn would gain if there were a scandal at Arbor. I didn't believe she'd be the one to cross Howard. If anything, she'd sweep the evidence under the rug, shredding documents to protect Howard. But I couldn't be sure.

Or it could be Nathan. I remembered Nathan telling us about how a financial mishap killed his dad. That was the reason he didn't put up with any funny business. Or so he said. There had to be a logical answer for Chadwick and Deenie's little conspiracy number, and I was determined to find out what it was.

Two hours later, Howard sent another text.

> Howard: Hi, sweetheart. I have to stay in Washington
> for a little while longer. Then I'm off to an appear-

ance at the New York office for a few days. Don't
wait up. Winky emoji.

Me: Good luck.

I didn't want a confrontation. My emotions were spiraling. I felt the pounding of a headache and knew I needed to get away from the office. I couldn't let anyone see me upset. I escaped onto the elevator, pressed the buttons, and kept my head down once the door opened. A few seconds later, I crashed into a sturdy body, encased in leather. "Oh! I'm so sorry. I wasn't looking and…"

"Hey, Leah. Are you okay?" Flustered, I looked up. Dylan, again. For someone who didn't work there, he was there a lot. It was impossible to control my despair. My face said what I couldn't. Dylan leaned in and swept his index finger across my lashes. "No one as pretty as you should be crying in the middle of the day."

"I'm not crying."

Dylan nodded his head. "Okay. You can go with that. My wet finger tells another story. Plus, I don't need to put a zoom lens on my camera to see that you're worried about something. Come on. Let's get out of here."

Dazed and filled with curiosity, I followed him. We walked through a set of sliding doors away from my usual entrance, around a bend to a courtyard of tables that I didn't know existed.

"I've been working here for months, and I never saw this part of the complex."

"Well, this place is crawling with secrets, isn't it?"

"I…" My lips began to tremble.

"My dad's been working at Arbor since the day they opened. My mom used to bring my brother and me here to have lunch with my dad, back when he never took a day off. I know where the bodies are buried. I actually know too much about this place.

What I can't figure out is what in the world you're doing here."

"Long story. I don't want to bore you."

"You don't seem like the boring type."

Our eyes locked. He was like a warm blanket, soothing my anxious heart. The sound of his voice was calming. I could just imagine what he sounded like with a microphone up against his lips. Or what those lips tasted like. No. No. No. *What is wrong with me?*

"I have to go." I scrambled to stand up. He grabbed my elbow to help. I was corporate Barbie today in my navy midi and nude crocodile pumps. He was rocker Ken. He knew how to wear a pair of Levi's. I'm sure Dylan didn't own a pair of designer anything. "Can you tell someone in the office I have a migraine and had to leave? Never mind. I'll text Reese."

"Leah, you don't have to do this, you know." His eyes pleaded for an explanation.

"I don't know what you're talking about."

"If you need a friend…"

"I'll keep that in mind." I gave a half smile. Dylan came closer and lifted my chin.

"Be careful."

I had promised Lily a pedicure and a college shopping trip. We were spending less and less time together, and I knew I'd regret it. This job had me clocking more hours than when I was a party planner. Graduation was around the corner. Time had flown by, and it was becoming a reality that Lily was leaving. I was thrilled she chose a college on the east coast, but an empty room was an empty room. Asher would start applying to schools in the fall. Life would be different. Who knew if any of Howard's promises would come to fruition? Would I even have a job? I put this morning's meltdown in the back of my mind, forgot the heat of Dylan's touch, and headed to the mall with Lily. A little retail therapy was good for both of us. I indulged more than usual and allowed her to get all the bedding and decorations for her dorm, as well as several dresses she claimed she needed for sorority pledging. I didn't want to think about my daughter playing beer pong at a fraternity house in a mini dress barely covering her *tuchus*.

Our feet were soaking in a bath of lavender bubbles when Lily casually said, "Mom, do you think you're going to marry Howard?"

Lily's candidness caught me by surprise. How much do you tell your eighteen-year-old that she hasn't figured out anyway?

"I don't know."

"Well, do you love him?" She didn't give me a chance to answer. Which was good. "If you ask me, Mom, I think you love the thought of him." Lily raised her eyebrows. "Dad doesn't hide his romances." I bit my tongue to keep from criticizing Louis's taste in women.

"I'm eternally grateful for what he did for your grandmother."

"Even I know that's not enough." How did I, a hopeful romantic, get a daughter so wise beyond her years?

"He's a nice man and a great boss, but I'm not making any plans." I had become a great liar. There was no playbook for this conversation.

"Well, maybe if you and Dad were both happy and remarried, you wouldn't hate each other so much."

"I think it would take more than that." Like a gruesome, slow, and painful death for Louis.

We finished at the salon and decided to grab dinner at Coco Bella. I called Asher to meet us, but he was busy on the phone with my brother, planning another basketball weekend, so he asked me to bring him a steak sandwich.

Lily began discussing her freshman schedule, and I was glad she wanted my input. "I decided that in addition to my journalism classes, I'm going to minor in psychology. So I can be like Peyton."

"That's a new development."

"Peyton has a way of knowing everything before everyone else. I want to learn how to do that."

"Peyton was doing that when we were ten years old. She didn't need college for that. But, if that's what interests you, I think you should pursue it."

"Serena said she overheard her mom and dad call you a gold-digging whore."

I felt a piece of romaine drenched in Caesar dressing get stuck in my windpipe. I reached for my iced tea and wondered if falling on the floor and needing the Heimlich would be the best move.

"I told her they were idiots, that you were super smart and a hard worker and didn't need anyone else's money. I also told her she had no room to gossip after her father had that DUI last year. That shut her up."

I was stuck between wanting to change the subject and wanting to know what else was being said about me. It never occurred to me that my kids would hear the gossip. I wondered if Louis had heard anything and would try to reduce support again. I was finally making enough money that it didn't matter. I also couldn't imagine a judge taking away a father's tuition responsibility just because his ex-wife was having a little (a lot of) steamy sex.

"People gossip. It's much more fun to make something up or run with an unconfirmed piece of juicy information than to verify the source of information. You should know that as a writer.

Please don't listen to any of it. People's lives get ruined that way, you know."

"I just thought you'd be interested." No. Another case of me thinking ignorance was bliss.

"Things are never what they seem, honey. Lies have a way of growing bigger the longer they're left unanswered. But that's all it is. Lies."

"Okay. What's going on with my article?" Lily's story was not only going to run in the *Garnet Springs Press* as a series on women in finance, but a local magazine wanted to run it as a feature for next month's issue. The paper was so impressed with her writing that they already asked her to submit freelance articles while she was away at school.

"I confirmed a date for the reporter to come to the office." I needed to find the right time to tell Howard.

We arrived home, and Asher came out to help unload the car. He was carrying shopping bags full of bedding, towels, and dorm accessories to the basement when he called out, "What's all this?" Cardboard boxes piled five high and five deep were positioned in front of the camp trunks. I had forgotten how many boxes of Howard's things were down there. Each time Howard came over, he brought more boxes, afraid to take a chance of Deenie doing something rash. But if he moved to Princeton, why didn't he take them with him? The list of questions I had for him was growing by the day.

"Howard's storing some stuff here temporarily. I'll get him to move it this weekend." I wasn't comfortable touching his stuff, and I certainly didn't want to break anything valuable.

Feeling guilty about being away and working so much, I suggested a game of Scrabble. It had been months since we had played. Lily beat Asher and me by a landslide. I put the game away and got into bed, exhausted. Howard had texted again: Goodnight. Miss you.

I texted back: Sorry. Busy with kids tonight. I didn't have the energy for anything else.

At the same time, Peyton texted; Are you ok?

I answered quickly: Fine. I left work early and spent all afternoon with Lily. Just like old times. I'll confront Howard when he gets back. Thanks for being there. Heart Emoji Heart Emoji.

> Peyton: I'm always here. See you tomorrow night.
>
> Me: What's tomorrow night?
>
> Peyton: You promised you'd come to Cara's party.
>
> Me: Shit. She gave me the cold shoulder for a week
>
> after I didn't come to the last one. How do I get out
>
> of this?
>
> Peyton: You don't.

Cara was hosting a party for her new best friend, Eden, an up-and-coming Pyramid sensation, and a few other consultants. It was the absolute last event in the world I wanted to attend, especially after Lily's distressing information that I was known as a gold-digging whore, but I had promised Cara during a weak moment, and it was too late to cancel.

I had no choice but to put on my best fake smile, whip out my credit card, and pretend to follow these lunatics on their journey of empowerment.

THIRTY-TWO

PARTY DOWN

*C*ara was in hostess mode and announced my arrival like I was attending a debutante ball. The house was transformed to look like a high-end boutique, with people selling everything from Tupperware to vitamins, workout clothes to lipsticks with staying power, and children's books.

A bartender served miniature espresso martinis. The patio had three kinds of charcuterie boards and a cannoli bar. Everyone had a drink in one hand and a credit card in the other.

"Is Heidi here? I saw her sweaters spread out in your living room," I asked, pretending I was interested.

"There's a new Sweet Sweater rep. Heidi's getting married again," replied Cara. "I'm so excited for her. She's super busy planning a wedding in Martha's Vineyard."

"Really?" I breathed deeper than I realized, which must have given off jealousy vibes.

"Try not dating married men, and maybe you could be planning a wedding, too," Peyton said while popping olives in her mouth.

"I don't need a wedding. And for the record. He's almost divorced. You know what? He might already be divorced." I laughed, but I knew it could be entirely possible based on Deenie's bombshell information.

Howard had called as I was on the way out the door. I mentioned where I was reluctantly going, and he said to use it as a networking opportunity. I told him I was way ahead of him on that idea.

I walked around the room, eavesdropping on each rehearsed spiel from the proprietors, trying to find the least expensive item I could buy. There were regional directors mingling, spreading news of the incredible good fortune bestowed upon them by being part of such a wonderful organization. They shared stories of being on the brink of bankruptcy until they became independent business owners. It was AA for shopping addicts, with everyone sharing a redemption story. I imagined this was like trespassing on a Scientology meeting. Was I the only skeptic here? The only one with any taste or knowledge? I wanted to stand up and scream: *Ladies, you're all being scammed!* But Cara would never forgive me. As if she were reading my mind, Peyton appeared with a fresh drink and a chocolate chip cannoli. "Behave."

"I'm trying."

"Try harder. These women are just trying to make a living. You, of all people, should understand. You sold your soul, too."

"These companies only want to recruit a downline of people. The products suck. It's a matter of time before they lose all their money. I lived through this with my mom. You know the damage it did. I wish there were a way to warn them."

"Okay, Pyramid Police. It's not your problem to solve. I know your mom's history, but I don't understand your fixation on bringing these women down. It's their money. They can invest it anyway they want."

"Aha… so you're finally admitting they're part of a Pyramid?"

"I'm just saying to be supportive like we are with you."

"I'm not doing something that's borderline illegal."

Peyton raised her eyebrow and gave me the side eye. "If you say so, Mrs. Madoff. Now find something to buy and be gracious to our host. I bought some yummy candles. Smell." Peyton opened up her beautifully wrapped package and gave me a whiff of grapefruit that was sweet and pungent.

"I suppose I could use a candle. Or two."

"That's my girl." Peyton winked at a woman wearing a pink power suit and a ponytail like Cara's, whom I did not recognize. I guessed it was a client, but Peyton would never betray that confidence in a public setting. She turned her attention back to me. "What happened with Howard?"

"Nothing yet. He's still away. It's giving me time to think about how I want to handle it. Or see if he brings it up first. You know the passive way."

"Haven't I taught you anything?"

"There's probably a logical explanation. I'm sure Deenie was trying to cause trouble. Friday is Lily's prom, so I'm leaving work early. Then Howard and I have dinner plans. I'll get to the bottom of everything. Promise. My new women's division is taking off. Howard was against it at first, but he was wrong. I've got a lot of strategizing to do. I can't wait to tell you about it."

"I'm so glad you found your purpose there. Maybe there will be a silver lining."

"Vivian's a hidden treasure of inspiration. I never expected it. Howard's not a fan. One more obstacle to work through."

"You were so worried about the mean girls not being nice to you, yet you pick even meaner men. You enjoy being treated like shit. I can't figure it out. I don't know if it's because of Louis or your mom or you're just a glutton for punishment, but you accept the scraps and then make excuses. You need to confront Howard. About all of it. If he's telling the truth, you'll know it. If not, you'll feel it in your gut. You're too old to play games and be in a relationship that's not honest. You deserve better."

"I'm a work in progress. There's just so much going on. But I can't wait to see my dad. He's coming up from Florida. Mitchell and Rachel are coming to Lily's graduation party. And then Louis is getting married, and the kids will be in Cabo for the wedding. It's a busy few weeks."

"Poor girl. Another future ex-Mrs. Perloff. Anyway, I can't wait to see everyone. How is Miss Broadway?"

"Rachel loves her life. She invited Lily to New York to see her latest show as a graduation present. Lily's really excited."

"That's terrific. Now go buy something before I sign you up for a monthly subscription of exfoliators."

A plate of tuna sashimi, another cannoli, a candle, and a set of Tupperware bowls later, I kissed Cara on the cheek, told her it was a lovely party, and begged forgiveness for having to leave early. I walked down Cara's driveway in time to see Ivy rummaging through giant containers in the trunk of her Suburban. Feeling guilty that I didn't buy any of her ugly workout clothes, I waved and asked if she needed help. She didn't expect me to offer, and I didn't expect to see her crying.

"Oh no, Ivy, what's wrong?"

"Nothing. Just trying to find a size for someone." Ivy faked a smile, reminiscent of our friendship.

"Are you sure?" I felt horrible. The black eyeliner that matched her hair, long and straight and flowing down her back like in a shampoo commercial, was smudged beyond repair. Ivy was always a good friend, and we spent lots of time together at birthday parties and school events. I started avoiding her when she started this business, and now I was regretting how insensitive I'd been. I watched her punch some numbers into her phone, shaking her head and going back to searching the gigantic containers. "Is there something I can do?"

Ivy lifted her head, deciding whether to trust me, and said, "Oh, Leah. Everything's a mess."

"What do you mean?"

"This." She motioned to the stacks of Rubbermaid containers bursting with garish prints. "GoGo Athlete. I'm out of stock of the good prints. Overflowing with bad merchandise and bad sizes. I think the only person fitting into all these extra-large pants is me. Barely," she said, alluding to her recent weight gain.

"You look fine," I lied.

"I'm not reaching my quota now that fourteen other women are selling the same stuff to my customers. The company won't send me what I need if I don't cough up more money for the next-level products, and I haven't gotten a payout for last month's orders yet. I'm sorry. I didn't mean to dump on you. I'm trying so hard. They sort of trap you so you can't get out. And then you're in debt up to your eyeballs. Just what I need with, well, you know."

After knocking on this business model for so long, I didn't feel the same sense of satisfaction I should have. But there it was, the problems I had suspected. There was no sense in rubbing salt in her wounds. "I'm sure you'll make it work."

Ivy shook her head. "I'm trying to sell out what I have. That's why I'm at the café all the time. They push you. I need to move what I have left and then decide what to do. I wish I had never gotten involved with Violet and Gray."

"Who?"

"Violet and Gray, the company that owns most of these independent retailers. Not the Tupperware, but most of them." Ivy smiled at my bulging bag of brightly colored bowls.

"Do you need to talk to a lawyer? My dad has some experience with this. My mom…" I stopped short.

"No, it won't work. This company's completely insulated. They don't care about me. Plus, I signed several licensing agreements. There's no way out except to take a huge financial hit. Or get into one of their other companies. That's what happens to most people eventually. It starts great, but then, well, you know how it goes. I thought I got in at a good time. I was making a lot of money. But now, they own me. They expect me to recruit more people."

I felt another dash of regret for not helping her out. She needed the money to pay her bills just as badly as I did. It wasn't the time to preach my poetic justice about what I thought. Ivy just needed a friend, the kind I hadn't been lately. "I don't know what to say. But if I were you, I'd get someone to fight for you. Legally. Or the Better Business Bureau."

I paused long enough for her to say, "And with Benji still looking for a job and Bailey leaving for college —"

"I'm sure you thought you were making a good decision at the time. It's possible to make the wrong decision for the right reason. We've all done it. See you at prom pictures?"

"Found it!" Ivy held the pink camo leggings with orange piping up for my approval. Her face relaxed, and the color returned.

"Ugh, Ivy, really?"

"Yes, they're hideous. I know." We giggled like the old friends we once were. "And prom pictures. Can you believe it? Yesterday, Bailey and Lily were in diapers," she said, licking her fingers and rubbing the eyeliner away. We shared a moment of unity. "And Leah, please don't mention anything to anyone, okay? It's actually in my contract that I can't say anything bad about them." I pretended to zip up my lips, flashed her an authentic smile, and went back inside to use the bathroom.

I let myself in through Cara's garage, noticing her car was missing and in its place were hundreds of boxes. Each box had a Violet and Gray logo on it. Something strange was going on.

A sweet honeysuckle fragrance permeated the powder room. I used the last guest towel and opened the vanity to get a refill. Stacked in size order were fifty boxes of candles. I knew Cara purchased a ridiculous amount of items from the consultants at the café and that she had the only split-level home that resembled a bed and breakfast, but this was over and above just trying to help someone out. I bumped into Cara on my way out of the bathroom.

"Oh, Leah, did you come back to get some more Tupperware?"

"No. But maybe you can explain this?" I opened the door to her garage.

Cara adjusted her ponytail and straightened her cardigan. "It's just a few gifts I bought for some friends."

"A few?"

"I can't talk about this now. Can't you see I'm hosting?" Cara whispered defensively.

The new Pyramid Girl appeared out of nowhere. "Cara, they need you on the patio." She tilted her head and said, "Hi, I'm Eden. Can I show you our line of Insta-firm neck creams?"

"Thank you. But I was just leaving." Plus, my neck is just fine.

THIRTY-THREE

STAND BY YOUR MAN

As I watched Toby pin a corsage on Lily, I couldn't help but think about this bittersweet sliver of time. Fleeting, yet rich with promise. Toby, Lily's camp boyfriend, flew in to escort her to the prom and go to the Jersey Shore with eight other couples for the weekend. I tried to ignore Louis as he made his way through the other camera-wielding parents to get some up-front shots of Lily and Toby. As soon as the kids left, I dashed out of Serena's backyard, simulating a smirk at her mom, who I now know called me a gold digger. And a whore. I wasn't sure which one I thought was worse.

Howard was picking me up for dinner, a welcome change from the usual meeting him somewhere forty-five minutes away, so no one would see us. I switched from prom mom to adoring girlfriend, showering and throwing on a black and white halter dress and a pair of stilettos. He had a lot of questions to answer.

At seven o'clock, Howard rang the doorbell and lifted me in

a bear hug, twirling me around in a way that made me feel dizzy.

"I missed you," he said, making me think everything I suspected in the past week could be nothing more than a cruel joke. Howard was dressed in slim-cut jeans and a well-tailored black silk button-down, looking more like George Clooney than a suburban dad. He opened the door of the Maserati and waited until I got situated before handing me a box of chocolates.

Before I could speak, he said, "Celebration time!"

"What for?" I asked, genuinely excited for him.

"You'll see," he answered, stretching out the syllables. He sang along with the radio, showing off his goofy side. Carefree Howard had returned to the building. I filled him in with details about Lily and Asher and their father's ridiculous wedding plans.

We crossed the Pennsylvania border and arrived in New Jersey. I saw the signs for Princeton University before he turned off the highway and into what looked like a deserted train station. "Where are we going?"

"You're about to have the best French food you've ever tasted." He grabbed a champagne bottle from the backseat and escorted me through a large oak door draped with ivy.

The staff was thrilled to see him. Howard ordered three appetizers. The waiter came over to pop the champagne bottle. Howard leaned in close to my face and whispered, "Case closed, baby. It's over."

"Oh my God. Are you serious?" I asked joyfully.

"Inquiry closed. Insufficient evidence. Insufficient data. Insufficient everything. I told you. They didn't have anything on me." His smile kept getting bigger.

"Do I still have a job?"

"Of course you do. Everyone loves you. And what you're doing with the wives. Unreal. I didn't think it would happen. Over a year of these bullshit accusations and the sons of a bitches in the SEC, they had nothing on me. Nada." He lifted his champagne glass. "To us, Leah, my one and only. I can't thank you enough for sticking by me."

My heart leaped out of my chest and took a seat next to us. So Chadwick had nothing. Maybe Deenie didn't either. I was about to bring up Deenie when Howard realigned his focus.

"Starting the celebration without me?" I felt a hand on my shoulder and looked up to see Eddie.

"Eddie! What are you doing here?" I asked.

"Celebrating with my favorite couple, what else?" He took a seat and motioned to the waiter for a champagne glass.

Eddie had an easiness about him; he listened intently as I spoke, often repeating the words back to me to be sure he got it just right. It was a trait I admired. He was complimentary, not to mention awestruck by what I was willing to do for Howard, and equally impressed by how I built my party business and sold it. Eddie couldn't be happier about what I was doing with the women's version of SHINE. When we met in Arizona, it was strictly business, talking about VG Industries and what the future held in his ever-growing business. Eddie spoke openly about his plans for a press tour and his timeline for launching new products, and was eager to hear my opinions about women customers and their shopping habits. But tonight, it was personal. He already felt like family, and I was thrilled that Howard included him in our celebration. Eddie imbued me with several jokes that I'd never remember in their entirety. I laughed uncontrollably, forcing me to postpone the touchy issues I was planning to bring up.

Two hours and a bottle of champagne later, we finished dinner with flaming crépes Suzette and my promise to Eddie that we would do this again soon. I followed Howard to his car. "I love that man. I can see why you're so attached to him."

"He seems quite fond of you, too. He's the closest thing to a father to me. I don't know where I'd be without him."

We pulled into a gated complex of townhomes. Howard waved to the guard and pulled his car into a reserved spot. I looked at him curiously.

"Surprise number two. You won't be needing that Realtor yet. This is one of Eddie's houses. It's in between rentals. I couldn't stay in that house with Deenie for one more minute. It was killing me. I should've told you earlier, but I've been preoccupied with getting this case closed." I had drunk more than usual, and the overall excitement of the night, Howard being vindicated, like a get-out-of-jail-free card, had me feeling like he could say anything to me at this moment, and I wouldn't care. There was no time to evaluate the house situation or remember what else I needed to discuss with him; my brain was mush. This was the Howie I fell in love with. The Howie I couldn't resist. I followed him into the bedroom, which was wallpapered in deep burgundy stripes. He lifted me into a large oak canopy bed that took up most of the space.

Howie kept kissing me and, in between kisses, whispering in my ear how happy he was. How he'd never felt this way with Deenie. How he loved me.

I pulled away and opened my eyes. I held onto the side of the bed so I didn't fall off. "What?"

"I love you. You knew that."

"No… I didn't. You never said it to me before."

"I didn't think I had to."

Three simple words seemed to wash away everything that bothered me. I was back on the roller coaster.

He took my clothes off and began to caress my body with a feverish thrill. Like he had something to prove, and I responded accordingly, permitting him to use my body as his private temple, bringing me to the brink of orgasm and then teasing me when he stopped. He was secure and demanding and left me screaming with pleasure.

We both dozed off with exhaustion. At 3 am, I woke up, an unfortunate perk from too much alcohol. The buzz had worn off, and unable to sleep, I traced Howie's face with my pinky, studying him without the alcoholic daze. So now I knew that Deenie only had it half right. He had moved some belongings to Princeton, but this was Eddie's house, not a colossal lie. Deenie's filing for divorce was all part of his plan. I felt a calm come over me.

Howie stirred. I whispered in his ear, "I love you, too."

"Mmmm," he responded.

I continued circling his face, running my hand down his neck. He was smiling in his sleep, his heart beating to an even tempo, grinning like a fat cat who ate an entire cage full of canaries. I wasn't sure I heard him correctly because his voice was low in between breaths.

"I knew."

I wish I had looked at a clock to watch time stand still.

"You knew what?" I asked, fearing I already knew the answer.

"Banyan Pharmaceuticals. It wasn't just a lucky hunch, and in the end, no one could prove how we had the information. I knew I could trust you. Now no one will ever know."

"How did you know?" I felt my pulse race.

"Eddie's wife, Sunny, stole the files from the nursing home

where she volunteered and gave them to Eddie. It was a multi-million-dollar acquisition by Banyan, but nobody could ever tie us to the corporation that owned them. We knew months before it was public. It was Eddie's quick thinking. Brilliant. Just brilliant."

"So you and Eddie were in on it together?"

"Of course."

"I don't think I want to know this."

"Then go back to sleep. We never have to talk about it again. We're free, baby. F. R. E. E. Like a bird."

Every part of me throbbed, from my head to my inner thighs. But the physical pain paled compared to the two simple words that now held the weight of the world. *He knew.*

He was free. This time. But what about the next time? He loved me. He was guilty. Both on the same night.

After his confession, Howard fell back into a deeper sleep, not a single care in the world. I went to the bathroom and threw up. Howard Gardner was not who I thought he was. Who I wanted him to be. But this was just the beginning. I realized then that this moment would always be the great divide. The before and the after. Before I knew he knew. And after. Nothing from before mattered anymore. It would always be the after.

THIRTY-FOUR

THE AFTER

As Howard's declared innocence quickly lulled him back to a peaceful sleep, it put my brain in overdrive, and I watched the sun come up over the golf course. He knew. Did it matter? Did it have anything to do with our relationship? The case was finally over. Could I trust him? I deserved an Academy Award for my performance over the next few weeks.

We got up early, put on our clothes from the night before, and got in the car. Not a word about the confession. Maybe I dreamed it. Perhaps he was bipolar. Maybe I'd play his game and pretend it wasn't an issue. After all, the case was officially closed. Now I wouldn't be questioned. I'd check the statute of limitations. He'd keep his license and reputation. We'd dance off into the sunset together. Problem solved. If only my head saw it that way. I just wanted to go home.

Howard stopped for coffee and bagels and pulled into the of-fice complex. The parking lot was empty.

"I haven't been here in a week, and I'm leaving again tomorrow for a speech at a stroke facility in Tennessee. They're interested in a collaboration."

"That's amazing. I'm so proud of you." I quickly added, "Your dad would be proud." Howard patted my leg and gave me another stressless smile.

"I've got to grab something from the office. Come in with me for a minute. I promise, one minute." He held up one finger.

We walked into the office together for the first time and, in my opinion, probably the last. He was whistling. It was the first Saturday in June, warm and restorative, the kind of day that instantly put you in a good mood. I heard Howard mutter a few curse words. Then, I heard him pick up his phone and continue cursing.

I made a split-second decision. "I need to check something on my computer." Howard wasn't listening.

"What the fuck, Nathan? What the fuck is going on now? Why can't I get into my fucking computer?"

I wish I could've heard the other end of the conversation, but I had work to do.

"What the fuck does that mean? Where the hell is Kai? You can't be serious! These guys have it in for me. What do you mean it's out of your hands?" Cue the heart attack signs. No one ever said this job was for the faint of heart.

"Well, who the fuck is it about then? How do you not know? No, I will not just leave the premises. Are you fucking kidding?"

I opened my computer to the new file for the wives and all the new women who transferred money over the past few weeks. Inside was their contact information, addresses, Social Security numbers, emails, account numbers, and account statements. I compiled them in a folder, quickly hit copy, and emailed a copy to myself and one to my dad. Then I did the same for the SHINE men.

"You need to handle this now, Nathan. That's what we pay you for."

I pictured Nathan on the other end, attempting to be diplomatic. Reasonable. He had a knack for not losing his patience. I walked out of the office and caught sight of two security vehicles parking in front of the door. I motioned to Howard, who looked like he might hit someone. He hung up the phone just as I saw the security guards leave their cars.

"What's going on?" I asked.

"Nothing. Just a bunch of incompetent people. Nathan swears he doesn't know anything. He was with me in Washington and claims it has nothing to do with me. He's never lied to me, so I'm going to assume it's a technical glitch. Let's go."

We got off the elevator as the security guards entered the building.

"Morning, Mr. Gardner."

"Morning, Sy. Morning, Tom. Working on Saturday?" Howard flashed his usual *I'm in charge here* smile to the two uniformed men.

"We've been instructed not to let anyone in the offices today. Orders from the top guys."

"I am the top guy." Howard was flexing his muscle card.

"Sorry, Mr. Gardner. It's coming from the New York office. Just protocol, but you can't be here. Strict orders to notify the police if anyone resists."

"Is that a fact? Police?" Howard was getting overly defensive.

Instead, I grabbed his hand and said, "Let's go, honey. Don't let something stupid ruin our weekend. As they said, it's nothing."

Howard shook his head and said, "Someone's going to pay for this," and stormed off to his car.

It didn't take long, but he resumed his composure, kissed me goodbye before he dropped me off, and promised to call when he got back from Nashville.

THIRTY-FIVE

AFTER AFTER

There was commotion in the basement. I had slipped into sweats, eager to relax with a book, a cup of tea, and a few extra-strength Tylenols to ease my massive alcohol/sex/confession-induced headache. I had a lot of soul-searching to do. Maybe a rom-com and some chocolate-covered pretzels would do the trick. Asher was sleeping at Louis's this weekend, and I didn't expect him home until Sunday night. I thought Lily was still away for prom weekend.

"Hello?" I called downstairs, not sure if an intruder was in the house. There didn't seem to be any forced entry. Mrs. Pomerantz would surely have alerted me if she wasn't already down there with a bat in one hand and a bottle of mace in the other.

"Uh oh, Mom... can you come down here?"

I made my way down the basement steps, stopping halfway to see Asher standing in basketball shorts and a Syracuse T-shirt knee-deep in Howard's boxes, which had toppled over. Binders, folders, and papers were strewn everywhere.

"Why are you home? I thought you had plans with your father and Jackie."

"They had a blow-out fight. You don't want to know."

"You're right. I'm not interested. I told you I'd move the boxes. Couldn't you be patient?"

"Sorry, Mom, I thought I could move one or two out of the way and get a head start packing all my camp stuff. I didn't realize they were so heavy, and when I tried to move one, they all came crashing down."

"This is someone's private property. It's family heirlooms!" I cried, defending Howard's right to privacy. I hadn't snooped. He said the boxes were filled with private mementos, and I believed him.

"Chill out, Mom. I'm sorry. I'll pick it all up." It was hard to yell at him. He rarely gave me any trouble.

"That's not the point."

"I'll put it all back. It's not like anything is broken. Jeez. Don't be so touchy. It doesn't look like anything fragile to me." That was true. It didn't look like pictures or family heirlooms at all. All I saw were piles and piles of paper. I picked up a file. Across the top, it read "2015 Financial Statement: Violet and Gray."

Violet and Gray… what the? I sat down and opened another file. Inside were pages and pages of reports, looking very similar to the type of reports I was analyzing for trades. I reached for another box.

"Mom, are you going to sit on the floor and read, or are you going to help me clean up the mess?"

I stood up and said, "I'm so sorry, Ash… I'm going to need your help to get inside these boxes." My heart was beating a mile a minute.

Together, we spread out all the boxes on the basement floor.

Half of the boxes were labeled *Violet and Gray*. The other half said *VG Industries*. It didn't make any sense. Why would Howard have VG analysis out of the office? I lifted a binder out of a Violet and Gray box. The cover was beautiful, featuring the Violet and Gray logo from all those business cards. I turned to the next page and started reading. "Profit and loss statement by category. Table of Contents: GoGo Athlete. EyeMazing. FOREVER LIP. CBD NATION. SummerBods. GlamourMe. ShakeTown." I turned the page. Over a hundred companies, many of them I recognized as either past or present vendors from the café, meaning one thing: The Pyramid Girls.

Asher got what he needed and dragged his trunk upstairs, along with his sleeping bag and a duffel bag filled with camp necessities. I sat back down on the floor and started reading. Violet and Gray was the company Ivy mentioned, the one she claimed she should never have gotten involved with. The logo on all the boxes in Cara's garage. For the life of me, I couldn't understand why these documents stamped with the word *CONFIDENTIAL* were in my basement.

I had become an expert at deciphering these types of analyses. I just loved figuring out trading patterns. An hour later, I realized that Violet and Gray was nothing more than a holding company for all these individual businesses. They were listed with different line items, but make no mistake, all the profits went in and out of one company, Violet and Gray. This was not uncommon. Ivy alluded to this; the only way out of one company is through another. I didn't understand when she said it. Now it was starting to make sense, and I didn't like any of it.

One report listed Violet and Gray companies, which were now defunct, and another listed each time a defunct business was rebranded with a new name. The paper trail had a paper trail.

There were boxes of legal filings. Cease and desist orders. Court documents. Better Business Bureau complaints and fines for running supposed pyramid schemes. Ledgers of accounting pages showing journal entries with a series of numbers identifying where the money was deposited. Bank account statements from Zurich. I was fascinated. But I was also getting nauseous. Howard knew my disdain for these companies. Why in the world did he have their financial records?

The only thing between me and a complete meltdown was my quest to unravel the mess in front of me. I finally opened a box that said *VG Industries*. It took a few minutes to process, and then my hand flew to my mouth. I screamed, "NOOOOOO!" This couldn't be happening. But all the evidence was sitting in my hands. Violet and Gray *was* VG Industries, and as I already realized, VG Industries was nothing more than a shell company.

The profit and loss statements spelled it out. Vitamin Global was not the balance sheet-healthy company that the stockholders believed it was. The company I was trading, VG, was a Las Vegas entity. It was easy to access shell companies and then do a reverse merger instead of an initial public offering. There was less scrutiny. They could uplist to the NASDAQ later. According to the statements, there were no profits, only debt. That was the data I used as the basis for executing trades. I knew those numbers by heart, and they weren't even close to these reports.

I thought about the offices on the second floor that were cloaked in secrecy. When I asked Howard about them, he said it was just the document storage facility. He must have lied. They must have been printing fake reports.

Every line on the ledgers showed a loss. The SHINE group

was being scammed to the tune of hundreds of millions of dollars. Luckily, under Arbor's compliance rules, the traders weren't permitted to purchase the securities we suggested for SHINE without approval. Reese and I joked about how we only wished we could make as much money, but Arbor had access to our investment accounts, so there was no way around it. Thank God we didn't even try.

No wonder my record was a hundred percent. I was being spoon-fed fake information. I couldn't believe it. Dear, sweet Eddie was the Pyramid King. And by the looks of it, Howard was Prince Fucking Charming, and I was the court jester. Set up to look like a fool. It all meant one thing. Howard and Eddie were running a fraudulent organization and illegally trading on erroneous information. And whose finger was the one pressing the button on every one of those trades? Yours truly.

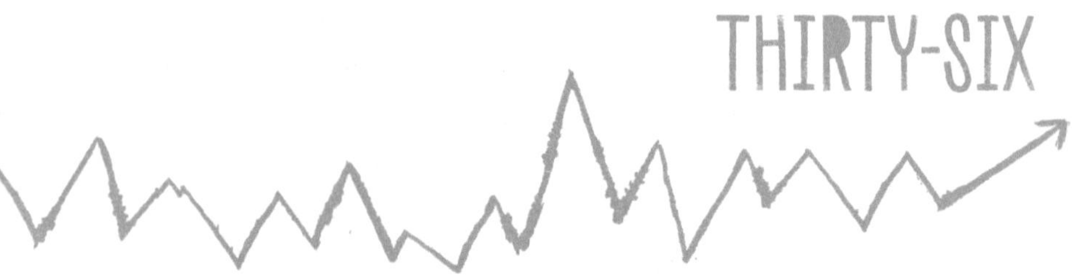

THIRTY-SIX

TELL ME LIES

I went upstairs and heard low talking coming from Lily's room. She wasn't due home until tomorrow. With Toby at UCLA and Lily going to Syracuse, their long-distance relationship was bound to be a challenge. I knew this was coming. I knocked gently.

"Don't come in."

"I'm coming in."

"I don't want to talk about it."

"How about just a hug?"

"Okay. Just one." I opened the door to see that Lily had taken all of her dance trophies off the bookshelves. The aqua blue sequined prom gown she had begged for was lying on the floor in a wrinkled heap. Lily's head was under her pillow, ruffled curls from her updo peeking out, and Asher was sitting on the edge of her bed.

"Why are you home?"

"Toby had an early flight." Asher was fidgeting with his phone and not looking at me.

"Who wants to tell me what's going on?"

"Jackie called off the engagement."

It took all of my energy not to laugh. "I see." I laughed anyway.

Asher joined in. "I don't understand why neither one of you can have a normal relationship."

"Oh, honey. There's no such thing as normal. Group hug and a Scrabble game?" Both kids enveloped me in a giant hug. I knew that no matter what else was going on, that right there was all that mattered.

I needed answers, and now I knew I couldn't trust Howard. It was time to take control of this situation before I was in a whole lot of trouble. I called Chadwick. He wasn't surprised to hear from me and wasted no time scheduling a meeting.

Lily was so upset about Louis and Jackie that she didn't notice the dark circles under my eyes. I spent the rest of the weekend explaining the situation to my father, who was positive I couldn't make any moves without a lawyer. I told him I emailed him a copy of all the accounts. "That's my girl!" he exclaimed.

My dad wasn't scheduled to fly in yet, but he could listen in and offer me guidance. It was time to bite the bullet. Peyton answered on the first ring.

"You're right. Snake charmer."

"What happened?"

"It hasn't happened yet. But it will be ugly. Sorry I doubted you."

"No problem, I'm used to it."

"I'll be at the café tomorrow morning for a meeting. If you and Cara have a few minutes for coffee, I'll fill you in. Or you can wait and see it all rehashed on TMZ," I joked.

"I'll see if I can juggle around some clients. And Leah?"

"Yes?"

"Told you so."

Chadwick was waiting for me in one of the café's private rooms. I arrived to see him nursing a cup of piping-hot green tea, his relaxed manner making this all a little easier. This time, I felt empowered and confident. I wouldn't be blindsided like last time. Chadwick was wearing tweed again, despite the June heat, and looked as though he should be smoking a pipe. He rose to greet me, and unfortunately, sitting next to him was Deenie Gardner, perfectly proper in a robin's egg blue Chanel blazer that matched her eyes, a white T-shirt, and a set of pearls.

"I'm sorry," I stammered. "But I thought this was a private legal meeting."

"Yes, ma'am. It is. But I think you should hear the information that Ms. Gardner would like to share."

I looked at Deenie sheepishly, guilt splattered across my face. There wasn't much I could say to her. She held her neck high, adding to her conviction in the shitstorm about to happen.

"I'd like to have my attorney on the phone while we talk."

"Absolutely."

I put my phone on the table and pressed the speaker icon. My father was already on the other end. "Your card says SEC Whistleblower Division. I'm not sure what you're looking for. The last time we spoke, you were evasive but mentioned VG Industries."

"There have been multiple attempts by an anonymous whistleblower to have us look into Mr. Gardner's interest and trade history with VG Industries. Originally, we didn't take the accusations seriously."

I nodded my head to acknowledge that I was listening. "Mmmm hmmm."

"Are you sharing your trades with anyone?"

"Excuse me?"

"Arbor's not the only brokerage house investing in VG. However, the trades are almost identical."

"I don't understand."

"We don't either. That's what we're trying to get to the bottom of."

"Why do you think Howard's involved?" I played it coy. My father instructed me to let them do most of the talking.

"We think he's the mastermind behind it. But we don't believe he's working alone. He didn't make the trades. You did. Someone at another firm is making identical trades to yours. We've been tracking them. Whatever you do, they copy you. Whatever you invest, they invest more. It's been going on for months."

I felt my face get hot. I took a drink of water. "I don't know anything about another firm copying my trades. That seems impossible."

"Leah, I think you should know something very important about your position at Arbor," Deenie spoke calmly and very softly. Her voice was soothing, like a lullaby, not someone who was out for vengeance.

I jumped in defensively, "I told you before, it was my idea to work there. Howard had confided in me about a possible SEC inquiry; it's over now, the case was dropped. I'm sure you already know that, but I thought maybe I could help out if he had a temporary suspension. I could trade for him. It seemed like a good idea at the time. I don't know what I was thinking. I didn't want to get anyone in trouble. And the divorce. He didn't want to upset you after, you know, your issues when you had to go away for a bit. To Nashville. He said you were so fragile. That's why he couldn't cancel the vacation."

"What are you talking about?"

"Look, Deenie. I'm sorry. Many people struggle with, you know, mental health."

"Mental health? Me?"

"He said you had to go back to Nashville for a tune-up."

"A tune-up? He said I needed a tune-up? And you believed him?"

"Well, since you suffer from—"

Deenie let out an uncharacteristic belly laugh and an inelegant snort. "Oh, sweetie, I'm not the one with mental problems. My sister lives in Nashville. So does Chadwick. And my mom, who hasn't been well." I saw Chadwick stare at her lovingly. "Tune-up. That's a good one. And cancel what vacation? Howard surprised me with the Turks and Caicos vacation on my birthday. In October. It wasn't scheduled before."

"It wasn't?" I put my hands up to my face and closed my eyes. "He said you were planning to separate years ago, and then you got pregnant with Addison." I opened my eyes. "So he stayed. But... I wouldn't have..." I was babbling now.

"WHAT? Leah? Do you know how old I am?"

I shook my head.

"Howard wanted another baby after his dad died. We had Addison by surrogate."

"I... oh my God..." Who lies about that?

"Let's get back to your position. Are you sure it was all your idea?" Chadwick asked.

I clasped my hands together, white appearing from my knuckles. "I mean, he had been telling me for months how smart he thought I was and how well I would do in the business; it was kind of an ongoing joke between us. But I had to convince him to work there. Not the other way around."

"At our last meeting, you were adamant that Mr. Gardner was not involved."

"I may have stumbled upon some documents."

"Does Mr. Gardner know you're here?"

"Oh God, no. Definitely not. Look, I don't want to be implicated in anything. My intentions were good when I got the job. I was ready for a change, a second act, you know what it's like… empty nest syndrome, and then, the timing, it all just happened simultaneously. And the offer on my business was too good to pass up. It seemed like it was meant to be. I'm not interested in being a whistleblower. I can't be responsible for getting Howard in trouble, but I don't want to take the blame for something I wasn't aware of. I want to get out and get back to my life." I was talking too fast and saying too much.

Chadwick nodded his head. "Ms. Samuels, innocent does not always mean not guilty."

My father interrupted from the speakerphone. "Leah, let them finish. Mr. Turner, we seek immunity in exchange for information Leah can provide to help your case. But it's clear she's strictly following directions given to her by her superiors."

Chadwick looked at Deenie and nodded. Deenie reached into her oversized Hermés, this one a pale blue to match her jacket, and pulled out a large envelope.

"About that offer to buy your business," Deenie said.

I stared at Deenie, perplexed.

"I told you, I sold to Daniel Ross, the DJ. He had investors. Why does that have anything to do with this?" My voice cracked.

"Leah, let's hear what they have to say," my father interjected.

Deenie continued, "I was reviewing our checking accounts and financial information for the divorce attorney." Her eyes met mine. Nine figures, Cara had said. *Nine.* It took all my strength to keep my composure. "Anyway, I came across numerous checks written to Daniel for Addison's Bat Mitzvah. I remembered Howard saying that the check was written out of the wrong account and that he had to write a new one. There was so much money going out of the accounts at that time that I didn't pay much attention. He handles a lot of the finances." I gasped, remembering the bounced check Howard had written to me. The one he blamed on his assistant. The check that started this all.

"But I inquired with the bank; there weren't any returned checks to DJ by Design or Daniel. Everything cleared."

"So, what does that have to do with me?"

"Do you know how much Daniel charges?"

"It depends on the package."

"Forty thousand dollars. The deluxe package. In other words, the 'can't say no to your daughter' package."

"Wow."

"Yes. Wow. But, you see, I have checks that cleared for more than ten times that amount. Some of them were written six months after the Bat Mitzvah."

"I'm not following you."

Deenie opened the envelope and dumped photocopies of the canceled checks onto the table. She looked through the pile and pulled out six checks, three written out to Daniel for one hundred thousand dollars, and five checks written out for fifty thousand each. She handed them to me. "Can you explain this?"

I looked at the checks. For the second time in forty-eight hours, I felt like I was punched in the gut. My name was on the memo on the bottom of the checks. I could hear my father's heavy sigh through the phone. I began to catalog my thoughts. I looked from Deenie to Chadwick and back to Deenie again. Their faces waited for me to process it.

Deenie said, "We did a little snooping with a private investigator. It seems super DJ Daniel has money problems, namely, a huge gambling addiction. He has bookies all over the country. Especially in Las Vegas. Even his deluxe package wasn't enough to get him out of this much debt."

"Daniel, a gambler? But how could you know that? And why would Howard care about getting him out of debt?"

"It seems our friend Daniel bet on everything. He was a regular at the casinos. He was probably doing online betting from his phone at Addison's Bat Mitzvah. It's quite common. The investigator's research proved he was well acquainted with Eddie through some unsavory people from his Vegas days. As some would say, Daniel doesn't have a pot to piss in. We think Eddie and Howard paid off his debts, paid him to buy you out, set up a shell company, and voilá, they have the perfect scenario to bring you in." Great, another shell company.

"Go on, show her the rest," Chadwick said.

Deenie slid a pile of copies of newspaper articles across the table. I recognized them immediately. They were about me. "Howard had these in his office drawer."

I was puzzled. "But why?"

"What can I say, Leah? He's a savage. He sees something he wants, and he goes after it. This time it was you."

"You mean the whole thing was a setup?" I felt a stab over my left eye.

"I'm not sure. I know he was enamored with you after the connection with your mom. He probably thought he was helping you."

"He was so wonderful to my mom. To a stranger. What he did was just so selfless."

"That's the Howard I fell in love with, too." Deenie looked at me wistfully. "But he's not that person anymore. He hasn't been for a long time."

I thought about throwing up in her Hermés bag. If I positioned myself just right, I could do it and not get any in my hair. Now, that would be a twenty-thousand-dollar statement. But it wouldn't solve anything. The early months of our affair washed over me. Howard's laissez-faire attitude when I mentioned I didn't have to negotiate the sale.

I thought about Daniel. The ten-year-old Kia. The trip to Atlantic City. Something about lady luck. Kenny Rogers.

I shifted my memory to Howard's plan to make the divorce look like Deenie's idea. He wouldn't look like the bad guy. It was all part of his supposed plan. He played me the same way, planted the seed that I was cut out for the business early on. How many times did he tell me how great it would be if we worked together? His perfect plan. Then mine. It had worked like a charm.

"Why would he do this?"

"For starters, you probably knew too much. Howard has a habit of bragging and eventually putting his foot in his mouth. You know, the old keep your friends close scenario. But Howard has to be the hero. He's a brilliant businessman. He always had the golden touch, but don't be fooled; he's the king of manipulation. Howard cherry-picks his associates and grooms them for his benefit. Classic narcissist. You're smart. He trusted you. Anything else was the cherry on the top for him. I'm sure he had feelings for you…" Deenie looked at me sympathetically, "Maybe does have feelings… but you were an easy target. I know his Modus Operandi."

I felt my face turn scarlet. A picture of Leopard-Lovin' Staci flashed in front of me, and I wondered if she had been an easy target, too. If it were possible to shrink into invisibility, now would've been the time.

"So now what?" I could hear my father scribbling notes on his legal pad. He probably already had a list of attorneys for me.

Chadwick said, "We need to know if you're on board. We'll give you specific instructions on what to do. We have the authority to block the trades on the other end. We're close. We need just a few more pieces of information to make a move. You may need to wear a wire."

"A wire? No. Daddy?"

"It may be necessary, sweetheart."

Chadwick interrupted. "What type of documents do you have?"

"Full immunity?" my father reiterated.

"Full immunity," Chadwick confirmed.

If I had any trepidation about this before, it had miraculously disappeared. The past few days had become a perfect storm of events, setting the wheels in motion at a speed I couldn't have calculated. Howard's confession was troubling. And this whole new set of accusations. The VG connection to Violet and Gray was shocking. I figured out the whole sordid operation was set up in Vegas, the breeding ground for this type of sham. The old investors were paid off with money from the new investments. Classic pyramid.

"Can you tell me who the whistleblower is?"

"I'm sorry. That's confidential."

I wished I could talk to Barry about this. However, seeing my name on those checks sealed the deal, unleashed a furor in me, and signified the end of this relationship. That part was inevitable. I no longer believed this was purely Deenie seeking revenge. But I needed to know one more thing.

"Deenie, why are you helping me?"

Deenie took hold of Chadwick's hand. Their eyes twinkled. They looked like newlyweds. "Because I know what it's like to make a mistake."

I couldn't figure out why she was on my side. Maybe I never would. There was no room for magical thinking. I had to make a choice. My choice was to be brave. Use my power. Because honestly, what other choice did I have?

Oh, and to nail the motherfucker.

THIRTY-SEVEN

FOREVER AFTER

We stood up to leave, and the stabbing pain over my eye increased. I knew a migraine was brewing. I had forgotten I had asked Peyton and Cara to meet me, and I almost walked past them. Cara jumped up from the table; her face broke into a radiant smile.

"Oh, dear Lord, as I live and breathe," she said in her hometown slang. "Chad! What a fabulous surprise! What in God's green earth are you doing up north?"

I looked behind me to see who she was talking to, but the person wasn't behind me; he was in front of me. She was talking to Chadwick. Now, I was utterly lost. My feet felt glued to the floor.

"Peyton, Leah, this is Chad. Chad Turner. From Nashville. Chad, you're a sight for sore eyes! I haven't seen you in, gosh, how long has it been? You're looking dapper, as always. How are you, sugar?"

Peyton was warm and friendly, accepting the introduction but much more focused on why I was standing between Cara's old friend from Nashville and the soon-to-be ex-wife of my alleged soon-to-be ex-boyfriend. I was speechless. Again.

Chad gave Cara a perfunctory kiss on the cheek. His demeanor changed from Chadwick Turner, SEC Attorney, to Chad, long-lost friend of Cara's. "I'm well, Cara, dear. It's so nice to see you. I was so sorry to hear about Johnny's accident."

Cara smiled sweetly, "Aww. Thank you. What brings you here?"

"Official business." He dropped his voice to a whisper. "Top secret stuff." He winked.

"Well, if you're involved, everyone must be in good hands," Cara said proudly.

"I'd love to stay and chat; however, I'm on the clock with an investigation. Perhaps we can find a time to catch up, but unfortunately, it will have to be next time. Please tell your parents I said hello." His face was gentle. If he wore a hat, he would have tipped it. "Ladies," he said as he walked away.

Deenie walked in front of me, removed the sunglasses that had migrated back to her face, and smiled at Peyton. I realized they'd never met.

"Hi, Adena. I love your jacket."

"Hi, Cara. Thanks. So good to see you." She put her sunglasses back on and followed Chadwick out the door. I slid into the booth next to Cara and Peyton, staking my claim on their friendship.

"What the hell was that?" Peyton demanded, her brain hard at work putting a hundred different psychological analyses on the scene she'd just witnessed.

"Wow. Chad Turner." Cara was still gushing.

"Who wants to go first? I've got clients waiting."

"Me, but first, Cara, I can't believe you know Chadwick. You know he's an investigator for the Securities and Exchange Commission?"

"Of course I know. He began as an investigator at his father's firm. Then switched to the SEC. My daddy sends me articles about Chad all the time. And Chadwick may use his formal name for business reasons, but he's just Chad to me. His daddy goes by Chadwick. I told you about him. That's the Chad that Adena dated at Vanderbilt. I told you he never got over her. I guess she finally forgave him."

This whole crazy affair just got smaller. Chad and Deenie, or Adena or whatever her name was, were in cahoots. Eddie and Howard were in cahoots. And where did that leave me? In the middle of a sleazy mess.

"Why were you meeting with an SEC attorney?"

"We're going to need a refill on the coffee. But first, I'm so sorry." I began telling Peyton and Cara what was going on, no secrets this time. Every. Dirty. Detail.

There's no manual for admitting to your kids that you're in the middle of a potential scandal. I decided that preparing them for the worst was the best option. I cooked one of their favorite dinners—a chicken and rice dish that my grandmom used to make.

"So, unfortunately, there may be some illegal activity at the firm. I may have made a mistake accepting a job at Arbor. It's the beauty of getting older. You admit your mistakes, make changes, and move on."

"Can I write another article?"

"Not yet." I must cancel the reporter that I scheduled.

"Does it have something to do with all those boxes in the basement?"

"Yes."

"Is this going to affect my going to Syracuse?"

"My lack of judgment will never derail your future. There could be fallout from some developments at work. However, I'm working with the right people to extricate myself from the situation. And I'd appreciate it if you didn't discuss this with your father."

"Okay, cool," they said in unison.

"Also, I won't be seeing Howard anymore."

Lily and Asher looked at each other and burst out laughing. Lily spoke, "Seriously, Mom, he's so not your type. Too flashy." Maybe they were more intuitive than I gave them credit for.

Lily said, "I guess the Scrabble thing was just a coinky-dink, as Grandpop would say".

"Just a coinky-dink." Clusterfuck.

Asher chimed in, "So I guess we lost two potential stepparents this week."

"I suppose so."

"What about my graduation party?"

"The party's still on." My dad was flying in first, followed by Mitchell, his family, and Rachel. A family celebration just in time for my world to fall apart.

THE CALM

Having Peyton and Cara on my side was the equivalent of a twelve-step program of accountability. Cara swooped in with her swift accounting mentality and helped me sift through the files, shedding light on the details I glossed over. We didn't speak about her Violet and Gray obsession. I think our friendship could only handle one screw-up at a time. Peyton took care of my vacillating brain, wrestling with whether to give Howard the benefit of the doubt. My anger fueled my decision-making process, making it easier to supply Chadwick with the information he needed to move the investigation along.

I went into the office every day and spent hours meeting with Vivian. I scribbled notes as she regaled me with stories of how she worked as a receptionist at a brokerage house in the sixties, and how her friendship with Muriel Siebert, the first woman to be allowed a seat on the New York Stock Exchange, influenced her career decisions. Vivian, like Muriel, was the lone woman in a crowded sea of male counterparts. She spoke of corporate raiders, criminals, and market crashes, all events she witnessed firsthand over the last sixty-plus years. It was *Mad Men* for Wall Street, but she survived despite it all. Her tenacity only made her more successful. I wished I had met her sooner.

"You certainly were a trailblazer, Vivian."

"The thing is," Vivian said, an unlit cigarette dangling from her crimson lips (she never actually lit them), "Women are resilient, like the market. They both will always bounce back. You need to know how to remain calm in between bounces."

It was a shame that no one realized the true legend there was Vivian.

Sergeant BadAss must have told Howard about my Vivian meetings because he questioned why I was spending so much time with the "old bag." I told him that Nathan instructed me to talk to her about Women's SHINE, and he backed off.

I kept my calls with Howard short and sweet, never letting on that anything was amiss. Thankfully, he was delayed in Nashville, so I didn't have to keep the façade up in person. The Nashville Stroke Clinic was merging with the Gardner Stroke Center, the beginning of a conglomerate of state-of-the-art stroke centers, and most importantly, another feather in Howard's cap and a nod to his commitment to honor his father. As Howard explained the details, his words dripped with exuberance. I considered allowing him the opportunity to explain himself, dispute the allegations, but deep down, I finally realized that he would only tell me what I wanted to hear, and none of it would be truthful.

I wasn't sure what would result from the information I provided to Chadwick, or even if they had a valid case. I understood that these matters could take years, and similar to the Banyan case, there was a chance that it would simply fade away. Chadwick reassured me that it wouldn't happen. I knew I needed to leave Arbor and distance myself from Howard sooner rather than later. My career was even shorter than Peyton joked about.

On Friday, Beau and Reese packed up early to get a head start on traffic to the Hamptons. I realized how much I would miss Reese. But, in a few years, he probably wouldn't remember the old lady who sat next to him. We had gotten close, but I didn't dare tell him my plans or about the unscrupulous behavior brewing. He wasn't happy I wasn't sitting at my desk all day, but when I was, if he looked closely at my screen, he'd see I was checking out the Friends and Family sale at Bloomingdale's.

Beau pulled out his phone to show me pictures of the house they rented in the Hamptons. It looked like an ad in *Town & Country*.

"You and the big man have to come up for a weekend. We'll give you the VIP treatment." Reese had figured out about my relationship with Howard. He was sworn to secrecy, although I was pretty sure the whole office suspected it by now.

"I'll check my calendar and break out the old tennis racket," I replied, faking enthusiasm, knowing Howard and I would never be gracing their guest room in the Hamptons. Or anywhere.

As Reese and Beau headed for the door, Nathan appeared, reminding us there'd be a mandatory meeting on Monday morning. Howard was scheduled to be back on Sunday. I knew I'd have to decide when I would resign. And I'd have to tell Vivian first.

Nathan was looking rather tired, and I wondered how much he knew. Unless, of course, he was the whistleblower. It seemed unlikely, but transparency could be subjective, and I was learning that nothing was how it appeared, especially in this business. My mind constantly changed as to who the whistleblower could be.

Right down to quiet, unassuming Zoe, who handled each day like it was a transcendental meditation retreat. She seemed way too calm for this business.

"Guess I'm coming home Sunday night. So much for an early Monday morning run on the beach," Reese said, throwing his BMW keys up in the air and catching them.

"I'll get a ride home. I'm not giving up my Monday morning run," replied Beau.

"Have fun. Don't forget the sunscreen," I called after them, evoking a laugh from Reese.

"Thanks, Mamacita."

Summer Fridays were a perk I never enjoyed in the party business and one I had eagerly looked forward to. The majority of our work slowed down by mid-afternoon, and nobody raised an eyebrow if you left early. Even Sergeant BadAss, who had unpacked a new suitcase of dirty looks, had taken the day off.

I walked to Barry's office, stopping at the door to listen to him sing a few bars from "Angie." He meshed into an instrumental solo, looking up from his guitar during the part that was about the dreams we held close.

"Have a good weekend, Barry."

"Gig in Asbury with D-man. You should come!"

"Maybe next week." I smiled.

Barry played a few more random chords on his guitar and said, "Leah, dry your tears…"

Suddenly, an urgent email notification from Chadwick appeared on my phone. There was an unexpected turn of events. I read it twice. An affidavit. Another witness. It was the beginning of the end.

THIRTY-NINE

STILL CALM

As the wheels of Howard's plane touched down, Chadwick and his men loaded the last of the contents of the boxes from my basement into their black Escalades. Howard texted: Can't wait to see you. More surprises are coming. XO

I texted back Sounds great. The less I said, the better.

My father had arrived and was outside conversing with Chadwick. I could see Mrs. Pomerantz watching from her second-floor window, thinking they were filming an episode of *Law & Order*. My father shook Chadwick's hand. I had provided what they believed was crucial evidence. There was no turning back now.

There were hundreds of cases against Violet and Gray, and their unscrupulous practices. Everyone knew someone who worked for one of these companies. They were as ubiquitous as the Starbucks on the corner, appealing to a similar demographic. It was hip. Scores of women, mostly financially strapped, wanted to control their destiny and become independently wealthy. The company preyed on women, but the promise of so much quick money often brought the husbands in, too. People re-mortgaged their houses, thinking this investment would provide them with years of income. Although some products were legitimate, the sales tactics were not; they preyed on consumers and owners alike. Promises of wealth and wellness surreptitiously captured the essence of what the masses were seeking.

"You know," my father said, "I found boxes of lipsticks stashed away years after Mom died. She was obsessed."

"I just wanted a little time with her. She prioritized her customers over her kids."

"We had plenty of arguments about that. It was important for her to have a job. It was the seventies—women didn't just start businesses by themselves—not like you did. No one understood the multi-level marketing pitfalls back then."

"How about the pitfalls of ignoring your kids? I didn't have a choice, Dad. She did."

"Don't be so hard on her. She did the best she could. She'd be so proud of you."

I kissed my dad on the cheek and said, "I hope so."

The multi-level business model never changed. With Violet and Gray, millions of dollars were made by those at the top, allowing VG Industries to siphon the profits into a shell company operating at a deficit. It was deception wrapped in a beautiful Violet and Gray bow.

My decision to turn over Howard's boxes was just one of the missing pieces of the puzzle. The investigation was more complicated than I could have imagined.

FORTY

THE STORM

It was a typical Monday morning, with an hour to go before the stock market opened. The air conditioning was on full blast, the TV blaring with CNBC's Andrew Ross Sorkin highlighting economic events over the past two days as we gathered in our usual cliques, sipping coffee, noshing on our favorite bagel, and discussing our weekends. At 8:45, Nathan called Reese, Barry, Brent, and me into the conference room. Howard's shades were drawn, implying he was in a private meeting.

"Effective immediately, we're taking a break from trading on VG Industries pending internal accounting issues. R&D is reviewing some new biotech companies that have recently come off private equity."

"Got it, boss. Whatever you say. Do you need my help on another team? Does Howard need another assistant?" Brent never stopped kissing up. Today, he wore a pale-blue quilted vest over a white polo, the summer version of his finance bro uniform. Brent tried to be likable; his comprehension of the industry was impressive, but he still reminded me of an unfortunate kid who once upon a time was stuffed in a gym locker.

"I've got a lot riding on these VG trades. Are there any exceptions?" Reese looked annoyed.

Nathan responded abruptly. "Two-week break. Minimum. No exceptions for anyone. Thanks to Barry, we have some new institutional business coming into the firm."

I smiled at Barry in appreciation as he flashed me a peace sign and a smile. The meeting was adjourned before 9 am.

When I got back to my desk, Reese pulled out a small box of cinnamon rugelach, fresh from a new bakery he found in the Hamptons over the weekend.

"You spoil me," I said.

"Just trying to bring a smile to your face. You seem stressed."

"I'm fine," I lied.

A few minutes after nine, a slight woman with tight brown curls, circular glasses, and a PRESS badge walked up to Beth-Ann's desk. I thought I heard my name, but I also heard a disturbance coming from the main reception desk. At that moment, I noticed the *Garnet Springs Press* logo on her mermaid green Hydro Flask. Shit. Miriam. The reporter assigned to Lily's story. I never canceled the interview. Before I could react, BethAnn's body leaped from her desk, banging into Miriam so hard the Hydro Flask hit the floor with a clanging that vibrated through the office. I didn't think BethAnn had it in her to move like that. Nathan ran out of the conference room, spilling his coffee on his polo and almost tripping over his loafers. Barry slowly opened his door to see what was transpiring, still munching on a poppy seed bagel. Howard's shades flew up,

and I saw him and two men I didn't recognize stand to attention. He picked up his phone and quickly put it in his pocket.
My heart headed into a tailspin. You don't fall out of love with
someone in a couple of days. I tried to get his attention, but he
never looked in my direction. The noise got louder, and suddenly, Zoe uncharacteristically screamed, "Oh my God! We're
on CNBC!"

I looked at the TV screen and saw the BREAKING NEWS
headline. The FBI vans circled the front entrance to our building.
A tall man in a CNBC jacket announced he was reporting live
from the Arbor offices outside of Philadelphia. I struggled to hear
the details amid the chaos in the office.

Another reporter announced loudly, "I'm Quinn Summers
outside Arbor Financial. The Department of Justice has just converged and is sweeping the office for records regarding an ongoing insider trading investigation." There was no time to react. A
group of DOJ agents swarmed our office within seconds.

The lead agent, a burly red-headed man with a matching mustache, spoke: "Ladies and gentlemen, please stay where you are
and step back from your terminals."

Nathan, looking more in charge than usual, said, "Do what
you're told. We have nothing to hide. This is routine and will be
over quickly." He took a handkerchief out of his back pocket and
wiped his brow.

Sergeant BethAnn, on the verge of hysterics, leaped into action again and tried to use her blazer to block the agents from getting into Howard's office. They held up some official documents,
and she reluctantly stepped aside.

Barry shook his head as if he had seen this all before, and
it was nothing more than a nuisance interrupting his morning

routine of reading *Rolling Stone*. He looked at me, concerned, and mouthed, "Are you okay?"

I shrugged my shoulders.

I tried to get Howard's attention again, standing on my tiptoes and waving my hand, but he wouldn't look at me. I was slowly giving up wearing high heels, finally choosing ballet flats for the office, and thought maybe he just couldn't see me. Howard was standing firm in front of his door, stone-faced. Several agents were inside his office.

Reese leaned over and said, "Jeez, who do you think did something shady? Or maybe Barry's office is getting raided for weed."

"No idea," I offered. "But I feel like I'm having an out-of-body experience. I can't stop shaking."

"Keep calm," Reese said. "I've seen this stuff go down before. It's usually nothing. Or a disgruntled client who lost too much money."

I glanced at the TV screen again, and it looked like there were an equal number of FBI agents upstairs in our accounting offices. I wondered if Leopard-Lovin' Staci was involved. Several agents were carrying boxes. I couldn't believe this was happening. Was it all because of me? I had no idea the SEC investigation was this close. I didn't think it was possible to plow through the evidence and get a search warrant this fast. I narrowed my eyes, trying to see the screen better. I thought I saw Dylan crouching next to an FBI van. No. It couldn't be.

As I watched the activity unfold simultaneously on TV and a few feet away, two DOJ agents spoke to BethAnn again, showing her a stack of papers. She reviewed them, turned around, scanned the room, and pointed at me. Her eyes were seething with revenge. Howard was watching. Why wasn't he doing anything to come to my rescue?

The DOJ agents made their way over to my terminal. Now, I was visibly sweating. I felt burning pains in my chest. I silently cursed Chadwick Turner and Deenie for double-crossing me, pretending they were on my side to get information. Didn't my dad say immunity? I had incriminated myself. I can't believe I trusted them. I couldn't go to jail. I had to take care of my kids. I wouldn't make it in prison. What in the world had I done? WHY WASN'T HOWARD COMING TO HELP ME?

The agents got to my desk, and I started to cry so hard I didn't realize they kept walking, and stopped at Reese's desk instead.

"Reese Hollander?" the red-headed man asked.

"Yes, sir. What can I do for you?"

The second agent, a portly woman with an earpiece and hair tightly secured in a topknot, revealed a set of handcuffs. "Reese Hollander, you're under arrest for suspicion of insider trading. You have the right to remain silent. Anything you say can and will be used against you in a court of law. You have the right to an attorney. If you cannot afford an attorney, one will be appointed for you."

I got hot and cold simultaneously and was convinced I was having a stroke. Oh, the irony. What were they talking about? Reese? Insider trading? It wasn't Reese. They had it all wrong. I wanted to shout *No! You've got the wrong guy!*

But Reese didn't resist. He nodded a few times in agreement and slowly pivoted so the red-headed agent could put handcuffs on him. When he finished, he turned around, winked at me, and said, "Take care of yourself, Mamacita."

"This is a mistake. Reese? Tell them! Tell them it's a mistake!" I was shrieking.

He shook his head as his shoulders slumped.

"Would you look at that?" Zoe announced loudly. "Hey, don't we know that guy?"

Everyone looked up at the screen. BREAKING NEWS had switched to a stately house in the Hamptons, where FBI agents had also arrived with a warrant for Beau's arrest. Beau, still wearing his running shorts and a sweat-laced Harvard T-shirt, was handcuffed without incident.

I turned back to Reese. "Why?" I asked in shock.

"For ZuZu," he said. As Reese was led out of the office, two agents wearing rubber gloves disconnected his computer and carried it out to black and white heavily marked vans. No one spoke; each of us was lost in confusion, our eyes now glued to Jim Cramer reporting the NASDAQ was plunging today and digesting the fact that Arbor Financial was national news.

Finally, Nathan said, "Please stay calm and return to work. I assure you that this is an isolated incident. And please, under any circumstances, do not give any statements to the media."

I wiped away the rest of my tears. If one more person said to remain calm, I was going to scream. My eyes searched for Howard, who had disappeared back into his office. I took in the scene. The finance bros were either staring at their terminals or gawking at their phones. It would take more than an FBI raid to rattle them. I told myself I was never stepping foot back in this office, grabbed my pocketbook, threw in the picture of my dad and kids, along with my box of rugelach, because rugelach should never go to waste, walked over to Sergeant BadAss, and said, "I won't be reachable." I didn't give her a chance to answer and deliberately strolled to Barry's office.

Pearl Jam was playing. Barry met me at the door and hugged

me. "Don't let the unthought known get you, kid."

"Story of my life," I said.

I looked around for the newspaper reporter, and she was nowhere to be found. Talk about a lucky break. I walked down the corridor to Vivian's office. Her back was to me, but I heard the ice clinking in her glass. She turned slowly. "Ah, looks like I'll need a double today. What doesn't kill you makes you stronger." Vivian took a long sip of her drink. "Leah, dear, you're as white as a ghost. Why don't you take a break, and we'll resume our talks in a few days?"

I nodded my head in silence. "Know your power," Vivian said as I stepped away.

I'd have to find a way to talk to Vivian and figure out what to do next. And if Howard wanted to talk to me, which, based on his reluctance to align with me during the showdown, seemed doubtful, he'd have to come to my turf.

A four-minute walk to my car, and already twelve texts appeared on my phone. Two from each kid, one from Peyton, one from Cara, surprisingly one from Ivy, who had seen the breaking news on TV, one from the *Garnet Springs Press*, two from my dad, one from Chadwick, and one from Howard, sent three seconds ago.

Don't be upset. Talk later. Love you.

I ignored the texts, hit the curb, before switching my car to reverse, and cranked up my seventies station just in time to hear Helen Reddy sing that she was a woman and knew too much to go back to pretend.

CHARGING BULL

By the time I pulled into my driveway, I was traumatized. My breathing was unsteady, and I wasn't sure I had the strength to get out of my car. My father, anticipating my reaction, was waiting to walk me inside. He had already spoken to Chadwick and had the lowdown on Reese. In retrospect, it was a brilliant plan, although I don't know how he thought he'd get away with it. The SEC had been monitoring Reese and Beau for months, connecting them through school records and social media. I learned that my unbeaten record of trading on Howard's information was the impetus for their scheme. Arbor's compliance policy required us to disclose trades we made personally and forbade us from buying securities deemed a conflict of interest.

Reese and Beau established a limited liability company unknown to Arbor's compliance department. The original plan was to mimic my trades. I willingly shared information with Reese. He also had my password to get into my computer. Reese knew I had access to confidential information, and he shared my trades with Beau. Technically, copying my trades was just immoral, not illegal. But it opened up a cache of trades they made that all came from insiders. Beau had deciphered the information I mentioned that was not yet publicly available. I never thought he'd use it to make illegal transactions.

Beau and Reese had agreed to invest a small amount of money and split the profits fifty-fifty. However, greed ultimately got the better of them, and the small trades quickly turned into hundred-thousand-dollar trades, using margin to leverage their bets. Together, they netted two million dollars in less than six months.

In addition to the joint account, Reese had, in a slimy attempt to undercut Beau, opened a second LLC at another brokerage house, also far from the eyes of Arbor's compliance department, yielding him an additional half a million dollars. Not bad for two guys in their twenties.

So, in a nutshell, Howard was using my naivety to place excessive trades, knowing the information was false, while Reese was using my *lucky streak* to line his own pockets. I was, inexplicably, the vital link between Howard and Reese.

Howard called three times, leaving messages begging me to pick up the phone. Peyton sat in my kitchen, helping me eat what was now known as the two-million-dollar rugelach. My dad was in the family room, taking selfies with my kids. Not surprisingly, the Maserati appeared in my driveway a few minutes before six. I met Howard outside. Mrs. Pomerantz was going to need to take her heart medicine.

"Jesus, Leah, I've been worried sick about you. Why aren't you answering my calls?" He reached in to hug me, but I stayed firmly planted on my feet, arms crossed, still rehearsing every-thing I planned to say. "What's the matter? You're not mad at me, are you? I have so much exciting stuff to tell you. This morning was scary, but it's just business. Hopefully, you won't have to wit-ness that ever again."

"What's the matter? Seriously? *You're* asking me what's the matter?"

"Honey, calm down. These things happen. Reese will get what he deserves. But it's a first offense. He's young. He'll work things out."

"These things?" I could barely get the words out.

"The guy has a lot of balls. Insider trading on my confidential information." A slip of incredulous laughter emerged from How-ard's mouth. The only logical thing I could think of was that How-ard was a psychopath. He didn't believe this had anything to do with him.

"What's the matter? Where do I start? Let me ask you some-thing. Did you plan this all from the beginning? At what point did you decide to make me your patsy? Before or after you fucked me?" My eyes seethed with anger.

"Plan what? I don't have any idea what you're talking about." He stepped back.

"Don't lie to me, Howard. I found out it was you who bought my business. Did you think I wouldn't find out? It's like you own me! I'm like one of your stocks. Did you think you could buy me and sell me at your whim? You used me. God, I can't believe I fell for this."

"Leah, please, I didn't use you. I thought I was helping you out. I thought I was doing you a favor." Deenie was right. Classic narcissist. Why did it take me so long to see it?

"By getting me involved with your illegal trading scams?"

"There's nothing illegal. Maybe Reese and Beau were doing something illegal, but they have nothing to do with us. You'd think you'd be grateful. Look at everything I did for you. You've got money to pay for college. You don't need to sit at home baking cakes and fiddling with papier-mâché. You've got better clothes. I was going to get you out of this crappy neighborhood and into a life of luxury. I loved you. You should be thanking me."

"There's nothing wrong with my neighborhood! Or my job! Or my clothes! Or anything else about me, for that matter! The only thing wrong in my life is you! You played me for a fool."

"You're looking at it wrong. I suppose Daniel confessed to you. I knew the kid couldn't be trusted. I'm sorry I didn't tell you. Eddie knew Daniel from his buddies in Vegas. That boy's a serious gambler. He would've had his knees broken and lost what little he had left if we hadn't bailed him out. This allowed him to set himself right. He kept his business going instead of gambling away thousands of dollars a week. And look what it did for you."

"Were you going to tell me?"

"Sure. When the time was right."

"What about VG and Violet and Gray?"

"What about them?"

"They're the same company!" My throat hurt from screaming.

"So what? Lots of companies are subsidiaries of other companies."

I thought about this for a minute. Was I losing my mind for nothing? Was this all about Reese? Was Howard innocent?

"You know how much I hate these pyramid companies, and you let me get involved with them by trading their stock. It's a scam. It ruined half of these women's lives. Desperate women!"

"Not exactly. If everyone had a personal vendetta against every company in the stock market, there wouldn't be any investing. You wanted this job. You practically begged me for it, remember? This is the thanks I get? What kind of job would you have gotten without me?"

"After you involved me with Banyan, I didn't have a choice."

"Oh, honey… don't play the victim here. *You* always had a choice." Maybe he was right. But he wasn't going to pin this on me.

"And what about SHINE?"

Howard chuckled. "Don't you get it, Leah? SHINE? It stands for **S**tupid **HI**gh **NE**tters. They should've known their profits were too good to be true. They were gamblers too. And they're so rich they can afford to lose sometimes."

"No one deserves that! You set me up. That's all this was. A setup for you to do more illegal insider trading. Just like you did with Banyan."

A look of *how dare you?* shot across his face.

"I don't know where you are getting your conspiracy theory, but you're wrong. I did all of this for you. For us." He muttered, "Jesus, you're just like Staci."

I stopped cold. "What?" And there it was. My lips formed a thin line. I didn't know if I could hold back.

"Nothing. Forget I said anything."

"Staci? Leopard-Lovin' Staci from upstairs, Staci? The one the firm paid off, Staci? Staci, who everyone talks about in a whisper, Staci? What happened with her, Howard, huh? Did she figure you out, too? Did she know about your little scheme? Does she know about your Howie Loans? Did you confide in her? Did you fuck her? Did you tell her that you love her, too?" I wasn't expecting Staci's name to come up. I don't know how such accusations fell out of my mouth. I would bet I just hit a nerve. I don't think I'd ever screamed so loud in my whole life. I was uncontrollable. Unhinged.

"Staci didn't mean anything to me. You do. She stumbled upon some information and tried to blackmail me. It's not what you think. Let's go inside and talk."

"You're never stepping foot in my house again! Do you hear me?"

"Please… I love you."

"You don't know what love is! You made me think there was something wrong with Deenie. That you were protecting her. You had to be the hero, didn't you? Poor, sweet Deenie with her mental health issues. A surprise pregnancy? How do you come up with the lies? Has anything you've ever said to me been true?"

It's interesting how fast a person's face can change when you hit them with the truth, exposing their guilt unexpectedly. Howard had that kind of face. The things I found so endearing became distorted. Kindness turned to deception. Strength turned to manipulation. He was nothing more than a fraud with a convincing pick-up line. A wolf in sheep's clothing, as my mom would say. And who knew how much he actually did for my mom. Maybe some of that was a lie, too. What a waste. Howard Gardner was going to drown in his greedy mess.

"I'm sorry you feel this way, Leah. You know, we could've had a hell of a future together. Just you and me. Partners." It occurred to me that I was his only lifeline. "We can still fix this. I promise. It's just business. Don't let a little misunderstanding ruin what we have. Now that the SEC is done with me, everything will work out. Just like I planned." His voice was soft. Sensual. And he was still trying to seduce me. He reached in to touch my face.

"I wanted this so bad. So bad. With every ounce of…" I had to stop crying.

"We can still have it. Don't you see? I don't know what you heard, but it has nothing to do with us. Please, beautiful. Trust me."

I stepped back. "You're running a Ponzi scheme."

"Business is one big Ponzi scheme. Think about it. Money in one door. Out another."

He didn't think he did anything wrong. "Don't you ever call me beautiful again. You only want to save your ass. But I know all about you, Howard. And Eddie, too. You're both nothing but frauds and criminals, and there's no way I'm going down with either of you. I never want to see you again. So, please, if you don't mind, get the fuck off my driveway!"

He didn't listen. Howard edged even closer to me. I could smell the cologne. I could feel his breath on me. It would be so easy to kiss him. One last time. "Come on, Leah, don't do this. I love you."

I held on to my senses. It wasn't desire or even anger anymore; it was rage burning inside of me. "I'm serious, Howard. Get away from me. If you ever come near me again, I'll… I'll get a restraining order." This time, it was Howard who stepped back, realizing he had misjudged me.

He looked defeated. He ran his hand through his hair. "It wasn't supposed to be like this. We lost a big donor. Eddie asked me to do him a favor. I couldn't say no. Not after everything he had done for me. And I got in over my head. But no one needs to know."

"You need to go."

"Okay, look, I know you're in shock. It would be best if you calmed down. Today was a mess. I'm so sorry you had to witness it. I'm playing golf with Eddie tomorrow morning. We'll come here and explain everything. I'm sure Eddie would love to see you. He makes a mean omelet."

"Don't tell me to calm down!" With all that was happening, the man was playing golf. Was he serious?

"You'll realize this was all a misunderstanding. Take some time to relax. If you still don't want to see me anymore, I'll respect that."

"Get away from me," I hissed. "Now." I looked him square in the eye; mine filled with a hate I didn't know I had.

"I understand." His face filled with despair. "But you'll change your mind. In the meantime, I'll take my boxes out of your basement. No sense in keeping my family mementos here. I don't want to put you out."

I could've had everything I thought I wanted. Instead, I felt pity for the man he'd never be. Did I love him? Or love the thought of him, as Lily said? I shook my head and headed towards my house. My family was watching from the window. I could see Peyton restraining herself from coming outside and punching Howard in the mouth.

And then, I stopped and turned. I looked at Howard one last time, trying to think of the perfect thing to say to end things. I needed to have the last word. It was my turn to call the shots. I needed my power back. He was so busy professing his love and his innocence that it never occurred to him to question how much I knew. Or how I knew it. The thought of the SEC or Deenie never crossed his mind. I didn't mention Chadwick. I didn't tell him his boxes were turned over as evidence. He'd find out soon enough.

All his lies jumbled into one as I watched a year of my life fade away. I wiped away the last of the tears streaming down my face. He didn't deserve them. Not now. Not ever. This betrayal was unfixable. It was over. I looked at Howard hard, studying the man who allowed me to make a fool out of myself, to lose my dignity. My self-worth. I could've lost everything. My body was filled with disgust. I finally realized I didn't need him to succeed.

"Please, Leah, say something."

I continued staring at him, emotionless, empty, like a rag doll that lost all its stuffing. There was only one thing left to say. "I quit. And I'm taking the SHINE wives with me."

Silence echoed in the space between us.

"Give me my boxes." Howard's lips compressed tightly. His nostrils flared.

I sauntered towards the garage and pressed the code. The door opened slowly. Howard stepped inside. Stacks of broken-down, empty cardboard boxes were scattered on the floor—Chadwick's people had only been interested in the contents. A single large box remained, the words HOWARD/FAMILY STUFF written on the side with a thick Sharpie. I knew it was the only box that actually contained family heirlooms. Placed on top was the burgundy box holding his father's Scrabble set, the corners split and more worn than when I found it. Howard picked up the box with shaky hands. He looked at me, bewildered, his face painted with anguish and fear. And in that moment, he understood everything.

<h1 style="text-align:center">FORTY-TWO</h1>

THE STORM Part Two

I slept late. How fortuitous that I had taken the rest of the week off to prepare for Lily's graduation party. Mitchell and Rachel were arriving tomorrow. I had a cake to bake and decorations to make.

My father entered my bedroom, opened the shades, and said, "Wake up, sleepyhead. I think you're going to want to see this."

Still drowsy, I followed him to my family room. He had a cup of coffee waiting for me, Sid style, extra sugar, extra cream. I noticed a bouquet of sunflowers arranged in a vase.

"Where did these come from?" I bent down to smell them.

"A hot rod in a leather jacket dropped them off early this morning. He said you could probably use a little sunshine today."

I was distracted by the hoopla on TV. It was another day of breaking news. My dad picked up the remote and pointed it at the TV, making the volume louder. I couldn't believe my eyes and ears. My heart sank a little as I saw his picture on the screen.

"Prominent businessman, Edward Grossman, collapsed today of an apparent heart attack at the Princeton golf course near his home. He was transported to Princeton Medical Center. No further information is known about his condition."

I looked at my dad with sorrow, a moment of sympathy for a man I briefly adored but barely knew. My dad used the remote to guide my eyes back to the TV. There was Howard, shielding his face from the cameras, being led away by the DOJ.

"In related news, Howard Gardner, president of Arbor Financial, was arrested outside Princeton Medical Center after accompanying his mentor and apparent business partner, Edward Grossman, by ambulance. Gardner, sixty-five, began his career at Slate Capital in New York and worked at Arbor for the last thirty-nine years. He is accused of ten counts of stock manipulation, fourteen counts of insider trading and security fraud, eight counts of falsifying documents, six counts of violating federal banking regulations, and two counts of racketeering. We'll continue to update you as more information is obtained." Were my eyes playing tricks on me, or was Dylan standing off to the side by the hospital entrance, a camera hanging from his neck?

"Daddy, I don't know what to say."

"I've been talking to Chadwick. Nice chap. Thorough. You know I like thorough. They had loads of information about what Howard and Eddie were up to. Years of accusations that their division couldn't validate until now." He embraced me with a stress-melting signature bear hug. "You did well, *ziskeit*."

My dad allowed the kids to stay home from school. He insisted he needed quality time with his grandkids. Miriam, the *Garnet Springs Press* reporter, was grateful to have arrived in the middle of an FBI raid and scoop the story before any other outlets. She asked Lily for assistance on a follow-up article. Just before noon, the doorbell rang. Barry and Chadwick stood shoulder to shoulder at my door. Barry had a shit-eating grin on his face.

"It was you?"

"Guilty as charged. Well, not guilty, but yep, I'm the whistleblower," Barry said coyly.

"I was hoping it was you." I released a huge sigh of relief.

"I've spent years tipping them off. They never took me seriously before." He looked at Chadwick, who shrugged. "But once you came on board, I could tell what he was up to. Never trusted the guy, and I've known Howard a long time."

"Almost as long as you've known me," Chadwick said, laughing.

"I'm so confused." They couldn't have been a more mismatched duo.

"I've known Chaddy here since some of my," Barry cleared his voice, "early brushes with the law. In my younger days."

"Are you going to stop calling me Chaddy?"

"Nope. Chaddy." Barry ribbed Chadwick with his elbow.

Chadwick shook his head. "I was a fledgling investigator, and this guy gave me a run for my money. I got him off more than once, and he promised to return the favor one day."

I couldn't believe what I was hearing.

Barry added, "I couldn't let you take the fall for anything Howard was doing."

"What about Nathan? Didn't he know anything?"

"Nathan was cautious about pulling the trigger too soon. He wouldn't go to the SEC until he was a hundred percent sure it was a solid case."

"I could've sworn I saw Dylan hanging around the FBI trucks at the office and again when Howard was arrested."

"I'm sure you did. He told you he needs to be in the middle of the action."

"Maybe we have more in common than I thought. Barry, I can't go back to that office. But I have some ideas. Will you help me figure out what to do next?"

"You got it, kid. Vivian will help too. She's quite taken with you."

SEC Interview #3

Howard Gardner

SEC: Mr. Gardner, did you share confidential information concerning VG Industries with Leah Samuels?

Mr. Gardner: No. She must have gained access to my computer when I was out of the office.

SEC: You're saying she acted alone? Are you protecting her?

Mr. Gardner: Yes. She acted alone. No. I'm not protecting anybody. I don't know what her endgame was. She had to know she'd get caught.

SEC: You stated previously that you had a brief romantic dalliance with her. Are you sure this wasn't an elaborate setup?

Mr. Gardner: Did I say brief? I don't recall.

SEC: You stated it was a consensual mistake. Is that all it was? Or was Ms. Samuels in on this the whole time? Were you acting together?

Mr. Gardner: Okay… so I lied. Big deal, we were involved. It was just sex. But this whole thing was her idea. I think she thought she was impressing me and that we would wind up together. But I'm a man. I'm human. I said what I needed to say to her to get her into bed. I was never going to ride off into the sunset with her.

SEC: Did she think otherwise?

Mr. Gardner: If she did, she was delusional. I hear she had quite the vivid imagination. Maybe she was conspiring with Reese. Ask him. She also had some cockamamie idea to start a women's trading division. Like I said. Delusional.

SEC: You state that you never discussed these trades and you did not provide any information, false or otherwise, to her that would have predetermined her trading?

Mr. Gardner: Correct.

SEC: Mr. Gardner, were you involved with buying Ms. Samuel's party business?

Mr. Gardner: No. I had a friend who bought distressed businesses. She was dying to sell, so I gave them her name. I figured I was helping her out. She should be grateful.

SEC: Is that it?

Mr. Gardner: Yes.

SEC: Last question. Mr. Gardner, what is a Howie Loan?

Mr. Gardner: I have no idea what you're talking about.

SEC: Thank you for your time today.

Mr. Gardner: My pleasure.

FORTY-THREE

FEARLESS GIRL

ylan's photographs made the front page of *The Wall Street Journal.* It was sheer coincidence that he arrived at Arbor during the raid when Reese was arrested. Dylan was so furious at Howard for involving me in fraudulent activity that he followed him the next day, assuming he'd catch Howard doing something illegal. The fact that he happened to be a few yards away when Howard got arrested, too, was another lucky break.

Louis showed up at Lily's outdoor graduation party, uninvited, with Jackie in tow. He thought it would be an appropriate time to announce that their wedding in Cabo was back on. Peyton kept her eye on him, making sure he didn't venture inside my house, and making Louis uncomfortable enough to leave early.

The next day, while my dad and Mitchell went out with all the kids, Rachel, Cara, Peyton, and I took a ride to the Jersey shore, taking Barry up on his offer to see his band, Vintage Whiskey, perform at an outdoor beach bar. The band was pretty good for a bunch of old-timers. But Dylan, as the lead singer and guitar player, brought the house down. He held the microphone close to his mouth; his body swayed along with the moonlit waves. He maintained eye contact with me, his voice raspy and full of emotion, and if I didn't know better, I would've thought every lyric was meant for me. His familiar smile sent a chill down my spine. I just couldn't keep my eyes off him. The beach air hung an imaginary wall around us. He continued singing, moving comfortably around the stage, rocking a frayed pair of Levi's. The tight sleeves of a faded blue Rolling Stones T-shirt constrained a pair of tan and muscular arms. I felt lighter than I had in months. After the set, Barry introduced me to the band members. He winked at me before walking away, and under his breath, I heard him say something about sometimes getting what you need.

In July, Barry finally gave the board what they wanted and retired; forty-seven years in the business was enough. He began teaching guitar, loving every stress-free minute of it.

Barry gave me updates on the case and reported that Don, my SHINE buddy, turned over evidence detailing records of the Howie Loans, and, if you did the math, the interest Howard charged was over thirty percent. Don returned his profits to a DOJ escrow account. Complex, I remembered Howard saying. It was complex and predatory.

Barry also told me that Rick, the café owner, was Eddie's son, which provided a pivotal location for the Violet and Gray scam to thrive. My father lined up his consumer law buddies to help the vendors who were in debt up to their eyeballs. Some vendors recovered their investments, some learned a valuable lesson, and others simply moved on to another company. Another promise of independent wealth. As W.C. Fields famously said, "There's a sucker born every minute."

Lily and Asher finished packing for Cabo. The wedding was a four-day event, and the kids were stoked with excitement. Louis arranged to pick them up and go to the airport together. My phone rang just as we carried the last of the luggage outside.

"You need to tell the kids the wedding's off."

"What? Isn't the wedding tomorrow?"

"Jackie took off with the contractor who's renovating our house." I burst out laughing. Karma did exist. "Hey, Leah, maybe now that we're both single, we could have dinner?"

"Fuck off, Louis," I said. I hung up on him and looked gloomily at the kids, "Sorry, guys. The wedding's off again."

Asher kicked his suitcase. "Oh my God. He's such an idiot!"

Lily added, "I should be writing about him next."

Before Lily left for college, we did one final shopping trip. Departing the shoe department in Bloomingdale's, Lily asked if she could purchase some makeup. We rounded the corner of the Chanel counter, laughing like children, when the saleswoman looked up from her register to see if we needed assistance. Standing behind the counter was BethAnn. She blinked twice, and a vein pulsated from her neck. I froze. She stared at me for a minute longer and then walked away in a huff, leaving Lily and me alone.

"Mom? Who was that?"

"Nobody important," I replied. "Nobody at all. Come on. Let's get out of here."

Howard's case was still pending. I never did hear from him again. His ego wouldn't allow it. It could take years to unravel the fraud he and Eddie were engaged in. FINRA moved to revoke Howard's license. The Department of Justice sought disgorgement and jail time for him and BethAnn, who was an accomplice. Knowing Howard, he'd get off with substantial fines. But he'd be back. Guys like Howard always came back.

Three months later

I stopped in the café, noticing the **Under New Management** sign in the window. Leonardo decided to back Ivy and her husband, Benji, allowing them to buy the café after Rick put it up for sale. Ivy put the original wall back up, giving the café a cozier feel.

I grabbed a tray of desserts and walked next door, using my key to open my new office space. The walls were painted a calming shade of sage green. Dylan stood on a ladder, securing an acrylic sign above the reception area. Peyton gave orders to the caterer (Leonardo). Cara decided where to place the abundance of flower arrangements that had been delivered.

Dylan stepped down from the ladder, kissing me on the lips as he whisked the dessert tray out of my hands. Peyton paused to give me a thumbs-up.

Tomorrow was opening day for The Women's Financial Network. When I pitched the idea to Vivian's colleagues at JB

Financial, one of the largest brokerages in the county, I didn't have a clear-cut vision of how a satellite women's division would work. Luckily, they were on board from the beginning, especially after learning about the seed money from the SHINE wives. Vivian coached me, and I hired a group of seasoned executives. In addition to investing, we decided to offer accounting, retirement and estate planning, and consultations on female entrepreneurship.

But tonight was the celebration.

Rita, Misty, and Natalia flew in. Gabrielle sent a giant fruit basket.

A bottle of Scotch from Vivian sat in a crystal ice bucket surrounded by a half dozen crystal glasses. Be Fearless, the handwritten card read.

The door opened, and the guests trickled in, a mixture of family, friends, former clients, and neighboring businesses. A small coterie of Yogette Coquettes, refined ballet wraps covering their sports bras. Miriam, the reporter, was there too, promising a feature story, in addition to six months of free advertisements.

I thought I saw the Matrix LED headlights of a Maserati circling the parking lot. It may have been my imagination. Or perhaps the lights were from a much further away place. A beam of energy. A sign of approval.

And then I saw them. Eden. Barbie. Heidi (fresh off wedding number three). Raina. Blair. Alana and Amanda (surprise—there were two of them), Lyssa. The Pyramid Girls. All lined up at my door with hopeful smiles. I was more than happy to help them.

THE END

AUTHOR'S NOTE

When I was six years old, my PopPop Martin propped me up on his lap next to a can of peanut brittle and a folded *Wall Street Journal* and began discussing the stock market. This evolved into his version of the Math Olympics, a weekly quiz that combined math and speed. Soon, I was able to recite whose face was on every piece of currency, knew how to calculate percentages, and could decide *which I would rather have*: thirty-one dimes, twelve quarters, twenty-five nickels, and ninety-two pennies, or a ten-dollar bill. I had sixty seconds to decide and explain why. This launched my life-long addiction (obsession) to numbers, charts, and all things stocks.

My grandfather, Martin Greenblatt, was a genius, especially when it came to the stock market. He graduated number-one in his class from Penn Law and the Wharton School of Finance in the late 1920s, but with the Great Depression brewing, he couldn't get a job as an attorney. Instead, he became a high school business teacher and taught investing to adults during night school. Unfortunately, starting in the 1930s, during the heyday of investing, the stock market ruled my grandfather's life in ways that proved disastrous. He became defined by volatile mood swings and cruel behavior, a pendulum mimicking the daily market fluctuations. I was told that when his broker called at four o'clock each afternoon, his demeanor shifted, and his frustrations were taken out on his family. Every conversation hinged on whether the market was up or down and which stocks to buy or sell, or in his case, never sell. It was enough to frighten people away, not just from him, but from the industry. But not me. By the time I came along, he had found his protégé in an innocent child.

Holiday dinners included discussions about compound interest, dividends, bond yields, and words I didn't understand. My grandfather had tremendous foresight. His investment decisions were impeccable, yet he drove a beat-up car from supermarket to supermarket to save a nickel. A lifelong hoarder, he lived for decades in a modest home in Philadelphia until his death. Depression-era mentality or Warren Buffett? Perhaps a little of both.

My parents continued the investment traditions, albeit with a layer of emotional resilience. Paper stock certificates littered my dad's home office. We took trips to multiple banks, scissors in hand, to cut coupons off oversized bonds. As a CPA, my dad had more ledger paper, adding machine tape, and mechanical pencils than an office supply store. This excited me to no end—*hand over the notebooks and binder clips.* While most kids were outside riding their bikes, I was in my bedroom playing "Bank" with piles of bank slips and check registers I had stolen during those bank expeditions, and using ledgers to keep track of everything: Babysitting money. Halloween candy. Allowance money saved for the Scholastic Book Fair. Money I earned selling bubble gum. In school, we were required to take industrial arts classes and make metal napkin holders, but not consumer finance to balance our checkbooks.

As a Journalism major, I did not take math or finance classes. Economics yielded me a grateful D+. I chose to do my stock obsessing in private. I waited anxiously for the newspaper to arrive, eager to peruse the stock listings, and years later, religiously watched the ticker tape on AOL. I inhaled news stories. Forced my kids to watch Suze Orman. Subscribed to financial magazines. Dated a bad stockbroker who eventually lost his license. Programmed my DVR to *American Greed* and *Mad Money*. I read books, watched news programs and movies about fraud and fraudsters, and could probably defend a PHD dissertation on Gordon Gekko, Sam Bankman-Fried, and Bernie Madoff. And then I became skeptical, convinced I could smell a scam a mile away.

My meticulous ledger-keeping served me well. I was the budget queen because I recorded everything. And when I got divorced, I was a step ahead of the game. As a business owner, I avoided Excel and QuickBooks. Instead, I listed each transaction, every piece of inventory, every customer, in a ledger book. My accountant loved that. (Read: Wanted to kill me.) But lessons in money, debt management, and investing stood the test of time.

In recent years, I was fortunate enough to have two men who took my love of numbers and the stock market to a new level: my uncle, Dr. David Greenblatt, and my dear friend and mentor, Saul Katz. Combined, they provided over 120 years of active stock-market wisdom. Their encouragement was life-changing. They were patient and kind, and non-critical, teaching me everything from how to pick mutual funds to how to analyze stock allocations. They may have created a monster. One who goes to bed checking the futures and wakes up in the middle of the night to check the pre-market. Who records investment patterns in ledgers inherited from her dad's stockpile from the 1970s. Stock market junkie is an understatement. It was inevitable that I would either get my financial license or write about it one day.

The problem is that the majority of women are often not taken seriously when it comes to money matters. How many women have been ignored, not looked at in the eye, or humiliated when they tried to buy a car? How many financial people have asked to speak to your husband? How many professionals assume *female ignorance*, enabling them to take advantage or overcharge? It's no wonder such a high percentage of single/divorced/widowed women have no retirement savings. No healthcare directives. No wills. Sometimes, it's a wake-up call too late.

A woman couldn't get a seat on the New York Stock Exchange until 1967. Nor could she get her own credit card or a mortgage without a male co-signer until 1974. Yet, sisters Victoria Woodhull and Tennessee Claflin opened the first female stock brokerage firm in 1870 (backed by Commodore Vanderbilt). The media treated them as novelties, nicknaming them Bewitching Brokers and Lady Bankers, describing their fashion sense and physical attributes, but barely mentioning that they made over seven hundred thousand dollars (equal to thirteen million dollars today) in their first six weeks. I didn't learn about them in history class.

Hetty Green, known as the Queen of Wall Street, the Wizard of Finance, and the Richest Woman in America, predicted the Panic of 1907. She bailed out New York City and her own husband, in addition to working with J.P. Morgan to save the banking system. She famously stated her investment strategy was to buy low and sell high, and never buy on margin. Known for her frugality, Hetty also held the Guinness World Record title of World's Greatest Miser. It was rumored that she washed only the dirty parts of her dress to save on soap. Hetty amassed a fortune investing in real estate, railroads, stocks, and bonds, which in today's dollars would be worth between \$2.5 and 5.4 billion—another trailblazer who is barely a footnote in the male-dominated world of finance.

On the flip side, the first Ponzi scheme was spearheaded in 1869 by two women, Adele Spitzeder and Sarah Howe. Their notoriety was hidden in the shadows, and so in 1906, Charles Ponzi received recognition for his crimes, lending his name to the money-making schemes we hear of today. Multi-level marketing and downlines existed long before the fictional companies I wrote about. But many of the tactics remain constant. Although I am aware that there are many legitimate ways to participate, my story only focused on the questionable aspects.

Stock Market Mistress began as a *what-if* story. What if you were desperate for money? Desperate for love? How far would you go? How much would you be willing to sacrifice for a love interest or a family member? It is a purely fictional story; however, during my research, it became so much more. I've discovered that many women don't even want to know about finance. *It's not interesting. It's too confusing. It's too stressful. I'll get to it. My husband does it. I have a guy. A friend of a friend. A brother-in-law.* This is all great, until it's not. Don't wait. Ask the hard questions. Read the small print. Check your statements. Do your due diligence. Have a plan. Find someone you can trust. Teach your children. And, most important of all, put yourself in a position of control.

Mistress: noun: to be in a position of power, authority, or control.

ACKNOWLEDGMENTS

It feels like this is the Oscar speech I've been rehearsing in the mirror for most of my life. There are many people to thank, and luckily, no music will be played to escort me off the stage before I finish. Independently publishing this book was harder than I imagined. It took trust, resilience, hope, and luck in choosing the right people, as well as fine-tuning my ability to bother my friends and family about book design minutiae.

I am fortunate to have Shel, my calm, unwavering, supportive spouse/lover/nusband/best friend, who became a chick-lit beta reader. He has patiently endured my too-late dinners, staying up through the night to write/edit one more chapter, turning every room except my office into a writing studio, and nonstop stressing over fonts, colors, and character names. I love you, Shel. Note: This is just the beginning.

Thank you to my *Criminal Minds* daughter, Marissa (look out Mariska Hargitay). If it were up to Marissa, every character would be a potential serial killer. She provided endless support with the website, design, analytics, promotion, and the launch of this book on her shopping platform. Thanks to her procrastination, in-depth character analysis, trend knowledge, and ideas, this book was pulled from the final stages of editing and rewritten to include the Scrabble storyline, ultimately strengthening and deepening the connection between Leah and Howard. Rissy, I am eternally GRATEFUL: seven plus letters — on a triple word would be eighty-six points! Also, to my son-in-law, David, for design input, promoting the book on the platform, and who, even without reading the book, had one-liners too good not to use.

Thank you to my wonderful son, Jason, for his expert technical support during all hours of the day and night and for graciously handling my I HATE COMPUTERS meltdowns. And to his wife, Brenna, for input on my cover design.

Thank you to my phenomenal cuz, Cindy Joy Marselis, editor, proofreader, computer expert, Word whiz, and reader extraordinaire. Cindy, words can't express how much I value all your help.

Reading has always been my escape; writing, my passion. Susan Bootel, my second-grade teacher, recognized that passion and nurtured it, encouraging me to join her young author group, where I could write stories that were bound and displayed in the school library. Her kindness and role in my pursuing my lifelong dream to be an author have never been forgotten.

Somewhere between reading Judy Blume, Judith Krantz, Sidney Sheldon, and Jackie Collins, I knew I was destined to write books. Far too many people rolled their eyes and said, "Sure you will." I finally decided to get my Master's in Fine Arts, but first had the joy of taking a class taught by the esteemed Vivian Grey. Vivian was instrumental in telling me that if I wanted to write, just write. And so I gave up the degree and wrote, joining her writers group in her dining room every week for four years until her death. These fellow writers were instrumental in providing hours of critique and motivation.

To my outstanding beta readers, your interest and diligence were sincerely appreciated. Lisa Altman, Abby Applebaum, Ellen Eisen, Sally and Danny Feldman, Alita Friedman, my sister and brother-in-law, Susan and Marc Kamenitz, Cathy Killian, Lorie Modelevsky, Sara Newman, Kathy Rosenberg, Rhonda Wise, and Lacey Yoder—your thoughtful comments were highly regarded and helped bring my story to life.

To my superb developmental editor, Jacqueline Friedland: I am amazed at how you attacked my story, which I was sure I had taken as far as it could go, and how you recognized the plot points that were hiding in plain sight. I was planning to delete an entire section, but you planted the seeds of a pivot, leading me to highlight minor characters and change the story's trajectory. Thank you for guiding me and making my story so much better.

To my impressive copy editor, Chloe Rosenberg: Thank you for your meticulous eye and for fixing my habit of switching tenses. You polished my manuscript flawlessly.

To Marci Senders, my fabulous cover designer and interior formatter: Thank you for your enthusiasm and your patience, for *getting me* from the very beginning, and most of all, for an eye-popping book cover. I may have to write another book just so I can use all your ideas. Your expertise in the industry was extremely helpful and made this process more enjoyable.

Thank you to Kim Broderick for proofreading and making my words shine — typo-free.

To my Uncle David Greenblatt, z"l, for teaching me things I

could never have figured out on my own.

To Saul Katz, who continues to be my investment guru and help hotline.

To my BFF Barbara Meranus, who has made decisions with me and for me for over fifty years. Hopefully, when you read this book, you will realize how much your influence is always present.

To Cathy Scharmett, editor of all things in my life, for always championing and supporting me, absolutely no matter what.

To Rachel Gordon from RayLynn Photography and Cindy Singer from Dylan Michael Cosmetics for an amazing set of author photos.

To the authors, readers, and reading community who promised to promote my book, thank you in advance. None of this would be possible without you.

Finally, a special thank you to all my friends and family who are not individually mentioned, but who knew I could do it and cheered me on. And to those who didn't believe in me, well, I did it in spite of you. This is a dream come true. The music can play now. *RLB*

www.ingramcontent.com/pod-product-compliance
Lightning Source LLC
Chambersburg PA
CBHW031114160726
47991CB00004B/1374